Ladies *of* the Shire

**Grosvenor House
Publishing Limited**

This book is published by
Grosvenor House Publishing Ltd
28-30 High Street, Guildford, Surrey, GU1 3HY.
www.grosvenorhousepublishing.co.uk

A CIP record for this book
is available from the British Library

ISBN 978-1-906645-71-7

www.peter-webb.com

Cover Photograph – Sara Hannant – www.sarahannant.com

Cover Design – Ben Rowe - www.benrowephotography.co.uk

Ladies of the Shire

Peter Webb

To my family; Doris and Dennis Webb,
who let me do it my way, Marjie, my harbour
light, and Ben, Kate, Jake and Robin.
Their lives and love have made me what
I am: this book is as much theirs as mine.

Acknowledgements

Many people have supported me with advice and their precious time during the production of this work since its inception in 2001. My inadequate thanks to: Chris Alexander, Claudine Conway, Mike and Rosemary Gaches, John Hardwick, Jenny Hope, Anne and Phil Howarth, David and Nik James, Eric Maclennan, Jill Rowett, Lynda Smart & The Leicester Mercury, Katie Stamp, and Jane Ward and the members of CYT.
My gratitude is in its completion; thank you.
My thanks are also due to Maggi Taylor, Ruth Pulis and my editor, "SH", at Grosvenor House Publications. I am in your debt.

Marjorie Webb

Nothing I own will repay what I owe

07.09.07

Contrary to popular opinion there are five and not two certainties in life, the other trio being:

The European Brown Hare, *Lepus capensis*, knows little of the ideologies contained within the lyrics of *Keep on Rockin' in the Free World*;

humans really are deceptively simple, fully paid-up members of the animal kingdom;

leatherjackets are considered unattractive beasts to all but another leatherjacket or hungry bird.

And this massive, four-wheel-drive, state-of-the-art tractor, pulling a six-furrow, reversible plough and its attendant rash of seagulls across a Leicestershire stubble field is about to prove the point.

The skeletal outline of the grubbed-out hedgerow, which once supported the body of nineteenth century British agriculture, is clearly visible across the field as, from the rear of this grounded trawler flows the tide of a different sea. The blades of the plough turn the golden stubble into turbulent waves of brown earth, and Richard, the Cnut of this seasonal tide, is giving this miracle of modern agriculture his due weight and consideration.

Sat well back in the seat, his leg folded over the seat's arm, one tapping foot up on the side window, earphones and iPod resplendent and seemingly oblivious to any level of concentration, he accompanies the tractor along an arrow-straight line from Forty-Acre Field's-end to Forty-Acre Field's-end.

Constantly being fed information by the tractor's computer screen and its rear-view camera, still, every now and then, he glances over his shoulder; checks plough-progress amongst the flurry of gulls.

It's a good day; sun shining, plough tilling, Neil Young giving it some; time for a chorus:

…Got styrofoam boxes for the ozone layer,
Got a man of the people says keep hope alive,
Got fuel to burn, got roads to dri-ive!
Keep on rockin' in the free world…!

A dozen yards ahead of this titanic nod to horsepower a doe brown hare starts up from the stubble and skitters off to a nearby hedgerow only to halt and hover, undecided.

From languorous indifference, Richard snaps into action, fast-halting the machine lifting the ploughshares snatching off his earphones and tossing them onto the dash-board in one fluid movement.

'Whoa!'

The massive tractor's computer screen flashes through several possible scenarios in a nanosecond, a visual, electronic incredulity at the sudden cessation of what had been, up until then, GPS plough-heaven. The engine sings its deceleration, quickly giving way to a duet of irritated gulls and strangulated Neil Young still insisting that we *keep on rockin'*.

Unclipping the iPod, Richard puts it alongside the earphones, swings out of the seat and dismounts his three-hundred horsepower ego-trip; his sudden premature birth from this agricultural womb causes the gulls to splinter away in blizzard formation.

Walking to the spot the hare had just vacated, he folds back a combine-missed tuft of barley straw; and there, snugged down in a lined form, the fur for which had been plucked not two days ago from its mother's chest, is a single leveret.

'Knew it.'

He sprinkles some loose straw over it, moves back to the thrumping tractor and the rear of the plough blades, gazes along the furrowed symmetry of the plough's legacy and, breaking off a clod of freshly turned soil, rubs it over his hands.

On the turn away he spots something in the furrow. It is the tip of…?… Richard draws out a huge, soil-clogged and rusty horseshoe.

Hand on plough-blade for balance, he knocks the horseshoe against the heel of his boot to dislodge the soil and turns it over in his hands. Even given the time it had obviously been in the ground it is still heavy.

'Some unlucky sod 'ad t' carry four of these and drag a plough be'ind 'em as well.'

He props the horseshoe on the tractor's rear light and returns to the hare's form. As he bends to complete his mission, his eye settles on something else…something lying just to the side of the hare's scrape.

'An' what's this?'

Dirt and grime rubbed from its surface reveals it to be an engraved disc with an age-peppered inscription……

23.09.95

'Break that up, boy!'

To the uninitiated, a pipe held between clenched teeth would make words sound different, almost foreign. To George, who had heard his father's voice with said vocal impediment all his short life, deciphering the sounds was easy. It was not the understanding of such statements that was the problem; it was the speed of his reaction in obeying them that was often amiss, as with most small boys.

Unable to hold up the Shire horse's massive hoof without his father's help, five-year-old George had been entrusted with the delicate job of removing the clack of soil. This compacted earth held its horse's hoof shape, even after the small grubby hand had loosened it with the smoothed wooden spatula blade, and George had watched as it hit the ground with a deep thud, thereby causing his father's instruction.

Geoffrey expanded the reasoning.

'That's where th' milk-wheat'll sprout if that's not loosed up.'

'Yes, Dad.'

George gave it a cursory kick. Further, exasperated remonstrations followed.

'Not like that! Break it…!…you've t' bury it! Y'r 'ands; use y'r 'ands!'

Picking up the clod, George uncovered a few gyrating worms and a self-righting beetle.

'It's full o' weekies, Dad.'

Geoffrey brushed the hoof with his hand and loosened further debris from it.

'Like th' soil that'll cover us all. I don't know, our George, what'll become 'f y'? You treat it right, that earth; if y' don't own it, it'll swallow you up an' leave no trace 'f you ever bein' 'ere.'

Crumbling the clod of soil, George let it fall to the ground.

'Yes, Dad.'

Geoffrey released the hoof.

'That's it. Now dig it deep, Georgie-Boy.'

George dug his hands into the soil and his small fingers crumbed its worked and nurtured quality with ease.

Geoffrey put a hand on his hip and, removing his pipe from his mouth, pointed its stem at the county in general.

'Land always wins in the end, son, remember that.'

'Yes, Dad; land wins.'

George stood alongside his father for a moment; his hand lifted to his hip as he too gazed across the landscape; then his gaze fell on the field. He looked up at his father and his hand traced a line across the field, the exact opposite to that which they'd been ploughing.

'Why do we plough this way, Dad? Why not that way?'

Squatting, Geoffrey indicated the lie of the field with his pipe as he spoke.

''Cos that's th' way th' water flows, lad, right down that slope an' into th' ditch at bottom. If we run th' furrows th' way you say th' water'd wash off all our soil, see.'

'All our soil?'

'Most, ar.'

'Where does water go from th' ditch then?'

'Out along with all the other t' th' river, by flood-meadows. That's why we don't plough there, ain' it, because th' river busts its banks an' it'd wash all crop away?'

'Then why…?'

'Need t' get on, Georgie-Boy!' Geoffrey stood up. 'These 'orses're ready f'r their tea an' talk won't butter no parsnips. We'll get across t' that line-marker stick then call it a day.'

'I put that stick in, Dad. F'r ploughin'.'

Geoffrey replaced the pipe and lifted his son onto the nearer Shire's back.

'Ar, y' did that, lad. Now set y'rself onto th' front 'f this pair o' patient souls an' let's get th' rest 'f this field broke up then 'ome f'r our tea as well. Call 'em, Georgie-Boy!'

Geoffrey flicked the reins.

George's voice called out loud and clear.

'Hie-On, ladies!'

The two Shire horses set off……

06.06.99

Reversing the hay cart, any cart really, was something George could do well, and here was an audience he could shine for.

As seasoned horsemen themselves the other men on *Fallen Oak Farm* appreciated skill, from whatever quarter. They may not always voice this appreciation, but they recognised it all the same.

Feeding the reins through nimble fingers, George gave a slight backward pull, clicked his tongue and gave a soft call.

'Hie, Chalky, Back-Back!'

The Shire horse leant into the task, her full-breeching leathers creaking under the pressure.

Standing at twelve feet high, the hay rick build was progressing well. Two-thirds up its height, a very old, very large door had been built into it, acting as a platform for the men to stand on and throw the hay to even greater heights. Projecting out four feet from the rick's edge, this platform was the point George was aiming for.

With the cart backing across the yard, and under the watchful eye of most of the other horsemen dotted atop and around the part-built stack, it was Reginald, as top-stacker, who directed operations.

'As y' are, young George, as y' are. Keep it left o' th' ladder; lovely job! Watch 'im that side, Daniel.'

Standing on the projecting door, Daniel, the farm's apprentice horseman, called back sourly.

'If it's such a lovely job let 'im do it on 'is own.'

'I said watch 'im, Daniel, now watch 'im!'

George backed the cart effortlessly and without any input from Daniel, to the unloading step and the waiting men.

Once there, he jumped from the driver's seat to the ground.

'That right, Mister Reginald?'

Reginald smiled at him.

'Ar, spot on lad. F'r a nine-year-old whipper-snapper y' do a fair job o' drivin'. Mind, you've 'ad a top teacher in y' dad. Why, y're as good as Daniel 'ere, an' 'e's seventeen.'

Daniel scoffed back.

'That'll be th' day! 'E's about as good as our sackless Edward over there an' that's no medal. 'E's a clear six-inch away from th' step on this side!'

At the mention of his name, Edward smiled vacantly as Reginald retorted.

'An' whose fault's that, Daniel? I told y't' watch 'im! Right 'and's always 'arder t' line up wi' th' rick in this part o' th' yard, you knows that. Take no notice, George; jealousy wears many 'eads, even one as big as Daniel's.'

Arthur and Jim, the two other horsemen, laughed out loud as Daniel snapped back.

'There's no competition 'ere, Reginald Price!'

Jim joined in the chatter.

'Ar, y'r right there, Daniel! Got that spot on; no competition…but you may mean summat different t' what we're thinkin'!' The laughter set off again. In an effort to avoid the banter, George moved to the horse's head as Jim continued, 'We'll throw from th' cart t' start wi', George; bit 'f 'eights what's wanted right now. You'll 'elp me thatch-off t'morrow, lad. This rick'll be done by then.'

George stopped in his travels.

'Yes, Mister Jim, but…won't Daniel be doin' it, th' thatchin'?'

Reginald joined in as Daniel pulled a face at the conversation's turn and its outcome.

'Never mind that Daniel. There'll be some f'r 'im t' do later…maybe. 'Bout time you learnt a bit an' y'r dad won't mind, eh?'

'No, Mister Reginald, thanks.'

He reached out to the Shire, a smaller than average grey, and she dropped her head in anticipated acceptance of George's approaching hand; he didn't disappoint.

'Chalky…Good lass.'

He folded the horse's ear gently and fondled it, creating a still moment in the grey's full and hard day.

- 4 -

15.11.99

Last ploughing day of the season was always a time for some celebration mixed with relief, and the close of this year's session was no different.

Prolonged dry conditions had made the ground harder than usual, the baked ground breaking up and leaving not so much a furrow as a scuffle. It also meant that horses suffered, for the bare stubble-ground was unforgiving and the soil, once turned, lay in large, brick-like lumps, making joints sore and muscles ache. Now, however, this track was easier on the horse's hooves, and what's more it led to home.

A tired-out George, sitting side-saddle on an equally tired-out Chalky on this fast-closing autumn afternoon, was enjoying the rocking motion of his steed…until his head dropped to his chest in semi-sleep and jerked him awake.

He adjusted his position.

Looking along the line of horses ahead he knew, even in his exhausted and groggy state that, Hiring Fair notwithstanding, this was how it would always be. Him, his father and the other horsemen working with the land, with the Shires and the seasons.

The line entered the yard and took up their respective places ready for the evening routine. Horses were tied to rings sunk into the mortar of the wall and the horsemen removed the tack and went into the small-stable block to clean up and arrange stables for feeding.

Geoffrey chivvied his son along.

'Way y'go, Georgie-Boy, get them feathers sorted.'

'Yes, Dad.'

Geoffrey called across to Edward.

'Edward, fetch water f'r George!'

Edward, a black brush in his hand, hovered uncertainly, working out where the buckets were.

Geoffrey saw his dilemma.

'Buckets're in th' usual place, Edward, where they always are? Far wall, th' drop-back, by th' barrels?' Edward's face showed realisation as Geoffrey walked over to him. 'Oh, an' Edward…?'

'Yes, Mister Geoffrey.'

He took the brush gently from him.

'You've not been back a few seconds an' y've done it again. Don't use these black brushes, they're f'r Governor's missus' cob only; understand?

'Yes, Mister Geoffrey.'

'I know y' f'rget these things but I shouldn't 'ave t' say it so often. That's three times in th' past week.' He held it up in the air and waved it. 'Black Brushes?'

Edward looked at it.

'Yes, Mister Geoffrey.'

'Don't use 'em. Right?'

Edward smiled at him.

'No, Mister Geoffrey.'

Geoffrey pointed to the small-stable entrance.

'Now, put it back on th' shelf in there an' fetch th' water f'r George, eh?'

'Yes, Mister Geoffrey.'

Edward remained where he was.

'Water. Far wall…by th' trough.'

'Yes, Mister Geoffrey.'

'Now; brush back.'

'Yes, Mister Geoffrey.'

Geoffrey indicated the direction Edward should travel and followed him into the small-stables, pausing to lean conspiratorially into George on his way.

'Keep 'n eye Georgie-Boy, will y'r. I know 'e's twelve year older'n you but e's just a child in 'is 'ead, remember that.'

'Yes, Dad.'

Edward returned to the yard and stood blinking at the surroundings.

George joined him.

'Edward? Water?'

Edward nodded in further realisation and went to fetch the water. George grabbed a couple of old brushes and together they started the yard routine.

It was only as they were finishing the sluicing and brushing-out of the last of the Shire's feathers and tails that George noticed Edward had one of the black brushes in his hand.

Scrambling over to him, he took it and said in a forced, hissed, whisper.

'Edward! 'Ow'd y'r manage that? You 'eard Dad, Mister Geoffrey. 'E said not t' use th' black brushes! Just!'

Edward looked at the brush in George's hand and blinked a couple of times, seemingly surprised it was there and even more surprised that he had been using it.

'Yes, Mister George.'

'No, not Mister George, Edward, just George. An' not t' use these brushes!'

'Not t' use brushes. Yes, Mister George.'

He stood looking, a puzzled smile on his face. George knew he needed to expand the point.

'No, not that y' can't use…' Edward was drifting, George could see it. 'Edward, listen! Look, it's not that y' can't use any brushes, just not these black ones!' He waved it. 'These!' George could see this was bypassing Edward. 'Just…don't, not these…just…look, f'rget it… an' don't use 'em again!'

'Yes, Mister George.'

Dipping the black brush into clean water and quietly placing it back on the shelf, George returned to the yard and, with finger placed to lips, whispered loudly.

'Edward? Shhhh!'

Edward smiled and did likewise.

Yard work done, the horses were led into their respective stables and the ploughmen set-to with the full brushing prior to bait being doled out.

George brushed and combed out the fast-drying feathering around Chalky's hooves, gradually working his way higher up her body. Standing at sixteen-two, slightly smaller than the other Shires, her reduced stature still meant George could not quite complete the grooming. He had reached his maximum when Geoffrey entered the stables from the tack-room.

''Ere, Lad, let's give you an 'and.'

Standing back, George watched his father begin to sweep the horse's back and rump with long, true brush strokes. The dust and hair billowed up, enveloping Geoffrey and starting him on a bout of prolonged, breathless coughing.

Daniel's head popped over the stable divide.

'Crikey, Geoff, that cough's gettin' worse. You'll 'ave t' stop smokin' that pipe o' yours.'

Moving away from the cause, Geoffrey made his hacking-coughing way to the far end of the stable. Followed by an anxious George, he reached the feed store and gradually managed to control his breathing.

'Alright, Georgie-Boy, just a bit o' loose chaff.' He looked back in Daniel's direction. 'I'll pack up this pipe when I'm passed off this land maybe, Daniel. An' what'd you do f'r a smoke if I did pack it in, eh?'

Daniel made his way slowly across, empty, tapping pipe in hand.

'I'll get by, which is more 'n you'll do; you're fit f'r th' knacker.'

Reginald and Arthur joined Geoffrey, Reginald indicating Daniel as he spoke.

'That's 'is answer f'r everythin'. Take no notice, Geoff.'

Geoffrey looked up.

''Ave I ever?'

'Not often, Geoffrey, no.'

Sitting on an upturned bucket, Geoffrey took out his pipe as Edward walked unsteadily past the men carrying two large, full buckets of water.

Daniel kicked out at him as he passed.

'Oi! careful wi' that water, stupid! My 'orses fust, don't forget, not like last evenin'! Leave that rubbish grey 'til last!'

George left the men and went along the aisle ahead of Edward. Daniel, intent on gaining free tobacco, failed to notice George opening Chalky's stall door for Edward who entered, put down the water and slipped quickly out, George closing the door after him.

Slicing some tobacco circles off a jet-black stick of un-cut shag with his pen-knife, Geoffrey began to pack his pipe as he spoke.

''Ave a little thought f'r th' workers, Daniel. I'm told she were th' first 'orse you 'ad when you arrived 'ere, what, five year ago? You've been 'ere a year longer 'n th' gaffer, eighteen month longer 'n me an' still learned nothin'. Can't believe you'd talk about Chalky like that.'

Daniel's reply dripped venom.

'Ar, they give me that grey alright; th' runt, just t' keep me in me place!'

'Well, what'd you expect? Y' were just a stable-lad; still are! Should think y'rself lucky y'weren't given a mule!'

'Would've been better off wi' a mule th'n that nag!'

Geoffrey shook his head in disbelief.

'Summat missin' in your intelligence I'd reckon then, Daniel, 'cos we all know that grey's worth two 'f

anythin' in 'ere. Way you treated 'er in th' past y' should
be grateful she even stays in stable when y' come in;
anyother else'ld walk out!'

Reginald and Arthur laughed out loud as Daniel,
ignoring this last, moved a pipe-twitching pace closer
to Geoffrey.

Arthur joined in, indicating George as he spoke.

''Er spirit's th' same as your little 'uns over there.'

Geoffrey smiled across at George who was
accompanying Edward still.

'Ar, 'e's not a bad 'un.'

Arthur chimed in.

'Not a bad 'un? Ha! Credit where it's due, Geoff.
Never you worry. You'll be able t' put y'r feet up soon
an' that lad take over. Way 'e works 'em 'e'll be 'avin'
'is own team soon; maybe put us all out o' work.'

Daniel snorted out loud at this suggestion.

'Pha! Out o' work; me?' He tapped the pipe a little
harder. 'You maybe Arthur, Reg an' Jim too…an' thick
Edward there, 'e'd be first gone…maybe not you Mister
Geoffrey but def'nitely not me, that much I know.'

Jim moved to join them all, laughing as he did so.

'Ha! I've a wonder y' can get through them stable
doors, Daniel, 'ead as big as that.'

'I know me own worth, Jim, an' it's a sight more 'n
Edward there.' Daniel tapped his pipe yet again. 'Can I
'ave a couple o' rounds, Geoff…Mister Radcliffe, I'm
out?' With no response, Daniel covered his
embarrassment by calling down the stable. 'An' you'll
'ave t' find a better nag than Chalky there t' keep up,
Georgie-Boy!'

'I'm not your boy, Daniel!'

Pipe now to mouth, Geoffrey looked up at George's reply as he replaced the plug of tobacco in his pocket.

''E's right there too, Daniel; 'e's not!' He lit up, inhaled the thick smoke deeply and coughed a single deep bark. 'Aha-ha! That's better.'

Daniel fingered his empty pipe.

'None spare, Geoff?'

'No. You reckon I'm not long f'r this world 'cos o' my smokin' so think on th' fact that I'm sayin' no t' save y' from a fate worse 'n death, Daniel, eh?' All the men laughed out loud again as Geoffrey continued, but this time with an air of authority that wasn't lost on Daniel. 'An' as f'r th' waterin' 'f these 'ere 'orses; that'll be th' first an' last time you give an order f'r th' care-rota in this stable, Daniel Long, not while I'm 'ead stable anyways. Understood?'

His face growing red with anger, Daniel hid it by pocketing his pipe and walking back to his horse's stall, spitting into the stable guttering as he did so.

08·10·04

'Whoa, Willow, Blossom! Stand-On now; Stand-On!'

A shirt-sleeved Geoffrey stood in the stubble, mid-field, mid-furrow and fast approaching mid-day.

Taking out his pipe and filling it, he watched the gulls as they circled in anticipation of the restart.

'You just wait on you lot, important business t' be seen to first.'

Walking to the horses' heads, he split an apple with his tobacco-stained pen-knife, sliced off a segment and popped it into his mouth, then shared the remainder with the horses.

'You're spoilt, y' know that? Both 'f y'r.

All three munched away in carefree manner as Geoffrey gazed at the landscape.

'By 'eck, girls but we live in a sixth-day county. God knew what 'e were doin' when 'e made Leicestershire, eh?'

He mopped his brow with his white-spotted, blue 'kerchief and made his way back to the plough, running his hand down Blossom's flank as he did so.

'Warm, eh? That sun's got some power f'r th' month, I know. Ground's well dry too.'

Back at the plough's stilts, with a match struck, a pipe alight and a set of reins to hand, the needs of all participants in this particular seasonal scene, horses, man, field and gulls, were satisfied with Geoffrey's simple call;

"Haul-On, ladies!"

—⦿—

In their cottage, George and his mother, Clara, were at the kitchen table, Clara just finishing off packing lunch into a home-made, olive green shoulder bag.

'You go careful t' th' field now. It's a fair step but be quick, y'r dad'll be ready for 'is snap, I know. There's a bottle o' tea in there, mind it's not broke; an' there's one 'f my biscuits in there f'r you too.' She handed the bag across. ''Ere. 'Way y'go.'

George took it.

'Thanks Mam. Dad said I've t' carry on th' plough while 'e's takin' 'is snap so I'll stay on an' come back with 'im at 'alf-three.'

Clara ruffled his hair with her hand as he moved to the kitchen door.

'Any excuse t' work 'orses, you.' She smiled at him. 'Ar, right, an' see y' bring that bag back wi' y'r...'

George was out the door and away.

'...Tea-bottle in one piece!'

—⦿—

The sudden fit of coughing overtook Geoffrey causing him to take his hands off the plough's stilts and push them into his sides.

Blossom and Willow sensed the alteration in pressure, felt the plough topple and, after taking half-a-dozen more steps, halted mid-field to await further instruction.

Snatching the pipe from his mouth as the coughing grew in intensity, the chest spasms took Geoffrey's body over completely…face turned red then flushed distorted blue…panic showed in his eyes…lack of oxygen waved its white flag…he dropped to his knees, then flopped face-first into the furrow, soil and rotting leaf debris filling eyes and mouth…the coughing fit made a marionette of his prostrate body as it reached a crescendo…then all was still.

—⁓—

George's pace quickened along the lane; he wanted to tell his father about the blackthorn crop and how the next frost would bring them to harvest state.

The field gate was open. He saw the horses standing, the spilt plough waiting…

'Dad? Snap, Dad!'

His arrival and call dispersed the recently settled gulls from the field.

'Girls? Where's master then?'

As he came into line with it, the odd shape in the furrow attracted his gaze.

'Dad!'

Running to the body he threw down the bag. Grabbing the now fast-cooling hand he rolled his father's body over.

'Dad, Dad!'

George looked around the field.

''Elp, someone!'

The two Shires snorted and rattled their harness.

'Dad! Dad… Mam!'

The discarded lunch bag and its leaking liquid registered.

'I've broke tea-bottle, Dad…'

—⁓—

The quietness of the house after the bustle of the past hour was tangible.

George's arrival home with Reginald and the two Shires caused the first domino to fall; his mother's appearance at the door swiftly followed by her initial, wailed reaction.

Then the moving of the body from cart to a rapidly cleared kitchen table; the hurried departure of Reginald to fetch the doctor; the arrival of Clara's sister, Rose; the arrival of Joseph, the farm's owner, and shortly after the reappearance of Reginald and the local doctor…and through it all the peripheral presence of Edward.

The death certificate was given in exchange for the doctor's promise that he'd inform the undertaker. Soon after, both Reginald and Joseph left to report on events to the other farm staff and their respective families.

Edward stayed on for a further ten minutes, moving to-and-from the lane and yard of George's house. Eventually, uncertain what to do, how to react, he too drifted away, back home.

With all concerned sightseers and officials gone, there entered into this haze of grief a level of stoic determination, of a job to be done with dignity and gentle care.

Sorting through clothing with which to dress Geoffrey, Clara and Rose's state of emotion was betrayed only by the occasional outward noise of loss.

In the kitchen, where from this day breakfast would never be taken without his father's presence, George sat holding the shrouded Geoffrey's cold hand.

After some seconds he stood gently, slipped the cloth clear then sat back and held the hand once more, unable now to take his eyes off his father's uncovered face.

Unconsciously rubbing the stiffened palm in a gentle massage, George eventually noticed this action and his gaze shifted to the dark stains on his father's fingertips. Taking a wet cloth from the bowl nearby, he began to rub at the stains, first one finger, then another, then another. Gradually his action gained in strength and speed, became all-consuming, frenetic…and now the tears flowed…and flowed.

Rose's hand on his arm and her calming voice halted his actions but failed to halt his tears.

'Scrub away all y'r like, George, you'll not shift it. That's th' soil 'e took away from a lifetime on th' land.'

From the doorway, Clara spoke in confirmation.

'Runs to 'is 'eart that stain, son. It's th' mark 'f a man. My ploughman.'

11.10.04

Churchyards had just been a part of the district that drifted by whilst other, more important errands were run. From now on, Allingham churchyard would hold a far greater magnetism.

The interment was witnessed by Joseph, his wife, Grace, and all the other farm staff excepting Daniel, who was conspicuous by his absence. Geoffrey's three bereaved family members gathered at the graveside to share this, the most intimate moment in their lives with these official mourners, plus the idle gaze of other interested local folk. Although Allingham was small and familiar, the church of St. Michael was of sufficient size to cater for the first-breathing-last-leaving of several villages round about.

Highly personal and private events like this became open, social gatherings as uninvited spectators reacquainted themselves with the celebratable or lamentable events now being experienced by their near-neighbours. In turn these events would become theirs; they knew this, but today they were allowed to reflect on their own inevitabilities without the cutting edge of personal involvement. Now, with the service over and the vicar's short, graveside eulogy given due consideration and comment by this caring mass of strangers, they gently moved away to continue shopping and chatter. Geoffrey's fellow horsemen moved off back to the farm too, and, shortly after, Joseph and Grace left the graveside allowing the inner-circle space to grieve without the corset of good form.

George was the first to move. He stepped forward to the fresh tilled soil, dug his hands deep into it and threw the gathered handful of earth into the grave. The soil hit the coffin and he stood at its edge blinking in surprise at the noise it made.

Time for niceties over and the bar at the *Plume of Feathers* beckoning, Robert Cott, gravedigger to the masses, moved rapidly in to finish his work. The shovel switched back and dug into the mound of soil only to stop as George grabbed the handle. Robert looked in surprise at the strength in such a youngster and had no choice but to relinquish it.

Stepping alongside the mound, George began to back-fill the grave, each shovel-full landing atop the coffin with a resounding full stop.

Clara now took hold of the end of the shovel, stopping George from completing the task.

'No, George, that's f'r others t' do. Say goodbye an' leave 'im to 'is earth, eh?'

After a look into the grave, George looked into his mother's face and nodded.

'Ar, Mam. Land's won.' He handed the shovel back to the gravedigger. 'Sorry, Mister Cott.'

Robert nodded in silent understanding.

George linked arms with Clara and Rose and this trio walked towards the churchyard's entrance, leaving an already very busy gravedigger to further work up his innate thirst.

Edward was standing by the open lych-gate and he raised a hesitant hand at George.

'Back in bit, Mam.'

He moved across.

'Yes, Edward?'

'Gaffer waits on y'. Told me…trust me…t' tell y'r.'

George nodded.

'Ar, thought it'd not be long. Thanks, Edward; I'll be along as soon as I see Mam an' Aunt Rose to 'ome.' He looked expectantly at Edward; nothing. 'Where, Edward?'

Edward stood looking blankly at George.

'Where does 'e want t' see me, Edward? Th' gaffer.'

Edward blinked, then the thought struck him and he smiled broadly.

'At 'ouse!' he said triumphantly.

George smiled at him.

'Thanks, Edward.'

Boarding the cart they had been loaned, the bereaved family set off back to the farm. In the yard, Reginald took over the horses and saw to their needs as the trio made their way back to their cottage. Once inside and with coats removed, George put the kettle onto the range and spooned tea into pot. Taking two cups and saucers from the overmantle cupboard, he placed them onto the table.

He saw the envelope, opened and read the death certificate for the umpteenth time, then replaced it.

'Not much in exchange f'r a life, is it?'

His mother called from the bedroom.

'What, George?'

'Nothin' Mam! I said I've laid f'r tea. Kettle's on! I'm away t' see Mister Joseph. Back in a bit.'

Without waiting for a reply, George set off across the yard to the gaffer's house.

—⚊—

Space and comfort. Those were the two words that came to George as he was ushered into the farmhouse by Grace.

'I'm just so sorry, George.'

'Thank y', Missus Grace.'

'Not all bad though.' George looked at her puzzled as Grace just nodded. 'Joseph and I have talked some. You'll see.'

She showed him into the kitchen and the waiting Gaffer and then left them to it.

Joseph shook George's hand and invited him to the table.

'A seat young George an' a cup o' tea an' chat, eh?' They sat at opposite ends of a large wooden kitchen table and Joseph poured two cups of strong brown tea. 'You'll take sugar?'

'Ar, thanks, Gaffer…er, three please.'

A smile passed across Joseph's face.

The two held a look across the table for a couple of seconds then, tea sugared and passed across, Joseph settled and began.

'Now, y' know I'd not see a family out 'f it…an' y'r dad were a top man. Ar, top man. Y' mother's said she'll vouch f'r y'…a lot t' learn but y' show some promise.'

'Yes, Gaffer.'

There was a short silence with tea-sipping accompaniment.

Eventually Joseph put his cup down.

'Tell y'r what. Me an' th' Missus Grace 'ave done a bit o' chat. Y' c'n keep th' cottage, same deal as y'r father, an' carry on wi' the 'orse work. I'll pay y'r 'alf th' rate, y'r only a lad yet an' y'll be learnin' on the job; got t' be worth summat that. You do us a good year an' we'll see about keepin' you on come next 'Irin' Fair…an' uppin' th' wage a bit; that gives y'r just under a year t' prove y'rself. 'Ow's that sound?'

Joseph could see the look of relief in George's face.

'Sounds fine. Thank you, Gaffer.'

'Ar. You're a good lad, George, allus said it. Just you keep on 'ard at it an' learn y' trade.'

George nodded.

'Yes, Gaffer, I will.'

08.03.06

Approaching this trio of stone-pickers on the damp potato ground as it was prepared for planting had been routine, but on this trip back up the field's length even a young man as naïve as George had clocked there was something on the bubble.

With George twenty-five or so yards distant, Jenny Clayson timed her movement to perfection. To fits of suppressed giggles from her partners in crime, Mary Suttcliffe and Victoria Ollerenshaw, a couple of innocent steps took Jenny into a direct line with George's path as she called out her opening remark.

'So, George, where's that grey; Chalky ain' it? Not seen 'er f'r a few days now.'

George was innocently surprised at her interest and slowed his approach to call back.

'Still in stable, Mrs Clayson, thanks f'r askin'. Not been well at all…losin' weight now, so I 'ear.'

'Y'don't know?'

'Well, no. I've not 'ad much chance t' see 'er this past week, lots t' get done an' Good Friday's less than a month off. Gaffer's been away a bit recent, an' now Mister Reginald's gone an' Daniel's runnin th' stable, 'e's taken t' sortin' 'orses f'r th' week's work 'imself now. I collect 'em from th' yard each day…could y' just…?'

'Ow long's that been then?'

'Erm… Past two week…er, Mrs Clayson, could…?'

'But y' clean up at close don't y'r?'

'Erm…ar, I do, but 'e's moved 'orses round a bit too. Chalky's at th' far end o' th' stable now, an' Daniel's said 'e don't want 'er disturbed; not now she's not well.'

George drew on steadily but slower now, closer to Jenny who pursued her objective with a terrier's tenacity.

'Things changed a bit now 'e's 'ead stable, eh?'

'Seems so. Wi' it bein' 'is job t' look after th' poorly stock 'e keeps 'is remedies an' potions close to 'is chest, just like most 'f 'em…err, Mrs Clayson, could y' clear th' way, please?'

Jenny stood her ground. She had no need to feign further equine interest now and moved on to the topic proper.

''E's a good-looker, y'know. Wha'd'y' think, Mary? Our George good enough f'r a local lass like y'rself, or is 'e f'r better things?'

Wiping her nose on her sleeve, Mary moved across to extend the barrier.

'Far too good f'r th' likes 'f a scrubber like you, Jenny Clayson, I know.'

George had no option but to halt the team.

'Whoa girls! Stand-On!' The two Shires drew to a halt. 'Mrs Clayson, Miss Suttcliffe, please? I've t' get on…'

Jenny showed no regard for George's obvious discomfort as she spoke over him.

'Watch out, George, looks like our Mary's clearin' th' field, an' I'm not talkin' 'bout stones neither.'

The women laughed at the joke and Mary shoved Jenny playfully on the arm and snapped back.

'Nothin' o' th' sort, Miss Guttersnipe. I'm a 'spectable single lady o' this shire; ain' I, Vicky?'

'Two outta three ain't bad.'

Mary looked across at Victoria.

'Meanin', Vicky Ollerenshaw?'

George was beginning to get nervous. The personal chatter was spiralling well beyond his limited social capabilities.

'Ladies, please, I…'

But Mary was having none of it.

'You just 'old y'r 'orses Master George Radcliffe! I think I might 'ave just been insulted, an' y'r wouldn't want that, you bein' a gentleman an' all, would y'r?' She turned back to Vicky. 'Meanin', Ollie?'

Straightening up from her work, Victoria moved in to complete the blockade.

'Well, Mary, y' single an' y're a woman…'

''Ere's th' pot callin' th' kettle…! Courted at seventeen, George, an' a race t' see who'd be first into church, 'er or th' baby!'

Seizing the chance, Jenny promoted her friend's cause.

'Looks like Mary's the only footloose-'n'-fancy-free lass in th' field, George. Wi' th' job 'f 'ead stable opened up now Reginald's moved on…well, y' could do worse.'

'Not much!' said Vicky, dismissively. 'An' any'ow, that Daniel Long's 'ead stable now.'

'Ha! That Daniel Long'll last about a week,' snorted Jenny. ''E couldn't tell a decent 'orse from a blowfly. No, 'e's just a stop-gap. Our George's destined f'r that one, mark my words, an' 'e'll need a good woman alongside 'im…failin' that, our Mary 'ere.'

'I c'n tell a good 'orse fr'm a blowfly.'

'She can! An' she's got prospects too, 'aven't y', Mary?'

'I 'ave, Jenny. I'm out t' be a dairy-maid, I am.'

'There y'r go, George. Th' choice is between our Mary, who's out t' be a dairy-maid an' can tell a good 'orse from a blowfly, or Ivy over there; an' sight o' that face 'ld stop a pig a chain distant.

Vicky looked across alarmed.

'Jenny, she'll 'ear y'r!'

'She'll not! She's usually three-parts cut, as deaf 's a parsnip…' She called her next remark across the field to a lady who was set slightly apart from the main body of stone-pickers. '…An' as pretty as a Landrace sow wi' rouge on! That right, Ivy?'

Straightening her back and looking up to locate the call, the said Ivy waved and smiled in their direction. In so doing, she revealed a mouth which was full of pipe and empty of front teeth, set in a face that had all the high colour, vein marks and bulbous nose of a heavy drinker.

Jenny waved back.

'Alright, Ivy?' Removing the pipe-stub, the best reply Ivy could offer in reply was several deep, throaty coughs, the gift of a lifetime's tobacco abuse. Jenny turned back to Victoria. 'That's a face only a mother c'ld love. Good job it were covered by a tit most o' th' time, eh? Chuck 'er in a spud-clamp an' unless she landed arse-up we'd never find 'er!'

Victoria and Mary laughed out loud and George looked the opposite way in embarrassment. Taking George's distracted gaze as cover, Mary moved rapidly round to him. As she passed Victoria she winked and adjusted her hand-hold so that, along with her well-soiled sacking apron still half-full of stones, she incorporated a handful of her skirt, lifting it well above her knee.

George's surprise at turning and suddenly seeing Mary so close only made her mood more coquettish.

'That's all y' get wi' dried-up marrieds, George; just chat.'

She altered her hold, spilling a small stone from her collection and letting go a very breathy, 'Ooooops,' as it fell, coupled with a dazzling smile. She slowly dropped onto one knee in order to retrieve the stone. Her loose-fitting blouse drooped down low at the neckline, fully revealing her unfettered and very large breasts. Gently picking up the stone, Mary stood up to look George in the eye. She was very close to him now, her face lightly stained where she'd wiped her soiled hands across it.

She leant even closer and whispered, 'What y' want is a filly wi' experience; show y' th' ropes...eh?' then moved back slightly, smiled and winked slowly at him.

Victoria and Jenny began to snigger and moved to join Mary. As they passed the Shires, Jenny slowed her pace and ran her hand provocatively down the rump of one of them.

'That's a lovely firm arse…'orse's ain't too bad neither.'

With the way ahead clear, a by now very red-faced George flicked the reins and clicked the team forward.

'On-On, girls. Haul-On!'

Both Blossom and Willow reacted immediately, moving quickly past the three women and forcing them to take rapid evasive action.

With drawn-out 'Ahhhs,' they watched him go.

Jenny sighed loudly.

'Hmmmm; that's coloured 'im up a treat Mary, 'e'll be goin' up 'n' down all day now.'

Mary sighed.

'Ooooo, I wish, Jenny, I wish!'

They all laughed as Victoria folded her arms across her chest, cocking her head to one side like a puzzled puppy.

'An' y'r right, Jenny, 'e 'as got th' best arse in th' trio. Look!'

Mary and Jenny copied Vicky's head position…then all three burst into further loud laughter.

—✲—

George returned to the farm a good deal later than usual. All the other horsemen had finished tending to their working teams and, unusually, even Daniel was absent. He tied his team up and patted Blossom as he went to fetch water and brushes.

'I'll maybe give Chalky a bit o' time after you two're sorted, eh? I'll give 'er y' best.'

The dry conditions meant the grooming was greatly shortened and it wasn't long before both horses were in their stalls, scrubbed and fed. He had not seen Chalky for five or six days, confined to the far end of the stable as she was. Daniel had decided to move her, reassuring George that she needed to be 'Out o' th' way,' and 'Given a bit o' quiet.' At the time, George had suggested that he could share the work, but Daniel had been adamant the grey be kept under his care. Disappointed as he was, George did as told.

Chalky had acknowledged his arrival earlier with a snort and hoof scrape and now, as George approached her stall, she lowered her head over the door and he responded to her whickered request with a gentle stroke of her ear.

''Ello, old girl. Long time-no see, eh? Been busy, we 'ave. Spuds t' get in an' Daniel's said y' need a bit o' quiet; just thought I'd see 'ow y'r was. Can't do no 'arm that, can it? Blossom 'n' Willow send their best…'

Her floor looked very low on bedding straw and George noticed her dull coat and thinning muscle. He joined her in the stall.

'Still not quite th' ticket, eh, an' still losin' weight by th' looks. Daniel maybe needs to up y'r med'cine, I reckon.'

He noticed her trough was empty, nothing unusual there, but her manger was too…and her water bucket was missing. George leant over the stable door and looked along the aisle.

No bucket in view.

'Someone's f'rgot y' water, lass. Good job I 'appened by, eh? I'll get some…' George looked at the straw. '…An' either they're bein' mean on th' beddin' or you're eatin' it. Best stop that or Daniel'll be fallin' out wi' y'r.' A further snort and hoof-scrape was the answer and George shook his head and patted her neck. 'You rascal. I'll get y' some fresh. Daniel'll not mind me 'elpin' out…an' I'll talk t' Mam about you; she'll 'ave an idea, I know.'

Fresh straw collected and shaken out, no sooner was it on the floor than the grey began to eat it.

'Oi, stop it now! Looks like y've lost y'r appetite 'n' found a donkey's; but y'r no better for it.' George looked over the stable door and along to the feed barrels again. ''Ave y' been fed; 'ave y'r…? Y' must've…'

The straw-munching continued. George looked closely at her eye. His face set as the thought occurred to him of what might have happened.

''Ave they missed y'r out…? Others might do, maybe, but not Edward, I know; 'e's not much mem'ry but 'e don't f'rget 'orses…'Old on an' I'll fetch rations. If I'm wrong then extra f'r once won't 'urt.'

Up in the loft above the stable, George filled his arms with hay and had to fight off the grey as he re-entered her stall with it.

''Ang on, 'ang on! Let me get it t' manger…you'll 'ave me braces snipped yet…'ang on!'

With a struggle he managed to load the hay into the manger and Chalky set-to as he went to the rank of feed barrels via Willow's stall.

'Just a loan, y' understand; y'r stable-mate's got a bit 'f a worm, I think.'

Dipping into Willow's barrel he tipped a scoop of mixed feed into a bucket. Chalky nudged him out of the way as she rapidly moved to the trough.

'Manners! Now, some water, eh?'

Past the hay-loft steps, he filled a bucket with water from one of the wall barrels in the yard out back. As he came back into the stable so he saw Daniel moving swiftly along the central aisle towards the feed bins.

'Evenin', Daniel. I thought you'd all finished.'

Daniel seemed surprised, flustered and annoyed to see George at that late hour.

'Radcliffe! What you doin' 'ere…wha'd'y' mean, all finished? 'Course we 'ave; long while ago we did. I 'ad an errand t' run…you're th' one is late.'

'Ar, chain split on th' back couplin' o' th' drag an' it took awhiles t' fix it.'

But Daniel wasn't listening.

'Y'were lucky I 'adn't locked feed bins; don't let it 'appen again.' He indicated Willow and Blossom. 'You finished baitin' them pair?'

'Ar, just…I hope it were alright, I just took some o' Willow's f'r Chalky…' Daniel's face dropped. '…I think she might need a bit 'f extra rations 'cos all 'er beddin's…'

Over to Chalky's stall, Daniel grabbed an empty sack in passing.

''Ave you been messin' wi' that grey? Will y'do as told? I said t' leave 'er t' me!'

'I didn't think it'd do any 'arm, Daniel.'

Daniel smacked the grey roughly to one side and removed what feed remained in the trough.

'Y' know nothin', Radcliffe!'

Putting the water-bucket down, George followed him.

'I know enough t' see that grey were 'ungry; I think…' Then he realised what Daniel was doing. 'Aye, Daniel, where's Chalky's feed goin' to?'

'A better cause, Georgie-Boy!'

'You put that back, an' don't keep callin' me Georgie-Boy, you're not my dad!'

Dropping the sack by his horse's stall, Daniel kicked over the full water-bucket in passing, re-entered the grey's stable and took out the hay.

'No, I'm not y' dad, y'r right there. If I were, you'd've picked a better beast t' work wi' than this runt!' Daniel carried the loose hay and piled it up at the base of the hay-loft steps. 'Y're a bit green t' be tellin' me 'ow t' run a stable, Georgie-Boy. Don't you forget, I'm 'ead stable now.'

'Only 'til they find a new man f'r Reginald…'

'An' that'll be never! Level o' wages our rogue 'f a gaffer pays won't fetch no one. So y've t' make it work wi' me, Georgie-Boy, an' y'r goin' th' wrong way about it, special if y' start cuttin' down on my 'orse's feed ration.'

Daniel went over to the row of open feed barrels as George pursued both him and the conversation.

'Your 'orse's feed?' Then the turn of events dawned fully on George. 'Y've not 'ave y'? But you said she needed quiet… an'…an' it's not your 'orse's feed, it's 'ers! Chalky's!'

Daniel pointedly drew a knife out of his coat pocket and flicked Willow and Blossom's feed barrel lids shut with it, locking both and underlining the point.

'Lock-up time! That old nag's f'r th' knacker within th' week, I say, so why throw good food after bad?'

Anyone else would probably have let it drop; not George.

'Because she's earned it, that's why!'

With an alacrity that took him completely by surprise, Daniel turned on a sixpence, grabbed George by the throat and slammed him back against the stable door-post, rapidly removing all the wind from George's chest. With his knife and bad breath very close to his startled face, Daniel growled slowly, deliberately.

'An' I say she's earned nothin' but th' knacker; now, leave it alone, you 'ear?'

With a single movement he swung George round and shoved him roughly against the opposite, inner stall wall, further winding him. Pocketing his knife, he spat out his intentions.

'I'll be emptyin' 'er stock-barrel Friday, after knacker calls. You call me to account wi' th' gaffer…or feed that grey from any 'orse's barrel, an' I'll cut you then th' nag, so I will!' Latching Chalky's stall in passing, Daniel left the stable, announcing over his shoulder as he went. 'Remember. Say nothin' an' take nothin'; Georgie-Boy!'

It took a while for George to recover from Daniel's reaction. Eventually he walked to the feed barrels, checked and called back up the stable to Chalky.

'Closed shop, lass!'

He busied himself.

Retrieving the hay and re-filling the manger, he slipped over to the back-field, stripped several scrub-mangolds and lifted a few scruffy turnips from his own garden. A hastily grabbed flop of grass from the field's edge completed his shopping. Returning to Chalky's stall, he dropped the makeshift rations into her trough. Chalky left the hay and nuzzled George out and herself in.

He re-filled the water bucket and she left her trough and drank deeply.

'Spoilt f'r choice now, eh?'

George picked up a brush and began to gently stroke her coat, his head buzzing with the recent revelations……

—⟞⟝—

'It'll be some groom t' set 'er right, young George!' Joseph's opening remark took George completely by surprise and he expanded the point. 'She's not been out f'r four days now, I'm told. Daniel's told us its kidneys an' 'e's reckoned on th' knacker. I'm not keen t' keep an old 'un like that 'angin' on in pain f'r th' sake 'f it so I'll be sendin' a note t'morrow f'r Friday collection.'

George's voice dripped contempt.

'Save y'r brass, Gaffer, she'll be starved by then. 'Er feed's missin' 'er belly by a stall.'

Joseph moved round to join him.

'Time an' a word, George Radcliffe, explain y'rself.' He saw the makeshift bait in the trough. 'An' them's not rations, where they from?'

'From 'ome an' th' back-field, Gaffer, 'er stable feed's goin' into other mouths. Been a gradual tailin' off t' nothin' f'r over three week or more, I'd guess…an'…'

George stopped, unsure of quite how to continue but Joseph was not about to let it hang there.

'Well? 'An'' what? C'mon, spit it out if y've summat t' say, lad!'

'Gaffer, if that 'orse 'as a kidney complaint then it's Christmas!'

'Oh, in th' presence 'f an expert, are we?'

'No, Gaffer, but…look, I mightn't know much but I know enough t' remember well what my dad taught me. Stand back a bit, Gaffer.' Joseph did so. 'Now, 'ow's Chalky standin'?' George looked at Joseph then nodded and filled in his boss's silence. 'Just like an 'orse? Ar, I agree. No stretchin' 'f 'er legs like she's about t' piss, nothin'. An', if it's kidneys, where's th' rose 'ips soakin', eh? Not in 'ere, that's f'r sure.'

'Your father taught y' well, lad.'

'Ar, Gaffer, an' Gypsies taught 'im.'

Running a hand down Chalky's ribs, Joseph looked along her side.

'Kidneys…? Well, maybe.' He looked at the mare that, having slaked her thirst, was now scrunching her way through the trough's meagre fare. 'Appetite looks good now…even if it is rubbish she's eatin'.'

'Y'r want more, Gaffer? If its kidneys then where's th' blood? There's enough piss on th' floor; look!' George kicked the straw to one side to reveal the stable's wet, cobbled floor. ''Ere's 'orse what's been locked in f'r four days now, not cleaned out proper neither, yet there's no blood; now why's that? Any 'orse wi' kidney problems'll shift some blood; y'd smell it comin' into th' stable…an' 'ow come an 'orse that's so sick is drinkin' like a fish…when it's offered to 'er that is.'

Joseph thought some more, then spoke with the voice of a mind made up.

'Right, what's a fact is she's thinnin' out. Daniel reckons its kidneys, you've made a convincin' case its not. Daniel says she's been fed an' cared for as usual an' you reckon not. 'Ave y'r seen 'er not bein' fed?'

'Well, no, Gaffer…'

'Badly treated?'

'No, Gaffer. Daniel keeps us all at bay while 'e gets 'er well, so 'e says.'

'Right, so you reckon one thing an' 'e reckons another. Maybe it's not kidneys but maybe it is summat else.'

'Gaffer, she's starvin' is all!'

Cutting across George, Joseph's voice showed his annoyance at having let the stable get this far out of his control.

'An' so says a boy! All this could cost me, an' we're not just talkin' money 'ere y' know!' George gave no reply. 'Silence; best policy that, Master Radcliffe. Now, this is 'ow it stands. I won't carry passengers, y' knows that. But I'm not a man t' begrudge a beast its victuals neither, particular a one as worked f'r me these past ten year an' 'ad as difficult a start as she did.'

'Never 'ad th' best 'f it, I know, Gaffer, but she's as willin' as th' rest 'f 'em. Never shirked 'er duty, even under th' guidin' 'and 'f our new 'ead stable.'

George's further reminder about Chalky's past output for the farm and of her early treatment by Daniel struck home. There was a further silence as Joseph looked from horse to stables then back to horse.

'Ar, that's fair comment, George; blunt, but fair. We 'ad a bad man in charge afore y' father arrived 'ere… afore I took over farm from mother.'

He paused and George was acutely aware the memories for Joseph were troublesome.

'Sorry if I've stirred up some bad things, Gaffer; would never do that if I'd've know'd.'

'No, I know that, George. Y' dad knew th' score, no 'arm passin' it on t' th' son… As she got older an' sicker, mother, so she let things go, but would she 'ave 'elp? Not 'er, not even from 'er own children she wouldn't. Proud she were, an' 'ard, but never on top 'f it; not f'r th' last three year 'f 'er life she weren't.' He stopped again and rested his hand on Chalky's shoulder. She lifted her head momentarily and he patted her. 'Left t' their own devices some o' them chaps were less th'n carin' wi' th' stock, Daniel in partic'lar. Y' dad soon sorted out th' wheat from th' chaff; one o' th' reasons I got 'im 'ere, 'is reputation. Was surprised 'e didn't get shut 'f Daniel as 'is first job, but 'e weren't that kind o' man…well, y'know y'rself. 'E give Daniel leeway on account 'f 'is age, try t' get 'im to improve; talked me round to it an' it made sense, but I reckon damage were done t' this poor bugger by then.' He patted Chalky again. 'An' now this lot.'

'You've 'ad a lot t' see to of recent, Gaffer, I know.'

'Should've seen it though, George; no need t' make excuses f'r me, lad; good 'f y', but no need. As things are, wi' my brother's farm over at Garston needin' a fair bit o' my time this past three week, I've 'ad t' trust t' Daniel. 'E's only been made 'ead stable on account 'f 'is time 'ere; that an', like y' father, my 'ope that some responsibility might curb 'im a bit.' He shook his head, maybe to clear his thoughts, maybe to form them. 'Even then it's only 'til things get sorted wi' a replacement f'r Reginald, 'e knows that; maybe that's th' problem…I don't know… What I do know is, all that aside, I'd expect t' be kept informed about progress from 'im. If not, then from Jim or Arthur…or y'rself f'r that matter, so 'ow come nothin's been said nor done 'til now?'

George put the brush to one side.

''Cos you'll not 'ear it while there's profit t' be made f'r other's favourites…an' I've only found out I'm right t'night. Daniel does all th' sortin' o' work stock now so there's no chance to follow up problems after the day's work.'

'Does 'e now. F'r 'ow long?'

'Past fortnight, Gaffer. I thought 'e'd talked it over wi' you?'

'D'y' think I'd be askin' these questions if 'e 'ad?'

'No, Gaffer.'

'Well then.'

'There's reason f'r it then. If 'ead stable puts out signals that an 'orse is gettin' anywhere near past it then them chaps, all 'f 'em, they'll find an excuse t' leave it be'ind an' spread th' feed out among their own. It's like watchin' th' buzzards gather.'

Joseph looked long at George.

'An' you think y'can set 'er right?'

'An' I can too.'

'Y' seem very sure about all this, an' the men'll not be best pleased you tellin' me about it neither, whether y'r right or wrong…'

'I'm right.'

'Are y' now? An' wha'd'y want done about it?'

'Me, Gaffer?'

'Well you're th' one as found it all out an 'ad th' courage t' chat t' me; so, wha'd'y want done about it?'

George thought for a while.

'Look, Gaffer, this 'ain't no time t' get grudges paid back. I reckon th' fact they've been rumbled'll be enough f'r 'em all, don't you?'

'Ar, y' y'r father's son alright. Right, I'll talk to 'em in th' mornin' an' I'll impress on Daniel that 'e looks t' th' stock more. Is 'e prime suspect or is it general?'

'Like I said, 'e's 'ead stable but I'd think th' spoils are shared equal, Gaffer.'

Joseph looked along the stable to the feed barrels then back to George.

'Let's nip this then. You've not got feed keys yet, 'ave y'r?'

'No, Gaffer, Daniel 'olds 'em all now. Y' said when I were sixteen I might be allowed my day-team's key on workdays.'

'Sixteen. An' when's that?'

'Month's time, Gaffer.'

'Month is it? Well think on this as an early birthday present. Work team keys'll stay with Daniel; I'll not serve farm nor 'im by takin' away all 'is input, y'r father were right about these things. An', as old as 'e is, Daniel needs t' learn 'ow things are an' the only way 'e'll get 'old 'f that is t' do it, but wi' a bit more guidance from me; if not then 'e's destined f'r deeper trouble. Chalky's keys you c'n 'ave.' Joseph pulled a set of keys from his pocket. 'I'll collect all th' spares, Daniel's too, so you'll 'ave the only other apart from me.'

He left the stall and swiftly returned with a sack which he threw to George, pointing to the trough.

'Get shut o' that stuff in there now then move that grey back to 'er old stall an' throw in some straw. I'll open up 'er feed barrel.'

George cleared a surprised grey's trough and led her back to her old stall, distributed some straw then followed to where Joseph was waiting by the feed barrels.

'Bring a bucket, lad; wake up! You'll not get enough in y'r 'ands!' George quickly gathered one as Joseph opened the grey's feed bin. 'Only a third full mind. She's already scoffed a bag 'f 'erbage an' we don't want 'er down wi' th' bloat afore y' get chance t' prove y'rself right, do we?'

After locking the feed bin, Joseph joined George and they stood for a moment in companionable silence as Chalky happily tucked into the feed.

'Right, lad, she's on 'er way. Feed 'er fair ration an' we'll see 'ow she goes on.'

'She'll do as well as any 'ere, I say…'

'Is that right? Well, f'r y' cheek, I say any extra bait she needs t' square 'er up'll come out 'f your wage. Still keen?' George nodded firmly and Joseph laid out the deadlines. 'Right, it's March now; you've 'til mid-April; a month.' He began to leave. 'If she improves an' gets fit, she's yours…an' it'll be my say-so that declares she's fit, not yours!' Stopping in his progress, Joseph turned to further emphasise the point. 'An' mark me well, Master Radcliffe, if she flounders, come May first it'll be you as'll call th' knacker out an' give 'im an 'and t' pole-axe 'er too…an' another thing, if y'r wrong about all this an' it ain't kidneys but is summat else, then that'll be 'app'nin' a damn sight sooner than May first, understood? That'll be a late birthday present you'll 'ave bought f'r y'rself…an' 'er.' He began to leave again, then stopped and turned back as the thought struck him. 'Tell y' what, get y'rself out early t'morrow. Pick up y' team an' be gone afore all others get 'ere.'

'But, Daniel sorts 'orses, Gaffer.'

'D' y' not know who you'll be out with?'

'Gaffer?'

'What're you on t'morrow?'

'Spud ground again, Gaffer.'

'Who'd y'r 'ave today?'

'Blossom an' Willow.'

Joseph began to leave again.

'Then that's who it'll be t'morrow.'

'But…Daniel…'

Joseph spun round to face George, his face flushed with annoyance.

'I'm Gaffer 'ere, Master Radcliffe, even though it may not 'ave seemed so th' last few week…!…An' no one's more aware o' that th'n me! Now, do as bid, get you out early t'morrow, afore all others get 'ere… I'll see t' Chalky's feed an' other information, leave that one t' me.' He began to leave with a purpose this time. 'An' you'd best tread light round them men f'r a day or two.'

Before George could reply, Joseph had gone.

He looked at the still munching grey.

'Y' could be mine, Chalky…did you 'ear 'im say it? I did. Get y'rself well an' y' could be mine!'

After she'd finished up her late supper, George gave Chalky extra hay from the loft then made his way back to his cottage.

---—⧓—

'An' what time d' y' call this? Tea's been on th' table since twenty minutes t' cold, an' food's too precious t' waste.' Clara pressed him for an answer with some annoyance. 'Well?'

Sitting down to a supper he could hardly finish in his excitement, George told his mother about the evening's events, toning down his confrontation with Daniel. Clara listened, gradually joining George at the table as her interest grew.

At the close of George's tale she poured him a second cup of tea and one for herself.

'So, a chance 'f y'r own 'orse then?'

'Yes, Mam, if I can get 'er fit. I told Gaffer I could, an' I can. I get feed-bin key t'morrow but I've only got t' middle 'f April t' sort 'er out an' I've t' pay f'r any extra feed needed t' get 'er there an' Daniel…'

Holding up her hand, Clara waved it in front of him.

'Slow you down! An' 'ave no mind f'r that pie-can, Daniel! 'E's as much use round an 'orse as gadfly.'

She got up from the table and went to a cupboard under the stairs.

'But, Mam…'

'You just 'old you up a moment.'

George sat and listened to the scrabbling and clinking that played throughout his mother's absence. Eventually she came back with a tall glass bottle in her hand and announced triumphantly.

''Orse tonic! Thought there were a bottle back o' th' shelf. Y' dad 'ld be proud.' She shook the dark liquid. 'An' the extra feed? Well, I've a little by.' She winked at George. 'Let's see what we c'n do b'tween us t' get you that 'orse, eh?'

09.03.06

Into the stables well before first light, George called in on Chalky.

'Start 'f our workin' partnership, lass, an' look!' He showed her the bottle of horse tonic. 'Fitness medicine! Few doses o' this an' you'll not be walkin' round that stable wall you'll be walkin' through it! I get feed-bin key t'day so it'll be me runnin' th' larder from then on, not that Daniel Long. Gaffer'll feed y'r this mornin'; show th' rest o' them th' way… Excitin' times, eh?'

He stashed the bottle behind a loose wall-brick at the rear of her stall and left to start the day's work with Blossom and Willow.

—⚓—

It was just coming on dusk when George and his team re-entered the yard after another day on the potato ground.

Joseph was standing by the gates.

'Y' late. 'Ere!'

He tossed a key to George who caught it, halting Blossom and Willow as he did so.

'Whoa girls! Thanks, Gaffer. That stretch by them alders took longer t' finish than I thought. Rain we've 'ad an' that narrow neck o' land makes th' turns 'ard…an' that stream's runnin' full too so 'orses aren't keen on th' drop. Nor me!'

'Ar, we should maybe put that corner t' summat else. 'Arvest's no easier in th' gatherin' than th' plantin'.' He paused, as if checking all was as it should be then continued, 'You'll notice yard's empty? All chores 'cept Chalky 'ave been done. I've seen to it she were fed this mornin', got Edward t' do it, an' I made sure Daniel knew about it too. 'Ad a face like squashed toad, but 'id it well 'cos 'e's crafty. Kept quiet 'cos 'e knows there's summat been said; realised that th' minute 'e got t' stable an' saw me waitin an' th' grey moved. It's also been made clear 'is diagnosis is suspect an' that 'er feedin's under your guidance an' my audience from 'ere on. She's your concern from this evenin' so she'll need cleanin' 'n' bait afore y' get off 'ome, right?'

'Yes, thanks, Gaffer.'

There was another silence and Joseph looked George over again; a recheck.

He sniffed.

'I want you away early again t'morrow, we all need a bit o' space after this mornin's chat. I've put Arthur on spud ground 'n' you on timber, up at Priest Wood. Some pine logs t' gather from th' far end; by Wilkes'?' George nodded. 'Right. Put 'em on th' centre ride, by the 'ollow. On y'r own up there so you'll not get much in th' way o' comp'ny.' He winked. 'Alright?'

'Ar. Thanks, Gaffer; what about Chalky t'morrow?'

'I'll see to 'er, not t' worry. I need t' be 'ere t' reinforce 'ow things are so I'll be in t' watch it done. Edward'll do th' chores again; I'll see to it.'

'Right, Gaffer; thanks again.'

'Ar.' Joseph began to walk back towards the farmhouse. After a few paces he returned to George. 'Tell y' what. Leave Blossom 'n' Willow in f'r Arthur t' use an' take Titan t'morrow. That way Daniel'll know you've chosen y'r own, an' our Titan'll keep you out o' mischief, I know. I'll get Edward t' lay out 'is evenin' feed early on; it'll be in 'is stall f'r when y' gets back. Pack a feed-bag now f'r Titan's mornin' bait an' take it t' wood wi' y'r; 'e'll not want feedin' at th' time you need t' be away.'

'Titan's feed? From where? Daniel's got all the other keys…'

'From Chalky's bin, where else?' George was about to say something but Joseph pre-empted it. 'Ar, I know what y' thinkin', 'It's all th' feed you've got an' I said you'll 'ave t' pay f'r extra…'! Y' c'n stop y' bleatin'. Edward'll give it back from Titan's bin t'morrow, right?'

George smiled.

'Done it all y'rself before, eh, Gaffer?'

'Ar. You young 'uns think y' know it all but I'll tell y' summat y' don't know about; what it's like bein' fifty-eight 'avin' been sixteen. Age don't make us no smarter nor no cleverer, lad, that much must've been obvious over the past little lot. What it does do is make us more able t' find our way through th' problems that come wi' it…an' there's plenty of 'em, trust me.' He tailed off suddenly, as if surprised he'd imparted so much inner wisdom then sniffed again as he left. 'Anyway, y've key an' a month; don't waste neither.'

'No, Gaffer, I'll not…an' thanks.'

'Ar,' was the only reply he got from the departing, tunelessly whistling, Joseph.

George clicked the team on into the yard. The farm was indeed devoid of other horsemen, which was welcome to George; he was aware he had not made many friends from that morning. Once inside he set about Blossom's and Willow's evening groom by the light of a couple of oil-lamps and a fast-fading evening. By the time he had finished with his working team it was full dark outside and George set-to on the impatient Chalky's needs. After a clean out and replenishment of straw and hay, George collected the concealed horse tonic and, going to the feed barrels, inserted the key into the lock…The growing he underwent as he opened that lock and lifted the barrel lid was huge and he felt a real swell in his breast. This was what he was now; a real horseman.

Mixing feed and some of the tonic from the bottle he returned to the grey's stall. Not surprisingly she was waiting at the door, and George had to force his way past her and try to keep her muzzle out of the bucket.

He poured in the mix and the grey dived in.

'Nothin' wrong wi' you a bit o' feed 'n' care won't put right.'

He replaced the tonic bottle and began to groom her. After ten minutes the only sound was the rhythmic sweep of his brush down her flanks and the grey's nose snuffling up the last of the grains.

Once satisfied, George patted her rump as he left.

'Nothin' but good in that lot, Chalky. Rack 'f 'ay's ready an' waitin', I'll see y' t'morrow.'

He took Titan's feed-bag and filled it from Chalky's bin. After closing and locking the lid, he snuffed the lamps one-by-one on his way along the central aisle and into the yard on a cloud-covered-moon night. As he passed the drop-back of the wall, where the four rain-water barrels were kept, a heavy stick slammed into his back!

Collapsing like he had been shot, even in his shocked state, George instinctively threw up his arms to give some protection as fists and boots rained in from his attackers. The beating only lasted a few moments before the ruffians faded into the dark and away…but it was a good one.

Dazed as he was, he remembered Titan's dropped feed bag and groped around in the pitch black until he found it. After scraping up all he could, with an immense effort he drew himself up the wall, using the barrels as support, and staggered to his cottage.

With the time well on, Clara had gone to bed, which was just as well, for George's reflection in the hall mirror was not a pretty sight; he knew if his mother saw him in that state she would have a fit.

A careful wash and tooth check in the kitchen prepared him for bed and he fell into it gratefully, aching in places he did not even know he had.

10·03·06

George was up and out of the house very early the following morning. Instructions from Joseph were the cause of his early rise, but he was as much in fear of what he might find in the stable, and of his mother's reaction to his battered state if she saw him, that made the early departure welcome.

On the one count he was not disappointed.

The sky had cleared now and, as he walked across the yard in the light of the morning-moon, he could see it was Chalky's carefully polished harness which had been dumped into the manure pile. He picked the collar out of the muck, brushing off what he could, and entered the stable with some trepidation.

Lighting the aisle's lamps he moved tentatively to Chalky's stall.

George looked in and saw that, although her water bucket had been overturned, several of the front slats of her manger snapped and the hay strewn around on the floor, the grey was unharmed.

He entered her stall and put his arms round her neck.

'Am I glad you're right, lass. They'd not dare 'urt y'r now they know th' gaffer's involved but I guess they'll make it 'ard f'r us. Just got t' get you well, eh?'

He checked. The tonic was still in its hiding place, but a look along to the feed stall did not hide anything. Even from this end of the stable and in this light it was obvious it was Chalky's feed-bin lock that had been broken. Rations lay spread over the floor mixed in with what looked like horse muck.

Hanging the collar and feed-bag on Chalky's door-post, George entered the feed stall. Judging by the temperature of the muck the deed had been done late the previous night. Separating it was a hopeless task. He gathered the mess and put it at the base of Chalky's feed bin. The smashed lock lay nearby, useless. George sharpened a sliver of wood, using it to slot through the hasp and into a knot-hole so as to hold the lid open.

Collecting fresh hay, George took some string and spent five minutes strapping together the broken manger slats, filled it, then filled and returned Chalky's water bucket too.

'I'm afeared t' leave y', lass, but there's work t' do…' Chalky nosed over the stall door and towards Titan's feed in the sack. '…No, no, that's not yours! That's f'r Titan later on.' He removed it. 'Edward's first in, early as normal; 'e'll feed you at a more civilised time an' 'e'll see the mess's been made an' re-fill y' barrel too; if 'e's given space from that Daniel 'e'd not see you 'urt nor starve.' He looked around the stable. 'Just make do wi' the 'ay 'til then, I'll feed y' this evenin' when I get back.'

He patted her neck and then, tacking Titan, he led him from his stable. Hitching up the chains to the massive Shire gelding they headed out of the yard, off to the wood and peace.

—⚏—

In spite of his stiffness the day had been a good one, even if the spectre of Chalky did keep returning to George. Gradually his beaten body eased and his mind was taken up with the task in hand. At the close of the day and although he knew he had done it, it was with some satisfaction he looked over the heap of pine tree trunks Titan had hauled to the central ride.

'Good job done there, lad. Gaffer'll be pleased.'

Arriving back from Priest Wood, George entered the stable yard riding atop Titan. He dismounted with a little difficulty and was about to begin Titan's evening clean-up when he sensed something was amiss…

Leaving the gelding tied in the yard, he entered the stables quietly only to see Daniel doing up his fly and jumping down from a barrel placed directly in front of Chalky's open feed bin.

'Daniel! You dirty, rotten sod!'

Daniel was ready for him in a trice. Even though George attacked with some spirit and landed a couple of blows, his condition and inexperience was no match for a seasoned campaigner such as Daniel. Several blows and a well-placed boot from him soon had George spread-eagled and gasping on the floor, blood coming from his mouth and above his eye.

Daniel, blood also leaking from his lip, grabbed a mound of dung left from that morning.

'Runnin' off t' th' gaffer like that…y' bastard! Wi'
'im watchin' I'm stood off that grey, but not off you!' He
threw the muck onto George. 'That's all you're fit for,
th' fuckin' dung 'eap, an' there's plenty more where that
come from, Georgie-Boy!'

He spat a mouthful of blood and froth onto George,
grabbed a handful of hay to wipe his hands, kicked the
door of Chalky's stall in passing and left the stable
without looking back.

Never had George hurt so much and it took several
minutes before he could get up. After sharing the
gelding's feed between both Shires and completing the
painful business of cleaning, George steeled himself
for the walk home. The journey from yard to cottage,
with George's fresh injuries on top of the bruising from
the previous night, plus the day's exertions, made his
head jar and throb with every step. But even though the
beating was bad enough, as he approached the front
door of his cottage, George knew the worst was yet to
come; it was still early enough for his mother to be up.

She was.

Her face a mixed picture of anger and concern, to her
great credit and George's relief, Clara, apart from her
first breathy reaction, said not a word when she first
caught sight of her bloody, rag-bag of a son entering the
kitchen. After a detailed and none-too-gentle inspection
of his injuries she motioned him to the kitchen table and
George sat, then entered into tentative conversation.

'Didn't think you'd still be up, Mam.'

'An' why shouldn't I be, after seein' all that blood in
th' kitchen this mornin'?'

'But, I tidied up?'

'Y' tidy like a man, now sit 'n' give me time f'r me temper t' cool.'

In a silence they could have bottled, Clara set-to with cloth and water to clean up his bloodied face. After the first scrape and with George not daring to utter even so much as a whimper, Clara swilled away the soiled water. Re-filling the bowl and collecting a bottle of iodine and some raw sheep's wool from a wall cupboard, she returned to the table.

As she lifted her son's face up by the chin and into the light, George saw the unmistakable glint of steel in her eye.

'Ayup, 'ere it comes,' he thought.

He was right.

'Is it that Daniel?'

'Mam…'

'Is it!?'

George eventually nodded.

'Right; we're t' see th' gaffer this very evenin'.'

'Mam…'

'I'll not be gainsaid, George!'

'Mam, that'll only make it worse!'

'An' this isn't bad enough?'

'It'll blow over!'

'No, that's just it, George, it won't!' She took in a deep breath the better to steady her temper again. 'Th' meek in'erit nothin' in this world, George Radcliffe, remember that; nothin'! They just get tramped on… Gaffer's this evenin', soon as you're bathed 'n' mended up. An' it'll be you as tells 'im, not me; this is summat you 'ave t' face.' Clara poured some iodine onto a ball of the sheep's wool. 'Now 'old you still.'

She slapped the soaked wool onto the open wound on George's forehead, causing him to suck in air through his bruised lips and ceasing his conversation.

With a little support from Clara, George walked across to Joseph's house in silence. Glad to be in the fresh air, it cleared his head somewhat and allowed him to concentrate on the forthcoming meeting.

Clara, also glad of the peace, was not dwelling on the meeting; she knew exactly what she was going to say.

—⁓—

Their knock on the side door was answered by Grace. Her gasp on first seeing George said it all and she ushered them into the kitchen calling for Joseph to join them.

Tea and preliminary explanations from Clara dispensed, Joseph looked across the table at George.

'If that's what y'call treadin' light then let's 'ope y' never stomp about th' place, eh?'

George could not suppress a smile, which he regretted straightaway as it re-opened the surface healing around his top lip. With the atmosphere eased slightly, Joseph moved on to address the matter more positively as George dabbed at the re-opened wound with a white-spotted, blue 'kerchief.

'So, George, what's t' do? Y'r mother's told all of the events 'cept the name of who it were as sorted you out last night, again t'night… an' who th' dirty bugger were who w's takin' a leak in th' feed barrel; I'm assumin' it were th' same f'r all three? Start fr'm th' beginnin'; who were it set about y'r th' night afore?'

George paused for a moment or two.

'I think there w' two 'f 'em, but it were too dark t' see either.'

'Two?'

'Ar, Gaffer, I think so, were dark…'

'An' t'night?'

'I just want 'orses t' be treated fair, Gaffer, that's why I left the feed bin open an' 'er rubbished food on the floor, f'r y' t' see…'

'What feed bin?'

'Chalky's, Gaffer; 'er food was spoiled, see. So I left…'

Joseph's eyes widened as an as yet unannounced realisation hit him.

'Is that right? Well feed bin were closed when I arrived.'

'Well I left it wide open, Gaffer…'

'Did y', now… Well that explains much an' I'll tell y'r now, answers'll not be forthcomin' 'til you own who it were as smacked y', will it?'

'No, Gaffer.'

'No, Gaffer. Now, I c'n just about figure you'd maybe not see who it were that give you a thumpin' last night; dark 'n' all just might excuse that. But I've never seen a night s' dark that 'ides th' face 'f a lamp-lit man, standin' on one barrel an' peein' into another, 'ave you?'

'No, Gaffer.'

'No, Gaffer. So. Who were it, George?'

'Gaffer, I don't know that I care! Others see it different, you know who! Chalky, she isn't bein' given a chance…'

Grace saw the set on Clara's face and the difficulties for George. Trying to calm the situation a little, she put her hand gently onto Clara's.

'You neither by looks of it. Joseph's told me what's at stake. A lot for you two, I'd think.'

Clara smiled gratefully at Grace.

'Not much f'r some, but all t' most such as us, Missus Grace.'

'Yes, we know. This hasn't always been our lot, Mrs Radcliffe. There were times, an' not that long ago…when Joseph's mother were running this farm, running it into the ground it turned out, an' we thought we'd be left with nothing…' She looked across at Joseph who was smiling and shaking his head gently at her. '…But we're grateful for what we have now, and I'd think you two deserve a bit of it as well.'

'That's my lady,' said Joseph simply.

A little pride burning in his reply, George spoke up.

'Maybe, Missus, an' thank you f'r y' concern. Look, I don't want t' sound ungrateful, I'm not, but I'm not beggin' f'r favours neither…'

Joseph quenched George's fire with a direct question.

'Were it Daniel t'night?' This concentrated minds and silence followed before he added. 'An' last night, were one o' th' pair 'im too?' There was a further silence and Joseph drove the point home. ''Cos if that's so then I've 'n idea who else. As f'r Daniel, I know 'is temper well, George. 'E's a mean streak as runs mighty deep in 'im an' 'e'll bear a grudge; mark me on that. 'E'll bear a grudge an' take it as far as 'e can then a furlong more; you 'ear what I'm sayin'?'

George knew a commitment was being asked for and he looked at his mother's set face, then across at Joseph.

'Yes, Gaffer, I 'ear.'

'Daniel?'

'Yes, Gaffer but it'll be just my word against 'is…'

'No it'll not; we'll 'ave Edward to 'elp us.'

'Edward, Gaffer?'

'Don't fratch yourself wi' that. I'll clamp it in th' mornin', an' you'll be there t' witness it. I'll send Mrs Clayson round this evenin'.' He looked across at Grace. 'A second cup might be welcome, Missus.'

Grace got up from the table, resting a hand briefly on her husband's shoulder in passing, and set about the making of a fresh pot of tea.

Joseph looked at Clara, then at George and his tone softened further.

'An' after tea, well, you'd best get off 'ome 'n' get some sleep, lad. Y' may well be doin' th' work o' three men come lunch, an' I'll tell y'r true y'don't look up t' much right now.'

In amongst the close community that was Allingham and district there were precious few secrets, and use of language to pass on those secrets was paid particular attention to. Word-of-mouth was the daily bread of contact for most folk and, from its nuance and timing, the county's inhabitants gleaned the stuff of life. It informed them of farming changes, local council directives, market alterations, food availability and prices and comprehensive information concerning the general doings of all their near neighbours.

When Jenny Clayson had visited each worker's house that Sunday evening and informed them all they were called into the yard at seven the following day, instead of the usual eight o'clock start and off-out, all the farm staff knew there were serious measures afoot. Any doubts they might have had about just how serious were quickly dispelled by Jenny who, when asked, confirmed that all the casual staff were called to the yard too.

That morning Joseph arrived with company; another man, who towered over even the well-built and tall Joseph, underlining the meeting's timbre.

Daniel, in particular, was keenly alert as Joseph introduced him.

'You all know my brother, David?' Then went straight to the detail. 'So, Daniel, what've y't' say f'r y'rself?'

Expecting an opening speech, this direct question threw Daniel. It was a good few seconds before he replied.

'About?'

Daniel was thinking on his feet, casting round for escape routes as would all animals that realise they are the target of the hunt.

Joseph sighed.

'Phh, are we to 'ave t' go through it all?' Nothing came back and he sighed again. 'Right. Beatin' on th' staff, stealin' feed from th' grey's bin, wastin' feed…'

Daniel talked over him.

'I've stolen nothin' 'n' touched no one, Gaffer! That grey's as good as in th' knackers' cart through no fault o' rations. I told y'r, it's kidneys!'

'An' I say it's not kidneys, I say it's all thanks t' you…' He paused for effect. '…An' Edward 'ere.'

This clever switch by Joseph stifled any further reply from Daniel and caught Edward completely off guard. A stunned silence followed this announcement for the farm's other staff were also genuinely surprised, as was George, and even Edward recognised there would be no help forthcoming from the assembled group; why should there be, they now knew where the axe was going to fall; Edward realised he had to say something.

The silence was cutting.

Eventually, he blurted out.

'I've not 'urt no 'orses, Gaffer, never to 'urt no 'orses…!…'

All but the simple Edward could see Joseph had another goal in mind, particularly Daniel. But anything he offered now would be so out of character he had to stay silent.

Joseph knew this and was seemingly showing no mercy.

''Orses, no. But 'elpin' Daniel give George a cloutin' the other night? Diff'rent matter that's only lessened by th' fact I know you'd not think it up on y'r own; y'r not that bright. Stupid way t' lose y'r employ on Fallen Oak after all these years, I'd say, Edward. What say you?'

Daniel had cottoned on to the trap Joseph was setting.

Edward, on the other hand, was completely snared.

'I works 'ere, Mister Joseph. Always works 'ere! I've not 'urt no 'orses! 'Ow…? Well…'ow was it me an' Daniel then? It were no moon…me 'at w's pulled, Daniel; like y' told us!'

Daniel stepped in towards him.

'Jesus, Edward…!'

David intercepted Daniel and gently, but very firmly, pushed him backwards then stood between him and the target of his anger.

Joseph looked around the assembled farm staff.

'See what I mean? Bright as a farthin' candle.'

Stepping across to Edward, George faced Daniel.

'Not Edward's fault, I'd reckon, Gaffer. Daniel's always been a bully to 'im; that right, Edward?'

The threatened child in Edward was well to the fore.

'Mister Daniel…?'

Joseph put the case to him.

'No use lookin' that way, Edward. 'E'll be th' same support as th' rope is t' the 'angin' man, even you should know that.' Edward stood rooted, his mouth gaping wordlessly as Joseph put the clincher on it. 'Neither bright enough nor brave enough.'

Only now realising the hole he had dug, Edward began to plead with Daniel.

'I said we were bad, Daniel, I said…!'

'Y' stupid bastard, Edward! Shut up, y' stupid, thick…!' David put his hand out to halt any idea Daniel might have of manifesting his rage, so he had to continue shouting around his bulk in his fast-rising fit of temper. '…Just you keep lookin' over y' shoulder! An' you, Radcliffe, I'll see you in 'ell f'r this!'

But Joseph had heard enough.

'An' I'll see you up th' road, Mister Long! I'll pay y'r up t' today, which is more 'n y' deserve, less one shillin' an' sixpence-ha'penny f'r that brass padlock y' broke an' another tanner f'r th' feed y' pissed on.' He looked at him in disgust. 'You disappoint me, Daniel. T' think I made you up to 'ead stable over Jim an' Arthur, an' all because I thought better of y'r, that you'd come up good.'

Daniel stabbed a finger in George's direction.

'Better 'n him, I'll warrant.'

Bloody, George may have been, but he was unbowed.

'So says nothin'! I've ploughed a straighter furrow than you, in th' field an' out 'f it!'

Daniel took a step forward again, froth spraying from his mouth in his rage.

'You bastard, Radcliffe!'

David stepped up closer to Daniel, the threat becoming implicit by his sheer size, and his voice boomed out.

'That's enough, Long! You 'eard th' gaffer! Best cut y'r losses an' move out; you've not many friends 'ere at present.'

Daniel saw that David was indeed very accurate in his summation, but going quietly was not his intention.

'Y' may think, just because y've got y' brother 'ere, y' may think y' safe, Gaffer; well you ain't…'

Joseph cut him off in mid flow.

'An' we say enough, Daniel! We're sick 'f 'earin' y'r! Save y'r energy f'r loadin' o' th' cart wi' y' furniture, an' make sure it is just your stuff y' load! David'll see you off. Back t' y' mother's I don't doubt, if she'll 'ave y'. Out by ten o'th'clock sharp!'

Standing his ground for a moment or two, Daniel eventually spat onto the floor in the centre of the group then strode out of the yard.

After a silence accompanied by the odd cough, Joseph turned to Edward.

'Edward, thanks t' George 'ere you've a chance t' redeem yourself…see y' use it; waste it an' y' gone!' He then faced the group of horsemen. 'You others, especial Jim 'n' Arthur, I'd've thought you'd at least 'ave said summat, if not about Daniel's badness then at least about that grey's condition; or were y' both walkin' about wi' y'r eyes shut 'n' y' feed-bags open?' Jim and Arthur stood silently as they braved the looks of all the staff and the continuing tirade of Joseph. 'Whatever it were, it took a lad, a lad you should've been leadin' mind, to 'ave th' gumption t' sort it out, an' 'e got little in return 'cept bruises from a bully. You've both much to answer for an' I'd reckon an apology's owed; not t' me, not t' George, but t' that grey! Do it, then get back out, there's work t' be done; both think y'rselves lucky y'r still 'ere an' doin' it! Eric?'

One of the casual staff answered.

'Yes, Mister Joseph.'

'Wi' Daniel missin' from th' day's chores, I'd be grateful if y' could stay on an' work timber, see if it fits out f'r us both. George 'as dropped a load o' pines on th' ridin' in Priest Wood, collect 'em up 'n' take 'em t' Gardner's mill, if y'r would.'

'Yes, Mister Joseph.'

'Afore that, take th' drop-cart an' put it outside Daniel's cottage f'r loadin'; bring the 'orse back 'ere. Day rate alright?'

'Yes, Mister Joseph. Thank you.'

Joseph nodded by return.

'Thanks're all mine, Eric. Right. George, you've much t' prove, I suggest you get on wi' it too; an' because you've got the other th' sack, from t'day you're 'ead stable. Don't let me or them 'orses down. See?'

Stunned as he was, George was acutely aware of the stares from the other staff.

Vicky nudged Jenny.

'Told y' so.'

Jenny folded her arms across her chest.

'No y' never, I told you!'

Mary nodded.

'She did, y' know.'

George spoke over them.

'Yes, Gaffer, an' thank you.'

'Ar. I'll take y' thanks f'r now, but y' may live t' curse me f'r it yet. Now let's all get out 'n' do a bit; all 'f y'r. Times've changed, look t' y'r own 'orses from 'ere on! George, farm'ouse in fifteen minutes, work rota an' wage t' sort out.'

'Yes, Gaffer.'

The horsemen scattered gratefully into the stables and began to get horses and kit ready for the day's work.

George moved across the yard to the corn barn and opened its doors as the other casual farm staff drifted out of the yard too.

'I did tell y'.'

'No y' never! Y' went on about Daniel Long bein' in charge!'

Vicky and Jenny went out of the yard still arguing. Mary, trailing along behind them, was loosening her waist-length hair prior to re-tying it. As she passed George she gave it a shake and him a huge smile.

'Bye, Mister 'ead-o'-stable Radcliffe.'

George flushed scarlet and entered the corn barn hurriedly.

After a brief discussion, Joseph and David left in the tracks of Daniel, Joseph nodding at the distant figure as he spoke.

'Get a note over t' Bryant t' drive 'im off...an' get 'im t' use one 'f 'is own Shires, David. I'll loan a cart but I'll be damned if I'll give 'im a chauffeur, nor no 'orse. An' keep an eye on what 'e takes; 'e's as like t' strip th' place.'

'Ar, 'e'll not be fussed what gets loaded; 'e'd rob th' beams if the 'ouse'ld stand up long enough for 'im t' make 'is escape. I'll see invent'ry's true, leave it t' me, Joe.'

The two men parted; Joseph back to his farmhouse and his meeting with George, David hot on the heels of the disappearing Daniel.

Three hours later with cart loaded, Daniel was ready to leave.

David nodded at Thomas Bryant, the driver.

'An' see th' cart gets back 'ere by four, Tom. No pubs, no parks along the way or e's as like to 'ave 'is furniture, our cart an' your 'orse sold, an' that'll be you in 'ock to us an' y' Gaffer. Four o' the clock mind!'

Thomas nodded.

'I'll see to it.'

Daniel said nothing, but David recognised the look of business unfinished on his face.

11

16.04.06

Joseph enjoyed these spring days. Dawn broke earlier, the weather was often good, and it also meant some spare time was to be had. Mid-mornings, with the farm staff and horsemen out of the way, were his favourite.

With the demands of his brother's farm now behind him, he could once more give his own place the time it needed; see how things were being cared for without being the subject of speculation or diversion, and what he had seen over the past few weeks had not disappointed him. With Daniel gone and George in charge there was a marked difference in the health and temper of both farm staff and livestock, particularly the horses. Harness and trimmings were gleaming, buildings and yard spotless, equipment repaired and renewed when it needed to be, and a regimented system of stock management started; the place even felt different.

Peering into each horse's stall, surveying the tack-room pegs and feed room layout, Joseph felt that, even to the gaze of the uninitiated, the whole stable declared its purpose.

'A place f'r ev'rythin' an' ev'rythin' in its place.'

As Joseph whistled his tuneless way across the yard, so George arrived through the main yard gates accompanied by Chalky who was pulling a large tree trunk.

'Whoa, Chalky! Stand-On.'

Joseph walked over to them.

'That th' Chestnut trunk f'r Wallace?'

George patted Chalky's neck.

'Ar, one 'f 'em. I've t' go back 'n' fetch the other two, an' Mister Wallace is sendin' over Nathaniel wi' a dolly f'r 'em at first light t'morrow. They're a fair size, as y' c'n see, so we'll need all 'ands t' pump then. I thought I'd leave 'em at th' back o' th' stable block, out th' way there but still easy t' get at.'

'Ar, that'll do, an' make sure we get good measure on 'em.' He continued talking as he moved around the grey, running a hand down her flank as he did so. 'I don't want t' do me neighbour down but I'm damned if I'll give 'em away! What's th' ground like top 'f Lloyd's Wood, still 'oldin' moisture?'

Knowing Joseph was stalling for time while he inspected Chalky, George played along.

'Spent s' long away we've forgot 'ave we? Mind, easy done, given all that sittin'-down-paper-work you 'ave t' do. Well, just t' jog y' mem'ry, that top gateway y' mentioned does still 'old th' moisture no matter what, an' last month's rain 'as laid well. 'Er 'ocks tell y' that.'

A glance at Chalky's muddied hocks would give any horseman unfamiliar with local conditions some information about the state of the ground on *Fallen Oak Farm*. For those who knew every portion of the land as well as Joseph there was much more to be read; George knew it…so did Joseph.

Any horse dragging a sizeable chunk of timber out of Lloyd's Wood, certainly something the size of the chestnut bole now lying in the yard, would be put through a real test of fitness and spirit. The steep riding, followed by what could only be termed as a wallow at the top gateway, soon sorted the Shires from the hunters. That Chalky had done it after only a month in George's care spoke volumes for both horse and horseman; Joseph knew this well. But he was not about to give it away, and he continued to look the mare over as he replied.

'Sittin'-down-paper-work it may be, Master Radcliffe, but it's what keeps you all in pay 'n' fodder, mind that.' He continued to assess the horse. 'Hm. Looks fit, I'll give y' that.'

Smiling at Joseph's persistence, George pulled at Chalky's ear; she dropped her head to his touch.

'Ar, she's well on 'er way. Blows a bit sometimes when she's under real pressure, but all-in-all she'll give a few good years yet, blind man c'ld see it.'

Straightening up, Joseph unsuccessfully hid the widening smile on his face.

'Ar, lad, y've a way wi' 'em that's f'r sure.'

George moved round to join Joseph.

'So y'reckon she's about right then, Gaffer? Looks, fit, does she?'

'Ar, just said so 'aven't I?'

George smiled.

'Then I reckon I've done meself a good deal there…y'r did say I could 'ave 'er, Chalky, didn't y', if I improved 'er in a month, an' as long it was you who said she were fit?'

Joseph shook his head.

'Ha! Thought that'd gone by y'r, should've known better.' He rubbed his chin and thought for a moment. 'Ar, I did say that, so she's yours, but I'll expect a good year from y'r.'

'An' you'll get it. I've never slipped my share in the 'arness so far.'

Joseph moved off out of the yard gate.

'Then see y' don't start this year!'

'Er…will we sort out paperwork t'day f'r 'er then, Gaffer?'

'Blimey, Radcliffe, don't let th' grass grow! D'y' look after th' farm's interests as well as y' look out f'r y'r own?'

'I do that, Gaffer; farm's my first thought of a mornin' an' my last at night.'

'A good woman'll soon change that, my man, mark me on that.'

'It'll take some woman t' best th' debt I owe this 'orse, Gaffer.'

Joseph laughed loud and shook his head.

'Ha-ha! Th' folly o' youth! I made th' right choice when I put you in charge, Master Radcliffe, so I did; an' you deserve that grey f'r that comment alone! Come up the 'ouse this evenin' an' we'll draw it all up.'

With that parting shot he was gone, whistling tunelessly as he left.

George rubbed Chalky's ear again.

'Did you 'ear that? We're a team, you an' me… a team!'

He collected the reins and clicked the mare on. With a fluid, forward lean that lifted her re-discovered muscles to the surface, she drew the tree trunk across the yard and out onto the field beyond.

'Two more, lass, an' we c'n call it a day.'

—⁓—

Gathering and drawing those other two tree trunks back to the yard took a little longer than anticipated.

To retrieve them meant a weave along the wood's steep central ride and an awkward, backward shuffle into its tightening tail. To make matters worse, the last of this trio of chestnut trunks was lodged into the ditch and meant the pick-up and first tow was a real struggle for Chalky. Proof of her fitness, if George needed any, was found right there and then.

Dusk was closing fast and the other horsemen had finished up the care of their charges when George and Chalky got back to the yard. With the last trunk aligned, he dropped the chain and tackles from Chalky's harness in the yard. Once working clothes had been swapped for a soft head-collar and Chalky tied to a wall ring in the yard, she relaxed into the routine that signalled the close of the day. Throughout the washing and grooming that followed, the grey stood still, her head swinging this way and that, her body-weight lodged on her left or right hooves depending on whereabouts George was working. She enjoyed the fuss, knowing this activity led to feeding time and a well-earned rest.

George stepped back to look at her.

'Y'know, y're not bad f'r what were a near-t'-death urchin.' He patted her neck. 'Tea-time, eh?' He stroked her ear and she dropped her head to his touch. 'Y've done a good job t'day, eh, my Shire lady.' He patted her neck again. 'Well done.' George untied her from the wall ring. 'Right, you fed 'n' bedded, tack 'n' chains cleaned; last check o' th' rest then I'm off 'ome f'r me snap. I'm that 'ungry me belly thinks me throat's been cut.'

With Chalky willingly following, George led her into the smaller of the two stable blocks. In through the main yard door, walking along the dimly-lit central aisle, George squinted ahead.

'Blimey, Chalky, who's turned these lamps down s' low? Y'could 'ide a black stallion in 'ere. I'll sort out some light in a bit.' Chalky halted and flicked her head up, the speed of her action pulling George's arm high. 'Whoa! Steady on, Chalky! What's up, not that black stallion is it…?'

George saw her nostrils were flared; this was no joke. The scent she had picked up made her very, very uneasy. To confirm this, Chalky now backed up, stomping her forefeet, dragging George with her.

'Aye, Whoa, lass, steady! Stand-On!'

George's strength was no match against Chalky's, but her trust in him was sufficient to slow her progress then stop it.

George stroked her muzzle and looked round the stable.

'What? What is it, Chalky?'

His senses homed in on it…on something different…something…?… methylated spirits.

At this same instant, George saw the arc of a lighted lamp at the far end of the corridor and, a moment later, heard the crash as of breaking glass and saw a pillar of fire shoot upwards. The flames lifted high as the straw was engulfed and in their dazzle a man standing by the loft steps was highlighted, fleetingly, in the fire's first greedy onslaught.

'Daniel…?'

This was all he had time to think, for the noise and sudden appearance of these flames dissolved any loyalty Chalky had mustered up for George. Skittling away with a firmness of purpose that would brook no opposition, she backed off toward the main yard door.

George leant his own urgency to her efforts and with Chalky back-peddling along the aisle for all she was worth; both she and George shot out of the stable block like a cork from a bottle.

Once outside, George forced her round and smacked her rump.

'Hie-On, Chalky! Hie-On!' George saw her away, shouted, ''Elp, someone! 'Elp!' and with that dived back into the stable.

Both stable doors had been left open, one by the departing Chalky, the other by the escaping arsonist, and the draught created by this had scattered the lighted straw, creating a fresh fire just inside the main yard door. Quickly pulling it to and stilling the air's movement, George ran the gauntlet of the drifting smoke, past the stalled and agitated horses. The original site of the blaze had a good hold now and it took an adventurous leap and scramble to get him through it, and out to the backyard where other water butts stood.

He drew in large lungs-full of air as he filled two buckets and scanned the surroundings. A disappearing, distant, shadowy figure registered.

'Daniel? Possibly?'

Then the noise of terrified horses reached him and cut short any ideas he might have of pursuit; with a bucket per hand, he ran back into the stables.

Unbeknownst to him, a lead-line of stray straw and hay had tempted the flames up the steps and into the hay-loft above but, oblivious to this, George gathered himself to douse the flames with the water. He only had to look from buckets to flames and back to buckets to realise he was in an unfair contest. Throwing the water, buckets and all, onto the flames, he ran into the tack room and grabbed a handful of head collars. Back onto the central concourse, he raced through the flames once more and along the aisle to Blossom.

He hung a head collar on her door.

'You just be patient, lass, two's as much as I can 'andle.'

Running back, he snatched open Willow's stall and put a head collar on her. On the aisle he tethered her to a ring doing the same with Titan, who kicked over his water bucket in his eagerness to escape.

'Steady now, Titan, steady, we'll all be right.' He looked at Willow. 'Just 'old you still my lass an' let a dog see th' rabbit.'

A glance both ways along the aisle told George that, even though the flames were higher by the door into the backyard, its escape route past the loft steps was closer and clearer. Decision made, the trio had barely moved towards it when the hay-loft fire of earlier completed its job and a section of ceiling dropped down in a roar of flame right in front of them. This not only cut off their chosen escape route, but the noise and brightness caused massive panic in both horses.

George was instantly lifted off his feet by their initial surge as they clopped loudly backwards along the concourse in their fear and surprise. His feet slipping, but still hanging on to the lead reins for all he was worth, George was flipped under their front hooves.

'Willow, Whoa! Willow! Titan…Ow! Ow! Steady!'

The narrowness of the aisle meant the two Shires were unable to turn, but it did not stop them from trying. As they cranked their heads from side-to-side in their efforts to face away from flames and into freedom, they flung George around like a rag doll. Slung over to the right for the third time in as a many seconds, George's feet slammed against a closed stall door and he managed to flick himself upright and swivel round to face the two Shires.

Leaning hard back on the reins and subjugating his own rising panic, George completed his control over what had threatened to be a charge from fire to frying pan.

'Whoa now, Titan, steady, steady, steady. Willow, steady now.' The two Shires responded to his calming voice. 'Now then…steady…steady…Hi-Back, Back!'

Pushing back on the two horses, George drew them alongside Blossom's stall where she stood all a-tremble.

'Stand-On now Titan, you too Willow; Stand-On. Hey, hey, Blossom, hey now; just steady.' Both reins in one hand, he reached across to her. 'We're alright, aren't we, eh, Blossom?'

She calmed at his touch and voice.

George let go a huge outward breath towards Willow and Titan's noses. Their eyes reflected flame, their stertorous breathing and involuntary muscular quiver reflected their inner state, but these two horses, either of whom was capable of dragging George and a dozen other men in any direction they pleased, now settled a little.

'Now then. Let's see what's t' be done. You Stand-On, Blossom, I'll not forget y'r. Willow, Titan, Hi-Back! Back!'

The two Shires reversed into the alcove opposite Blossom's stall. The merry blaze at the site of the collapsed ceiling meant escape that way was now impossible; even with the flames and thick smoke obscuring the main yard door this was obviously the only way out.

George took an even firmer hold on the halter ropes.

'We 'ave t' go through that way, no choice, an' right now. You Stand-On, Blossom, I'll be back.' George rattled Willow and Titan's lead ropes. 'Trot-On! Trot-on!' All three set off, along the aisle, straight at the flames and smoke. 'Now, don't stop...Trot-On! Trot-On! On-On, Titan!'

Blinded by acrid fug, to their great credit and George's everlasting gratitude they moved swiftly toward the smoke-blurred doorway. As they approached it, so George pulled back on Willow's halter and forward on Titan's lead rein then, releasing it, he whacked the gelding's rump as he passed his slowed stable-mate.

'On-On! Trot-On, Titan! On!'

Titan was spurred on by George's rallying call and smack, but it was the spurt of flame to his left-rear that really served to kick him on faster. Two thousand three hundred pounds of eager-to-exit Shire horse crashed through the un-latched door as if it were matchwood, snapping the top half off its hinges. Titan was rapidly followed through it by George and Willow. As soon as they were in the yard the fresh-air hit him and George let go of Willow's rope, doubling over in a fit of coughing.

It was this scene that greeted Edward as he entered through the yard gate leading Chalky, who was not exactly keen to be re-entering the scene of her recent scare.

Edward let go of Chalky's halter and ran over.

'Mister George? Mister George! What's goin' on? There's a burnin' smell…what's that?'

Controlling his somersaulting lungs, George pointed at the stable.

'Jesus, Edward, th' stables're on fire! Can't y'see?' He indicated the three horses now milling in the yard. 'Take 'em out!'

'Where…out?'

'Out! Take 'em out! Anywhere! Out th' gate! Let 'em up th' lane, they'll not go far, then run an' fetch th' gaffer…now! Small stable's on fire! I'll get Blossom!' Edward's widening eyes confirmed to George he'd cottoned on to the seriousness of the situation. 'Move, Edward! 'Orses out an' get 'elp; get th' Valiant! Fire! The gaffer…fetch th' gaffer!'

Much to George's relief, Edward began to chivvy the willing horses out of the yard.

Taking off and dipping his jacket into the yard trough, George draped the sopping garment over his head and re-entered the stable to rescue Blossom……

12

17.04.06

The early hours of the following morning saw the yard in a state of calm chaos and end-of-scene activity.

The Valiant fire-pump with its attendant hose-piping, hand-pumps, empty buckets and scattered wet blankets were distributed amongst the hurriedly rescued tack, tools and horse-care kit. Smouldering timbers laced the yard with lazy smoke, and the handful of locals who had answered the alarm call were salvaging what they could so they could finish up and salvage some of their lost sleep. The farm's horsemen and casual staff, Mary Suttcliffe and Victoria Ollerenshaw included, were completing the dousing of the last of the embers, their faces blackened by the ash still drifting round the scene.

Standing in the yard, Joseph, his jacket singed and one pocket torn away, and George, smut-covered and draped in a sopping-wet shirt which had the front torn open and most of the buttons missing from it, were surveying the wreckage.

Outside the yard, tethered to a field rail like so many cowboys' horses, the rescued Shires stood contemplatively munching on the remnants of some wet hay dumped near to keep them occupied. The new carter, Cedric, and the new stable-lad, Martin, were sifting through tack prior to breaking up the horses' al fresco supper before taking them into the large barn, where makeshift stalls had been hurriedly constructed.

Surprisingly, given the intensity of the initial blaze, a fair proportion of the small stable block was still standing, even though it was unfit for horses. The larger stable block next to it was, miraculously, undamaged.

With the fire now out, Joseph felt safe in dismissing the helpers.

'There'll be bonuses, special, f'r you all; my appreciation, see.' He looked across the yard. 'Mrs Ollerenshaw?'

Victoria, soaked blanket in hand, looked up from her steady thrashing of a particularly stubborn piece of glowing timber.

'Yes, Mister Joseph.'

'When's Mister Ollerenshaw back from 'is away-work?'

'Day after t'morrow, Mister Joseph.'

'Right, well you'll kindly inform 'im of what's 'appened 'ere an' that I've some timber repairs f'r 'im t' see to; soon as 'e's free; by mid-week 'ld suit.'

'Yes, Mister Joseph. Thank you.'

He turned to George.

'Y'sure y' didn't see who it were?'

George hesitated for a split second before answering, shaking his head as he did so.

'No, Gaffer, like I said earlier, not t' be sure, no.'

'Daniel?'

'Gaffer, I can't be sure, an' that's th' truth.'

'Educated guess?'

'Can't do that, Gaffer. Outcome o' this'll be serious f'r them as gets caught, an' if I'm t' point th' finger I'd 'ave t' be certain sure.'

'But y'r saw someone?'

'Not someone, just a figure. It were dark, lamps w' turned right low so not much flame.'

''Cept th' bugger what razed this lot.'

George smiled without humour.

'Ar, 'cept th' bugger what razed this lot. Everythin' 'appened s' fast, Gaffer. I just saw th' body in them flames as I went inside…then Chalky kicked off.'

'Ar. By, but we were lucky Edward 'appened back when 'e did. If it 'adn't've been f'r 'im frettin' whether or no 'e'd filled up th' water f'r Titan you'd've been on y'r own for a fair time longer.'

George smiled.

'Good job 'is mem'ry's poor then, Gaffer, 'cos water was in stall waitin' f'r Titan t' kick it over in 'is panic t' leave.'

Behind them, Mary and Victoria got ready to go as, outside the yard, the farm horsemen gathered the Shires together and Joseph explained to George the early evening's events.

'No one were more surprised t' see 'im at 'ouse than me. Missus Grace an' me, we were contemplatin' goin' t' bed an' 'eard th' thumpin' on th' door.'

'Ar, sorry 'bout that, Gaffer. I just 'ad t' trust t' luck 'e'd remember what t' tell y'r. I did give 'im a lot 'f instruction, an' in a damn 'urry too!'

Vicky and Mary, shoving each other on their giggling way out of the yard, approached the deep-in-conversation George and Joseph.

'Go on, Mary! Dare y'.'

Joseph talked on.

'Well 'e remembered some. 'E just stood at th' door two-foot from me. I wondered what 'e wanted at first, 'is mouth gapin' like a grounded fish. Then after a few seconds 'e just pointed back 'ere, yelled out, 'Fire!' at th' top 'f 'is voice an' buggered off! Left me t' work out th' detail f'r meself…near deafened me! Lucky 'e remembered the important bit, eh?'

Mary flicked her hair ostentatiously.

''Night, Mister Joseph! 'Night, George…nice shirt!'

They burst into a fit of laughter and Joseph called after them.

'I don't know what's so funny you two… ' Then his attention was diverted by the horsemen as they led Blossom and Willow across the yard. 'All finished, Arthur?'

Arthur relinquished his rein to Martin and called across.

'Ar, Gaffer, finished an' bedded down.'

'An' you've not put Dagger too near them mares 'ave you, Edward?'

Edward, following Blossom as she went through the barn's door, stopped as his name was called, unsure and surprised at being addressed directly about horse-care.

'No, Mister Joseph…on 'is own; new wall.'

'New wall? Wi' what?'

George interrupted.

'Rustled up some o' that timber fencin' back o' th' yard t' close 'im up safe, make 'im more comf'table; that an' some extra straw.'

Joseph turned back to Edward.

'Fixed secure, Edward?'

'Yes, Mister Joseph'

'Who did it? You, Jim?'

'No, Gaffer, George did.'

Joseph looked from Jim to George.

'When were there time f'r you t' do that?' Joseph, shaking his head, turned away from George and called to the men. 'Right, back 'ere at six you lot! Not you, Arthur! I want you over t' Bowman's by first light an' pick up some 'ay wi' th' cart. Don't worry 'bout th' time; if I know Alec Bowman 'e'll be up an' about by then. Let 'im know what's 'appened 'ere an' that I'll settle up by Statutes…take the large waggon, an' take Dagger; scent o' them mares'll prime 'im well f'r the exercise, I reckon.'

'Yes, Gaffer.'

Arthur turned to leave but Joseph carried on, stopping him.

'Once that's dropped off, get up t' Lloyd's Wood an' draw down those oak boles from th' bottom o' th' ridin', them one's as were felled a couple o' winters ago, y' know the one's I mean?'

'Yes, Gaffer.'

'Good. They'll be fair dry be now, an' we'll need all of 'em. Drop 'em at sawmill, tell Gifford they're f'r beams an' that we'll need 'em within th' week, ready f'r Mister Ollerenshaw.'

'Yes, Gaffer.'

'Tell 'im I'll send a pattern an' measurements later in th' day…' He turned to George. 'Y'r first job t'morrow, George, that, an' we'll start t' draw up plans f'r th' rebuild f'r Mister Ollerenshaw t' follow…' Then he turned back to address Arthur again. '…Y'can finish f'r 'ome then, Arthur, that'll be enough f'r anyone in a day.'

'Ar, Gaffer. Right!'

'Th' rest of y', don't be late; we've a deal o' tidyin' t' do.'

The other men chorused back across the yard.

'Yes, Mister Joseph.'

Joseph gazed across at the wreckage then turned his attention back to George.

'So, no idea at all?'

George shook his head firmly.

'No, Gaffer…I did see a figure but, like I said, it all 'appened s' fast, an' 'orses were my first thought.'

'As they should've been, y'r spot-on there, lad. Well, we'll find out, never worry. I'll call in t' police later an' talk it through.' He put his hand on George's shoulder. 'An' well done. Bad as it is, you've saved me some fair cost 'n' trouble, George. I don't f'rget things like that.'

13

The bitterly cold weather was relentless leading up to Christmas and into the New Year. Even Titan, the fittest of the farm's Shire horses, began to look jaded from the punishing schedule in the sometimes brutal cold.

As the conditions worsened so the amounts fed to the working horses were increased and supplemented with beans, maize and, of course, the replenished tonic used by George's father, as well as on-demand supplies of hay. Once a week and under supervision at first, Edward was promoted by George to be in charge of making up a hot bran mash for evening feed as a treat, adding some diced apple and carrot on occasions. But, even with this feeding regime, plus his knowledge and skill applied daily to keeping her fit, George remained concerned about one horse's condition; Chalky's.

Over the past two years, the occurrence of her breathing difficulties had become more frequent, the effort needed to cause it, less, and her recovery time longer. George was under no illusion that the hardships she had suffered as a youngster under Daniel's stewardship had taken its toll; good feed and dedicated care would not cure her of that.

So it was, on this bitter January morning, George entered the newly re-built small stables to find, not entirely to his surprise, the old grey Shire dead in her stall.

He leant over the stall door.

'Work bust y'r 'eart, eh? Huhh… My poor old Shire lady; sorry to 'ave let y' down so many times.'

He entered, knelt down and took hold of her ear; an ear that now lacked the customary warmth of old; but he stroked it all the same.

'You 'ad a few extra years, lass, an' not one 'f 'em spent at grass; not fair that…but at least y' were 'ere…wi' a friend.'

He patted her neck and stood up.

'Best get th' gaffer. 'E'll not want remindin' but I know 'e'll want t' see you off.' He walked slowly to the entrance, passing Blossom en-route. 'Look out, girl; we've a lass down an' still th' best part o' winter t' get through yet. Could be some 'ard times ahead.'

The chalk-board feeding chart hanging by the door had the names of the farm's horses written on it. Their ages and health were all well known to George and, as he scanned the list on his way out, he shook his head.

'What we want on this farm is new stock.'

Late that afternoon the knacker-cart collected the carcass and, old though she was, it still took five men and a hauling rope attached to Dagger to heave Chalky's body up onto the cart. Once this was done, the horsemen left to continue their work, leaving George and the knacker to complete the paperwork and payment. Finally, and much to George's relief, the job was finished and he was left alone in the yard.

As he watched the cart leave George thought that head-stable wasn't much fun right now……

14

12.02.09

George had taken over Titan as his main workmate now, but even though he had given it the best part of a year to adjust, still it was not the same. It was a man deep in thought that Joseph found as he entered the stables on a chilly February noon.

Sat eating his snap, his back against one of the main stable supports and lost in concentration, George failed to hear Joseph until he spoke.

'Afternoon, George.'

Snapped out of his reverie, George spilt his sandwich on the floor.

'Afternoon, Gaffer! You give us a start! I were in a diff'rent county then.'

'Penny for 'em?'

'I'd be robbin' y', Gaffer, honest. Did y' want summat special?'

Upturning a bucket, Joseph sat next to him.

'Ar, a bit. I know y've plenty on, George, but 'Irin' Fair Speakin' Time's due in three 'r four month, any thoughts on which way you'll swing?'

'Blimey, Gaffer! Y'r a bit forward ain't y'?'

'I know, I know, just need t' get a couple o' things in order, before I commit t'…t' summat.'

Pondering this mystery for a few moments, George re-gathered the contents of his sandwich.

'Well, Gaffer, I've no ties now as y' know, what wi' Mam away six months o' th' year at 'er sister's an' the old grey gone. I 'ad thought I might just try me luck at th' Fair come September. Nothin' definite, just a thought. 'Course, I would've let y'r know early enough…just not quite this early…say…mid-August…?…y' know; at Speakin' Time, as we usually do?'

Joseph smiled at George's explanation.

'No side t' you, George, as ever, speak as y' mean. Ar, right; straight back by return. I've 'eard 'f a couple o' useful fillies up f'r sale, not that far from 'ere. What say we go 'n' 'ave a look-see? Can't do no 'arm, an' if we like 'em enough an' they're within my purse, then I'll buy 'em f'r th' farm, give you sole charge 'f their breakin' 'n' trainin' an' let y' work 'em up f'r a bit o' showin' 'n' breedin', eh? Th' farm could do wi' some new stock…an' now we've th' man t' manage 'em.'

Whatever George was expecting it certainly was not this.

'Bugger but y'know 'ow t' sow a diff'rent crop, Gaffer, I'll give y' that! That's a mighty temptin' offer…I don't know what t' say.'

Standing up, Joseph righted the bucket and offered his hand.

'Thank you 'n' yes, that's all as required. Deal?'

They shook.

'Ar, deal. Thank you, Gaffer.'

Rubbing his hands together, Joseph left the stables whistling tunelessly, leaving George to contemplate the remains of his ragged sandwich.

15.03.09

Joseph moved excitedly from foot to foot as he waited by the yard gates.

When he saw George appear round the lane's bend leading the two horses he fair left the ground as he pointed along the track.

'They're 'ere, Edward! They're 'ere!'

Trotting across the yard, Edward stood behind Joseph to watch the procession.

'Big, Mister Joseph, ain't they?'

'Ar, an' they look better than I remember; a real good size f'r three-year-olds. That grey'll stand nineteen-two when full growed or I'm no 'orseman.'

George slowed slightly as he approached the yard, talking quietly to them.

'Steady-on, now, girls. Nothin' 'ere to 'urt.'

At the yard's gateway they all paused, both horses snuffling the air, surveying the scene, taking stock.

Joseph spoke quietly as he looked them over.

'Y' made good time.'

'Ar, they'd brought th' grey over t' th' bay's farm last week like I asked, so they've been stabled next to each other since an' 'ad chance t' meet. Nice quarters. Quiet, just like 'ere, an' well looked after. That made th' trip back a lot easier, I reckon. Th' leadin' reins 'n' 'alters'll 'ave t' be returned but they said anytime next week'll do.'

'No trouble on th' journey?'

'No, not a bit. Ground work's been done well, Gaffer.'

''Ad they managed t' get tack on 'em? They said that'd be likely but depended on th' year an' 'ow they muscled up?'

'Ar, on each 'f 'em. The grey's even pulled a dolly a fortnight ago. Lovely temperament, both, an' they weren't a bit bothered by me leadin' 'em off. So, wha'd'y' think, Gaffer, will they do or shall I take 'em back? 'Orses that is, 'alters 'ave t' go back whether we keep Shires or no.'

Joseph's grin said it all.

'By, you'll 'ave y'r 'ands full wi' those two, Georgie-Boy! I just told Edward 'ere, that grey'll stand nineteen-two or I'm no judge 'f an 'orse.'

'A ladder, Mister George. Use a ladder…'

Edward's voice tailed off in surprise at what he had said and Joseph's smiling reaction to it.

''E's right too, y'r will need a ladder! Edward, stop bein' clever. Get over t' those stall doors an' open 'em up…' Edward was about to set off at a gallop. 'Slowly, Edward! Slow…lee… They'll 'ave George's arm off if y' spook 'em an' they decide t' cut 'n' run!' Edward backed away toward the stable block with some reverence and Joseph moved round the back of the horses. 'Away y'go, George, I'll bring up th' rear.' As they set off across the yard, he added. 'From this view,

I'd say that's some 'andful 'f 'orseflesh you've got there, take my word f'r it.'

One of the improvements George had asked for when the small stable block had been rebuilt was to triple the width and double the height of the stable entrance and, because of this, both horses showed no alarm when they entered through its wide main doors.

George sighed.

'That went well, knew I were right t' make it bigger. Can y' take one, Gaffer?'

'I'll take th' smaller bay if that's in order. That other bugger's goin' t' grow into a bloody dragon; I'd rather keep 'er a week th'n a fortnight!'

George stifled a laugh.

'That's it, Gaffer; make me feel easy about th' next few month…'

Joseph gently took the one halter rope and George coaxed the grey forward with soothing words and clicks of his tongue. She halted at the open stall door and it took a couple of minutes to reassure her that all was well but, after patience and quiet had been applied, she eventually went in. Stripping the rope slowly off the halter, George closed the bottom of the half-door gently behind him.

On it was painted:

4426 - SCARSDALE SILVERGIRL
CLOWDY

The grey filly moved up to the closed door and George reached up towards her ear. She flicked her head away as George smiled.

'Alright, lady. Plenty o' time t' get used t' that. Good lass, Clowdy. You're 'ome now, an' look who's livin' next door.'

Taking the rope off Joseph, George walked the bay into the next stall. Having seen her companion enter her stall she was easier to coax in, and George soon had her halter rope off and the door closed.

On it was painted a different name and number:

141142 - STUNTNEY CHARLOTTE DIMENT

Diment moved to the side of her stall and Clowdy joined her. They touched muzzles through the bars that filled the upper half of their dividing wall and all three men stood and looked at the horses for quite a few moments.

George broke the reverie.

'It'll still be in order f'r me to 'ave Edward 'elp out wi' th' routine f'r these two, Gaffer?'

'Ar, as agreed. Mornin's'll be f'r these two, an' Jim'll cover routines elsewhere, but just you make sure Edward don't do nothin' stupid. Bit like askin' a cat not t' steal cream from th' dairy, I'd reckon. 'E's prone t' stupidity is our Edward as y'well know… 'e knows it too.'

'It's just a bit o' careful 'andlin' is required, like these two. 'E'll be fine.'

Joseph turned to Edward.

'You 'ear that, Edward? Mister George says you'll be fine.'

Edward took his gaze from the two Shires.

'Yes, Mister Joseph…'Orses.'

Rolling his eyes at George, Joseph sighed and raised his voice.

'You're to 'elp out Mister George 'ere, Edward, right? Don't do nothin' clever; just pay attention an' do as you're told.'

'Yes, Mister Joseph. I'll be best friend.'

'Ar, I'm sure y'will, Edward, but do as y'r told first, you 'ear?'

Edward moved his gaze back to the two Shires.

'Yes, Mister Joseph.'

George diverted the conversation.

'Well, my girls, up to us not t' waste th' gaffer's cash now.'

Joseph made to leave the stables.

'Y' right there.' He turned back with an afterthought. 'Oh, by th' way, you'll 'ave 'eard…about Daniel Long?'

Edward moved closer to Clowdy's stall, pretending not to listen but wanting to hear the conversation all the same.

George stood puzzled.

'No, Gaffer, what were that?'

'Set about Elizabeth Ferris, apparently. Y'know Graham, 'er brother?'

'Ar, a bit, what 'appened?'

'Grace 'eard, by way 'f Mrs Kent. Graham got back from sheep market ten days ago; found 'Lizabeth in their kitchen, a damp cloth to a swollen eye an' bad bruisin' to 'er side.'

'Didn't know they was courtin', Gaffer. When were this?'

'Day afore yest'rday an' I'd 'ardly use th' word courtin' t' cover what Daniel 'ad in mind. She's only a young-ster; what is she, seventeen? Well, I guess she'd not 'ave much idea about th' Daniel Long's o' this world?'

'No, poor lass. I'd not 'ad contact wi' 'er but I know Graham; not well, like I say, but know 'im. Useful 'orseman, so I'm told. 'Ow is she?'

'Bit 'f a mess by all accounts, y' know what Long were like. By all intents 'n' purposes Daniel would've been a dead man 'ad Graham found 'im. Gone missin' I 'eard, so no surprises there.'

'All news t' me, Gaffer.'

'Ar, me too, I only 'eard from my Grace. Graham kept it quiet by all accounts; didn't want 'Lizabeth t' be branded, if y'know what I mean, but as y'know...' George joined in with Joseph and they finished the sentence together, '...there's not many secrets round 'ere.' Joseph smiled and continued, 'Too true, an' an association wi' that scoundrel does nothin' for a body's reputation. Mary'd not press charges 'cos 'f it, so th' bugger's got away clean.'

Edward shuffled uneasily from foot-to-foot as George shook his head.

'Poor lass. An' folk wonder why I prefer 'orses.' George sensed Edward's mood change. 'Though, look-in' at these two there may be a surprise 'r two 'ere yet, eh, Edward?'

Edward looked up and smiled and Joseph turned to leave.

'Ar. My you're goin' to 'ave a busy year, what wi' this pair, harvest an' ploughin' still t' be done an' now Edward on top 'f it all.'

Taking hold of Joseph's arm, George stopped him and shook his hand firmly.

'Best job in th' world, Gaffer; thank you.'

'Early f'r thanks yet. Let's see 'ow autumn pans out, eh?'

Watching him go, George called after him.

'Best job in th' world, Gaffer!'

Joseph stopped, then turned back to George and Edward.

'Ar, we might live in th' country but we do see life.'

He left the stables whistling tunelessly.

16

28.05.09

By early May, George had the two Shires well drilled in the niceties of tack, behaviour and almost all of the main commands.

Each morning, he and Edward led them into the large grass paddock behind the stable block to take them through their paces. Working first with one then the other, Edward proudly holding the resting horse in between whiles, George stamped his authority and expectation on each them. Gradually, he increased the time Diment and Clowdy trained together until they started to think as a team, George included and, towards the end of the month, he was sufficiently satisfied with their progress to let Joseph see them in training.

George took them through their routine and Joseph nodded in recognition as each familiar command was called, but even he was impressed by how much the Shires had learned in such a short space of time, and also at the speed with which they responded to the given commands.

'By, but they're a sharp pair, George. T' come 'ere wi' th' barest work done on 'em an' to 'ave come on this far?'

'Whoa girls! Stand-On. Sharper 'n their trainer, I reckon, Gaffer. I'm learnin' from them!'

George unhitched the dolly and, calling Edward over, began to remove the horses' working tack; to Joseph's surprise, they put soft head collars on the waiting Shires. With Edward holding open the gate, both horses stood their ground and George looked over to Joseph, who sensed something special was afoot.

'Just a little extra, Gaffer; playtime sort 'f.'

George put up both hands, one to each horse's head, and both of them dropped their muzzles so that he could rub their ears. He then quickly sat on the ground and waved both his outstretched hands slowly.

'Drop, Girls! Drop and Still.'

Both horses lowered their bodies to the floor then flopped onto their sides and lay down quite still.

After a few seconds George got slowly up onto one knee with his palm resting softly on Clowdy's muzzle.

'Diment, Hie-Up-Hup!'

Diment got up quickly but Clowdy still lay on the floor.

George stood up and removed his hand from Clowdy's nose.

'Clowdy, Hie-Up-Hup!'

Now Clowdy got up too and shook herself.

George stood back a little, aware that Joseph's mouth was wide open in silent surprise, and called out.

'Home-Home!'

Both horses instantly broke into a smart trot, one each side of George, off through the gateway and past Edward.

Joseph was finally able to voice his thoughts.

'What the 'ell, George?'

'Relax, Gaffer, they're only goin' t' one place.'

When they got to the stable yard, both horses were standing patiently by their wall rings. Joseph looked at them in amazement.

'Well I'll be damned! If that aint' th' smartest thing I've seen in many a year. 'Ow on earth did y' find time t' get that lot into 'em?'

'They've set their own time-table, Gaffer; no pressure involved. This pair're as sharp as razors, pick things up almost before I've taught 'em. Just a bit o' time, a bit o' patience…an' the 'elp 'f Edward 'ere.'

At the mention of his name, Edward grinned with pride for he was inordinately proud of these two horses and of George's recognition of his involvement in their training.

George whistled and called out.

'Back-Back!'

The two horses moved back and apart to allow Edward to open the wide main doors. With George leading Clowdy and Edward Diment, they entered the stable-block and the two Shires walked into their respective stalls.

George winked at Edward.

'Feed 'em up, Edward.'

Edward began to prepare their food and Joseph turned his gaze from the horses to George.

'Give you another month an' you'll get 'em t' feed theirselves!'

'Not quite, Gaffer but it makes th' sessions fun f'r them an' me. Keeps 'em…well, keeps 'em sharp…as if they need it, eh?'

As impressed as he was, Joseph calmed proceedings.

'All well 'n' good, but never mind circus tricks. 'Aymakin' next month, will they be ready?'

'We've done plenty o' cart 'n' chain 'arrow work. They start regular day-work sessions from t'morrow, 'aulin' that timber out 'f Lloyd's Wood; those big pine trunks y'r wanted?'

'Ar. I wondered why they'd not been brought down yet.'

'Left them a purpose, Gaffer. Ideal f'r these two t' tackle. 'Course, they'll be on a dolly f'r starters. They'll move on from that t' th' large waggon wi' some field work thrown in f'r good measure, but, t' tell th' truth they're ready f'r mowin' now, Gaffer.'

Joseph scoffed playfully at George.

'Is that right?'

'Ar, it is. They're ready now, Gaffer.'

Joseph believed him, but he wasn't about to throw praise about.

'Ar, I c'n see a glimmer o' promise there. I'll look forw'd t' seein' 'em on th' field, that'll be proof.'

George held his gaze.

'An' we'll look forward t' welcomin' y'there too.'

Joseph reached into Diment's stable and she nuzzled his outstretched hand.

'Well done you two. Y've made this chap look good. Edward! A small bonus f'r y'mother, at the 'ouse, f'r y'r 'ard work wi' these two. Pick it up from Missus Grace when y've done 'ere.'

He winked at George.

'No bonus f'r you, George, just a season 'f 'ard work.'

George smiled at him.

'Don't need no bonus, Gaffer; these two're all th' bonus I could ever want.'

Looking wistfully at the two Shires, Joseph smiled.

'Ar, I know…by, if I were thirty year younger.'

He left the stable whistling tunelessly as George and Edward began the grooming and feeding routine.

17

28.06.09

Haymaking started out gloriously and the fine weather kept on throughout.

Once the dew had risen and moved from mist to clouds, George, Diment and Clowdy would set out and complete a full day's work cutting or turning hay, and George had it confirmed that he had become involved with a highly talented, very clever pair of Shires. The more they worked together, the more the trio understood each other, pre-empted each other almost, and the more fluid became their performance.

This twenty-eighth mid-day of June found the team mowing the nine acres of grass at Crab's Field in glorious sunshine, all three and the machinery in perfect, chattering harmony.

A pair of crows worked over the cut sections of the field, their raucous cacophony rasping over the song of skylarks. Parties of swallows dive-bombed the field's now homeless insect population, and a kestrel was eagerly searching the same trimmed areas for disorientated mice.

Sun was shining; mower was mowing; birdsong filled the field; it was a good day, no different from the five days leading up to it, except in one respect; today Joseph was coming to watch the team work.

Turning the team at the bottom of the slope, George saw Edward enter the field almost at a run.

When he was still two chains away, he began to shout.

'Mister George! Mister George! Gaffer, 'e's died-ed! 'E's dead!'

George hauled in the horses and the mower cackled to a halt.

'Whoa, girls! Stand-On. When, Edward? When were this? I saw 'im this mornin'…!'

In-between panted breaths, Edward blurted out the details.

'Just…breakfast…Missus yelled shep'erd…fetch doctor. 'E did…but too late…now what's us now farm's finished?'

His mind racing, George moved round to Edward.

'Calm down now, Edward, let's sort out what's to 'appen when th' time's right. I'll un'itch th' cutter, you draw th' blade then we'll get over t' th' farm an' see what's t' be done.' He could see Edward needed to concentrate his mind onto the practicalities. 'Edward? Edward! Missus'll want some 'elp, I reckon, an' we can give 'er that 'elp. You an' me.'

'You an' me 'elp, Mister George?'

'Yes. Now, I'll un'itch th' cutter, you draw th' blade an' y'can lead Clowdy in f'r me, eh?'

'Lead Clowdy?'

'Ar, lead 'er back, t' th' farm. I'll bring Diment an' we can see what's t' be done, but we need t' be calm about this, Edward, calm. Th' Missus Grace'll be our first thought, eh?'

'Missus Grace…yes, Mister George.'

It only took a few moments to unhitch the two horses and for the sombre procession to set off for the farm.

—ᴡ—

By the end of that surreal day, George was feeling particularly tired but, of course, his mother needed to hear of the events; out at market that day, she'd only heard the news on her return home, so wanted chapter and verse.

He told her of their arrival back at the farm. The sombre panic coupled with an undercurrent of hysteria that Grace had so nobly held in check. How he had sat with her until the arrival of David and the eventual, constant comings-and-goings of other family members, friends and interested parties; of how he had slipped quietly away once he saw Grace was being cared for…and of how much the whole series of events reminded him of his own father's demise.

'Was summat 'f a struggle, Mam, I don't mind sayin' it.' Clara pressed her hand onto his head and nodded in silent understanding as he continued, haltingly at first. 'Funny thing is…y'think…y'think all these events, these 'app'nin's, Dad dyin' like 'e did an' all that, y' think they're gone; they're th' past an' this is now, an' some'ow they don't matter…no, not don't matter…that they've forgotten y'r…but they've not. They're just sleepin' an' all it takes is a day like t'day t' wake 'em up…not very good at this Mam, sorry; y' understand?'

Clara nodded.

'Every day, George.'

These last admissions stalled the conversation for a while and Clara left George as she visited the pantry as much for mind's occupation as anything else. On her return into the kitchen with butter and a pot of hedgerow jelly, she placed them on the table and stood for a moment. She sensed another layer to George's tale. Finally, with bread, knife and breadboard collected and delivered to the table, she began to prepare a sandwich.

'An' you? What's to 'appen now?'

'Well, th' farm's…'

'No, George, not th' farm! What 'appens t' you now?'

George thought for a long time before answering.

'It's not a snap decision, this, Mam…what I've been thinkin' on. I've 'ad it in mind f'r a while, an' what wi' you tellin' me only a fortnight ago, about wantin' t' be away at Aunt Rose's permanent now…?…An' then this…it all seems t' be fated some'ow…just forced things t' th' surface a bit quicker that's all.'

He stopped talking, the kettle boiled. Clara made tea, laid cups, saucers and sugar on the table. They sat in silence as tea brewed then she filled George's cup and put a slice of the fresh bread and butter on the table alongside the opened pot of jam.

'Thanks Mam, not 'ungry though, sorry.'

'The jam's O-seven, best o' th' crop.'

''Onest, Mam, thanks.'

'That's alright, maybe in a little while.' She readied a cup for herself. 'What does it mean f'r you then…these ideas you've 'ad. What are they?'

Sighing deeply, George wiped his 'kerchief across his mouth.

'I reckon t' try my 'and in the 'Irin' Fair. It's been wi' me f'r a few month now, even while we were sortin' out Clowdy 'n' Diment...' He stopped talking as the thought process rolled on and it was another few moments before he could continue. 'Y' wouldn't believe 'ow good they are, Mam. They're far more an 'orse than I'll ever be a man, if y'know what I mean.'

Clara poured her tea as a distraction.

'I know, George, I've seen y' workin' 'em remember, but 'orses or no, you've t' decide what's best f'r you. If it suited, then most bosses 'ld drop y' f'r an extra farthin' profit, remember that.'

George looked up from his tea.

'By, you're an 'ard woman, Mam.'

'Been round th' track a-whiles, George; these lines weren't got from a life o' powder 'n' silks. Maybe Gaffer, Mister Joseph, maybe 'e were a bit diff'rent than th' run, but 'e's not 'ere anymore, rest 'im, an' you just watch. Surplus stock, both man 'n' beast'll soon get shifted from Fallen Oak when a different boss takes over.'

'Maybe.'

'No maybe about it, George. I know 'ow it works. So, 'Irin' Fair then?'

'Ar. Speakin' Time's almost due. I doubt I'd've thought on it more than a per'aps, but now...wi' gaffer gone, an' you an' Aunt Rose...I reckon time is good.'

Clara ruffled his hair with her hand.

'Whatever y'think is right.'

George looked out at a view that had been a part of his life for as long as he could remember.

'I'll tell th' Missus Grace straight after th' funeral. She'll 'ave enough on 'er plate 'til then. I 'ope she understands.'

His mother patted his head again.

'You tell 'er true an' treat 'er wi' care an' she'll understand. She knows you as well as most, Georgie-Boy.'

18

Each tendril of growth that had snaked loose of its shrub parent was laden with an explosion of flowers and a cascade of perfume; trapped in the lane's track, the combination verged on the giddy.

Holding Clowdy's lead rein and heading out of the yard, George spoke to her and to Edward, who was alongside, leading Diment.

'Best dog-rose year I c'n remember, Edward; late along th' lane too…looks like it waited for 'im; Gaffer 'ld be an 'appy man t' see it; were 'is favourite.' Clowdy snorted and shook her head causing her bridle and its incumbent brasses to rattle and sing. 'Wish 'e could, eh, lass? Me too.'

Edward echoed the sentiment.

'Me too.'

The sun blazed down and, although the pull of the hearse was no effort to the Shires as they eased their way along the lane, even this easy walking pace, in this heat, was sufficient to bathe them both in lather.

With both horses parked under the deep shade of the beeches in the churchyard, George and Edward joined the mourners, all of whom were grateful to exchange the sun for the church's cool interior. But the chilled beams of

Christendom were only a temporary escape from the furnace of the graveside. Back into the full glare of the sun for the interment, the use of handkerchiefs for mopping tears was rapidly outbid by the use of handkerchiefs for mopping perspiration. The walk back, even with an empty hearse, re-lathered the Shires and both horses were relieved when, after arriving back at the farm, the chains were slipped and the hearse collected.

Standing at their customary places in the yard, George and Edward sluiced both horses down, using several buckets of fresh, sun-warmed water they had readied that morning. Even the usually impatient Diment, never happy to have any obstacle put between her and the trough, basked in the pleasure of the damping-down.

A scrape over and rough cloth-dry completed, George left their early feeding to Edward and walked over to the farmhouse and his pre-arranged interview with Grace.

She was standing in the kitchen, looking out onto the back-yard of the house. George thought, in the face of all the last few days had thrown at her, how noble, how much a lady she looked.

'Missus Grace. Thank you f'r seein' me so soon… after…'

Grace smiled at him.

'Best to get things sorted as soon as is possible, George. There's a quiet time just now, family know we have t' talk. Folk've gone back t' sort their own affairs then they're due back here t' meet our solicitor at four o'clock; time t' talk, eh?'

Letting him into the kitchen and inviting him to sit at the table, George accepted the proffered glass of home-made lemonade and, taking a swallow, spoke haltingly.

'I 'ope this is in order, Missus Grace…I did say, that if y' wanted t' postpone it…'

She smiled at him kindly.

'Not at all, George. I was glad to hear you wanted t' settle matters immediately not let them linger on…and I think I know what this is about…' She looked out the window then back at George and sighed. '…No, I'm pleased you did this. Joseph always admired your sensibility an' no-nonsense ways.' She settled herself into a chair. 'What can I do for you, Master Radcliffe?'

George talked Grace through his thinking over the past few months, aware throughout by her smile and frequent nodding that she seemed to have foreknowledge of his thoughts. He talked about his mother's desire to be with her sister, how he felt his time on the farm had run its course and the probability of his attending the Hiring Fair, and of just how much he owed to Joseph.

When he'd finished a silence fell between them until, eventually, George concluded as best he could.

'I 'ope what I've said 'as caused you no more distress, Missus Grace. Last thing I'd ever want t' do. 'Course, I'll stay on 'til th' season's finished an' wheat's in, whatever 'Irin' Fair throws up. Just that I needed t' tell y' sooner not later…felt it weren't right, y' know, t' leave things unsaid when I knew about 'em. Seemed t' be cheatin'…lyin' like…t' you…y' know…that I knew an' you didn't. So I 'ope you'll understand. Gaffer were always good t' me an' I don't want t' bite the 'and, but…'

'But you want t' better yourself?'

'Yes, Missus…it's difficult.'

'Nothing wrong with ambition, George. My Joseph knew you were of a different stamp t' the run of it. You'll go far, my lad.' She looked long at him, then continued, 'No; no, you move on, better y'rself. With no children to follow, Joseph's brother, David, will take on the farm now and I reckon it'll not be just stock he'll want t' change. He'd like to keep you on though, said as much to me only day before yesterday, but if you've a mind t' move on then 'e'll have to think again.'

George shuffled uncomfortably in his chair.

'Just wouldn't be th' same, Missus, no offence t' Mister David.'

'And, on his behalf, none taken.'

There was a short silence.

George cleared his throat.

'Ahem…I 'ope y'don't think I'm bein' funny, Missus Grace, but y'know what I'll miss th' most?' Grace looked at him intently but remained silent. ''Is whistlin'…I'll miss 'is whistle.' He could see the beginnings of tears in her eyes. 'Sorry, Missus, didn't mean t'…'

She dabbed her eyes with her handkerchief.

'No, George, it's right you should say, and it pleases me you have a memory of my Joseph; never in tune, was it?'

George smiled at her.

'No, Missus Grace, never; but it's th' sound o' this farm t' me.'

There was a lengthy silence and then Grace placed her hand on top of George's.

'One other thing, I'd like you to return for th' reading today, George. Four o'clock?'

Surprised by this sudden contact, George now looked puzzled.

'Readin'?'

Grace smiled and patted his hand then sat back.

'Of th' will, George.'

'Will?'

'Best if solicitor tells you. Four o'clock then?'

Rising from the table, George said his farewells.

'Yes, Missus Grace, I'll be there.'

'Thank you, George.' She nodded at him. 'You were a real tonic for my Joseph. He told me, many times.'

She smiled a smile of lost opportunities and a future alone.

George felt his chest fill up and he began to leave and speak hurriedly.

'Four o'clock Missus Grace thank you.'

He left Grace still sitting, neatly folded handkerchief in hands, hands gathered neatly in lap, world strewn in tatters.

—◊◊◊—

As solicitors go, Mister Catchpole Senior of *Catchpole and Catchpole, Solicitors and Oathtakers of Leicester (1804)* was a decent enough fellow. Not that George had any prior knowledge of such folk, but he was made most welcome, both by him and Grace when he arrived back at the farmhouse.

In all, four family members had gathered to hear the reading but apart from David none of them was known to George.

He felt twinges of embarrassment as the contents of the will were read, almost like an eavesdropper, and he feigned disinterest and endeavoured to distance himself from the parlour party…

The view out the window was straight across Grace's Meadow; on down to the river at the far side of the field…swifts were zipping across the blue…larks floating on a parachute of song… On the far horizon…? Yes, a falcon…a merlin possibly…?

George was snatched back from his reverie by the sound of Mister Catchpole's voice.

'And now to Shire horse 4426, Scarsdale Silvergirl, known as Clowdy, and Shire horse 141142, Stuntney Charlotte, known as Diment.'

Now he was paying attention.

'These two Shire horses were bought for the use and betterment of Fallen Oak Farm and its stock. All work and improvement of these said Shire horses has been completed to my entire satisfaction by my Head of Horse at Fallen Oak Farm, Mister George Radcliffe. As witness to his input into their present ability and of my friendship of the said George Radcliffe, I wish them to continue on with the said Head of Horse, Mister George Radcliffe as his own, personal property for no sum and without let or hindrance from this date of witnessing and in perpetuity.' Mister Catchpole stopped reading and looked at George. 'Do you understand, Mister Radcliffe?'

George looked round in his embarrassment.

'No, Sir…not entire like.'

Grace leant over to him.

'The horses, Diment and Clowdy? They're yours, George; your team. Joseph left them to you.'

George looked round the room again, at Mister Catchpole then focused on David who was nodding at him.

'Mine?'

Mister Catchpole turned the will round towards George and pointed at a paragraph.

'And all the tack that goes with them, Mister Radcliffe.'

George spoke hurriedly and in a forced whisper.

'But…Missus Grace, I'm leavin' end o' th' season, 'Irin' Fair, I said. I can't stay on 'cos gaffer's left me 'orses, even them two.'

Grace interrupted him with a voice that was both loud and clear.

'Then Diment and Clowdy go with you, George. Wherever you go, they're yours…'in perpetuity'.'

19

12.10.09

George's heart sank as he saw just who was waiting for transport.

For all things natural, October was the beginning of the year's slowdown. In the case of Jenny, Mary and Victoria however, the exact opposite applied. October was the month of the Statutes; Hiring Fair Day. With the tempting promises this twenty-four-hour experience offered to these three ladies speed was of the essence; they intended to make every second count.

With George still twenty yards distant from the trio, Mary's shouted greeting reached him.

'Mornin', Georgie-Porgie!'

This simple statement immediately had all three ladies convulsed in fits of laughter.

'I'll never understand 'em,' thought George. As he called the horses to a standstill outside *The Oak*, George tried to tackle the hysteria head on. 'Whoa, Clowdy, Diment. Stand-On! You three ladies not been drinkin' at this early 'our 'ave y'r; not drunk already?'

Amidst more laughter, Mary retorted.

'We're drunk alright, George Radcliffe, but only on th' thought 'f our journey to Alling'am wi' you on this beautiful autumn mornin'.'

Shoving Mary playfully against the cart, Jenny giggled.

'Listen to 'er! She c'n do wonderful things with 'er tongue can our Mary.'

And Victoria joined in.

'If gossip's anythin' t' go by!'

The laughter shrieked off again.

George jumped down from the waggon and dropped its back-flap.

'Load up, ladies, please. Where's Mister Ollerenshaw an' Mister Clayson?' He looked around as he placed the wooden box-step on the floor. 'An' Graham?'

Elbowing her way past the other two and onto the step, Victoria offered her hand to George.

'Who, Graham Ferris? 'E's not on at this stop now. You're t' pick 'im up at 'Odges Farm, by them wych-elms at bottom o' th' track.'

George felt the touch of doom as Victoria grabbed his hand and almost man-handled him into helping her onto the waggon. His voice now held an almost plaintive quality.

'An' Mister Ollerenshaw…Mister Clayson?'

'Did y' not know?'

Victoria lifted her skirt high and placed her foot onto the back of the waggon. Showing plenty of thigh, she turned to Jenny and Mary and winked at them as she gripped George's hand tighter.

'They tell this boy nothin' do they? Master Ollerenshaw left f'r th' Fair at four-thirty this mornin', an' if I know mine 'e'll be well soused by now.'

Propelling her forwards and onto the waggon on hearing this news, George let go of her hand as fast as was decent, only to have it grabbed immediately by Jenny, whose voice followed on with the knell of no-husbands.

'An' my Master Clayson's over in Derby, 'edge-layin' f'r Lord Cardigan's man, so 'e'll miss it too…all t'gether now, girls…'

Victoria and Mary joined in from on and off the waggon.

'Aaaaah!'

Then all three set off into peals of laughter again.

Now George was clutching at straws as his voice rose over their hysteria.

'But…where's y' children, Missus Clayson, an' yours, Missus Ollerenshaw, aren't they comin' t' th' Fair?'

'Yes, 'course they're comin'! Wi' Mary's mum at midday! Gives us a mornin' to us-selves…don't fratch y'self about it; you'll see 'em all on th' return though, if y'r that worried on their welfare.'

The three women laughed loud again as Jenny gushed.

'We're th' load, Master Radcliffe, just us shy 'n' innocent girls, so be very gentle wi' us. Promise?' She pushed her breasts against his bare arm and George reacted, practically lifting Jenny from step to waggon against her volition. She was surprised and thrilled by this. 'My, y'r very strong, aren't y'?'

A panting and eager Mary held out her hand for similar treatment.

'Is 'e, Jenny? Is 'e very strong?' She gripped his upper arm as he helped her up onto the step. 'Oh! 'E is strong, Jenny! Y'r right…!' Dropping her hand from his upper-arm she gently brushed George's genitals. This caused him to jump back and lift her onto the waggon in one and the same instant, and with surprising alacrity. As the colour rose in George's cheeks to a brilliant crimson hue, Mary added, '…An' big!'

The shrieks of laughter set off again. George was now in some lather of embarrassment as he moved rapidly to the front of the waggon.

'Please, ladies, please! Y' must be'ave! We'll be th' talk o' th' village at this rate!'

Daring anyone in the surrounding county let alone village to challenge her, Mary stood, hands on hips.

'Let 'em talk! It'll be f'r all th' wrong reasons! It's Fair-day…' She paused for effect. '…Y' know what that smell is? Breathe it in girls; it's th' scent 'f sloe-gin, 'ome-brew an' new dresses, eh?'

George took the reins as he called back to them.

'I'd reckon it's th' scent 'f a crisp, frost-blown James Grieve, Miss Suttcliffe.'

His statement halted all conversation. The three ladies stared open-mouthed at him then at each other.

George flicked the reins.

'Walk-On, girls, Walk-On!'

The two Shires set off, their sudden movement catapulting Mary backwards onto Jenny's lap and setting the three ladies off into fits of laughter…again.

George rolled his eyes heavenwards.

'Never understand 'em. Not in a million years...
Long day f'r some, Diment; long day.'

—ɯ—

He was never so glad to see another body as he was to
see Graham Ferris waiting at the appointed place. As the
waggon drew closer to Allingham so Jenny, Victoria and
Mary began to work themselves up into a glistening of
excitement, all three determined not to miss a stall or ale
house from town's edge to centre; George was even
more relieved when was able to release the ladies on the
outskirts of the town. Calling to them as they set off in
their eagerness, George's voice rose as their distance
from him increased.

'Don't f'rget, seven-thirty at The Old Mow. Outside,
not in...!...an' be sure y' there...!...wi' partners! 'Cos
if not you'll be walkin'!' Shaking his head as they folded
into the crowds, he turned to Graham. 'That's some
representation o' th' ladies 'f our shire, Graham, eh?
Alling'am watch out is what I say.'

Graham smiled back.

'Ar, boys in p'ticular. Anythin' past puberty'll suit.'
At this, Graham moved to the front of the waggon and
said, conspiratorially. 'Can y' drop me at Town 'All,
George, please?'

'Ar, I can. Y' got business there? Not that y' need t'
tell me. Just...if I c'n 'elp...trouble 'r anythin'.'

'That's mighty good 'f y' George thanks; I'm in no
trouble, but...' Graham moved to sit next to George as
they set off through the increasing throng of people and
traffic. 'Business...? Ar. Not t' make too much noise

about it…' He looked around again and dropped his voice even further. '…I'm lookin' t' join th' police force, if they'll 'ave me.'

'Blimey, Graham! 'Ow long's this been an option?'

'Awhiles now.' Graham smiled sheepishly, nervously. 'I think I'd be alright at it. What d' you say?'

'I reckon you'd be a godsend round 'ere, an' that's f'r true.'

'Y'think they'll take me then?'

'Snap you up! Foolish not to.'

Holding out his hand, Graham shook George's.

'You're th' first t' be pleased f'r me, George Radcliffe, thank you. M' gaffer, dad, most o' my friends they seem t' think I'm joinin' the enemy. I'm not. I just want to 'elp folk, y'know, folk like our Lizzie.'

Each considered this from their own understanding.

It was George who broached the subject first.

'I 'eard, from my late gaffer, 'bout th' trouble. You'll not know it but I've 'ad my fair share o' bother wi' that Daniel Long over th' years. 'Ow is Elizabeth these days?'

'She's well now, thanks. She's walkin' out wi' Norman Preston…from Maidwell Farm?'

'Ar, I know of 'im. 'E came to us a couple o' summers ago to 'elp wi' the 'arvest. Didn't 'ave that much t' do wi' 'im; 'e were stackin' an' I were on cart, but 'e seemed a decent fellow by all accounts.'

''E is that. Good f'r our Lizzie 'e is.'

''Ave y'r seen anythin' 'f Mister Long Esquire since the event?'

'No, an' no point in dwellin' over it now. It'd only upset our Lizzie, an' she's put it be'ind 'er. Water's shifted since an' there's a decent man lookin' out f'r 'er now... Back then though, 'e knew what the outcome 'ld be if our paths 'ad've crossed. Wouldn't've put it right but it would've made me feel an 'ole lot better.'

George nodded.

'Ar. Y'must've 'ad a job keepin' y're 'ands off 'im, eh?'

'Too true, but I'm glad the opportunity never come up. Never knew then 'ow things were goin' t' shape up f'r me; but now? Well, I've a clean record; never made no trouble an' I'm damned if I'll lose my chance o' join-in' police over a snake like 'im. That way th' bugger 'ld win.'

'I reckon that's th' best choice; don't give 'im th' pleasure.'

'Ar, an' who knows, I may 'ave th' chance t' get even, bein' on th' right side o' th' law an' all, eh?'

'Y' may well at that! There's one thing f'r sure, 'e'll be on the opposite, an' 'e'll as like be th' same this year as last, so you'll not 'ave t' waste much time waitin'.'

'Short-odds on that, George.'

'Well, th' very best t' y', Graham. Force'll be gettin' a good man an' y' gaffer losin' one. 'E knows does 'e, y' gaffer?'

'Told 'im a couple o' month ago, at Speakin' Time. 'E asked me if 'Irin' Fair was t' be a change f'r me an' I said, "sort of", then surprised 'im wi' me answer. 'E thought I was meanin' another farm! I reckon 'e'd've upped th' yearly wage t' keep me, not wantin' t' sound big about it. But when 'e'd sorted out what I meant, well, 'e weren't best pleased, let's just say that.'

'They only ever see y' value when y'r leavin', 'ave y'r noticed that?'

'Too true, but nothin' 'e could've said would've made any diff'rence.' Graham stopped and, taking a sheet of paper out of his pocket, he coughed nervously. 'Ah-hem! Err, look, George, y' couldn't do me a favour, could y'?'

'Ar, if it's in me power an' don't get me into no trouble; what y' want?'

''S like this, see. M' gaffer, when 'e 'eard about this, well, like I say, 'e weren't best pleased an' 'e refused t' sign th' paper that says 'e knows me an' that I'm a decent sort o' chap, nor wouldn't give me no ref'rence neither.'

'What, nothin'? Well you are a decent chap, Graham, an' that's f'r true; th' miserable bugger! So what's t' do then?'

'Well, you know me, I know not well, but well enough t' know I'm no mad-man nor nothin' like that; I was wonderin'…I was wonderin' whether you'd sign t' say as much?'

'Is it really what y' want?'

'It is, an' I'll not be put off.'

'Well, Graham, I'll sign it, an' gladly, but will they accept my name on it; I'm a nobody, y'know?'

'Not so, George. When you 'ad that fire on your place a while back, folk said you acted well an' sorted out things before too much damage were done, risked y'r life f'r th' stock an' all; y' gaffer, Mister Joseph, 'e spoke very 'ighly of y' t' m' gaffer, coppers too when 'e reported fire.'

'Well that's news t' me, Graham, first I've ever 'eard about it.'

'Them's the facts, George, so I'd be real 'appy to 'ave y' sign f'r me.'

'Well, I'd be real 'appy t' sign f'r y' too; give us it 'ere. 'Ave y' summat I can use t' put me name on it?'

'I 'ave.' Graham took out a pencil from his jacket pocket. ''Ere.' George signed the sheet and gave both back to Graham. 'Thanks, George, I owe y' one; more mebbe. It's in pencil so police may come round an' check it were you as signed; that alright?'

'Anytime they like. I'm lookin' f'r new pasture, but I'll be in th' near county, so let 'em know that an' I'll be glad t' back up my sign wi' some chat.'

'You're a pal, George, y're old gaffer spoke true.' Graham looked nervously at the paper again. 'D' y' really think I'll get in?'

'No doubt about it! What say you, Clowdy?' Clowdy tossed her head and snorted. 'Seal 'f approval right there, Graham. Ayup, 'ere's Town 'All, Whoa, Girls! Stand-On!'

Graham pocketed the paper and dismounted.

'Thanks f'r th' lift, an' y' sign…an' the encouragement, George, means a lot.'

'Think nothin' on it, Graham; least I could do.'

'You're a pal. Seven-thirty at The Old Mow?'

'Ar, but I'd get there dead on th' money if I were you. Summat tells me those girls'll be creatin' a ruckus an' whoever's about that they recognise'll be dragged into it f'r sure; that'll be y'rself if y're early.' George stopped for a second then his face lit up. 'Oh, there y'r go,

Graham, good trainin' for y'. Riot control! See y' later, P.C. Ferris!'

Graham waved in return as George moved off deeper into the town centre.

—ᴍ—

The roped-off area for horses and transport was already fairly full when George arrived. After unhitching Clowdy and Diment, settling them with feed and water and making sure the duty boy was well versed in their care, he took his whip and set off back into the market square. The whole town was abuzz with people, many of them even at this early hour a little the worse for drink, but the banter was good natured even if some of the language was a little ripe.

At the market square, George moved through the crowds looking for a spot in which to stand and meet the hiring bosses, some of whom were already milling around the outskirts of the square eyeing the prospective employees. In the distance, George noticed Daniel heading for the *Black Dog Inn*, walking with a fellow he recognised. From their demeanour they were probably on the verge of sealing a hiring.

Standing in a likely spot, time slipped by; George exchanged the odd general comment with other acquaintances in the square, talking horses in particular. David Cley, one of the recognised horsemen thereabouts came across to chat and George mentioned he had seen Daniel earlier.

'Wi' that Mister Arch from Grove Farm, if I reckon right, an' up f'r a fast'nin' penny too.'

David considered this for a moment.

'Well one thing's f'r certain, George. Arch is as rough as th' package 'e's 'Irin' so it's a good job they're gettin' t'gether; means only two people are mis'rable 'stead o' four!'

Such small talk and banter continued to fill the time and, in between whiles, George was approached by several farmers from the district, but no bargain had been struck. Lunch was beckoning when a well-dressed gentleman approached him with hand held out.

'Good afternoon.'

George shook it.

'Afternoon, Sir.'

'It's Radcliffe, isn't it? George Radcliffe.'

'It is that, Sir. Y'seem to 'ave the advantage 'f me, Sir, for I don't know you…although y'do seem familiar. You local?'

'Several miles further up the valley, Shirley Lodge Farm?'

George nodded in recognition.

'Oh, yes, I've 'eard 'f it; near Mister Arch's farm. That's Mister Carter's place, I believe.'

'Yes. I'm Mister Carter, Henry Carter.'

'Well good afternoon, Mister Carter. What can I do to 'elp y', Sir?'

'Well, very obvious really. I was well acquainted with your late Master, Joseph. Awful to hear of his sudden death…'

George slapped his whip on his boot.

'That's it! Th' funeral! I saw you at th' funeral!'

'Yes indeed, I was amongst the many there; dreadful business… Well, as I say, we've taken on a few extra acres so now we're looking for a horseman for the farm.'

'We, Sir?'

Henry indicated a young lady standing a way off from them whose presence had escaped George until then.

'Yes, my daughter, Emily and I.'

Emily was dressed in an autumnal coloured dress and bonnet and George stared across at her. Seeing she was the centre of their attention, she nodded at them, then looked away.

He was snapped back to the present by Henry's continued conversation.

'Joseph spoke very highly of you and I'd heard from his widow, Grace, that you were to be seeking work outside of Fallen Oak this season? I thought we might discuss terms.'

George smiled at Henry.

'May be a bit complex, Sir, but we c'n try.'

The two men then began earnest discussions and Henry's face gradually grew more perplexed as the conversation developed. After listening to George for a while he shook his head and stood back a pace.

'I wondered why you'd not been snapped up by now. Well, I have to be honest, Mister Radcliffe, I'd not be looking for a second worker until later in the year, probably harvest time.'

'Yes, Mister Carter, I understand. Way o' th' world, that, as I've found out t'day.'

'Well, you shouldn't be surprised at that, and as far as Shirley Lodge is concerned…well, we know it's a fair drop for you from the acres of Fallen Oak to our back-yard, but the terms you've set mean it's a lifetime's investment in yourself that you're risking, here or anywhere else for that matter.'

'I know that, Sir, but Edward…'

'Yes, Mister Radcliffe, "but Edward ". Have you officially left?'

'Yes, Sir, I 'ave.'

'Would they take you back?'

'Only if I ask, Sir, an' I'll not be doin' that. Times right f'r a move, I told Missus Grace that; meant it then, mean it now.'

Henry thought for a few moments then spoke slowly, deliberately.

'I'll be honest with you, as things stand at present and even with the recent increase in our modest acreage, we would only take on extra staff for the season's demands. Since the loss of my wife five years ago we've scaled down the farm's output. Emily and I have done it all since, or rather Emily has. I've just been a passenger for much of that time; she's been the driving force there. But now we've taken on these four new fields, Forty-Acre……well, Emily needs the help, hence my overtures to you, you see?

'Yes, Mister Carter, I do.'

'You know as well as I do that, of course, extra help is always useful but not always affordable, particularly when that extra help isn't quite the full shilling. No disrespect meant to Edward, of course.'

'An' none took, Mister Carter. 'E were th' first out f'r that very reason when the old gaffer, Mister Joseph died, an' 'is brother, Mister David, took over th' runnin', but I'd vouch for 'im as under my care.'

'Well, what's to do? I'd be a very pleased man to have you on the staff, I'll make that plain, but what you ask is a lot.'

George thought on for a while then spoke his thoughts out loud.

'Y' know I'm fetchin' my own team, Sir, so that should account f'r some.' He stopped and thought some more as Henry nodded in agreement but kept silent. 'An' as f'r 'ousin', Sir, well Edward'ld prefer t' stay on at 'is mother's an' cycle t' work, summat 'e does now, so that'd be no change an' no cost t' you. In fact Shirley Lodge is that bit closer to 'im than Fallen Oak were…other direction, but closer! I'm a single man, Sir; we could some'ow look on Edward as my pledge!'

'What, as a bodager? A bodager's employ is seasonal, Mister Radcliffe, you know that as well as I do, and their pay comes out of the employed man's wage. You want Edward to be employed on the farm throughout the year…'

'I'd vouch f'r 'im, Sir, an' my word's my bond, you must've learnt that much from Missus Grace.'

Henry frowned and rubbed his brow.

'Look, Mister Radcliffe; George… Yes, Grace spoke very highly of you, but…the thing is, it's more difficult than just where he lives and who vouches for him, surely you see that?' George was about to interrupt but Henry held up his hand. 'I know, I know, he'll not get much help elsewhere, I know that, but this brings much in the way of responsibility to Shirley Lodge.'

'An' I'd take that responsibility for you, Sir!' George paused for a moment to collect his thoughts. 'Look, Mister Carter, apart from what Missus Grace 'as said you don't know me from a bull's foot, I understand that. So, all you 'ave…all we 'ave t' go on is a friendship wi' my late gaffer. Well one thing I c'n tell y' Sir, is that I'll not let y' down an' I'll not shift my responsibilities to any other shoulder. Without this as a start 'e'll just be so much waste. Daniel Long, one o' th' chaps at Fallen Oak, 'e finished off what little God'd given Edward. Left 'im wi' no pride nor no confidence; th' last thing 'e needs now is no work.'

'I understand that, George, but…'

'Y' said a bodager's pay would come out o' my wage? 'Ow about…'ow about if y' pay me two-thirds o' th' salary on offer, Mister Carter, an' add the other third to 'is wage. Would that be acceptable?'

'What, for the whole year?'

'F'r th' 'ole year, yes, Sir.'

This last stopped Henry altogether. He shook his head and smiled at George's persistence.

'If you feel you'd be prepared to work for that sort of reduced salary, then yes, but it's a slice of money you're giving up.'

George pressed home the advantage.

'Ar, but it's mine t' do with as I please, an' if y' knew an' respected my gaffer as y'did…well…then I reckon we'll go well together, Sir.' Henry smiled and nodded again as George continued, 'One thing, Sir, if y're agreeable, I'd be much obliged if y' just make out you've 'ired him on th' staff for 'is abilities, such as they are. No need t' mention our arrangement is there?'

'Yes…yes, very well. You're blunt and to-the-point but a fair and decent fellow for all that; Joseph was right.' Henry offered his hand to George. 'Then for my part we've a deal, Mister Radcliffe, and Edward's a very lucky man.'

'Thank you very much, Sir, I owe y' much f'r that an' you'll not regret it, not f'r a moment.'

'Time will tell, Mister Radcliffe. Can you excuse me while I see my daughter and make the explanations, then, if she's agreeable too, we'll away to seal the bargain?'

'Yes, Mister Carter, 'course.'

They shook hands again and Henry walked across to Emily who was still waiting patiently. As they entered into a discussion, Emily threw several glances George's way. At the close of their conversation she looked long at him and smiled. Smiling shyly back at her, George could not hold her gaze. He looked across the square and waved at an imaginary acquaintance.

Henry moved back to him.

'Right, well, the staff of Shirley Lodge Farm is unanimous in their acceptance of our arrangement, and I know Emily will be glad to relinquish the day-to-day to another. It's been a burden for her, even though she'll not admit it. Will you explain to Edward there's a vacancy you've heard of with us then send him over to the farm by the end of the week, Emily will fill in his duties for him.'

''E's quite slow, Sir, so she'll need t' repeat stuff for 'im afore 'e catches 'old.'

'Yes, I'll tell her; she'll know exactly what to do.' He rubbed his hands together. 'Right, after all that, I believe a drink's in order! Emily will meet me outside The Old Mow in about twenty minutes. A fastening penny awaits, I believe, Mister Radcliffe.'

They shook hands.

'Lead on, Mister Carter, I'm as dry as a wooden dog!'

The two men moved through the crowd and into the public bar; just twenty minutes later they both emerged into the street.

George saw Emily sitting on a bench opposite. She was talking to another woman with a couple of children in tow and George now noticed her animated face and warm smile. As he and Henry stood at the doorway, she looked up at them and her gaze locked onto George's.

The moment was broken when Henry took George's hand and shook it.

'So, a start in two weeks time then. Emily will see the stabling and cottage are ready and you can move your furniture in at the same time as your team. I hope for a long and fruitful partnership, Mister Radcliffe.'

George smiled, still glancing at Emily.

'Thank you, Mister Carter; I do too, an' thanks from me an' Edward…'

'Georgie-Porgie! Georgie! Whoo-hoo!'

The dulcet tones of Victoria Ollerenshaw rang out, filling the ears of just about every other inhabitant of

Allingham, and Henry was brushed aside in their eager onslaught as George was surrounded by the three ladies. All of them were much the worse for drink, but Mary was by far the most drunk as they arrived in a bundle, shrieking at the tops of their voices. Jenny's chatter remained the loudest as she parked Mary at an angle in the pub doorway.

'Oh Georgie, we 'ave missed y'r! What y'r stuck 'ere on y'r own for?'

'You need a drink…Oh, look, it's old man Carter!' squealed Victoria. ''Ow are y' me old love?'

George tried to gently intervene.

'Casual farm staff at Fallen Oak, Mister Carter…'

'But nonetheless proud an' willin',' retorted Victoria.

'Some more willin' than proud, eh, Mary?' added Victoria.

This set her and Jenny shrieking with laughter again. Mary just sloped smilingly in the doorway, a line of dribble escaping from her lower lip, her eyes holding the glazed look of a hypnotised goat.

Henry smiled at Victoria and touched his hat.

'Pleasure to meet you, ladies.' He turned to George. 'Two weeks time then, Mister Radcliffe.'

Jenny spoke over them.

''E wants a good woman round 'im 'e does…'

George answered Henry.

'Yes, Mister Carter, two weeks.'

Now Jenny grasped what had just been said.

'Two weeks? Wha's two weeks…? You've not tempted 'im away, 'ave y'r? 'E 'as, Vicky, 'e's stolen our Georgie-Porgie…What's our Mary goin' t' do now?'

Still slumped against the tavern doorway, Mary rallied slightly at the repetition of her name and gamely wiped away the drool.

'Whasss t' do now?'

George tried to steer the conversation onto a better route.

'Nobody's tempted me, Mrs Clayson. I'm away 'cause I choose t' be!'

Henry decided a tactical retreat would be in order.

'Goodbye, Mister Radcliffe. Ladies.'

He walked over to Emily, Victoria's voice loudly pursuing him.

'But our Mary!

Jenny focused on the departing couple.

'Is that that Emily Carter over there…? Is it?'

As Emily was watching them, and had probably heard every word, George tried to be quietly firm.

'Yes it is, Mrs Ollerenshaw, now please, keep y' voice down. I've never said anythin' to encourage…'

Mary slipped down the doorpost and George lunged forward to catch her, causing Mary to shriek loudly and Victoria and Jenny to both yell over it, attracting even more attention their way.

'Did y'see 'ow fast 'e was, Jenny! An' strong too! Did y'see, Mister Carter?'

'I did, Vicky, I did!' shouted Jenny. 'That was our Mary's swoon f'r love if ever there were one!'

As he wrestled with the dead-weight that was the inebriated Mary, George saw Henry take Emily's arm as they turned and walked away. At the same instant, Jenny and Victoria surrounded George, further knocking him off balance as they declared their concern and undying love for Mary, their dislike of Emily and their insistence they should all have another drink to get over the shock.

Emily took a glance back, just in time to see this rowdy quartet lose its balance completely and crash through the doorway of *The Old Mow*!

—⁓—

The journey back from Allingham was a much more subdued affair.

Victoria had her spouse on board so, had she been awake, her style would have been somewhat cramped. As it was, she and Jenny were slumped, snoring gently together, both of them percolating a hangover that was created by alcohol, stimulated by excitement and which would be of cataclysmic proportions.

Mary was still semi-awake but a great deal less voluble than usual; no excitement or any other emotion was involved, it was solely down to drink.

All the children were exhausted after their day and slept in various pockets of straw scattered around the waggon as, with all the authoritative slur that drink bestows, Graham and Arthur Ollerenshaw vied with each other over who loved Leicestershire more.

Glad of the quiet, George was enjoying the sinking of the sun when Mary diverted sufficient wind from flatulence to voice-box in order to shout out from under the straw.

'Georgie-Porgie's been talked away...t' Shirley Lodge...! We saw 'im...an'...an'...'er...that Emily whisherthing...bet they got y' cheap, Georgie!'

She slumped back.

'Thank God they know nothin' about Edward,' thought George.

Raising herself up from the straw, Mary launched one last hurrah.

'An' Edward's goin' wi' 'im!'

George shook his head.

''Ow the 'ell did she know that?'

Letting go a huge belch, Mary smiled broadly and generally, then fell back into the straw again.

For the rest of the journey home, George could feel the eyes of the other passengers, those still able to focus that is, burning into his back in their curiosity.

20

Settling into the new routine at *Shirley Lodge Farm* took only a few days for George, Edward, Diment and Clowdy.

Every detail had been catered for and George was greatly impressed by the quiet composure of its running, the condition of its agriculture, buildings, farm implements, the transport and livestock; all were in top order. The cottage turned over to George was spotlessly clean, had been installed with gas lighting and held a small stock of essential provisions for him to use until he sorted out his own supplies.

Stabling had been put aside for him with the other three horses on the farm. One brown Shire gelding, Ben, a black hunter mare, Polly, and a dun general hack, Carmen. All the horses were in immaculate condition, as was their hunting and work tack, and George was also surprised and delighted to see that gas lighting had been installed in these stables too. Whoever was in charge knew a deal about agriculture and a lot about horses and their care, and George said so during his first full meeting with Henry.

'Place runs itself very well, Mister Carter. Yard an' stock're in top order; y' keep y'rself very busy.'

Henry shook his head.

'Not just me, George, as you might remember from our meeting at the Hiring Fair. Put the vast majority of it down to my daughter, she's the one that makes all the major decisions.'

'I see, Sir. Will she be joinin' us?'

'Unfortunately she'd arranged to visit my sister today, otherwise she would be. Delegated her second in command to have this preliminary chat, but I've to report back.' He smiled and gave George a knowing look. 'And it'll have to be a full one.'

'I'm sure we'll be able to give a good account of ourselves, Mister Carter. Y' seem at ease with it all, Sir.'

'Have to be, George. I'm not a youngster anymore, as you can see, and the loss of Harriet, my wife, was a huge blow; was my right-hand, we did it all together, but she'd taught our daughter well. Was a natural progression for Emily to take over the running of the farm and my involvement has gradually dwindled to my present role of occasional help and chief cashier… No, no, I have to say I'm not troubled by it…taking my arthritis into consideration.'

'Well, first look around says Miss Emily knows 'er 'orses an' 'er farmin', Sir, an' that's a fact.'

'As I say, a good teacher, her mother.'

Henry looked towards the farmhouse as if half-expecting to see his late wife come out the door and down the path.

'Y' must miss 'er, Sir; not wantin' t' get above myself, but I remember 'ow much I missed my dad when 'e left us.'

Henry switched his gaze from closed door to George and smiled.

'Yes, I do miss her. A lot.'

'Ar.'

'Right, George, now, the Forty-Acre paddocks. What's the best way to run them, do you think?'

'Well, Sir, I think th' divisions're about right; 'edgerows're good but'll need some work this winter. I'd suggest we get Master Clayson over an' let 'im set about layin' 'em.'

'Right.'

'We're a bit pressed f'r time t' get it all in work this year, Sir, so I suggest we turn over both top sections; th' ley's been there long enough an' a crop o' spuds off it'll do it good. Lower end loses th' moisture nicely, so spring barley should prosper well there. Leave th' left 'and section as grass an' take off 'ay this time round. Wi' a bit more time next year we'll be able t' rotate it in. Certainly not reckon on anythin' late 'arvested there, 'oldin' th' wet like it does…as f'r th' rest 'f it, well, we'd best get on.'

'I'll get a message over to Clayson today; let's hope he can fit us in. You're quite right, we are late, but those blackthorns are getting way above themselves.' Henry smiled and nodded. 'Done your homework well, George, and I'm sure the boss will be pleased…. Do you think you can get it all done before Christmas?'

'Well, I'd not want t' work 'orses too late in th' year on some 'f it, as I said, an' it'll need some graft t' prepare it, but we'll give it a good go. I thought I'd get along t'morrow an' make a start, if that suits, weather 'avin' been dry an' all.'

'Yes, absolutely.'

'So t'morrow then. We should get first cut done in a little over fourteen days then we'll work it over an' see 'ow it breaks up through winter.'

Henry rubbed his hands together.

'Good, George, good. Well, I'll get back to the house. If you need anything you'll know where to find me, and Miss Carter's always on call.'

The two men parted, Henry to the farmhouse and George to the stables where Edward was scrubbing the buckets after feeding.

'Right, Edward, we're t' look out th' ploughs an' chains. Turn over Forty-Acre paddocks t'morrow so we need t' make sure all's well. Right?'

Edward put the bucket down and grabbed his jacket.

'Yes, Mister George, all's well.'

George smiled at him.

'You've time t' finish scrubbin' out though, Edward. Ploughin' t'morrow, eh? We'll not be leavin' this very minute.'

'Yes, Mister George, ploughin' after buckets.'

''Ere, I'll 'elp; get it done th' sooner, eh?'

'Yes, Mister George, then ploughin'.'

21

31.10.09

To the accompaniment of a horse-tack-orchestra, George walked Clowdy and Diment along the lane to their second ploughing stint on the Forty-Acre.

Over the rise ahead another man appeared with a single Shire horse and low cart; it was Daniel Long. George halted to allow him room to get past. As they drew level, so Daniel halted his horse.

George looked across and nodded.

'Daniel. Mister Arch's man I 'ear, so near neighbours then?'

Wiping his nose on his jacket sleeve, Daniel sniffed.

'Not by choice. I 'ear y' swindled the old man out 'f a pair 'f 'orses; them pair if I'm not much mistook.'

'Ha! Always a one f'r lettin' y' mouth move off before the 'arness on y' tongue were tight. So much you know.'

'I know enough t' know you're not as smart as y'make out, Radcliffe. Anyone who saddles theirselves with an idiot as a workmate…'

'Meanin'?'

'Guess.'

'If y'r referrin' to Edward, then let's stop it right there; understand this well. 'E knows you're still in th' district but nothin' 'f y' whereabouts; let's keep it like that. What 'e does an' doesn't do is no concern o' yours, an' I'll thank y't' keep right away from 'im, understand that well too.'

Daniel recognised a different George now and although he continued to grin, the facial expression was less human, more simian. George had nothing to add and was beginning to leave as Daniel finally spoke.

'Radcliffe?'

George stopped.

'What?'

'Y' never said, 'bout th' fire…never told th' gaffer; made trouble f'r me.'

George turned to face Daniel nodding gently in realisation.

'Was never certain who it were; not 'til now.' George's thoughts flicked back to the events of that night and in a split second, his anger rose then subsided. 'No 'orses 'urt or we might be talkin' a different endin'. As things were, an' even if I'd've known it were you, 'ow much more trouble could y' be in? You'd lost y'r job, th' cottage an' y' good name…not much 'f a drop that last one, I know, but I reckon that'd be enough on a man's back.'

Daniel's eyes narrowed.

'An' y'think, what…I owe y' summat, is that it?'

'There's nothin' o' yours I want, Daniel Long, not even y'r acquaintance.'

Daniel dragged the phlegm back in his throat and spat into the hedgerow.

'Ar, just as well. We may well be seein' a bit 'f each other as I intend t' set me cap at Miss Emily, so I'm glad me 'quaintance 'ain't wanted. Clear?'

'Ha! Clear as mud, as usual. I'll do 'n' go as I please, Daniel. You're no worry t' me now, I'm me own man; an' so's Edward, remember that. As like you'll slither y' way onto th' farm an' there's not a lot I c'n do about it, but I'll tell y' this…' George pointed to his heart and head. '…From 'ere an' 'ere…' Then pointed straight at Daniel. '…If I so much as catch you makin' yourself known to Edward, I'll be on y' like a burr; an'…as f'r Miss Carter…well, I'm not sure you'll get much in th' way o' change there, but that's f'r 'er an' you t' find out. Whichever way it goes, I expect y't' treat 'er better than the other females you've 'ad under y' command.'

'Meanin'?'

'Like that old grey, Chalky, an' I'd guess that bay mare in your 'ands right now…an' from what I 'eard a while back, Mary Ferris?' George saw Daniel's face twitch a little and knew he'd made his point. 'Like all'f 'em, Miss Emily'll deserve better… An' don't you forget this; she's my gaffer's daughter. Like anythin' else on this farm, I'll not see 'er ill-treated.'

Daniel was rumbled but he tried to bluff it out.

'She'll get what I give. Just you keep out th' ring. Now, I've work t' do even if you've not.'

'That'll be a first then.'

Daniel slapped the reins onto his horse's back.

'Walk-On!'

146

The bay mare jumped forward at the volume and abruptness of the command and set off hurriedly.

George stayed for a few moments watching them go, not quite sure how he felt about the conversation and its revelations.

—⁓—

Mid-afternoon found Diment and Clowdy running this, their last arrow-straight line of the ploughing session, seemingly unaided. Pressing the stilts firmly, forcing the plough-share into the turf and turning the green to brown as he created a sea of fresh soil, George walked gently behind them. The flock of seagulls that had been following him all day were seemingly still hungry. Dipping, weaving, robbing many an invertebrate of longevity as they filled their bottomless appetites, they flurried around him in snow-storm hysteria.

This was the sight that greeted Henry and Emily as, on their way back from Allingham, their cart cleared the hill's brow on the lane that ran alongside the Forty-Acre paddocks. It was Emily who had suggested they go via these fields, just to see how things were going. Unaware he was under their watchful gaze, George continued with his ploughing, the whole unit working as one. From their elevated position, Henry eyed the level of craftsmanship on display and turned to Emily.

'That's as straight a line of ploughing as you'll see this side of heaven. He's got them so well trained; I swear they'd grow crops without him.'

Emily smiled.

'It's an affinity, Father. He has that effect on all sorts around him. You remember Mister Grice's Mastiff, caught your prize ram last year?'

Henry snorted in derision.

'Ha! If Grice wasn't the only farrier nearby I'd've insisted it should be shot!'

'Father, don't be so cruel! Scampers round George like a puppy. He has that effect on things.'

Henry looked at her and raised an eyebrow.

'Hm. George, is it?'

—⁓—

Henry was crossing the yard in near full-dark when George arrived through the gates leading Diment and Clowdy.

'My, you're late on. I hear you've been over to the farrier's. Not problems with the plough were there?'

'Y've seen Edward then?'

'Yes, he's not long gone. He was full of smiles, said he'd done a bit of ploughing and that you'd gone to Grice's; puzzled me a bit I must say.'

'Nothin' t' sweat over, Mister Carter. Edward did a part run f'r me at th' close, just t' get a feel o' th' ground f'r t'morrow. Diment dropped a shoe on 'im, at least I reckoned it were this last run, could've been earlier an' I failed t' spot it, 'er bein' furrow side an' all.'

'You'd not miss a thing like that, George, I know.'

'Maybe not. Any'ow, we went back but couldn't find it nowhere; dusk closin' fast as it were. I sent Edward back 'ere t' finish up. Did 'e manage it?'

'Yes… He never mentioned anything about a shoe, just your visit to the farrier.'

'Well, 'e wouldn't, Mister Carter. 'E tends t' forget detail; things slip 'is mind, as y' know, like 'im bein' 'ere a regular 'alf-hour afore 'e's supposed t' be; earlier some days.'

'Yes. Does he not know how to tell the time?'

'No, don't think so. 'E just uses th' sun an' 'is stomach.'

'So buying him a watch wouldn't be much use then?'

'No, Sir. I tell 'im most days t' tell 'is mother about 'is start time or if 'e's not wanted 'til late after lunch, but by th' time 'e's at 'ome 'e's forgot. Well that's th' same as me goin' t' th' 'smiths; 'e'd know I was goin' but not remember what for.'

'Well, he's just left. Got the stable routine done, he said. I've just checked and he has, so now I'm on my way back to the farmhouse.'

'See, 'e remembered some 'f it. Like I said, I sent 'im back 'ere t' finish up, save me time so's I could walk this pair t' Grice's; you ask 'im what the day's been like an' 'e only gives y'r 'alf th' tale. Lucky t' find Grice in an' furnace up, otherwise I'd've definitely lost part o' t'morrow. I've no doubt th' shoe'll turn up.'

'I don't suppose that Mastiff of his was about when you got there?'

'What, Bridger? Err…no. Not that I saw any'ow. Why, what makes you ask?'

'Oh, nothing, just something Emily said earlier. Well, g'night, George… Are you on target?'

'Ar. Edward an' Ben'll be out wi' me from t'morrow so, shoes bein' willin' an' all, we should get a few good runs in.'

Henry rubbed his hands together.

'Excellent! Good night then.'

'Night, Mister Carter.'

They parted, Henry to home, George to stables.

22

26.06.10

Hauled by Diment and Clowdy, who were beginning to lather up with the effort and heat, even at that early hour, the cart's hay-bustle swayed gently to the movement of wheels on uneven ground.

As he approached the farm, George could see the small, busy figures in the yard ahead. At haymaking the other local farm workers would all join forces for the stacking of the hay, and this blazing hot June day in this blazing hot June week was the Carters' turn. Excellent timing with the weather, the only cloud on the horizon being that Daniel Long was amongst their number.

When the list of men involved in the farm's hay-making had been presented to George two days previously, he had been very surprised to see Daniel included and had asked Henry why this was. Henry's reply was entirely pragmatic.

'Harold Arch may not be a friend, George, but he is a neighbour. We'll be expected to do the same for him in a week or so at Grove Farm. I'm not so bad a neighbour as to forego reciprocation.' Henry saw the set of George's face. 'I know Daniel of old too, George, remember that. His reputation reached even here, but it is beholden on us to support our neighbours, and although I'm not entirely happy with the arrangement…'

George confirmed the point.

'No, Mister Carter, an' neither am I! Does Edward know 'e's 'ere?'

A little taken aback at George's abrupt comment, Henry smiled all the same.

'Joseph was right, there's no side to you at all. Not yet, George, no, Edward doesn't know. We thought it best to keep it as quiet as possible. I well remember our conversation back in Allingham. Indeed it was Emily who told me to make sure there would be little or no chance of them coming into contact except by total accident. She suggested I assign Edward to loading in the field for our haymaking, Daniel to stacking in the yard and, when we get over to Grove Farm, for me to leave Edward here to cover our needs.'

'That's very good o' you, Mister Carter, an' Miss Carter too. I just 'ope there's no accident.'

'Look, George, I took Edward on but with the full understanding that his presence must not interfere with the running of the farm!' He stopped then added in a more conciliatory tone. 'I understand your reservations George, and so does Emily, but we have Harold Arch's surety that Daniel's got the better of the drink and has settled in well there. After a long chat, I was reconciled to the needs of the farm and satisfied with the working arrangements organised by my daughter; on that I trust her implicitly.'

'That's very thoughtful o' Miss Carter, Sir, an' I'm not ungrateful, just…'

'Rest assured, George, Daniel knows full-well that at the first sign of trouble he'll not only be away from here, he'll be away from Grove Farm too. I've informed him of that myself. If that happens, he'll have run the gauntlet of just about every farm of any size in the neighbourhood, and that'll mean a move away if he's to find land work again; last thing he wants, I'm sure.'

'Old dogs 'n' new tricks, Mister Carter…I've worked with 'im afore, remember.'

Henry smiled at George.

'Yes, I'm aware and I'm also under no illusions, but we need the help if we're to get all the fodder in during our allotted week. You were right to leave that section of grass in the Forty-Acre paddocks, but added to our usual amount of hay it puts us under some pressure, you know that yourself.'

George nodded in agreement.

'Ar, I know, Mister Carter.'

'We need the help, George, and I can give you my word that I'll take no nonsense; expect you to take the same approach and also take Mister Arch's assurances that all will be well; Daniel's too.'

George nodded.

'Right, Mister Carter, you're th' gaffer an' I'll be guided by that. Will y' thank Miss Carter on Edward's an' my be'alf f'r 'er kindness? Y'c'n both be sure I'll give Daniel every chance but th' farm comes first, an' if 'e gives so much as an ounce o' bother, 'e's gone.'

'Good to hear, George. You have my absolute support on that. Emily's too, as in everything else to do with the farm.'

With the work started and the staff distributed as Emily had arranged, the rick-building began and the yard stack grew rapidly for the crop was heavy and of top quality.

George, seated here atop the loaded hay cart, knew he had the best of it for he could appreciate even the smallest breeze, whereas working in the yard on such a day was hot and stifling. The walls surrounding the yard banned all air movement and the temperature of the sun and the dust from the hay meant for uncomfortable working conditions, even though plentiful supplies of home-brewed cider and farm-produced bread and cheese kept the men well fettled. George had not sampled these delights yet and he was looking forward to his first taste; Emily Carter's beer and cider had something of a reputation locally. Diment and Clowdy too would be given some light nourishment and be able to slake their thirst in the cold spring running into the yard's trough.

In the yard, Daniel, as top stacker, had a bird's-eye-view of the surroundings. This meant he was the only person to see Emily enter the stable block through the field-side door. He glanced around and moved to the edge of the stack. Below him, Michael Calloway, another local farm labourer was on the next level down.

He indicated the shrubbery in the corner of the field to Michael.

'Just got t' go away over yonder.'

Michael nodded.

'Oh, right. I'll come up.'

Slipping off the stack, Daniel made his way round the side of the barn and into the stables. He saw Emily at the far end, amongst the horse tack.

'Missus?'

Lifting a saddle off a spar, Emily jumped at the suddenness of Daniel's arrival.

'What is it, Daniel?'

'I wanted t' ask who you w' walkin' out wi'.'

Emily frowned for a moment.

'Not that it's any of your concern, but there's no one at the moment.'

'Then it may as well be me.'

'Don't you think you should ask?'

'I've done all but, Missus. I've passed y' several times in Alling'am, been 'ere, on th' farm f'r two days now an' tried t' make y'see me as I am but y've ignored all o' that.'

Emily smiled.

'Well, setting aside those briefest of meetings in Allingham when, I have to be honest, your presence has passed me by, and the even briefer time you've been here, my further lack of interest should've been a clue, don't you think?'

Daniel blinked and stood for a moment or two, the only sound being the dull chatter of working men out in the yard and the arrival of the next loaded hay cart.

'Well? What's y'r answer, Emily?'

Emily tried to make the point a little clearer.

'What you lack in some of the social graces you make up for with your brevity, Daniel, so I'll be as brief. No, thank you.'

'Not good enough f'r y', eh, day-man like me?'

This was becoming irksome.

'Your social position has nothing to do with this, Daniel! You've asked me, I've given you a civil reply. Now, can we remove from this? I'd suggest you should be back out in the yard or you'll be missed…'

Before she could complete the sentence, Daniel moved in very rapidly, grabbing her by the wrist. The force of his approach knocked the saddle from her grip and it toppled to the floor.

Emily spoke loudly and firmly.

'Daniel, stop this foolishness now!'

Daniel clamped his hand over her mouth.

'I want t' show y' what y'r missin' Emily.'

Pushing her back against the stable wall, he tried to plant a kiss on her lips…

Hearing the door open, Daniel let go of Emily and she moved to the side of the stall, picking up the saddle as she went.

George took the scene in at once.

'What's doin' 'ere then?'

Having the moment spoilt did nothing to improve Daniel's temper; the fact it was by George was a red rag to this particular bull.

'Clear off, Georgie-Boy!'

'I've told you before, Long, not t' call me that; y're not my father! Y're not fit t' walk under th' same sun as 'im. Now, if y' value y'r employ 'ere, or anywhere else f'r that matter, you'll be out o' that door quick-sharp!'

Daniel was at a pitch of rage and embarrassment as he moved rapidly towards George.

'I'll fuckin' knock you through it, Radcliffe!'

Side-stepping the blundering move with ease, as Daniel stumbled past off balance George felled him with a single, massive punch!

The silence was instant.

Still clutching the saddle, Emily moved out of the stall.

'Thank you, Mister Radcliffe; George.'

George looked up from the comatose Daniel.

'That's alright, Miss Carter, I've been wantin' a reason t' do that f'r years. You've done me a favour; thanks.'

'Oh…I see…have I?'

'Yes, Miss Carter, you 'ave.'

'Oh, well I'm pleased to have helped…and it's Emily.'

George looked at her.

'My name? It's Emily.'

'Yes, Miss Carter, I know…I work 'ere, remember?'

There was a short silence.

Emily cleared her throat.

'Ahem. Erm, can we keep this to ourselves, please? I'd rather it wasn't to become common knowledge. You know what folk are, gossip and such.'

Smiling at her, George looked over Emily's shoulder towards the window.

'I would, Miss Carter…'

'Emily.'

'Sorry, Miss Emily; I would if it were anywhere else, but this is just outside Alling'am, Leicestershire?' Emily turned and saw the line of farm-worker faces pressed against the grimy windowglass as George continued, 'It'll be in Kent come lunch. No secrets between us in this village, Miss Emily, you ought t' know that by now. We may look out f'r each other but we chatter a lot too.' He indicated Daniel's still prostrate form. 'I'd suggest y' leave th' barn now, Miss Emily. 'E'll be out f'r a good few minutes yet but 'e's not likely t' be in a good mood when 'e does come round.'

He began to leave as Emily said.

'Is that all we're going to do?'

George turned back and looked at Daniel again.

'I'll see Mister Carter now, Miss. 'E'll pay 'im up an' scuffle 'im off, if 'e's still about t' be told by then that is. What Mister Arch decides t' do…'

'No, no, I mean…with Mister Long…just leave him lying there, like that, on the cobbles?'

George shifted his gaze from Daniel to Emily.

'Ar. What did y' want, give 'im a pillow?'

With that he walked out the barn and gently closed the door.

23

08.12.10

Because the bust-up had happened in full view of the farm's guest labour, news travelled back to the haycock field almost as fast as Daniel hit the floor and, when he first heard, Edward was horrified and amused in equal measure. After George had calmed him and explained that Daniel was now about as welcome as a plague of rats, Edward was partially mollified, certainly less agitated.

Shortly after this incident, George heard, through Michael Calloway, that even Mister Arch could not countenance Daniel's behaviour, Michael adding that, knowing how big a rogue Arch was, to be fired by him was probably the zenith of Daniel's career. Edward's relief was therefore complete when George informed him Daniel had left for pastures new; George's comment that he hoped those pastures would be China amused Edward greatly and somehow the days lacked shadows for him from then on.

As his time at *Shirley Lodge Farm* moved on, George's contribution towards the farm's development grew and, of necessity, contact with Emily was increased; but, because these meetings were wholly farm oriented the presence of Henry was always needed. As bankroller, historical font and unofficial gooseberry, Henry's attendance kept all chat on a strictly business footing. There were accidental meetings between the couple of course, and these chance meetings meant opportunity presented itself for them to develop their friendship; it was George's shyness and work-load however that prevented anything other than good mornings being exchanged.

The year's glorious June days lengthened into July and August, each month vying with the other to pack in the most sunshine. As is often the case with blistering summers however, there followed a brutal opening to winter which continued unabated, freezing root-and-branch in the lead up to Christmas. Field-bound livestock had to be given extra rations, and George was grateful that their hay-crop had been so plentiful.

Now, on this December morning and with Edward on potato clamp duties, it fell to George to deliver feed to the cattle housed on the hilltop, in the lea of the woodland known as Miller's Belt.

As he crossed the yard to get Diment and Clowdy out for the cart, so Emily left the stables leading Peggy, almost bumping into a surprised George and causing an involuntary impulse to override his usual monosyllabic greeting.

'They're not 'untin' in this, are they, Miss Emily?'

Emily was also surprised by the meeting-and-greeting and found herself replying by return before she realised it.

'No, George…er, but, but hounds still need to be run, as you know.' She indicated Peggy. 'And this frisky madam too. I'm, er…do you know John Quinn? The Whip? He's father's cousin, and an invite came the day before yesterday, so I'm out with him and the Master…to exercise them. There's a few of us, we'll be out by Curtis' for the morning; flat there and big enough hedges to keep hounds confined.'

George looked at the hunter.

'Peg looks set for it. Take care she don't fix 'er mind on them 'edges f'r a bit o' steeplechasin'.'

Emily laughed.

'No, you're right. She doesn't take kindly to being cramped up for too many days without a run, but there's no worry of bolting from that particular quarter; this young lady does as she's bid.'

George smiled at her.

'Wi' you in charge I don't doubt it.'

There was a short pause, then Emily spoke.

'You out to the cattle up at Miller's Belt, George?'

'Ar. Snow's blown three-foot deep on th' rise there so I'm takin' some 'ay, as you've already worked out. Not lookin' forw'rd to it though, Miss Emily, that track an' all, but they'll not last another day without, so it's a case o' frost-cogs in an' get on with it.'

'Oh, that's why you were at Mister Grice's on Wednesday! Father said you'd taken the horses there and I mentioned it was only two weeks ago you'd had them re-shod. I complained about the extra expense; sorry George, penny-pinching, I didn't think. You've had screw-shoes put on them?'

'Yes, Miss Emily, an' sorry 'bout the extra expense…'

Emily smiled and nodded.

'No, no, I should have realised, my apologies.'

'Just seemed a sensible thing t' do…an' we did discuss it at last meetin'.

'Ah, sorry, must have not been concentrating; sorry.'

'No apology needed, Miss Emily, you've plenty t' think on without me fussin' over frost-cogs. I just suspected this end t' th' year, past experiences see? Can't claim any credit f'r it though. I weren't the only other at Grice's 'avin' 'em fitted, I c'n tell y'. Seemed 'alf th' county 'ad th' same idea.'

Emily smiled at his description.

'And very sensible too, but even with their fancy footwear, I don't envy you the trip…just go carefully.'

There was an awkward silence.

George cleared his throat.

'Uhh-uh! Well…you just be steady too, eh?'

Emily watched George disappear into the stables and her thoughtful walk across the yard leading Peggy was slower than usual.

—⋙—

George was indeed glad he had fitted the horses with their frost-cogs. If the walk up the sloping track that led to Miller's Belt with the loaded cart had been tricky, it was as nothing compared to the return down it.

After the fall of fresh snow, the track and steep bank it topped was an unbroken eiderdown of white. On the upward journey the weight of the hay had steadied the waggon. Now it was empty, and the thick snow covering on top of the frozen ground that hid the brick-hard, ruts-and-stone packing of the track made it behave like an over-excited puppy. As a further reminder of what may befall the unwary, the gently bubbling, summer stream sixty feet below the track was now a swollen winter torrent of icy water that gushed and rinsed like a black scar.

Measuring their hoof-fall carefully, the journey was tortuously slow but George, even though leading, left the pace to his horses; they knew their own footing after all.

Given their gentle progress, then, it came as a complete surprise to all when one of the waggon's rear wheels lifted high onto a snow-covered boulder… flopped off it, bounced violently and skittered across the frozen and slippery narrow track towards the top of the bank. Off it shied, straight through the single-strand wire fence, snapping a post and dragging all with it. The ground offered little or no purchase, not even to the horses in their snow-cogs, and neither Diment nor Clowdy were a match for this sudden change of agenda or the speed with which it happened.

'Haul-On, Girls! Haul-On! Hup! Hup!'

But even with George helping them they could do nothing to halt its progress. At the top of the bank the waggon teetered on the edge of balance for a split-second, seemingly undecided, before gravity and motion took proceedings in hand and sent it tobogganing over the edge and down the precipitous slope. Scrabbling for all their worth and even with George heaving on their collars, all three swiftly followed on, the snow slipping and cascading around them, completely obscuring visibility as the waggon gathered further speed.

'Whoa…! Bloody 'ell, girls! Whoa!'

His devilish prayers were answered when their downward travel came to a sudden stop!

'Drop 'n' Still, girls! Still.'

The two horses lay where they were, as much from the shock of it all as from George's command.

Gradually the snow haze settled and George was able to see their predicament. Draped on either side of a thick ash tree, the wire-tangled waggon was still attached to the Shires, but only by leather reins, hauling chains and fence wire, the draw-spar having been snapped and now dangling at right-angles. Thirty feet below, the snow-swollen stream flushed and crashed over the boulders.

'Drop 'n' Still, girls.'

George crawled round to inspect the damage. There were no wounds, but although Clowdy was virtually free from entanglement, Diment was well tied up.

He placed his palm gently on her nose.

'Diment, Still; stay Still.'

Loosening Clowdy's umbilicals, George called to her.

'Clowdy, Hie-Up-Hup!' She rose unsteadily to her feet and stood shaking a little. 'Stand-On, Clowdy. Diment, Still; Drop 'n' Still.'

A further inspection of the grey showed no obvious injuries apart from shock, and he moved back to the waggon to see if the same freedom could be granted to Diment but it was obvious, even from a cursory glance, that she was well-and-truly snared. He moved back to the mare.

'Can't do a lot unless I c'n tie off th' waggon, lass, an' t' do that I need t' be in two places at once.' He looked up the bank's slope. 'We'll 'ave t' get some 'elp, girls.'

He placed his palm onto Diment's nose again.

'Diment, Drop 'n' Still.'

Taking Clowdy's collar strap in one hand, George urged her up the bank. Diment moved slightly as they left but could sense all was not well and obeyed George's last repeated command.

'Diment, Still; Drop 'n' Still!'

Half-scrambling, half-dragged, George quickly found himself at the top of the bank. Turning Clowdy down the track he slapped her rump.

'Home-Home, Clowdy; Home-Home!'

Clowdy moved off towards the farm and George went back down the bank to reassure Diment and see what could be done to free her…

—w—

As she hacked the last mile of her journey home, Emily felt the temperature begin to plummet further and was glad of the extra layer she had donned before leaving. A mixed flock of fieldfares and redwings had gathered on the muck-heap in the farm's yard, underlining just how severe conditions must be to entice these normally shy birds into such close human contact.

Although she had enjoyed the taughtness of the weather, Emily was pleased when the Master had called a halt to exercise for it seemed even hounds were feeling the cold; she certainly was. Now back in the relative warmth of the stables it had taken her a lot longer than usual to prepare Peggy for bait and bed because her gloved fingers were so cold and stiff.

Emily noticed Diment and Clowdy were still out as soon as she entered.

'And in these conditions,' she thought. At least she had been doing something pleasurable; cold, but pleasurable, and she did not have to rely on ungrateful cattle to set the timetable.

'Brrrr!'

The sound and shudder left her involuntarily. She concentrated on getting her final chores done as quickly as possible. Gradually the feeling came back into her hands and the warmth from Peggy, plus her own grooming efforts soon had her body radiating heat. She finished and patted the hunter.

'You're the best crock-bottle I've ever had, lady.'

Sliding the bolt on the mare's stall meant home, hot tea and a slice of the walnut cake she had baked yesterday.

The warmth gathered by Emily was immediately dissipated by the bitter cold of the yard as she moved her shivering way across it. She was only half-way when Clowdy walked briskly in through the open gateway.

'Clowdy? Clowdy! Whoa, Girl, Whoa!' Emily took hold of the Shire's halter and stroked her neck. 'Now then, steady girl. What's up? Where's Master, hm? Where's George?'

The morning's conversation came back.

'Is he still out by Miller's Belt? Is he?' She looked out of the yard at the crepe-paper whiteness. 'In this cold?'

There must be something wrong, she knew it and also knew that, in these conditions, time was all. Emily let go of the halter and Clowdy took a couple of steps toward the gates; that confirmed it for her.

'You Stand-On there, Clowdy, Stand-On.'

Grabbing two long lengths of leather rein as she quickly re-entered the stable, Emily was back with Peggy, who had yet to finish the feed in the trough. Slipping one rein onto the surprised mare's halter she led her out into the yard. Clowdy was stood waiting. Jumping onto her hunter's bare-back, Emily slipped the other rein into the grey's collar, took it in one hand and called to her.

'On-On, Clowdy, On-On!'

Clowdy paused for a moment, then turned and trotted out of the yard alongside Emily…

—ᴍ—

George had massaged Diment's limbs in order to stimulate her circulation and then began again to tentatively remove the wire-and-leather cords that connected her to the waggon but it voiced its disapproval by groaning and slipping further down the bank. Diment had, understandably, struggled to get to her feet when this happened only causing further movement from the waggon; it was now on the verge of dragging both horse and man closer to the tree-trunk and into imminent danger of being whipped round it and away.

'Steady, Diment! Drop 'n' Still! Steady, lass, Steady.'

She had settled to his voice and command but George was far from happy with their situation and very unsure how much longer they could remain there before fate decided the outcome for him.

On the verge of risking an all-or-nothing release he heard, to his immense relief, the approach of horses above him even in that covering of snow.

Clowdy had realised where they were heading and was now in front of Peggy by the length of her lead rein. Dismounting, Emily needed no guide to see where the problem lay; the snow told its own story.

'Oh, no…not in the stream…oh, please…' she muttered. She moved warily to the top of the bank and patted Clowdy who was looking down the slope. 'Steady, Clowdy; Stand-On.'

George's voice floated up from the snow.

'Clowdy? Clowdy, you back already?'

Emily's head spoke a grateful prayer as her voice spoke in answer.

'Yes, and with the cavalry too!'

Hearing Emily's voice, George patted Diment.

'Soon be out now, lass, 'elp's arrived. Miss Emily, that you?'

'Yes. Are you alright?'

'Now you're 'ere, I couldn't be better.'

Emily smiled at the comment.

'What should I do?'

'Can y' come down t' me? Watch out! It's treach'rous slippy!'

'Yes. Wait there.'

'Not likely t' be movin' about much, trust me.'

'Yes, alright; stupid thing to say, but do it all the same. Clowdy, Stand-On.'

'Y' knows th' commands?'

After the briefest of pauses, Emily replied.

'Er…some…Heard you use them…er, odd times, sort of overheard them, er, a little…'

Her voice tailed off as she started down the slope, finding out very quickly that George's warnings were well founded.

Slipping and sliding, she catapaulted down towards them, only just managing to catch the tree trunk in passing.

'Said it were slippy. Welcome, come in, good t' see y'r.' Emily was about to say something but George repeated. 'No, really, Miss Emily; it's good t' see y'r.'

There was a moment of silence.

'Right, George, what's the best way out of this?'

'Steady th' waggon first, I'd say. But you not me, if that's alright, Miss. I'll need t' stay wi' Diment, keep 'er calm.'

'Right.'

Diment was showing signs of discomfort from the cold and fright as Emily slid across to the waggon, reviewed the situation and reported back.

'No chance of untangling Diment bit-by-bit without the waggon moves away, George. It'll either drag her round that tree-trunk or tighten the remainder before I can get it all released, and she could lose a leg if that happens.'

'Ar, we found that out earlier, didn't we, lass. Suggestions?'

'The only thing is to support the waggon as best we can, get Diment out of these wires, then release everything in one go.' Emily looked back at the waggon again. 'Have you a knife?'

'Ar, 'ere.' He handed her his pocket knife. 'Careful wi' it. I may not be good at much…well, I w's meant t' be feedin' cattle an' ended up 'ere, but I c'n edge a knife.'

Putting the knife into her coat pocket, Emily smiled at him.

'I'll leave all the important couplings alone for you to sort out later. Let me release what I can, what's safe, and we'll fashion what I get free into a rope. I'll go back up top and use Clowdy and Peggy to steady the waggon, then you can slip the remainder off Diment…what do you think?'

He looked across at the waggon then down at the stream below.

'Ar, I reckon. Put Clowdy be'ind though, an' tie it to 'er collar, Peggy c'n act as brake…' George looked at her. '…Can y' do it?'

Emily smiled at his concern.

'I'm out of any other ideas.'

'Me too. Let's get on; this mare's goin' t' die 'f a chill if we're not fast out.'

Decisions made, George stayed by Diment to reassure her as Emily moved across to the waggon. Checking each leather connector with George before she released it, Emily used his knife, which was indeed very, very sharp, to cut them free.

Much of the wire from the fence was coiled but loose and, by bending it back and forth, she managed to snap off a couple of good lengths. Clowdy's chains were free from earlier work done by George, and Emily also managed to release one of Diment's without too much complaint from the waggon. After ten minutes, Emily guessed she was in possession of sufficient lengths of leather, chains and wire to reach the track. Returning to George, they began to tie each length to the other.

This was the worst job. The cold had penetrated their bones to the very marrow, and what would have normally taken a minute or two took several. They completed the tying in companionable silence, saving energy for the work in hand, and eventually Emily was able to return to the waggon and tie their make-shift rope to a front wheel.

It was only then she broke their silence.

'Right, back up top, quick as I can.'

'Ar, but I'd rather it were slow an' you alright than fast an' you 'urt…if y' see what I mean.'

Fresh snow began to fall as Emily nodded, giving George the broadside of her smile, then headed up the slope to Clowdy and Peggy. At the top she turned the horses and attached the improvised rope to Clowdy's collar. She then took both lengths of stable reins, tied them together and joined the two horses with a stop-knot around Peggy's neck and a straight run to Clowdy's working-collar.

'Ready! I'll move them on. You call the halt when we've got the slack out as I shan't be able to see from here!'

George's disembodied voice floated up to her.

'Gently though, Miss Emily. Clowdy's used t' th' game but Pegs'll find it all a bit strange…no gallopin' now, eh!'

Emily smiled in spite of her nervousness.

'Spoilsport!'

She took hold of Peggy's head collar and led her on until the rein connecting the horses tightened then she halted the mare.

'Ready up here!'

'On your start call then, Miss!'

She breathed in deeply.

'Hie-On, Clowdy! Hie-On!' Clowdy moved forward, gradually taking up the slack. Emily clicked at Peggy and pulled gently on her head collar. 'Peggy, Walk-On!'

Gradually the line between Clowdy and waggon tightened until the Shire was taking its full weight. As soon as George saw the waggon shift fractionally uphill he shouted from below.

'Whoa, Clowdy! Stand-On! Stand-On, lass!'

Clowdy came to an abrupt halt. Working as rapidly as his frozen fingers would allow, George untangled Diment and even though the waggon made to slip downward once or twice, Clowdy's strength and Emily's mongrel rope held firm. After a feverish few minutes, he had released the last remaining strands of wire, chains and leather and Diment was free. His gentle voice reassured the mare.

'Diment, Still; stay Still.'

He moved round her, rubbing her limbs in an effort to get the circulation moving then, taking hold of Diment's collar, in a firmer voice, he called to her.

'Hie-Up-Hup! Diment! Hie-Up-Hup!'

Gradually, slipping twice in her efforts to do George's bidding, Diment rose from the snow, her limbs stiff and chilled.

Standing dutifully by Peggy's head, Emily could only listen to the events below but, after a few moments of silence and to her great relief she heard George's voice.

'Right. All clear 'ere, Miss Emily. We'll be up in two shakes 'f a lamb's tail.'

It was at this point that the slippery surface and weight of the waggon, a decent pull for two Shires, began to tell. With a sudden, graunching sound, Clowdy's snow-cogs gave out, two of them snapping off under the strain as she slid back across the track and towards the precipice. Peggy and Emily, no match for Clowdy's backwards movement and off-balance bulk, were dragged back with her as Emily called out.

'Clowdy! Peggy!'

Hearing Emily's shout and seeing the waggon begin to slither down the bank; George guessed what was happening above him on the track.

'Clowdy, Hie-On! Hie-On girl! Hie! On!'

Hearing George's command, Clowdy scrabbled at the ground and managed to gain a tenuous foothold. Taking her cue from this, Emily urged Peggy to walk on and take up any slack.

The shift in the waggon and its connecting rope now loaded extra force on one side of Clowdy's collar, trying to wrench her head round, and she pulled forward as much to obey George's command as to relieve its pressure. The waggon steadied and George called up again.

'Stand Tight-On, Clowdy! Good lass, Stand Tight-On!'

With what remained of her snow-cogs digging into the frozen ground, Clowdy obeyed, leaning forward slightly, her muscles standing out in her efforts, her breath streaming from widened nostrils in clouds of condensation.

The falling snow-flakes grew bigger as Emily pulled on Peggy's halter and tried to add her own weight to the equation.

'George! Hurry!'

George took hold of Diment's collar.

'Hie-On, Diment! Hie-On, On!'

Her first movement was a real effort as her limbs were stiff and uncooperative, but to George's insistence, Diment gradually moved up the hill, dragging George with her, out through the gap in the broken fence and onto the track. George released his hold on Diment and the mare stopped at the edge, shaking slightly, breathing hard and obviously not fit to help solve the present predicament. He moved swiftly round to Emily as the snowfall increased in its intensity. Taking hold of Clowdy's collar he spoke rapidly.

'That waggon'll 'ave t' go, there's no way we'll get it back up, sorry, Miss Emily. You'll explain t' y' father, will y'?' Emily smiled at him as he continued, 'Can I 'ave me knife back, please?' He took it. 'I'll cut that length o' rein by th' fence. Clowdy'll take most 'f it, but sudden loss o' th' waggon'll cause both 'orses t' come on y' fast so be careful, an' watch out f'r them 'ooves, eh?'

Emily arranged herself for the outcome which, she figured, would be rapid.

She was right.

The knife-blade hovering over the rein, George shouted to Clowdy.

'Haul-On, Clowdy! Haul-On!'

Clowdy stiffened, taking two steps forward as the second knife stroke was completed and George rattled off his next command.

'Stand-On, Clowdy! Stand-On!'

She halted immediately and, acting as a two-way brake, the grey locked her two thousand pounds of solid muscle into a rigid anchor point as the loss of the waggon's weight and the sudden slackness of all connecting ropes transmitted through to her. But Peggy, still straining forward and unused to such shenanigans, and Emily, still holding onto her mare's halter, were totally unprepared for the sudden change in weight. The connecting rein dipped and both hunter and holder rocketed forwards only to be snatched back as the force that was the forward-sledging Peggy was checked by the immovable object that was Clowdy.

Below them all, intent on its own journey, the waggon paused for a post-release breath; then the cut-free rein shot away past George's face with a whip-crack as the waggon slithered and bounced down the slope. To the sound of a waggon smashing to pieces on the stream's rocks, Emily tried to dodge the oncoming Peggy. Even by staggering away and throwing herself to one side, however, she was still in danger of being trampled by her own horse. Peggy now completely lost her balance. Slipping onto the snow-covered floor in the surprise of it all, and to George's further yell of, 'Look out, Miss Emily!', the hunter's hooves flailed and scythed, missing Emily's head and shoulder by a fraction.

Emily was up immediately encouraging Peggy to her feet. The mare stood shivering with the cold and suddenness of the events; Emily's breath came out in gasps as she looked at George's expression and realised how close she had been to some real harm.

The silence that followed all this activity was absolute and then suddenly, Emily and George began to laugh in their relief. Gradually the laughter subsided and they were left, still looking at each other through the falling snow across the width of the track.

'Peg's alright?'

'Confused but fine, George, thank you.'

'You, Miss Emily?'

'Me? I'm just confused, George.'

George moved to Peggy's head and the still smiling Emily.

'I'll 'ave t' get Diment 'ome 'n' rubbed down, Miss Emily; she's 'ad some cold in 'er.' He paused and surveyed the scene. 'Phew, there were some close calls there. Thank you, Miss Emily. That's three favours I owe y' now.'

Emily's eyes narrowed a little.

'So deep in debt…you could just call me Emily and pay back one of them.'

'Yes…Emily.'

Emily moved in very close to George and he could taste her warmth through the bitter cold.

'You could offer to kiss me and pay back another.'

Gently brushing the settled snow from Emily's face, George leant forward and planted a light kiss on her lips then moved back.

'That's two.'

Emily pressed her hand onto George's cheek, pulled him closer and whispered,

'Ask me to marry you and we'll call the debt paid.'

- 24 -

29.04.11

As weddings go it was a low-key affair; just Clara, Rose, Grace and Henry, with Edward as best man, attended the ceremony.

There was a general invite to local farmers and workers to attend the celebrations afterwards though, and upwards of sixty people turned up to drink the couple's health and wish them well.

It was a great relief, to George in particular, when the evening wound to a close and he and Emily were serenaded across the hundred yards that separated Henry's farmhouse, where the reception was held, to George's cottage, now their married home and snug retreat.

The doorway was decorated with spring flowers and greenery and it was to loud applause, and the ringing sound of a hunting horn courtesy of Uncle John Quinn, that George picked Emily up and carried her over the threshold......

10.05.12

The tummy rubbing helped Emily with the immediate pain but the ache itself seemed to be settled in for the day; again.

George rested his hand on Emily's spherical belly.

'There y'go, Lump.' He pulled the bedclothes back over Emily. 'Y' bound t' get a few more o' these, I s'pose, Em. Wi' ten days t' go they'll probably get worse, not better. Nothin' t' be done f'r it an' midwife's well informed so she knows all th' detail; ought to, she's been out 'ere often enough.'

Emily plumped her pillows and sat up.

'Well thank you for the reassurance, George Radcliffe. Quarter to six of a morning is not the time to tell a woman in my delicate state that there's "nothing to be done for it", that she's "being demanding" and that "things will only get worse!"'

Getting out of bed, George put on trousers, began to pull on shirt and walked to the door.

'Just tryin' t' be 'elpful's all.'

He just managed to dodge behind the open door as the pillow bounced off it and Emily called after him.

'Tea! Tea to ease my aching condition; I demand tea, slave!'

His shirt over his head like a shawl, George popped back round the door.

'Certainly, Your Majesty. Will that be served here in the boudoir or in the withdrawing room?'

'Neither, I'll have it in the kitchen, with the common herd.'

'Careful, Madam, you'll be giving the servants ideas above their station.'

Emily laughed as George pulled his braces over his shoulders, further tightening the shirt on his head. He tugged his forelock and disappeared from sight.

She flipped the bedclothes back, slipped both hands under her tummy to act as a cradle for the weight, and called out.

'George? Are you still happy with Sarah for a girl and Henry if it's a boy?'

He answered from the stairs.

'What's wrong wi' Lump?'

Dropping her feet over the side of the bed, Emily sat there.

'George, be serious; are you?'

'What, bein' serious? I think so.'

'No, stupid, I mean happy with the names!'

'Ar. I said so didn't I?'

Emily waved her dangling feet to-and-fro.

'Ye-es. I just wondered. I mean, they were both my choices, you just nodded in agreement.'

'What else am I s'posed t' do?' George re-appeared round the bedroom door, properly dressed now. 'Say I don't like 'em 'n' demand summat diff'rent?'

'Such as?'

He paused for a moment, a puzzled expression on his face. 'Such as? Such as…nothin'.'

'Well you must have other names in mind, names you'd prefer otherwise you wouldn't now be demanding something different.'

'I 'aven't demanded anythin' diff'rent.'

'Yes you have, you've just brought it up; you said you wanted something…'

George moved into the room.

'I didn't bring it up, you did…! You asked did I like th' names y' chose…'

'See, there you go again; "the names you chose".'

'But…they are th' names y'chose! An' you asked if I liked 'em an' I said yes.'

'Well, do you?'

'Yes! Look, d'y' want any tea or shall I get on wi' work?'

'Only if you're sure.'

'About what, th' tea?'

'No, you soft 'aporth, about the names.'

'I'm sure, Em, as God's my witness, I'm sure! Now; d'…y'…want…tea?'

Emily snuggled, smiling, back down under the blankets.

'Yes, please; and be quick about it!'

George left the bedroom. Half way down the stairs he stopped, shook his head and muttered.

'I'll never understand 'em.'

Emily sat up fast.

'Understand who, George?'

'Crikey, you've the 'earin' 'f a bat.'

'Never understand who?'

'Women, I'll never understand women. You.'

'That's because we're mysterious.'

Walking back up the stairs, George reappeared in the bedroom.

'I'll wear a bloody trench through 'ere, so I will.' He stood at the door. 'Mysterious? There's nothin' mysterious about it. Mystery I c'n work out, it's women I can't.'

Emily sat up, dragged her pillows up behind her and patted the bed solicitously.

'Sit down and tell me what you don't understand, my little troubled one.'

George stayed by the door.

'You. Women.'

'Such as? Example, please.'

'What, now?'

'Yes, now. You seem to need to fathom the mystery, so, example, now.'

George thought for a moment.

'Right…erm…I don't know…' Then his face brightened. 'Right, last week, Wednesday, we go shoppin' to Alling'am, f' lace, f'r them curtains we still 'aven't got up in th' kitchen.'

'Is this a general complaint about my domestic skills because if it is it's unfair, I'm pregnant……'

George sighed.

'It's got nothin' t' do wi' y' domestic skills nor y' pregnancy; it's about th' mystery that surrounds goin' t' buy lace in Alling'am!'

Emily tucked the bedclothes tight around her legs and waist so they formed an outline to her body.

'Well; you tell a poor tale.'

'That's because y'keep interruptin' me.'

'That's because you tell a poor tale.'

'No it's not, it's because y'keep interruptin' me!'

'And you lose track.'

'No, I don't! Y'keep interruptin'…'

'Because you lose track.'

'I…do…not…lose…track, Em! Now, d'y' want to 'ear it or not?'

Emily made a movement with her hand over her mouth to signify that her lips were sealed.

George sighed.

'Right…' Then paused and looked blankly at Emily. 'Where were I?'

'Allingham? Buying lace?' Emily put her hand to her mouth and muttered through her fingers. 'Sorry, George, do go on.'

'Ar, right. Well, we're in Alling'am…buyin' lace…an' you picked some up in Gifford's an' said t' me, "That's perfect!" Then y' put it down an' I said, "What y' doin'?" an' you said, "I'm goin' t' look at what else there is!"'

Emily smoothed the coverlet, completely non-plussed.

'So?'

'So? We did the other two shops that sell lace in Alling'am; Brakes, an' Cooper 'n' White'ouse, didn't we?

'Yes.'

'An' come back wi' nothin'!'

'Yes, that's right.'

'Well there you are then!'

'Where are we, exactly?'

'Em…we came back wi' nothin'!'

'We came back with nothing because there was nothing else to come back with!'

'But…?…in th' first shop y' said you'd found summat that were perfect!' Emily smiled as George floundered on. 'Well…I mean, 'ow much more th'n perfect can y' get than…well, perfect?'

Emily looked at him, smiled again and sighed.

'Haaaa, such simple things, men.' She snuggled back down under the bedclothes. 'Tea, please.'

Blinking in the glare of a conversation he had not fully understood, George slowly left the bedroom.

'Right, thanks f' that, Em. Explained it all so well; my mind at rest, I'll go 'n' make tea f'r y',' adding as he went down the stairs. 'An' Robert or Rebecca.'

Emily threw back the bedclothes.

'George!'

—⁓—

By half-past three that afternoon, Emily knew this was no ordinary tummy-ache.

George had told her he would be in the yard or the paddock at the back of it for the day, so it was not much of a walk to find him. As soon as he saw her, George knew this was her time too.

Ushering her back to their cottage, he ran to the farmhouse, announced the imminent arrival to Henry and got him to sit with Emily. Telling Edward to finish for the day and be sure to let his mother know why, he got out the small cart, hitched up Diment and set off to collect the midwife, calling in at his aunt's house on the way to inform Clara and Rose and asking them to make their way to the cottage.

By the time he got back all the relevant people had arrived and George felt Emily was in good hands. It was Clara who suggested he occupy his mind by tending to the horses.

Returning to the stables, George was surprised to see Edward sitting with Clowdy.

'Edward? What y' doin' 'ere? I thought I said t' stay 'ome?'

'Come back t' do 'orses.'

'D' y' not remember me sayin', about stayin' 'ome?'

Edward's face registered a frantic search, then he smiled.

'Come back t' do 'orses, Mister George.'

'Ar, so y' said. I would've done 'em; there were no need t' cycle all th' way back 'ere… Did y' tell y' mother why you'd got back early; about Missus Radcliffe an' th' baby?'

'Yes, Mister George. I told 'er.'

'About th' baby?'

'Yes…told 'er, said Missus Radcliffe were with babies…like our sow back awhiles.'

He smiled broadly at George, happy in the safe delivery of the message.

George sighed.

'Right. Thanks f'r that, Edward. Well, y' can go back 'ome if y' like, there'll be no more work t'day…not f'r us any' ow.'

There was a silence and Edward gazed around the stall.

'Come back t' do 'orses.'

'Yes, I know, y' said.' George could see there was an impasse here. 'Right, if y'like. I'd be glad o' th' company t' be 'onest. You start on Clowdy seein' as y're in there with 'er, I'll do Diment, eh?'

Edward smiled broadly.

'Yes, Mister George. 'Orses. Time'll pass.'

'Not fast enough f'r Missus Radcliffe, I'll warrant.'

Working on in companionable silence, George and Edward gave a thorough grooming to all the horses and did, indeed, partially lose track of time.

At twenty five minutes past nine that evening, they received the news from Clara that George had a bonny wife, now mother, and a fine, healthy baby girl.

'One, Mister George?'

'Ar, just th' one, Edward.'

'Our sow, she'd fourteen.'

'Lucky I didn't marry a pig then, eh?' Edward laughed. 'Right, Edward, this calls f'r celebrations…f'r th' new baby o' course, not th' fact I didn't marry a pig.'

In the yard, George scooped two tin mugs of spring water from the trough.

'T' baby Sarah, Edward.'

'T' baby.'

He and Edward drank a toast.

'Not pig.'

'No, Edward, not pig.'

Edward's face clouded over.

'Will she roll it?'

'What?'

'Our sow rolled 'ers, killed-ed four.'

'No, Missus Radcliffe won't be rollin' on 'ers; leastways, I 'ope not. Right. I'd best get in and see t' mother an' baby, you get off 'ome. An' y' c'n tell y' mother th' news…it's a girl, not a piglet…an' no work t'morrow; mark me on that. No…work…t'morrow!'

'Yes Mister George; no work.'

'Right. An'…thanks f'r y' comp'ny tonight, Edward, it did 'elp.'

'Yes, Mister George; an' me.'

George watched him cycle off and shouted as he rounded the yard gates.

'No work t'morrow, Edward!'

Edward raised a hand as he disappeared round the yard wall and George returned to the stables to close up for the night. In with Clowdy, he patted her neck.

'So, Sarah it is then, eh, Clowdy-lass. G'night you lot. Edward'll be in t' feed y' t'morrow mornin'.'

26

29.06.14

Emily saw copies of the *Leicester Daily Mercury* stacked neatly in their wire frame outside the village shop and picked one up.

The front page held the usual adverts for farm equipment and domestic help and she opened and leafed through it.

The headline on page seven stopped her short.

AUSTRIAN HEIR SHOT.

DOUBLE ASSASSINATION.

BOMBS AND BULLETS IN SERAJEVO.

A STUDENT'S CRIME.

CALLOUS CONFESSION OF THE MURDERER.

Leaving the sleeping Sarah in her pram outside, she took her shopping bag and entered H.J. Hall Provisions, serenaded by the shop door's spring-bell. Mrs Abram was by the counter talking at the elderly owner, Mister Hall, and Emily closed the newspaper as she approached them, placing it on top of another pile of *Mercury*'s.

'Morning Mrs Abram; Mister Hall.'

As Mister Hall drew breath Mrs Abram seamlessly switched object but not subject.

'I were just sayin' t' Mister 'All 'ere, Mrs Radcliffe, dreadful business isn't it, 'im dead 'n' all?'

'Yes, indeed. Assassinated too! World's a dangerous place when there's lunatics abroad…'

Mrs Abram's face showed real shock at this revelation.

'Assinated! Y'think 'e were assinated, Mrs Radcliffe? Well, I don't know; who'd do such a thing?'

Emily picked up and reopened the paper.

'Well…yes…it says who killed them both here… look…'

Mrs Abram looked askance at Emily.

'Both?'

'Yes, the Archduke and Archduchess…'

'I don't know about no dukes nor duchesses…? 'Ave y' not 'eard news? Panel Doctor? Died, Sat'day night!'

'Oh, I see…erm, no, no, I'd not heard, Mrs Abram. You mean Doctor Davis? Oh, my goodness… How did he die?' Emily took the shopping list out of her bag and handed it across the counter. 'Couple of additions to the usual list, Mister Hall.'

Mrs Abram was glad to have someone else to report the details to and Mister Hall was once again cut off before he could reply.

'Doris Willard said 'e fell off 'is bike, well not so much fell as cart-wheeled, over that five bar gate, bottom o' Wells Lane!'

A determined Mister Hall talked loudly over Mrs Abram.

'Morning, Mrs Radcliffe! This the lot?'

'Yes, thank you, Mister Hall.'

He left the counter to collect the various items as Emily turned her attention back to an affronted Mrs Abram.

'Over the gate? I'm not sure I understand you. How on earth did he manage that?'

Mrs Abram threw a look towards the departing Mister Hall then folded her arms across her chest and took up the stance of self-important herald.

'Well, y' know 'ow much 'f a toper 'e were, well, 'e were on 'is way 'ome from th' Dog 'n' Duck, as usual, on 'is bike, as usual, skin-full, as usual... unusually someone 'ad been a good countrym'n an' shut th' five-bar gate at th' bottom there.'

Mister Hall returned with an armful of items and put them on the counter. Emily pointed to a small brown bag in their midst.

'Not that tea, Mister Hall, thank you. Sorry, should have said. We've a mind to try the one in the blue bag, same measure though, please.'

'Yes, Mrs Radcliffe.'

Mrs Abram leant over the items in inspection.

'Change o' tea is it, Mrs Radcliffe? Stick wi' what y' know, I say. No good ever come o' choppin' an' chang-in'; our Panel Doctor c'n vouch f'r that!'

Mister Hall rolled his eyes at Emily and left the counter to change the tea and collect the remainder of the shopping on the list.

Emily turned back once more to Mrs Abram.

'From what I remember, that gate's always left open. Everyone round here knows what Doctor Davis is like and how he gets home; it's not been shut for four…'

Mrs Abram cut across her.

'Years. See, no good ever come o' choppin' an' changin'. Yes, well it were shut Sat'day night last.' She paused to consider this event for a moment. 'Must've been a stranger t' the area…Well, down that 'ill 'e goes three sheets t' th' wind, freewheelin' as usual, when, wallop! Over th' gate 'e goes!'

Emily raised her eyebrows at the news.

'Goodness me!'

'Snapped 'is neck an' gate's top bar in one movement; an' them gates ain't cheap.'

Mister Hall's voice came from the bowels of the shop.

'Will that be the large carbolic, Mrs Radcliffe?'

'Yes, please, Mister Hall. Well, I'm sorry to hear all that, Mrs Abram.'

Mrs Abram was not about to say any more, obviously feeling what she had said was enough for anyone to digest at one sitting. There was a short silence as Mister Hall returned with Emily's last few items of shopping and began to tie the string around the blue parcel.

'There's only a quarter of the blue tea, I'm afraid, Mrs Radcliffe…'

Mrs Abram butted in.

'See. No good ever come o' choppin' an' changin'.'

Mister Hall talked over her.

'…They'll not deliver on a Monday, but I know I'll be getting more t'morrow.'

'Thank you, Mister Hall, can you charge me for the whole half-pound now though, please; oh, and don't forget The Mercury here.'

She lifted the newspaper off the counter.

'Yes, Mrs Radcliffe. I'll just reckon it up for you.'

Emily returned to Mrs Abram.

'Well, that's all very unfortunate. We can get most things from Mrs Ridley at Moor Cottage; she's always got a good stock of potions. Failing that, there's always Cooper's chemist in Allingham, but that's quite a journey for the older folk hereabouts. Where do you suppose we get the big medicals now? Queen's Nurse?'

Mrs Abram launched into what seemed to be a well rehearsed speech.

'That's what I says t' my 'Arry only this mornin'. I said. "'Arry," I said, "Queen's Nurse is all well 'n' good, but it's no ringer f'r a Panel Doctor, an' a Panel Doctor wi' a broke neck in this part o' th' county's neither use nor ornament," I said. "We can't all go traipsin' over t' Lichfield every time we're in need o' th' big medicals now can us?" I said.'

'No, not at all, that's…'

Mrs Abram interrupted Emily's agreement.

'Well, they'll 'ave t' get someone else in that's all, an' sharp. There'll be cattle t' castrate in three month time an' winter's not that far away, there'll be plenty o' back 'n' chest pain t' sign off.' She paused as a thought struck her. 'An' t' think I paid that drunken sot eight pence three-farthin' only last week f'r 'is call out t' see to our 'Arry…after that terrier o' Clarke's bit 'im while they were out rattin' a month ago; snappy little sod! If I'd've known what were to 'appen…'

Mrs Abram stood up straight and nodded sagely in confirmation of her tale as Mister Hall returned with the bill.

'That'll be six shillings and thre'pence please, Mrs Radcliffe.'

Emily paid him.

'Thank you, Mister Hall. I'll call back for the extra tea about twelve-thirty tomorrow.'

He wrote out and gave her the receipt.

'Yes, Mrs Radcliffe. Thank you.'

Emily gathered up her bags and made to leave.

She turned back towards Mrs Abram and Mister Hall, lifting the paper as she spoke.

'Dreadful business, this Serajevo thing, isn't it? Never rains. Our doctor and the Archduke and Archduchess killed on the same day, what an awful coincidence.'

Mrs Abram looked from Emily to Mister Hall and then picked up a newspaper from the counter.

'Were they ridin' a bike too?'

27

11.07.14

The heat of the day had gradually taken its toll and George had been ready for his lunch and the chance to sit for half an hour now. Seeing Emily enter the field of hay he was cutting on the Forty-Acre, he let out a huge sigh. Moving to a gap in the hedgerow, he called across to Edward who, with Ben, was turning yesterday's cut grass in the adjacent field.

'Edward! Y'want t' set off back 'ome f'r y' snap? Hour or so? Tie Ben up 'ere!' He indicated the shade thrown by the first in the line of elm trees that were interspersed along the hedgerow. ''Ere, Edward! I'll feed 'im!'

Emily was carrying Sarah and twenty yards distant from George, put her on the ground where she stood uncertainly for a few seconds.

'Off you go, Sarah, go to Daddy.'

Making a shaky start on the uneven surface, but gaining in confidence at each step, she staggered her way to George.

'By, but she's gettin' on famous f'r th' scrap she is! T' Daddy, Sarah. Come on our lass!'

Diment and Clowdy looked on with studied interest as Sarah tottered her way past them and on to George who stepped forward and swept her up in his arms.

Sarah gurgled with laughter as he buried his face into her neck.

'Hug-lee, Sarah! Hug-lee for Daddy!'

Emily walked past them and into the lea of the hedge and George pecked her passing cheek.

'Ready f'r this, I am.'

Attaching Ben's rein to the fence line that ran the top of the ditch, Edward ducked under the rail, dropped down into this ditch and reappeared in the hedge's gap.

He waved at Sarah.

''Ello, Miss Sarah. 'Avin' snap?'

Sarah looked up at him.

'Snap with Daddy.'

Emily looked across at her daughter.

'And Mummy. I'm the one who made it all, Sarah.'

'Daddy work!'

'Mummy too, you cheeky gosling.'

Sarah looked from Edward to Emily.

'Edurd got snap?'

Edward rubbed his tummy.

'At 'ome, Miss Sarah. Snap's at 'ome. Alright t' go, Mister George?'

'Yes, Edward, I've just said so. An' take an hour; an…hour. Don't forget, not like yesterday. Y' must 'ardly've 'ad chance t' swallow th' last mouthful afore y'were back in th' field. An hour, right?'

'Yes, Mister George. Hour. Bye, Miss Sarah, Missus Emily.'

Emily waved.

'Bye, Edward.'

He set off through the gate as Emily put the basket down and began to unpack the Radcliffe family's picnic lunch.

George watched him go.

''E'll be back in about forty minutes; I'll put money on it. 'E's got no conception o' time…I'd buy 'im a watch but 'e'd not know 'ow t' use it; forty minutes, you see.'

Sarah buried her face into George's neck.

'Hug-lee, Da-dee, hug-lee!'

George laughed out loud at this and repeated it.

'Ar, hug-lee Daddy, eh!'

—⁓—

Gathered under one of the hedgerow's huge elm trees, the family began to relax as the warmth worked its magic on them. George had his back against the elm's trunk, Emily her back against George's upper arm. Ben, nose-bag now empty, was teetering on the edge of a doze and Sarah was sitting by the heads of Diment and Clowdy, watching intently as they finished off the contents of their nose-bags. The swallows provided the summer entertainment as they flickered and swooped over the field of fresh cut grass, feasting on evicted insects. Picture-perfect…

Into this still-life of rural bliss, Emily introduced the topic of the threatening hostilities.

'All the talk is of war, George.'

'Ar? Maybe in all that stuff y' read but not 'ere it ain't, Em. Not in Forty-Acre it ain't. Just th' buzz o' them bees an' th' noise o' that wheat growin' in th' next field; any other talk you 'ear ain't about war, Em, it's about farm-workers' low wages.'

'The world's bigger than Forty-Acre and farm-workers' pay, George; bigger than the farm too. I read that our man, Mister Asquith, he says it'll not come to that, but if it does he said he was sure the leaders and brave men of this country won't shirk from their duty.'

George took another swig from his tea bottle.

''E's goin' too then is 'e, our brave man Mister Asquith, our leader? Goin' t' march on the enemy. Got a wand, 'ave y'r?'

'George, it isn't a fairy-tale. The reports in the paper and the village gossip... Don't you see, with Mister Asquith making speeches like that, it may come that you'll have to go too?'

'Ar, that's right, don't need no wand accordin' t' th' tale you've been readin'. Simple t' sort it; I'll call on 'im an' we'll go t'gether, 'Erbert 'n' me, 'oldin' 'ands 'n' whistlin' an' 'appy tune, all us brave men...Ha!'

Emily was not amused and her voice underlined the fact.

'George! I'm concerned, and so should you be!'

George put his hand on her arm.

'Steady now, Em. Y' should stop readin' that stuff if it upsets y' so.'

'But it's everywhere, newspapers, talk in the shops, everywhere, George, don't say you haven't heard.'

'Nowhere near as much as you, Em, an' I don't give what I do 'ear anywhere near as much thought. Market talk is all about the price o' bulls an' the drop in sheep prices, that an' wage levels.'

'Farmers! The rest of the world can go to the devil as long as they don't have to pay a farthing more for their cattle feed!'

'Alright, Em. If it makes y'feel any better, I'll be concerned too, but mine'll be 'cos I know th' brave folk your Mister Asquith's sure'll be doin' their duty 'n' dyin' f'r their country'll be th' likes 'f me 'n' mine; there'll not be a toff in sight.'

'Thoughts like that tell me you know more than you let on, George Radcliffe.'

'Maybe. Don't do t' dwell on it. Enough to concern me is whether we'll be able t' get all this 'ay in afore the weather breaks; that's plenty t' be goin' on wi' f'r now.'

Their idyllic moment was gone now, and Emily was cross with herself for having broken it. She began to gather up the lunch things and pack the basket roughly.

'Men! Why can't they just talk over their differences without killing people?'

'Because talkin' don't let y' snatch the other country's land 'n' money, Em. Only fools're glad t' see war; pity is they're th' ones in charge.'

Emily stopped her displacement packing.

'And the killing?'

'People is just animals, Em; needs must as th' Devil drives. Give 'em th' right circumstances an' folk'll do some fierce defence o' themselves or their own when events demand.'

Emily began to fold the cloth but her irritation only made her folding haphazard.

'I can't imagine killing someone, can't bear the thought of you having to do that; can't imagine it, for any of us.'

George took one end of the cloth from her and they folded it together.

'Let's 'ope it don't come t' that, eh, f'r none 'f us.' George stopped in his folding. 'Wonder what 'appens when they've got everythin', Em? What'll they want then?'

Emily took the cloth from George and restarted her packing. After a few moments she stopped and looked across at her daughter. Diment was trying to reach the final grains hidden in the deepest recess of her nose-bag and Sarah was teasing her with a wand of grass. The scent of fresh-cut pasture and the panorama of forever spread out in front of her.

It was idyllic, the whole scene…but she could not shift the images she had conjured up.

'But if it does…will you go, George?'

George sighed at the topic's reintroduction.

'Em…'

'Will you, George?'

'Y' mean I'll 'ave a choice? 'Cos if I do, I choose Asquith's lad goes instead o' me… Eh, there's a thought, Em. That'd stop it in its tracks, eh, if it were their brood that were sent off first, t' deflect th' bullets from us country folk. Eh?' There was no reaction from Emily, and George put his arms around her. 'Tell y' what, 'ow about we get some grains t'gether this evenin' an' start t' make y' beer f'r th' winter, eh? I saved some o' that barley from Topper's Rise, good stuff f'r beer. 'Ow about we do that, eh?'

Emily nodded and smiled, but there was no happiness in it.

—⁂—

The day perspired to an end and that evening Emily, accompanied by a pram-sleeping Sarah, joined George in the yard.

'I'll do the ladies, George; you get the grains sorted.'

He smiled at her, pleased to have her company and more pleased that her low mood of earlier had seemingly gone.

'Ar, right. I was goin' t' give 'em a full soak, that still alright?'

'Of course, though I expect Diment will be irritable. It's past her feeding time.'

'Ar, she's never keen on 'avin' 'er feet done when 'er belly's callin'…just you watch out f'r that tail. I'll fetch buckets 'n' such then I'll flail out some good stuff, eh?'

'Yes. Alright.'

He turned but Emily grabbed his arm.

'Sorry; about this afternoon, George. Just came out.'

He turned back to her and took both her hands in his.

'Nothin' t' be sorry for, Em. Y' were right an' I'm sorry too. I should've thought a bit afore spoutin' off.'

'Then we're both sorry and it's a good day.' Emily kissed him on the cheek. 'Buckets, please; full ones.'

Returning the kiss, George went to fetch two buckets of water.

With Emily started on the washing, George went into the barn and, after sorting some of the held-over barley crop, began to flail it for their beer making.

With both ends of the barn open to allow what miniscule breeze there was to waft through and dissipate the chaff, the shafts of the evening sunlight were picked out in the dust and, after a while George stopped as he focused through this golden haze onto Emily in the yard.

Both Shires had been sluiced down and the water had dampened Emily from head to foot. That, and the result of her efforts made her thin summer dress cling to her body, highlighting her figure in the evening's light, and the pools of water glistened and rippled their tinted caress over the sleeping Sarah.

George devoured the scene; it was perfect.

Propping the flail against the door he walked across the yard to Sarah. Picking her up, he held her very close to his chest. She stirred but remained sleepy.

'Hug-lee, Sarah, hug-lee for Daddy.'

Emily looked at them, a cloth in one hand, the other wiping the water from her face.

Getting up from the kitchen table, George went towards the pantry.

'Tell y' what; wha'd'y' think, Em, beer be ready?'

She got up from the table too.

'Should be, George, been just over a fortnight; might need a skim though.'

'Are th' spent grains 'n' 'ops in th' bottom o' that set o' drawers in th' cellar, Em?'

'Yes. I laid them out there after we'd strained off; put them with some rolled oats. They should be well finished by now.'

'Right, well if they're dry enough we'll maybe add 'em t' th' 'orses mix this evenin' then.'

'Yes, that would be useful about now, I'll need those drawers for our apple crop fairly soon. You cut the top and I'll let father know we're about to try it.'

The late afternoon had been herald to a stunning sunset, and the Radcliffe family had stood outside the kitchen door to watch the sun burn its way through the branches of the distant Miller's Belt only to be doused by the wave of the hillside it stood on.

During this spectacle, Sarah had gradually slumped into a deep sleep in George's arms. Putting her to bed,

George and Emily had returned to the kitchen and Emily's offer of tea had been outbid by George's suggestion they try out the beer and Emily's rejoinder that Henry be invited to sample it too.

After skimming the top, George poured out three mugs of the deep brown liquid.

''Ere's to a lass who knows 'ow t' brew a drop o' good, Mister Carter.' They each took a drink. It was very good and very potent. George smiled at Emily. 'Spot-on, Lass. Ready t' drain off, I reckon.'

'Yes, let's do that, then you and father can take the grains out to the horses. That alright?'

Henry smiled at them.

'What, take the grains out? Yes, but not me. You go, Emily. I'll stay on here and sit for Sarah.'

George frowned a little.

'You sure, Mister Carter?'

'I am. My leg's giving me a bit of gyp… I've brought my paper along…you'll have noticed there's rather a lot going on; Grantham's farm's up for sale so there'll be a bargain or two to be had there, and the weekly bull sale, I want to go through that too; good time to catch up with it all. I'll be fine here, really.'

George nodded at him as Emily squeezed Henry's arm.

'Thank you, father.'

George and Emily strained the liquid from the copper into the several crock flagons they kept for their beer, then collected the half-bucket of used barley grains and hops from the drawer which was, indeed, dry.

A final check on Sarah revealed her to be fast asleep and, leaving Henry relaxed in his newspaper and second glass of brew, they strolled across the yard to the stables.

'Just an 'andful, mind, Em. I want 'em t' cut straight t'morrow. We'll add th' rest in wi' their other feed.'

The horses all shared in a portion of the mix, then George added the rest to the large feed bin. Leaning over the edge, they both began to stir this into the bulk feed with their hands.

They were very close. George could feel Emily's breast pressing and sliding against his arm as she moved her body to-and-fro to combine the ingredients.

He stopped his movement.

She sensed immediately what was about to happen and was ready to let it…

—⁓—

Emily got up from the straw stack, re-arranging her blouse and skirt. George lay where he was watching her dress.

'By, my lass, you're some 'andful o' woman.' She sat near him now, leaning over to kiss him, her blouse still undone, the curve of her breasts visible through the gap. 'Can't believe y' belong t' me.' She smiled and stood up; brushing her skirt clear of straw she began to tie her hair back, then she curtseyed.

'Glad to have been of service, Sire. I'll go in and see to Sarah. Father will be wanting to get off home too; you stay on if you want.'

'Ar, I'll be over in a while. I'll just check water.'

She began to do up her blouse buttons.

'Right. Oh, I'll be leaving early for market tomorrow, so not back until noon. Will you be at the farm for lunch?'

'Ar.'

'Right, well, if we don't see each other before then, can you collect the eggs and kill a cockerel for Sunday?'

'What 'appened t' romance?'

'You've had your romance for the next month, my man. It's back to a life of poverty and cockerel strangling from now on…' George laughed again as Emily threw some straw and flicked the hem of her dress at him. 'You magnificent beast, you.'

George lay and listened as Emily went down from the loft then out the stables. A few minutes passed then he got up and followed her down.

After checking and topping up Diment's bucket, he saw Clowdy's water was still two-thirds full and was about to go out along the aisle when he noticed Clowdy's hayrack.

'By, that looks temptin', Clowdy. 'Ow about…?' and with that he entered her stall, climbed up into the hayrack and lay down in the scented warmth of a summer meadow.

22·08·14

He was woken by the dual alarm of Clowdy whisking hay over his face and noise coming from the yard.

'Stop it, Clowdy.' He sat up in the manger. '…What's all that racket then?'

He looked out of the stall window. Gathered in the yard were a collection of men he either knew from the local farms, or who knew him through his trips to Allingham.

'Got visitors, lass.' He looked around the stable. 'An' no Edward yet? First time 'e's not been early f'r work since I've knowed 'im.' The noise of chatter outside continued, 'Wonder what they want on a Sat'day, as if we don't know?'

He rolled out of the manger and left Clowdy to her compressed hay in peace.

In the yard he was greeted by Arthur James, Robert Clarke, and brothers Cecil and John Mayhew, all of whom were local farm staff and who should, under normal circumstances, already be hard at work. The other three men, Sandy Barclay, Henry Jefford and Thomas Main were local council workers and known only to George as casual acquaintances.

George was immediately wary but his cheery greeting belied his inner concerns.

'Mornin' each!'

Arthur was the first to speak.

'George. Looks like you've slep' in them clothes.'

'Ar, maybe…'

But Arthur was not interested in the reply; he had a head full of news to impart.

'You'll know Sandy, 'Enry an' Tom?'

'Ar, we've met once or twice. What c'n I do f'r you all?'

'War's up, George, 'ave y'not 'eard? We're all goin' to enlist, join th' party. Even your Edward's goin' t' try now we'd told 'im all about reasons an' th' chance for 'im t' be an 'ero.'

George's wariness had been justified and, after hearing of Edward, this wariness was coupled with even greater suspicion. He looked at them all as he spoke.

'Edward never mentioned it…when'd y' get chance t' chat then?'

Henry Jefford joined the conversation.

'This mornin'. There were a gang 'f us by th' milepost at Crean's Cross. I reckon 'e must come that way t' work?'

George answered, trying to remain composed, although inside he was seething.

'Ar, 'e does. That explains a lot. 'E must've taken it to 'eart then, your chat…I doubt they'll take 'im. You all seem eager; y' must be th' first.'

'No, we're well be'ind! I 'eard Daniel Long's already gone.'

'Daniel y' say? I 'eard 'e was up f'r a job-change, from Broad Farm this time, so 'ostilities is timely f'r Mister Long, I'd say.'

Now the element of surprise was George's for it was obvious from the men's faces that this was indeed news to them.

'Where'd you 'ear 'bout Daniel, then?' asked Cecil. 'Far as I'd 'eard, Mister Birch were satisfied wi' 'im.'

'From my Emily. She 'eard by the whip, when she were out early cubbin' wi' th' Belvoir last week; Lantern Farm's got a couple o' litters needed trimming up, cubs'd been practicin' their chicken-killin' skills. She 'eard Daniel'd been thievin' again; so that's cubs an' Daniel!' The joke caused no mirth amongst the men and George finished his discourse to their indifferent silence. ''E'd taken up wi' a maid from th' big 'ouse, that's 'ow 'e got t' their silver. Set about 'er when she threatened t' tell, I 'eard, so no surprises there then.'

Cecil pursued the point.

'We'll, I've 'eard nothin' in th' local about it, not even from Constable Ferris. 'E's a reg'lar an' we all know what 'e thinks on Mister Long.'

'No, well you'd not 'ear neither. Maid wouldn't press charges… That's th' second time t' my knowledge that 'e's smacked a woman an' got away wi' it. I'd like t' see 'im try it on round 'ere.' The men exchanged glances. 'So 'ow come you're all so eager? I'd 'eard it were just single blokes an' them as lost wives they've called up.'

Robert showed George a sheet of paper.

'Gaffer's said we c'n go, special permission.'

George waved it away; he knew what was on it.

'You all got one?'

They nodded as Sandy took a similar sheet from out of his pocket and flashed it in George's direction.

'Council's given all us workers th' chance t' join up wi' full pay; no fences to us, but we'd go with or without. Why should others 'ave all th' fun?'

George laughed.

'Ha-ha! Fun? Y'think it'll be fun then, Sandy? You too, Robert?'

Robert took on the role of spokesman.

'Ar, 'course… Don't want t' be thought a coward, do we. I don't doubt there'll be some paintin' jobs t' do with some, like in Leicester, but not wi' us, eh, lads?'

They all murmured their agreement as George queried Robert further.

'Paintin'?'

'Ar. Tar-'n'-feather job.'

'When was that then?'

Pleased the tables were turned and he could impart news to George, Cecil filled in the details with a smug grin.

'You not 'eard 'ere yet, George? Albert Stockard, come back from there Tuesday-last. Went t' bid f'r a new bull an' said there were a couple o' chaps who'd talked against th' call up, said they'd be damned if they'd go.' The men all murmured their disgust as Cecil continued, 'They'd been well covered 'n' tied up in th' centre o' th' market almost afore they'd finished their cowardly chat; a lesson t' them…an' others.'

'Cowards, eh?'

'They were.'

'Did y' tell Edward about this?'

'Course. 'E needs t' know 'ow world works, what's expected.'

'Which is?'

This halted conversation for a few seconds, then Robert replied slowly.

'Well…what's expected is that we do our duty, George, what other is there?'

'An' what 'appened t' free-choice then, Robert?'

'Simple folk like 'im 'ave no grasp o' free-choice, George, you knows that. An' folk like us, we've no need 'f it, none 'f us! There's only one choice an' there'll be no cause to avoid it neither. We 'eard they're gatherin' local battalions in Liverpool 'n' Manchester, don't want Leicester t' be thought a city o' cowards, do us? Over t' France f'r a few months 'oliday, gi' them Germans what for then back 'ome in time f'r Christmas they say.'

George smiled.

'Who says?'

'Our government men.'

'Do they?'

'Ar, they do.'

'Seem to 'ave a lot o' knowledge then all'f a sudden. Unusual f'r government men, that.'

There was a short pause.

Arthur looked from his companions to George.

''Ow about you, George; you'll be goin'?'

'I can't just leave, Arthur! Farm's still got t' be run. There's just th' three 'f us 'ere y'know, not like you lot, all part 'f a bigger system such as you are. Y'c'n pass th' reasonin' onto y' gaffers an' th' workload t' th' remainder. Not me. There's stock t' see to an' arrangements t' make. I need t' think this one through… an' I'll 'ave t' talk to Em…'

All the men now had their say, phrases tumbling on top of each other, George all the while trying to make his point.

'What's to ask 'er about?

'Y'will be goin' George, won't y'?'

'…She's away at market yet, 'til lunch…'

'Y'will be goin' though, won't y'r, George?'

'…She'll 'ave 'eard though, an' Mister Carter too.'

'But y'will be goin', won't y'?'

George stopped the explanation.

'Ar…'course…but folk t' see.' There was a further, awkward silence. George broke the moment. 'Right! Got t' get mowin'. I'll be seein' you in th' queue, eh?'

The men muttered their farewells and sauntered out of the yard, leaving George in the empty farmyard.

—ɱ—

He was waiting in the kitchen when Emily returned from market. She knew straight away there was a bigger reason than the plucked cockerel and trays of eggs arranged neatly on the table.

The small-talk drifted through the unload from bags to pantry shelves then, once Sarah had been sat at the table and given a crust of fresh bread to chew on until lunch proper, George informed Emily of the morning's events.

'You'll 'ave 'eard they've done wi' th' talkin'? They want t' go ahead wi' th' killin' now.'

'Yes, I met Mrs Stallard in the market.'

'Information's been driftin' in all mornin'. You 'eard about Leicester then, th' tarrin' 'n' featherin'?'

'Yes, I did. Mrs Stallard was telling me about her sons, Richard and Martin? They've both volunteered.'

'Ar? Well there's plenty others 'ave gone t' th' Town 'All t' join up an' all, whether through bravado or fear, I'm not certain. Most 'f 'em were 'ere in th' yard earlier. Daniel's gone,' they both said, 'There's a surprise!' together and laughed without humour as George added, 'An' Gordon Smart was 'ere not ten minute ago t' tell me 'e'd seen Edward there earlier. You 'eard 'e'd tried t' join up too?'

'I heard; Mrs Abram told me. Source of amusement to many, she said. What happened to get him there?'

''E'd met a crowd 'f 'em at Crean's Cross; they told 'im th' lie o' th' land an' off 'e goes…not turned up 'ere yet; too scared…either that or too ashamed.' Emily's face showed her sadness and concern as George continued, his voice rising slightly in his anger. 'Them bloody blokes! 'E should never 'ave gone! Should've come 'ere first, I could've saved 'im the embarrassment!' He stopped and steadied his temper, then spoke more softly now. 'Gordon gi' me th' details. Know what 'e said when they asked 'im why 'e wanted t' join up?'

'No.'

'So's 'e could be an 'ero.'

'Oh, Lord, George…what was he thinking?'

'So Gordon said. Thinkin'? Not Edward, Em. Doin' as 'e was bid, as usual. Don't know 'e's ever found 'is own voice. Obvious to all but Edward they'd not take 'im on active service 'cos 'f 'is 'ead. Trouble is Edward thinks 'e's normal an' it's th' rest 'f us're a bit strange. Ha! There's odd bedfellows…army tellin' a bloke they don't want 'im t' volunteer t' get shot at 'cos 'e's mad. Edward w's really disappointed by all accounts… confirmed their diagnosis, I'd say.'

Picking up something in George's tone of voice as he recounted the tale, Emily, although fearing the reply, pressed on with the conversation.

'Father says he'll be able to stay on here. And you?'

'What, y' father's said I c'n stay on 'ere as well? Good.'

'You know what I mean, George, you've a wife and child and they only want singles and widowers, don't they?'

'They've only called up singles and widowers, Em, but that don't mean they don't want us all t' join.'

'Yes it does.'

'No it don't, Em. There's an 'eap o' diff'rence between bein' called-up an' peoples' expectations 'f what a call-up means.'

Emily felt a rising panic enter the pit of her stomach.

'What expectations? They've not called you, George, and I expect nothing. You've a farm to run, people still have to eat, and Edward's staying on here…'

'I c'n see y'don't understand th' military mind, Em. Edward's stayin' 'cos he's too simple t' go. I'll be expected t' go 'cos I 'ave just th' right amount o' simplicity; y'see?'

'No, I don't "see" George.'

George leaned against the shallow crock sink.

'The military require a certain level 'f intelligence, Em, but not so much as means y'c'n see through their plans.'

'What plans? What do you know of their plans?'

George looked at the sink's single, cold-tap.

'Glad I put that in, Em, saves a lot o' carryin' come wash-day… fill th' bucket an' just a short stroll t' th' range, eh?'

'George! Never mind the beastly tap! Garden well was fine, and I'd revert to it in exchange for this discussion we're having at present. I asked what you know of their plans!'

'You'll thank me f'r that tap one day.'

'George!'

He paused for a moment, then launched into it.

'I know enough t' be sure their plan is f'r us all to up sticks, gallop over t' th' Town 'All, throw on a uniform an' spend from now 'til Christmas gettin' shot at! That's their plan, their expectation…an' the expectation 'f most other folk round 'ere too…'

Emily's panic was rising as she tried to interrupt.

'George…never mind expectations, George, you've not been called…!'

Sarah picked up the tension between her parents and stopped eating to watch them as George talked over Emily.

'Good plannin' that. Take all the 'alf-sensible folk 'n' leave th' totally insensible ones like Edward be'ind t' run th' country. Nothin' changes, does it? I'll as like come back 'n' find 'im as Prime Minister; mind like that'd fit in well.'

'Is that what you want?'

'What, come back 'n' find Edward as Prime Minister? No. No, Em, it's not what I want.'

'Make a joke of it if you want, but I say they'll not take you, George! You aren't what they want. Father will sign no releases; you've a farm and family here.'

But flippancy was far from what he had intended and all Emily's fears were realised in his frustrated reply.

'So 'ave th' rest 'f 'em that's gone t' join up, Em! Jesus love…! Look at th' list! Eric Abbot, married wi' one on th' way; gone! Th' Stevens'? Married an' breedin' like rabbits, Bob Stevens; gone. Albert Stock, 'e's in an' 'e's got a wife, four kids, a crabby mother-in-law, seventy acres o' plough an' two-dozen scrubby sheep t' look out for! I 'aven't noticed that flock o' blokes comin' back from th' town weepin' they've not been signed up, 'ave you?' Emily took a breath to reply but George continued over it. 'No, you've not! All that's gone's been taken in, wi' open arms…th' Council…th' bloody Council f'r Christ's' sake! They've told blokes t' join up an' they'd keep 'em on full pay 'til they get back "'Ome by Christmas". When tight-fisted buggers like that start throwin' money about y' know just 'ow serious it all is!'

The strength of George's outburst had shocked Emily and there was a long silence, George looking out the window, Emily looking at Sarah.

Emily spoke quietly, fearing the worst.

'And you?'

George was calmer now, but his voice held no respite for Emily's darkest thoughts.

'Oh Christ, Em… D' y' think f'r one minute they don't want me? Ask y'rself, will they turn me down? I'm a fit, skilled 'orseman. Ask y'rself, d' y' think I'll not be snapped up?'

Sarah began to get agitated at the atmosphere in the kitchen and her eyes started to fill. Emily saw her daughter's apprehension and calmed her voice.

'Lunch time soon, Sarah; boiled cookie-egg and toast soldiers.' She turned to George and dropped her voice to a coarse whisper, indicating Sarah with her eyes as she spoke. 'Of course they'll take you, George, but only if you turn up to ask them.'

But either George missed the subtlety or was not prepared to modify his response nor his voice's volume.

'An' if I don't?' He repeated it unnecessarily. 'If I don't, Em?' Then he cruelly guided it home, quieter, his voice now holding a tone of recognised inevitability. 'You tell me, Em; what 'appens if I don't? Tell me a way out an' I'll do it.'

There was no reply Emily could think of.

It was a tearful Sarah who broke the silence.

'Mummy, why was Daddy shouting?'

Moving quickly over to Sarah, Emily picked her up.

'George, stop it, please…what are we doing? Shush now, Sarah.' She calmed Sarah while George continued to stare out the window. After a few moments and even though she did not want to hear the answer, she asked the question; she had to. 'Do you want to join up, George?'

There was another long pause.

'No, Em. No, I don't…but I will.'

'Why, George…?'

'Because Daniel's joined up, Em!'

'Daniel has no choice…!'

'Because Albert Stock's joined up! Because even Edward, Em…simple, gentle, Edward, who's got no understandin' but just "wants t' be an 'ero", even 'e tried to f'r Christ's sake!' He stopped for a moment as if his interest had been diverted, then continued, but quieter now, 'Because I don't want you t' be married t' the only bloke within a fifty mile radius 'as opted f'r th' quiet life nor our Sarah be th' daughter'f a father who's known county-wide as a coward. Don't you understand that?'

Her face drained of colour, Emily came straight back at him.

'If they change the rules and you have to go then so be it. But right now you don't have to and right now I only understand that I love you, George, and I don't want you to go; not never, but not now.'

Blinking in the glare of Emily's distilled honesty, George's only escape from its truth was to leave. He did so, slamming the kitchen door as he went.

Holding a now crying Sarah, Emily watched through their window as George crossed the yard and entered the stables.

'Shush-shush now, Sarah, shush.'

With two sets of chains in tow and leading Diment and Clowdy, George emerged from the stables.

Emily bounced Sarah a little.

'Look! Look, Sarah. Daddy Radcliffe going cutting! Diment and Clowdy look smart don't they? Shush now, Sarah, shush.'

30

07.10.14

Proof that animals sense changes in atmosphere and mood was granted to George, Emily and Sarah on the morning of George's departure for the armed forces. As they entered the stables, Diment bounced and whinnied and Clowdy pressed against the stall door, making it creak; something out of character for both horses.

George pushed his hand against the grey's head.

'Hie-Back, Back, Clowdy, Back!' She moved a pace away from the door. 'Crikey, girl, you'll 'ave that door over! What's up wi' you, eh?'

Emily picked up Sarah.

'If you need to ask that then you're not the horseman I married, George Radcliffe.'

George stroked Clowdy's head.

'Ar, I know. Dodgin' the issue. They know a lot more'n we give 'em credit for.' George looked long at the two horses. ''Ad it all planned, Em; all planned. Take a foal out 'f each o' these two, run 'em on an' start th' Shirley Lodge line.'

'When was this, you never mentioned it?'

'No, well, I didn't want t' start summat we couldn't finish. Made the enquiries at market a couple o' month ago. Was goin' t' talk it through when I'd got some firm offers; glad I didn't mention it now, so much more disappointment.'

'I'd not have been disappointed, George. I just wish you'd've given me a bit more warning, I could've helped.'

'Ar, I know, you've a way wi' stock, Em, an' don't think I was bein'…selfish, I weren't. Just needed t' see what were on offer then get y' t' gi' th' final verdict once stock were known. I'd even sorted out a couple or three stallions f'r us t' consider f'r Clowdy. One were Mister Bullock's over in Staffordshire; 'im as bred Draughtsman?' He patted Clowdy's neck. 'She'd be about right soon too. What are we, two weeks since y'r last season, lass, an' last chance o' th' year too? Another week 'r so… All too late now, but I 'ad it all planned.' He patted Clowdy's neck. 'What a waste…promises 'n' pie-crusts.'

Folding his arm around Emily and Sarah, George held them both close.

Clowdy dropped her head into their midst. A moment later and Diment leant around the side of her stable door and in towards the group.

George stepped back a little and took in the view.

'Take care 'f each other my Shire ladies. Back be Christmas, eh?'

31

10.04.15

Unlike the last two billets, where he had voiced serious misgivings about some of the conditions for the horses, the tented stables at Lille were not too bad. At least there was room for horses, feed and bedding to be kept under cover and dry.

Army routine had been easy for George to slot into; the early starts and constant workload were just a carry-on from his life back in Leicestershire.

The other members of his troop were a varied lot. Mostly friendly, and with the majority of them having horse experience they had a common bond, a point of conversation…and an in-built, gentle level of rivalry.

George walked his two Shires out from their stall and the shimmer on each of their coats and leathers glistened, even under the dulling effect of the part-canvas. But today an addition had been made; on each horse's bridle was attached a highly polished, regimental tunic button.

Samuel Gordon, one of the men George had taken an instant shine to and who had reciprocated his offer of friendship, gave a low whistle.

'Phoooo! 'E's even got brass on 'em, look; you'd think they were goin' to a show not a battle!

Jesus, Radcliffe, where the 'ell you get them buttons from?'

'Same place as 'alf th' battalion Sam. Souvenir badges, they say, though souvenir of what is beyond me. Pound-f'-pound, there's more weight o' metal bein' shipped back 'ome than there is enemy shells bein' fired right now!'

'Y' see an' 'ear nothin but them 'orses, do y', Radcliffe? They're f'r sweet'eart badges, f'r wives an' girls back 'ome; do you not know?' George shook his head in denial. 'Sliced in 'alf an' wi' a picture in 'em they make a nice keepsake…but you? Sweet'eart badge or no, y've got yours on full display, on a couple o' nags if y' please, rubbin' their noses in it. If Sergeant sees that 'e'll 'ave y' crimed, an' smartish.'

'They aint' nags, Sam, an' no 'e'll not. Respect, pride an' a good bridle, that's what you got to 'ave f'r y'r 'orses, even 'e knows that.'

'But they ain't your 'orses, George, they're the army's!'

'Course they're mine! Y'talk about 'em like they're a bit o' spare kit them field-guns keep needin'.'

Walking round to George's side of the stalls, hands behind his back, Sam addressed him and the other members of the troop as if he were giving a briefing.

'It's touchin'. 'E's so naïve ain't 'e?' He glanced at one of the horse's hooves in passing. 'Why d'y' think they've branded 081114-7 'n' not Lady or Toby on their 'oof? I'll tell y'r why. They don't want us t' get attached to 'em, that's why. Why?' Sam pointed to the crow's foot brand on the horse's rump. 'Because they're wearin' th' symbol o' carrion on their arse, boys, that's why! Because, like as not, they'll be dead t'morrow; you'll thank y' lucky stars it's them not you, an' 'ave t' get issued another pair fr'm Stores. That's why.'

George shook his head firmly.

'No, Sam, y' wrong on all counts. That's not what'll 'appen f'r two reasons. First an' most important, I'll be with 'em. I c'n tell y'r now, as wretched as this life we 'ave at present is shapin' up t' be, it's better 'n bein' dead, so I'll not be puttin' them or me in any danger. An' second, Stores is f'r storin' things. If they was f'r issuin' things…' Sam and the other horsemen joined in with George to chorus the end of the quote. '…they'd be called Issues!'

They all laughed as Sam resumed his mock briefing.

'F'rget everythin' else but remember two things, Radcliffe.' He scanned the other troops. 'Th' rest 'f y' too an' you'll not go far wrong. One: Wars is dangerous places t' be. Two: 'Orses is kit!'

George began to walk his two Shires out of the tent.

'Not while they're wi' me, they ain't. I'll call 'Orse **081114-7** Dolly, an' 'Orse **151014-3** Rose. They're mine f'r th' duration, Sam.'

'Or th' next whizz-bang.'

'Jesus, Sam! Th' least y'could do is show a little compassion, even if y' don't mean it.'

'F'r what?'

'Y' need a reason? It's my birthday in a couple o' weeks' time; give us some'f y'r usual string o' cheerful chat, eh?'

Patting the passing rump of Shire 081114-7, Sam moved back to his own stable.

'Well 'appy-bloody-birthday, George! Y'll find y' present buried in one o' them shell-'oles. I'm givin' y' me compassion; y'll recognise it easy, I've used me string o' cheerful chat t' wrap it up with.'

32

18·06·15

George clicked on Horse **210315-5**, Topper, and Horse **300415-1**, Glen, as they struggled to drag the field gun from the ditch.

Forced into it by the nearby explosion its twisted tow-bar kept digging into the bank, its metalwork jamming on the hawthorn hedge's roots, which meant they had a real fight on their hooves to drag it out, and without any help from its wheels. With George's encouragement and some frenzied turns with the spade, after fifteen minutes the team were finally successful. The gun rasped out of the ditch and flopped onto its wheels.

'Well done, lads!' He gave their regimental tunic buttons a rub then patted their necks. 'Another brigade victory f'r keepin' goin' what we all wish'ld stop, eh, Topper? Don't know who's dafter…'

He checked harness, fixings and the gun's condition before attempting the journey back to the repair tents. The wheels were in one piece at least and, after clearing the torn grass and mud from the moving parts, George walked to the ditch to make sure nothing had been left behind.

Looking over the frazzled hedge, he eyed the agriculture of war that ran up to the town of La Bassée;

cratered fields, charred grass, scarred buildings. After a cursory glance along the ditch he returned to the horses and patted them again.

'That's some strange 'arvest over yonder, lads. Not even room f'r a skylark t' nest.'

—ᴍᴍ—

'Look, Sarah, a skylark. See?'

The speck above them was buoyed on a fountain of song and Sarah, seated atop Clowdy's back, shielded her eyes and repeated to the summer sun.

'Sky…lark.'

'Yes. Daddy's favourite.'

'Daddy sees?'

'No, Sarah, not that one. Another maybe.'

Emily returned her gaze to the horses and her thoughts returned to last autumn…

Those periods of instruction, just before George's departure as he took her through Clowdy and Diment's idiosyncrasies, the tweaks he adopted to work them at a level that so impressed everyone, had been more than just horse-training sessions, she knew it now.

Standing in this Leicestershire field, in the summer sun listening to the serenade of a skylark, she could almost feel George's arms around her waist. With the bird acting as conduit, she realised that, back then she had not only been feeling the horses emotions, reactions and intentions through those reins, but George's too…and now it was too late to pull it in, embrace it, to hold on to it as life itself…and that the purpose of this closeness had been just a hastening of their parting. It had never fully occurred to her until now…and her eyes began to fill.

She took out a handkerchief.

'Mummy cries?'

'No, no, Sarah. Just the sun…from watching the skylark.'

Sarah looked up once more into the bright blue and squinted.

Emily walked round to the horses' heads.

'How are you bearing up, Clowdy, my lady, eh?' Clowdy flicked her head and rattled her harness. 'I'll bet. I know just what you mean; been there.' She returned to the mower. 'Let's get this mowing done, baby Sarah. This lady wants home and tea; that's a long day for her right now. Look, Edward's almost turned Low Meadow and we'll be holding him up.' Waving across at Edward, who waved back, Emily picked up the reins and clicked the team on.

'Hie-On, ladies!'

Diment and Clowdy reacted, setting off through a sea of sweet grass and scented flowers……

33

14.07.15

He never thought he'd be grateful to a caltrop.

Horse **210315-5**, Topper, and George, had been trawling back to Drocourt across the charnel house of the recently evacuated battlefield. The tide of mayhem was on the ebb, so only sporadic firing applauded them as they moved across the open ground. At distant points, other soldiers, horsed and on foot, were clearing up what they could of the devastation. Machinery and arms were being assessed for re-use; the wounded and dead, man and beast, being transported to hospital or heaven.

With a salvaged tool-box in tow, they had been making good progress when Topper shied suddenly and snorted loudly. George saw immediately he was favouring his left-front and had guessed what it was. Lifting up the gelding's hoof, he could see the spiked sphere embedded deep into the sole.

'Steady, old man, steady. That's some creation o' th' Devil you've picked up there, an' used by someone 'as supposed t' be in God's image, eh? You just Stand-On an' I'll get it sorted.'

He moved to the tool-box, lifted the lid, bent into the box, the shell-of-straydom landed… And there he was; saved by a caltrop.

Sheltered by horse, lid and box, George was still pushed over by the initial blast. Quickly up, surprisingly with the pliers in his grasp, he surveyed the damage, knowing, even before he looked, that it wouldn't be good; he was not disappointed. One rear leg twisted round the other, one front leg shattered, Topper was lying on his side. The blast had temporarily deafened George so sounds were muffled, but he could hear his heartbeat clearly as he arrived at the horse's side.

Kneeling down, he gently lifted the one rear leg over the other to arrange it more neatly. Topper reacted, whether in pain or the ease of pain George was not sure. What he was sure of was the horse was on the edge of Christendom.

He patted Topper's neck.

'No more work f'r you, old chap. Time's up, an' y'r better off out' f it, believe me.'

He felt more than heard the thud of horse's hooves through the ground and looked up to see a mounted soldier trotting his way. Turning his gaze back to Topper he fondled the horse's ear.

'Christ, they're like bloody vultures. Y' Nemesis arrivin', old man.' George took a deep breath and called across the field to the mounted soldier. '…Vet detail!'

The mounted soldier arrived at George's side in a very short time.

'You're a lucky bugger! I was 'alf-expectin' y' t' 'ave most o' that tool-kit embedded up y'r arse.'

'No, not my time. 'Is though. If y'ready then I reckon 'e is too; poor sod.'

'Allus ready!'

'Jesus, no need t' be so perky about it!'

The Vet's Assistant was annoyed.

'An' no need f'r you t' pull me down f'r doin' it neither! This is me doin' th' job no one wants t' do but everyone's glad t' see gettin' done!'

'That's a mangled reasonin' if ever I 'eard it.'

'Mangled it may be; true it def'nitely is.' The V.A. soldier dismounted, led his steed a few paces away then, from out his saddle-bag, he pulled a smaller black bag. He untied its top and took out a metal spike with a short wooden handle. Back alongside George he pulled his right sleeve back. 'Now, c'n I get on?'

'Wi' what?' George indicated the spike. '… That?'

The V.A. soldier looked at the spike in his hand, then at George.

'Ar, what else?'

'Not 'im nor no 'orse o' mine; not wi' that…thing.'

'Your 'orse? What y' talkin' about, your 'orse? This is an army 'orse, soldier, an' in the army this is 'ow it's done!'

'I know that, but not t' no 'orse o' mine, I said!'

The V.A. sighed long.

'Phhhh. I see. Your 'orse; right. Then 'ow d'you expect me t' put "your 'orse" out 'f 'is misery then… Mister Gabriel.'

'You've a pistol?' The V.A. looked down at his side-holster. 'Then use it.'

'What? Bloody hell, you'll 'ave me up on a charge! D'y' know 'ow much a bullet costs?'

'If y' that worried, I'll pay f'r th' bugger meself.' George took a pace between Topper and the V.A. 'But

229

charge 'r no charge y' not using that spike on 'im; an' all th' while we chat 'e's suff'rin'.'

The V.A. could see he'd have to give way.

'Bloody 'ell but you've a funny way o' showin' concern f'r this poor sod!' He bagged the spike, looked hurriedly around the immediate vicinity then took out his pistol. 'An' it'll all mean th' same to 'im, y'know that, don't y'?'

'A dignified end f'r a comrade-in-arms is what it'll mean.'

George stood to one side as the V.A. took a second swift look around the field then hurriedly fired the pistol into Topper's forehead.

The horse's demise was instantaneous.

He re-holstered the pistol.

'Satisfied are we?'

'Just.'

'Ar…well, God's got 'im now, alright?'

George scoffed.

'God's got 'im? Ha! There's no God 'ere, soldier, nor within a million miles 'f anywhere near! God's just excuse or reason we use f'r never acceptin' th' blame f'r th' messes we make. Sooner we accept responsibility f'r ourselves th' better this world'll be.'

Studiously ignoring George's outburst, the V.A. returned to his horse with the re-wrapped spike. With it back in his saddle-bag, he took out a notebook from his pocket and, moving back, stooped to look at the horse's right fore-hoof.

He spoke out loud as he wrote.

''Orse **210315**…'

'Topper.'

Looking up from his writing, the V.A. sighed large again.

George repeated.

''Is name's Topper.'

The V.A. shook his head then began to write and repeat.

''Orse **210315**…'

'I said 'is name's Topper, now write it!'

The V.A. spoke to the panorama.

'Jesus, 'e's off again…' Then he addressed George directly. 'I can't! 'E's 'Orse **210315-5** as far as the army's concerned; that's 'is call-up date, that's 'is number. I'll get shot if I write down anythin' else!'

''Is name's Topper, I don't care what th' army want t' call 'im! Now, f'r 'im an' me, an' maybe a bit f'r y'rself, write 'is name down!'

The V.A. soldier hesitated and George stepped forward, snatched the notebook and pencil from him and began to write as he spelt out loud, pressing the pencil deep into the paper.

'**T O P P E R**!'

He finished and threw the notebook back which the V.A. juggled then finally caught.

'No offence meant, just…they deserve better.'

Both men stood in silence for a moment. The V.A. closed the notebook and moved to his horse.

'They deserve better? F' Chrissake, mate, so do us all! Bloody 'ell, you wanna get y' priorities sorted out!'

'I 'ave; I sometimes think I'm the only sane person livin' in this mad world.'

Back at his horse, the V.A. soldier pushed the notebook back into his pocket.

'What's in a bloody name, 'e's dead now ain't he? An' doin' it th' way you wanted…an' writin down some soppy name made such a diff'rence to 'im, didn't it?'

'It did make a difference to 'im! T' you an' me as well, don't y' see that?'

'I just see another dose o' carrion f'r them dogs that 'ang around the village, that's what I see.'

George shook his head slowly.

'Well I'll tell y'r it did make a diff'rence…to 'im if not you, an' if y'can't see that then there's no 'ope nowhere. It's th' way Topper deserved it.'

The V.A. soldier remounted.

'Well, Topper's now a deserving but very dead 'orse, private; congratulations. An' name or no-name, don't f'rget t' remove th' tack, their…'

George cut in.

'I know, I know, "…their regiment's on it ". It's not th' first time I've done this y'know?'

'The way you're goin' on it could be y'r last.'

'Bloody 'ell! Look around y', man! Every day c'ld be me last! Inventin' another way t' die out 'ere's 'ardly revolution'ry.'

'Well my invention is that I'll get shot if I don't remind y' t' get th' tack an' numbers; an' f'r Chrissake don't mention about me usin' a pistol on 'im.'

Without another word the V.A. horseman rode off to continue his mission of mercy in other parts of the field.

Leaning forward, George lifted Topper's front-right hoof.

He looked at the caltrop.

'A crow's-foot in y'r 'oof t' match th' one on y'r arse; bugger if Sam weren't right.'

He removed the caltrop with the pliers; pointless, but he did it all the same, then looked after the disappearing V.A., around at the local scramble of life in death and finally at the horizon.

'God's got 'im…? Well, if y' love y' creation then you've a funny way o' showin' it, an' 'Orse **210315-5**'ll want an explanation when y' meet up, an' that'll be sooner rather than late; do me a favour, call 'im Topper, eh?'

Taking off tack and collar, George piled it up ready to carry back.

'Who's th' vulture now then, George Radcliffe, eh; who's th' vulture now?'

34

13.08.15

Drifting back into the yard at the end of a day's log-hauling, Emily tied Diment and Clowdy to their respective wall-rings and went to fetch water and brushes prior to scrubbing down. As tired out as she was the routine still demanded that little extra effort.

Clearing Diment's hooves of debris, she sluiced and scrubbed her feathers; it was at this point in the process that the mare began to bridle. Any obstacle put between Diment and the waiting trough was bad news; water sloshing over her feet was about as bad as it got. Agitating from one hoof to the other, lifting one then the other high, moving towards Clowdy then suddenly moving back, Diment tried every trick to avoid the cleaning-up process.

As Emily threw the last bucket of water at her hind left, so Diment sidled quickly across to Clowdy again and the water landed harmlessly onto the yard stones.

'Diment, Stand-On! You're a bad lot; now I've to get another bucket!'

'She's naughty, isn't she, Mummy?'

Sarah stood in the yard's gateway in dressing gown and outdoor shoes, a small doll in her hands.

'Oh, Sarah! Where did you spring from? Yes, she is naughty. Anywhere near feeding time and she forgets all her manners!' Henry appeared behind Sarah and picked her up. 'Hello, Father.'

'Evening, Emily. We heard you arrive and Sarah wanted to say 'night before she went off to bed. I see you got those two pine trunks down to the gate.'

'Yes, and now Madam here wants her supper!'

'How did Clowdy cope?'

'Very well, all things considered. Got good support from her workmate but she's not quite the ticket… and Sarah's right.' Emily slapped Diment's rump to guide her away from Clowdy. 'You're just a big, spoilt baby, aren't you, Diment, and greedy with it. Now you've to wait even longer while I get more water and so has Clowdy, and that's not very fair on her is it?' Emily walked over to Sarah and Henry with the buckets. 'I'll not be long, Sarah. Half-hour and I'll come and snuggle you in. You alright 'til then, Father?'

'Same as every day, Em.' Emily smiled at the comment as Henry chucked Sarah under the chin. 'We do a good job together, don't we, Sarah?'

'Grandpa sings me songs, Mummy.'

'Songs? What, nursery rhymes?'

'Yes, new ones.'

'New ones! I didn't know you knew any, Father! That must be lovely, Sarah. Now, if you let me get on with these two, I'll be up to snuggle you down, I may even join in.'

Sarah beamed at the prospect.

'Yes, Mummy.'

Henry made to go back to the house.

'There'll be some supper in the kitchen for you, Emily, I think you've earned it.'

'Same as every day, Father.'

Henry smiled.

'Touché.'

With Sarah returned to the ground they walked hand-in-hand back to the farmhouse.

Replenishing the bucket, Emily swilled off Diment's remaining hoof then walked the Shire a few yards away from Clowdy and retied her.

'Now you wait there and drain a little. Bait'll be served only after you're both done, brushing down too, you know the drill by now.' Diment moved slightly to the side and snorted, dragging a hoof across the yard stones. 'You can fratch all you like! Not until Clowdy's done, same as every day.'

Clowdy was always the more patient of the two, particularly when it came to having her feet done, but today she seemed ill-at-ease when asked to stand on three legs. Concerned at Clowdy's obvious discomfort, she stood back and looked at her conformation.

After running a hand over her side, Emily went to her head and took a long look into her eye.

'No more for work for you, my lass. Time's up, I reckon.'

Finishing the other two feet as quickly as possible, Emily soon had both horses groomed and, much to

Diment's delight, tucking in to their evening bait. After looking Clowdy over once more, Emily made her way out of the stables to home.

'I'm tired out, girls, see you tomorrow.'

—⁓—

She let herself into the kitchen. The fresh bread, boiled egg and salad were laid out on the table and she picked up a radish and bit into it on her way past.

'You'll regret that later, Emily Radcliffe.'

Hearing no sound from the living room, she moved to the bottom of the stairs. A murmur was audible and, as she slowly climbed them the sound of her father talking grew in volume and clarity. She smiled and sighed.

'Nursery rhymes…ahhh, lovely.'

Then the couplets Henry was speaking became ever clearer.

'…What's this I see before my eyes?
A German sausage in disguise.
I grasped it, damn and blast it,
It's a turd!'

To Sarah's shriek of delighted laughter, Emily shouted up the remainder of the stairs.

'Father! That's not a nursery rhyme!'

26.02.16

There did not seem to be enough space to slide a cigarette paper in between the wreckage that littered the field outside of St. Mihiel. Everywhere George looked were the charred, still-smoking remains of discarded munitions, men and mules.

Nearby lay Horses **101015-7** and **030615-2** and George was busy removing their tack and muttering.

'Never met 'til now, an' I'm late by th' looks. At least y' spared th' ministrations o' th' Vet's Assistant, eh? That's some strange name f'r th' knacker, an' some bloody strange choice f'r you an' all.'

—∿∿—

'On-Lee-On, Diment!'

Diment wheeled left-handed to draw the long-barrow drill round for the return run.

'Good lass! Stand-On now, Stand-On!'

Emily checked the amount left in the seed box tray.

'Enough for another couple of runs, Diment, then we'll fill again.' She flicked the clats of soil from off her boots, checking the mare's feet as she went, and Diment dropped her head. Emily gave her left ear a rub. 'Hello, Madam.'

She took George's penknife out of her pocket and the feel of its familiarity and association rushed her right to his side, wherever he was. Taking an apple from her other pocket, she cut it and offered one half to Diment.

'Here you are, greedy.' Diment sucked it in gratefully. 'Chew it! Chew it! Goodness me!' Eating the other half herself, Emily reached up to rub Diment's ear again. 'That ground's still sticky after that rain of last week and drying out very slowly, don't you think, lass?' Diment tossed her head and shook it. 'Miss your partner these days, eh? Me too.'

She looked across at the remainder of the field.

'Well, this'll not buy the baby a new bonnet, will it? Best get it finished, one horse or no.' She gave Diment the core. 'Extra treat.'

Back at the drill, she picked up the reins and gave them a flick.

'Haul-On, Lass, Haul-On!'……

03.07.16

Picking his way through the wreckage strewn across what was once a field of wheat near Boise-le-Prêtre, the Sergeant got within hailing distance.

'Steady wi' all that! Bugger me…call y'rselves 'orsemen! We'll 'ave t' get another team over or yer'll kill them poor buggers!'

George, with a new pair of horses, and Samuel with his usual team were trying to pull out a bogged-down tank with a broken caterpillar. They stopped in their efforts and relaxed as Sam called back.

'Then it'll save th' shells gettin' 'em! Tanks! They've done nothin' yet an' already we're 'avin' t' bail 'em out. Two teams can't pull this bloody monster free an' now y'want t' get a third…an' they'll not do it neither. Not any number'll do it.'

George addressed Sam and the approaching Sergeant.

'Y' think not? I've a pair 'f 'orses at 'ome'd do this on their own, Sarn't. A grey, Clowdy, stands nineteen-two an' a bay, Diment, eighteen-two; 'er match f'r strength if not stature…'

Up alongside them now, the Sergeant pointed at the stripes on his arm.

'Listen up! This is yer Sergeant speakin'! Them 'orses you'm waxin' liquorice over ain't 'ere at this precise moment are they, Private Radcliffe?'

'No, Sir!'

Sam replied fast.

'I'll pop back 'n' fetch 'em if y' like, Sarge…'

The Sergeant wheeled round.

'There's only two types o' sarges in this mob, Private Gordon; pas-sarges an' sau-sarges got that?'

'Yes, Sarn't!'

'An' if anyone's goin' t' pop back anywhere t' fetch anythin' it'll be me, Gordon! Mark my words, you pair o' useless individuals, yer'll be glad they invented these things in time. Save all this sloggin'.'

George offered his opinion and that of most of the serving soldiers if truth be known.

'We've got 'em now, Sarn't, an' what're these poor sods doin' now if not sloggin'? They've 'ad no real rest f'r seven days now. 'Orses gettin' less in number so doin' twice th' work. Wire, caltrops 'n' stray shells sortin' out the unwary, all th' while 'orses bustin' a gut pullin' these new-fangled…tanks, that get stuck th' minute we 'ave an 'eavy dew, an' on top o' that their grub's gettin' poorer. Is there no way we c'n at least up their rations?'

The Sergeant put his arm around George's shoulder.

'We all 'ave t' suffer, Private, we're all on short rations…that single rasher o' Lance-Corporal bacon we've been havin' every mornin' passed y'r by, 'as it?' He released him and barked. 'There's another intake 'f 'orses due in about six week or so; maybe then grub count'll go up, 'til then we…do what?'

George and Sam replied together.

'Make do, Sarn't!'

'That's right; we make do, because we're what?'

'Soldiers Sir!'

'Quite right, we are, but in your case we use that statement in its widest possible sense.' The Sergeant moved away from them. 'Now, wi' yer permission Privates Gordon 'n' Radcliffe, I'll fetch another team over…Dig round th' back there!'

He strode off leaving George and Samuel, now armed with a spade apiece, to continue their struggle with the tank.

37

15.08.16

'Take the post from Mister Combest, Sarah, will you, please; Mummy's hands are all wet.'

'Yes, Mummy.'

Sarah ran to the kitchen door and the postman dropped below it, then leant over the half gate and into the kitchen very quickly.

'Boo!'

After leaping backwards, giggling and chuckling at the surprise and fun of the prank, Sarah took the letters.

'Ere y'are, Miss Sarah. Could be y'call-up papers, eh?'

'Thank you, Mister Cobmest.'

Wiping her hands on a cloth, Emily joined her at the door.

'Combest, Sarah, Com-best. Thank you Mister Combest. Call-up papers? I hope not. Where would the farm be then, without my main helper?'

'In a pretty poor shape, I'd say, Mrs Radcliffe. Good mornin' t' y' both.'

The postman got astride his bicycle and rode out of the back yard.

Emily took the letters from Sarah and, flicking through them, sat at the kitchen table. Her face paled slightly; one letter was the bearer of military franking and was opened with some trepidation.

She read, slumped into the chair and flopped the letter onto the table.

'Mummy alright?'

'It's a general call up for the horses, Sarah. The Military need them for the war.'

'Ours?'

'Everybody's, I'd think.'

'When, Mummy?'

Emily reviewed the letter.

'Next week…twelve o'clock, Wednesday.' She looked up at the calendar hanging by the stove. 'A week today.'

Moving to Emily's side, Sarah looked at the letter.

'All the horses?'

'Most; the best certainly.'

Sarah thought for a moment.

'Can we hide them, Mummy?'

Emily smiled at her.

'Oh, Sarah. If only.'

Arriving at exactly twelve o'clock, the black car pulled up just outside the yard and two men stepped out to be greeted by Emily, Sarah and Henry. One man was in uniform and carried a small, black tin box. The other, be-suited, carried an attaché case.

After a brief greeting the uniformed man asked to see a copy of the farm's last, original livestock inventory which he scanned as they were escorted into the yard, explaining the procedure to Henry as they walked.

'Of course we in Remount Division realise our records may be out of date, Sir, but we have a good idea of the stock numbers. This inventory, the Shire Horse Yearbook, and local reports inform us of changes in stocking and land use and so give us all the information we need to keep an accurate check.'

'How accurate?'

'Well, put it this way, Sir. There are some who are unpatriotic enough to think our stock records are so out-of-date they can hide their stock from us; imagine!'

'And they get caught, no doubt.'

'Every time, Sir; every time. You're dealing with the military now, not some local market dealer… Ah, here we are!'

They entered the yard and it was spotless, as always. The suited man smiled.

'Ah, excellent. Made an extra effort I see, Mister Carter.'

'No, it always looks like this. You can't keep good stock in poor conditions; even those on the periphery of the horse world should know that.'

'Ah, yes, quite right, Mister Carter. You run a very tight ship here.'

'Me? No, not at all. This is all my daughter's, Mrs Radcliffe's, work. She does all the management here, horses and agriculture. My arthritis precludes me from most of it these days, I'm afraid.'

'Ah-hem, err…' The suited man looked at his notes in an attempt to re-gather his ruffled pride. 'Ah, indeed, ah-hem…but, as I see from the farm's history notes, not so tight a ship as to have escaped the odd still-born foal?'

Gathering Sarah to her as she spoke, Emily faced him.

'Yes. These things happen, even in the best-kept establishments…and my daughter doesn't need reminding of these events, thank you.'

The suited man cleared his throat again.

'Ahem! Well…yes…shall we get on? Can you parade the present stock for me please…Mister…' He looked at Henry who shook his head and indicated Emily again. 'Err…Mrs…?'

Emily replied smilingly.

'Radcliffe.'

'Yes, right, Mrs Radcliffe.'

Waiting for a beat or two, Emily replied, still all smiles.

'Certainly.'

One by one she fetched the stock from the stables and tied them to the wall rings. The two men gave each horse a thorough inspection, checking their notes against the farm's inventory and ticking them off from theirs, writing the horses details and descriptions on a set of forms as they went.

After some confidential conversation, the suited man left his military companion and handed Henry a sheaf of papers.

'Could you sign here for me, please, Mister Carter?'

'Shouldn't that be Mrs Radcliffe? She's the farm's head of stock.'

'No, Sir. Head of stock she may be, no offence, but not head of the household, Sir, and it's head of the household to sign. That'll be you, unless there's another man on the farm?'

'No, my son-in-law is away serving, and I've said that Mrs Radcliffe is…'

'That'll be you then, Sir.'

Henry looked across at a speechless Emily and shook his head as he took the papers. He began to sign as the military man began his speech.

'Thank you. As you'll see the hunter will stay.' He pointed to the sheets. 'And here…' Henry signed again. '…As will the dun hack. The skewbald mare is a new purchase, I see. She stays too, bit old for our purpose, I'm afraid…'

'That's good news to us, she's only sixteen.'

247

'Precisely, Mister Carter. Sixteen. Too old for us at this juncture. Ideally we'd like them a lot younger, between three and six is ideal, and if we can get a good number of six-month to one-year-olds…'

Henry interrupted.

'As young as that! Not expecting an early end to it all then?'

The military man ignored it and talked on.

'…Six-month to one-year-olds, then we have an opportunity to bring those on to take the place of stock that can no longer do the work.'

'Worked to death one way or the other.'

The suited man ignored Henry again and pointed to the sheets.

'And…here… Young stock repays the effort put in to get them working to our exacting standards, Mister Carter Not spoilt by thoughtless owners and so far easier to train.' He pointed at the forms yet again. 'And here…' Letting go a world-weary sigh, Henry signed again as the suited man continued, 'The grey mare…' He consulted his papers. 'er…4426, Scarsdale Silvergirl, and the bay mare…' He read again. '141142 Stuntney Charlotte, and the brown gelding, no number for him, just Ben, will do very well. Class Five HD and the perfect age. You have very good stock here, Mister Carter…and Mrs Radcliffe of course. Well reared, especially the grey and the bay…' He scanned the papers again. 'Diment and Clowdy is it?' He looked at his uniformed companion. 'Quaint names. They'll do us good work for the war effort, I'm sure; excellent structure and temperament. Your own training?'

Emily was stunned. Of all the scenarios she had rehearsed, this was not amongst them.

'Err…Yes. That'll be down to my husband.'

The man in uniform smiled at her.

'Indeed. Away serving, you say?'

Still trying to come to terms with the enormity of their visit and its outcome, Emily looked from Sarah to Henry.

'Err, yes…since the outbreak.'

Sarah had shown real courage as she listened to the details reeled off so matter-of-factly by the suited man. Like all small children she had no say, no control over events and outcomes that affected her directly. Faces gave her the most information. From these she could ascertain how words she did not understand affected those closest to her. All she could do was listen and watch, try to understand and imagine, and ride the roller-coaster of her confusing emotions. Looking at the individuals involved in this event she knew her mother was on the verge of tears, and now Sarah's game of emotional brinkmanship was on the edge of collapse too.

The man in uniform gave begrudging approval.

'Hm. Commendable.'

Releasing the first tears, Sarah's youth allowed her the luxury of voicing her feelings too.

'But, Mummy, they're Daddy's horses! They belong to Daddy! Diment and Clowdy…and what happens…?'

The suited man was untouched by this outburst, but the uniformed man locked his attention onto Sarah when she uttered this cry.

Emily stepped across him and rapidly scooped Sarah up.

'Yes, they are Daddy's horses, and they always will be, Sarah, but some have to go into the army now. They have to…and you never know, they may bring Daddy home just that little bit quicker.' She looked at the uniformed man, and he could see she was seeking support. 'Isn't that so?'

He looked sheepishly at her.

'Er…well, er…it's not…'

He could not hold her gaze and his suited companion interrupted his difficulty.

'We're not allowed to divulge any information about the condition or state of the war, Mrs Radcliffe, secrecy is all.'

'Ha!' Henry scoffed from behind them.

The decision's enormity was now fully realised by Emily. Carrying Sarah with her, she moved over to Clowdy's side.

'And they will be together, the grey and the bay, Clowdy and Diment? They're a working team, trained together and…'

The suited man took back the sheets from Henry and began to write on his own notes.

'Thank you for that information, Madam. I'll note it in the forms, and rest assured we know precisely what we're doing. All proven working teams are kept together wherever possible; it makes solid, military sense.'

'"Over by Christmas" notwithstanding?'

Ignoring Henry's comment, he handed back the altered chit and, opening the tin box, took out a chequebook and handed it across to his companion. Writing an amount on it, he tore out the cheque and gave it to Henry.

Henry looked at it. Shook his head.

'My thirty pieces of silver then, is it?'

There was another awkward silence.

Snapping his attaché case shut, the suited man began to leave the yard in the direction of their car.

'We'll collect on the date stated. You'll note we've paid the current going rate for livestock, less our administration fee, of course.'

'Of course,' echoed Henry.

'No need for tack, we'll supply them with everything they'll need. No charge for that, you'll be pleased to hear, Sir. Goodbye.'

'You sure? You've taken most of what the farm has to offer, why stop there? Have a look around, help yourself.' He looked again at the cheque. 'At this rate you'll be getting a bargain!'

Emily put her hand gently on his arm.

'Father, there's no point.'

As he passed them, the man in uniform gave what Henry described later as a pompous salute.

'That's alright, Madam, we're used to the feeling of resentment from some quarters.'

Emily was still stunned, but Henry was not about to let it go at that.

'Hasn't gone deep enough yet then 'cos you're still taking the best of them and expecting us to feed and rebuild a nation with what's left. Like all military and politic folk, you don't listen!' He turned to Sarah. 'No voice, Sarah, remember that. You, me, these horses, we've no voice.'

Emily squeezed her father's arm again.

'Father, please…'

The suited man stopped and turned to them, an edge of command in his voice.

'Oh, and, if you're thinking of being out when we call in order to dodge the call-up, please, think again. We've had a similar experience with a particular farm a little ways away from here, but near enough for the unpatriotic epidemic to spread to others. So, let's just reiterate; next Thursday. That's a week tomorrow. Goodbye.'

Emily turned to Diment and Clowdy as she felt the single tear run down her cheek.

They dropped their heads as she and Sarah nestled in between them.

'Oh, my ladies…my poor Shire ladies.'

39

Horsemen must all look the same to a horse. But to Emily, standing in the kitchen and seeing them enter the farm, these two horsemen looked particularly sinister, and the drab, olive-brown cow-gowns they wore did nothing to enhance their appearance.

She took off her apron and called out.

'Sarah! The military men are here for the horses! Come and see them off.'

'Yes, Mummy!'

Sarah came into the kitchen and Emily adjusted Sarah's collar as she spoke.

'Now, do you remember all the things we talked about last week?'

'Yes, Mummy.'

'Good girl. Both Diment and Clowdy, and Ben of course, but especially Diment and Clowdy will want us to be brave for them, won't they?'

'Yes, I'll be brave.'

'I know you will, Sarah, you're a Radcliffe.'

'Like Mummy.'

'Like Mummy, yes; and Daddy.'

'And Daddy.'

Emily took her hand.

'Right. Edward's spent the morning giving them all a good brush so they'll look splendid, let's play our part, Sarah; send them off happy.'

Out in the yard they joined Henry and Edward. Emily was surprised to see two other men, accompanied by three horses, gathered just outside the yard.

The man they assumed to be the lead hand of the group approached them.

'I'm Baxter, East Midlan' C'llection Co-ordinator, Remount Division.' He gave Henry a sheet of paper. 'Three t' collect 'ere, that right?'

Henry took the proffered sheets.

'Strange uniforms. Are you in the army, you four?'

'No, we just 'andle th' collection o' stock f'r th' army in this district, as I said.'

'Are they all to be together?'

Baxter looked across at Emily.

'What, Missus?'

'The horses from here and those others.' She indicated the group. 'Are they all to be together?'

'Yes, Missus, they all travel t'gether. No cause served by gettin' 'em from 'ere one day then comin' back t'morrow 'n' collectin' neighbours' stock, now is there? Waste 'f our time an' scarce resources, I'd say.'

'From what I understand of the military that'd be no surprise!'

Ignoring Henry's remark, Baxter authorised his standing.

'Can we get 'em out 'n' sorted then, please, Sir, we're runnin' late as it is?'

Emily, pursuing her point, indicated one of the other horses in particular.

'Excuse me, Mr Baxter is it, but the Cleveland Bay, is that Gent, from Hive Farm? Mrs Grove's place?'

'Don't know any Gent... Cleveland Bay from 'Ive Farm? Ar, that were th' place, weren't it, Fred?'

One of the other horsemen, finger in mouth as he gnawed at its nail, answered.

'Yeah.'

Looking at his sheet, Baxter ran his finger down the listings then nodded.

'Oh yea, 'ere 'e is; Gent. 'Orse **310816-3** now though, not Gent.'

'**3108**...? But...that's her carriage horse, Gent.'

Fred took his nibbled finger from his mouth and interrupted Emily, grinning broadly.

'Y'right there, Missus, an' that's what 'e were doin' when we come across 'em the other side o' th' brook yonder. In th' shafts 'e were. We soon took 'im outta them. 'E's 'Orse...?'

He looked at Baxter who read the details again.

'**310816-3**.'

Fred echoed it.

'Ar, 'Orse **310816-3** now.'

Henry was incredulous as he addressed his next question at Mister Baxter.

'What, you took him away from her while she was driving him?'

'Well not exactly while she were drivin' 'im, Sir. We stopped 'er first, otherwise we'd've been trampled on, wouldn't we.'

255

'Do you think that was the right thing to do?'

'It were th' right thing t' do, Sir. Remounts'd paid 'er a visit not four week ago.'

'But, she's over sixty now is Mrs Groves.'

'Age don't enter into it, Sir. She'd 'ad fair warnin' we were collectin' t'day an' 'ad still decided t' go out shoppin', again. Were only luck we caught up wi' 'er…I've just said, she weren't in last time Remounts called neither, not from th' information we got anyhow; that were a month ago.'

'Ahhh, so this was the lady your companions visited; Mrs Groves! And of course, you knew instinctively this was her horse?'

Fred's voice chimed in, tinged with further sarcasm.

'Well th' name, 'Ive's Farm Dairy on th' side o' th' cart were a bit 'f a give-away.'

Henry was not amused at Fred's continuing sarcasm and he turned towards him.

'Yes. I'm aware of that. She's a near-neighbour of ours, but forgive me if I say it, you are not locals are you, and that could've been any horse!'

'Ho, no Sir. One thing we know about is 'orses; it's our job, an' description we'd been gived from when assessors first visited 'er fitted 'im perfect.'

He indicated and Baxter read from the sheet once more.

'Brown, Cleveland Bay geldin', No Book number, Sixteen-two, White star on fore'ead, White socks on opp'site legs…'

Fred then closed off his companion's speech.

'So, it were a case o' goodbye cart 'ello army fer…?'

Fred looked at Baxter again.

'Gent.'

'Ar, fer' Gent.'

Emily was amazed.

'So, let me get this straight. You stopped her, took her horse and left her with the cart?'

'Yes, Missus.'

'Where?'

'Other side o' th' brook; I've said just.'

Fred saw Emily's expression and he looked across at Baxter who endeavoured to justify their commentary.

'Like Fred said, Missus, she knew we was comin'. Were out th' time collection were first organised, so Remounts'd already 'ad a wasted visit to 'er. Y'can't keep puttin' off th' military, Missus; war needs 'em an' they've t' go, no excuses.'

Henry involved them both.

'Well, whatever reasoning you two put on it, I think that's an appalling way to behave…'

Now Baxter was defiant; his tone said so.

'So's dodging th' call-up, Mister…' He looked at the sheet. 'Carter…I'm sayin' war needs 'em an' they've t' go!'

'Yes, I know, I heard the first time, but to leave that lady with a cart and no means of getting it home!'

'Fair warnin', Sir, she'd 'ad fair warnin' an' th' cheque; these folk want it all they do, but not this time; ho, no. What's paid for's ours; we 'ave the authority, Sir.' This seemed to cover all explanations and returning to the job in hand, Baxter looked at the list and confirmed his authority over the situation. 'No fuss 'ere, though, I c'n see that. C'n we get 'orses out, please? Three in all; one a Scarsdale 'n' one a Stuntney 'cordin' to our notes.' He turned to Fred. 'Been lookin' forw'd t' this, ain't we, Fred?'

'Ar, we 'ave that.'

After a short pause to prepare herself for the inevitable, Emily motioned to Edward who left them and went into the stables.

Ben was led out first and Edward relinquished him to Fred who, taking off the horse's head-collar and lead rein, pushed them back into Edward's arms and replaced both with military issue kit. One of the other R.D. men moved across carrying a measure and took the rein. As Ben's details were being confirmed, Edward and Emily returned to the stables.

'Right, Fred. Shirley Lodge Farm… Brown geldin'?'

'Ar.'

'No Book number; measure?'

Ralph helped Fred to measure Ben.

'Seventeen-one, Ralph?'

Ralph checked it.

'Ar. Seventeen one.'

'Seventeen one.' Baxter wrote, then looked up. 'Bobbed tail, Fred?'

'Ar.'

'White on lower nose?'

'Ar.'

'Dark t' black feathers on all four feet?'

'Ar.'

Baxter turned the page.

'That'll be 'Orse Number **310816-4**…'

All conversation stopped abruptly as Diment and Clowdy were led out into the yard to a collection of gasps and whistles from the assembled men.

Fred, in particular was very impressed.

'By 'eck, these're some 'orses. Waited all week t' see this pair, ain't we, Boss, an' worth th' wait. That grey's summat t' see or I don't know an 'orse!' He looked over Baxter's shoulder and squinted at the notes. 'No need f'r descriptions 'ere, Boss. A Scarsdale an' a Stuntney in th' same yard? Not often that 'appens along. Missus, that's some pair o' mares y've got there, take my word.'

Emily smiled at him.

'So glad you happened along to tell us.'

Fred waved the sheaf of paper, his ace in the pack.

'Ar. Your loss an' army's gain now though, Missus.'

'Was there any call for that comment, Mister Baxter?'

The men ignored her, engrossed as they were in hurriedly swapping head collars, checking descriptions and confirming measurements. The only difference from Ben's treatment was that, this time, Edward took the new reins back from Ralph and held on to them very firmly, and his quiet insistence would brook no opposition.

All Ralph could offer was a quiet, ''Ave it your way, but they'll be mine at th' finish, mate.'

Details read out, confirmed and noted, Fred, to signify all was at an end, raised his hand to stroke Clowdy's head.

'All done, lass.'

Uncharacteristically she flicked it away to avoid the contact.

Baxter moved across to him.

'Ha! Got you understood, Fred; shows she's some quality in 'er! Welcome t' th' fold, 'Orse 310816-5…an' you, 'Orse…310816-6…'

'Diment and Clowdy.' The two men looked at Emily so she expanded the point. 'Their names. It's Diment and Clowdy; Diment is the bay, Clowdy the grey; she's 4426 Scarsdale Silvergirl, Clowdy…'

Their interest broke and, writing as he spoke, Baxter concentrated back on his paperwork.

'Not anymore, Missus. Army runs their lives now, so it's 'Orse 310816-6 an' 'Orse 310816-5 from t'day.'

Henry shook his head.

'You're so very wrong there. Not to us they aren't. They'll always be Diment and Clowdy.'

Baxter sniffed.

'Ar, right, suit y'rself, Sir. Ralph, John! Best get movin', time's gettin' on!'

This call was the finish for Sarah. Once again, shifted to the periphery of control but in the vortex of events, she could only add her tears as input.

Ralph handed his reins to John, stepped over and chucked her under the chin.

'Don't worry, little 'un. Big adventure over there, an' they're good stock so they'll 'ave that on their side.'

Emily took Sarah in her arms as John joined in.

'He's right, y'know. Just look out f'r a postcard, eh?'

'Look on th' bright-side; it could've been knacker cart what came for 'em, eh?'

Fred realised his attempt at lightening the moment had failed when Emily replied simply.

'It is.' She turned to Sarah. 'Brave now, Sarah. Remember what we said in the kitchen? They need to leave happy.'

Sarah gulped back her tears.

'But I am being brave, Mummy.'

'I know you are Sarah, I know, I didn't mean you weren't.'

There was an awkward silence as Henry signed the release form.

Baxter pointed to Edward in an effort to regain his authority over the situation and turned to Emily.

'Is 'e goin' t' move, or are we to 'ave t' walk over 'im then?'

Since taking the reins off Ralph, Edward's grip had become tighter as the conversation and time had moved on. Now the whites of his knuckles confirmed the effort involved in maintaining his vice-like grip.

Baxter now called across at him.

'Oi, mate! You'll have t' let 'em go or you'll lose that arm!'

Emily stepped between Baxter and his view of Edward.

'You know, for someone who does this for a living you have all the compassion of white nettle. I'll talk to him.' She moved towards Edward but turned round after a couple of steps. 'Do you have any understanding of just what horses like this mean to us?'

'Yes, Missus, I do.'

'Do you?'

'Missus, I'll 'ave you know I work wi' 'orses an' 'ave collected f'r the army f'r twenty year now, as 'ave most o' these men 'ere wi' me, an' I c'n tell you we know 'orses!'

'Then what happened to you; to you all?'

'We know all about 'orses, Missus.'

'Oh yes, I realise you know how to tack them, drive them, herd them, know when they're lame, what to feed them and when, but what happened to you all that you know so much yet understand so little?' No one replied. 'What happened?'

This time, Baxter repeated his maxim with a weary tone to his voice.

'Missus; war needs 'em an' they've t' go.'

'And that's it, is it? You think that, like you, we consider them to be just machinery for the war effort? Well you're wrong, they're not! And they're not just your blessed military issue; not Horse **3108**-whatever either!' She scanned the men. 'Don't you remember them?'

'I'll 'ave you know I've 'andled military's 'orses f'r twenty years, Missus!'

'Then might I suggest those twenty years you've spent collecting for the military have done you a disservice, Mister Baxter, and if you can't see that then you're lost; all of you. These horses are our horses…and because we're supposed to have the superior intellect they deserve to be called something better than a number! Do you not see that?'

Now nothing came back.

'I feared as much. You just go on about your job and pass your glib comments. You come here and boast about how you took an old lady's horse from its shafts, never giving a thought to how big an event like this is to her, to us.' She looked at Edward. 'To him.'

Henry moved to her side.

'Emily, there's no point.'

'Maybe not, father, but it has to be said.' She nodded towards Edward. 'For him if no one else.' She turned back to the men. 'You may do this every day, Mister Baxter, but this is the only day it's ever happened to him, ever likely to; ever. He's known those two since they were fillies, helped train them with my husband and this is a devastating loss for him.'

Baxter looked defiant.

'I'm sorry Missus, but we 'ave a job t' do an' 'e'll 'ave t' move…an' I've no idea about 'is 'ist'ry,' he nodded towards the horses, 'nor theirs f' that matter.'

'Well done, Mister Baxter. For the first time today you're quite right; you have no idea.'

With Sarah still cradled in her arms, Emily walked over to Edward.

'Edward? Edward, it's alright, we all feel the same but they do have to go.'

Sarah took her head from out of Emily's neck.

'Brave, Edward, like me.'

Edward shifted his fixed gaze from horizon to Sarah.

'Yes, Miss Sarah, brave.' He looked at the horses and then at Emily. 'Will they be 'ome, Missus?'

Emily shook her head.

'I don't know, Edward, but I do know that if they return to anywhere in England then they'll find their way back here. Do you think so too?'

Edward smiled.

'Ar, Missus. Be 'ome soon.'

She took his hand and gently eased it free.

'Let them go, Edward.'

The reins dropped but, as they moved away, Emily realised Clowdy had taken hold of her coat between mumbling lips.

She laid her hand very gently on Clowdy's muzzle.

'You take care ladies; both of you.'

Emily pulled gently on the coat and the lips and material parted.

Ralph quickly collected Clowdy's reins as Baxter called out.

'Ralph, grab these! Fred! Get that other 'n' lets get on, we're an hour be'ind as it is; dinner's callin'.'

Taking Ben's and Diment's lead reins, Fred joined Ralph and walked all three horses out of the gates. Once together the whole group turned and set off along the lane leading away from the farm.

After several seconds, Henry broke their silence.

'Sarah, my girl, you were very brave and very grown up.'

Emily smiled at Sarah.

'Grandfather's right, Sarah, you were brave, Edward too. Come on; let's see what we can do to rescue Mrs Groves, eh? Edward, get Carmen and Lizzie out and we'll step out along the lane to the brook.'

'Yes, Missus.'

'Mrs Groves can use Carmen until she gets sorted with another. You go too, Sarah, lead Lizzie out for Edward.'

Emily put her daughter down and, taking hands, Sarah and Edward made their way to the stables as Emily moved over to Henry. In the distance the dust-shrouded, swaying mass of horses disappeared round the bend in the lane.

Emily swallowed her tears with some determination and took her father's hand, her other using the handkerchief to wipe her nose.

'Never thought it'd come to this, Father; you?'

Henry stared at the now empty lane.

'No…but we should have guessed. Greedy beast is war, Em.'

40

21.09.16

'The best view 'f Étain we've 'ad this week.'

George looked over to Sam, who was racking bridles.

'Wha'd'y' mean, Sam? We're inside a bloody big tent; all we can see is tent!'

'Exactly, George!'

Laughing loudly, another of their troop, Brian Tanner, joined in.

'Y' get worse, Sam! No use tryin' madness f' y'r escape papers, they'll not know th' diff'rence!'

A soldier entered the tent at a run.

'Troop Walkers're 'ere wi' th' new intake!'

The soldiers made for the entrance as one, voicing various remarks.

'Thank Christ f'r that!'

'About bloody time!'

'More grist t' th' mill.'

Sam winked at George.

'Better f'r us than th' poor buggers what've just arrived, I'll warrant.'

Out in the makeshift stockyard the horsemen were gathering to inspect what they were expected to work with. Thirty or forty horses were milling around in the strange new surroundings, unsure and uneasy.

George called back to Sam as they joined the other soldiers.

'Bet they're a load o' pit ponies an' 'acks, Sam…!' A whinny and hoof scrape across the stones caused George to look up and across the gathered livestock. '…Clowdy?' Sam and Brian looked in surprise as George rapidly pushed his way through the assembled block of horses. 'Clowdy…!…Diment!'

'What, George?'

'Those're mine! My Shire ladies!'

Both Diment and Clowdy began to snort and stamp the ground with their forefeet, recognising George's clear voice even above the clatter in the yard.

Brian nudged Sam.

'Ayup, Sam, 'e's off again.' He shouted to the fast-disappearing George. ''Ow many times you've t' be told, these ain't yours, they're the army's!'

Sam and Brian followed, Sam shouting as they did so.

'Christ, th' shells 'ave finally done their job, Brian! 'E'll be needin' a strait-jacket, a straight-'ome-jacket…an' I'm just th' man t' fetch it f'r 'im!'

Alongside Clowdy and Diment, George was beside himself with amazement and joy.

'No, I mean these! Th' one's I've told you about! These're my Ladies! My Diment…my Clowdy!'

Their raised voices drew the Sergeant across to them as, arriving at George's side, Sam and Brian could now see both horses fully. Clowdy and Diment dropped their heads to George's touch, and he stroked and pulled their ears.

'Jesus, girls, what've they done t' y' manes an' tails…
That's some cruel 'aircut!'

Sam stood back from the two Shires, all the better to see them.

'Bloody ding-dong! There's some 'orse-flesh if ever I saw it!' He looked at their front hooves. 'Orse **310816-6**, 'n' 'Orse…**310816-5**; I'll give y' me watch for 'em, Radcliffe!' He drew his sleeve up to reveal a solid gold wrist watch. 'Me wrist watch, Radcliffe! Not many o' these about…rarity; solid gold! Got me name writ on th' back but y'c'n soon scrub that off.'

Their heads sagging in the ecstasy of the greeting, George continued rubbing the ears of both horses.

'Not f'r a sack-full, Sam, not f'r a bloody sack-full! An' mark it well, all'f y'r. There's no numbers 'ere; this is Diment an' this is Clowdy.'

By this point in the proceedings, the Sergeant was amongst them and had caught the last part of the chatter.

'There'll be no buyin' an' sellin' 'f army livestock 'ere, Private Gordon…' He stopped short as he saw the two Shires basking in the fuss. 'Bloo-dee 'ell, look't that grey!'

George patted Clowdy's neck.

'My Shire ladies, Sarn't…what I told you about.'

'So, these're them then; them wonder-'orses! They actually exist! Who'ld've thought it, eh? Of all th' bloody places t' team up… Couldn't leave 'em where they were could yer? By God, they'll not thank yer f'r this, Radcliffe, reunion or no.' He looked around at the assembled men. 'Still, best warn fam'lies back 'ome eh?'

Brian looked puzzled.

''Ow's that then, Sarn't?'

'Well, look around yer, Private Tanner. Does this war look like it's over?'

'No Sarn't.'

'No, Private, it don't, but, accordin' to all th' tales Radcliffe's told about these two it'll be over next week! Be a bugger t' fight yer way through this lot f'r King 'n' country only t' get 'ome expectin' a cuddle an' surprise th' missus shaggin' th' milk-boy!' The men laughed as the Sergeant moved in to stroke Clowdy. 'Well, Radcliffe, aren't yer goin' to inter'duce me?'

'Yes, Sir. This is Diment, this is Clowdy. Ladies, say 'ello to our nice kind Sergeant!'

Clowdy shook her head and snorted and Diment scraped her hoof twice, much to the Sergeant's amusement.

'Bloody 'ell! Party tricks an' all!'

'Yes, Sir.'

'Well, Radcliffe, I reckon yer spoke true, there's some bridle-full 'f 'orses 'ere. I suppose now yer'll be wantin' t' run…' He looked at their front right hooves and winked at George as he spoke. ''Orse **310816-5**, an' 'Orse…**310816-6** into th' routine 'ere y'rself? Get 'em used t' th'…little surprises that we 'ave t' put up with, eh?'

'Would be a good thing, Sir, if y' could see y' way clear.'

'I could…but only if Gordon 'ere wills me that wrist watch 'f 'is, the one 'e promised yer not two minute ago.'

'Sarn't! My mother give me this wrist watch!'

'Sacred t' th' mem'ry 'f yer grey-'aired old mother is it, Gordon?'

'No, Sarn't, it's sacred t' th' fact it's solid gold!'

'An' which yer was willin' t' give away f'r a couple'f 'orses just now!'

Sam nodded sagely, emphasising the facts.

'Yes, Sarn't. A pair, of 'orses; an' what a pair 'f 'orses.'

'Be very careful, Gordon. As your superior officer an' in the face of Radcliffe's refusal, I feel th' best I c'n do is 'onour yer offer and I can assure yer, y' refusal will undoubtedly incur th' wrath o' this kindly Sergeant! Now, wrist watch?'

Sam tried to deflect the conversation.

'Reminds me o' that lass I met in St. Mihiel a while back. She offered 'er 'onour, I 'onoured 'er offer, and so, all night long I was on 'er an' off 'er!'

The Sergeant spoke over the laughter.

'Summat else y' need t' learn, Gordon. In this battalion, I tell the jokes an' you lot laugh, now, f' th' last time 'f askin'; wrist watch?'

'Yes, Sarn't! It's yours!'

'I'll look forward t' bein' called t' th' readin', Gordon, thank yer.' The men laughed again and the Sergeant turned to George. 'A very early Christmas present then, Radcliffe, but remember, if this war ain't over by December twenty-sixth, I'll set yer on mule duty 'n' give them pair t' Gordon 'ere!'

'Thanks, Sarn't, we're in y' debt; maybe they'll pay y' back one day.'

'Payment?' He glanced around the yard. 'These buggers pay every day o' their lives wi' us, Radcliffe; you 'f all people should know that. Remember, th' rest 'f yer, we should be payin' them! Now, let's break up this mothers' meetin' an' sort these sods out; take any longer an' they'll turn back t' wild stock!'

The men dispersed to divide and manage the new horses.

George stayed behind, holding onto the reins as he stroked Diment and Clowdy.

'You must be a present from my Em; old team back t'gether then, eh, girls.'

41

14.11.16

Ancre Heights, just outside Beaumont Hamel was surrounded by sodden fields turned by a different plough; sown with the seeds of a future generation and fertilised with their blood and bone. Through this morass of extinguished possibilities, Diment and Clowdy were hauling a field-gun to a repair quadrangle nearby. Occasional shells were landing around a hill top in the distance cheered on by bursts of gunfire, but George's preparation of both horses for the battlefield had them working as if through birdsong.

Collecting the field-gun had been particularly difficult, requiring George's help with spade and lever when the gun became bogged down. So much so that, when they reached the repair area on the outskirts of the base, all three were regally spattered with mud and sweat. Pausing for a much needed breather, George dipped his 'kerchief in a puddle and wiped their faces with it, cleaning the mud off the regimental tunic button fastened onto each halter too.

'Gets just about everywhere, don't it, Clowdy, eh?' He picked up the reins once more. 'What we wouldn't give f'r th' Forty-Acre an' an 'ay tine…' He flicked them. '…Haul-On, my ladies. Haul-On!'

Zigzagging around the various depots that made up the tent-and-timber village, Diment and Clowdy dropped the field-gun in amongst other machinery in need of repair. Unhitching them, George gave their ears a rub and told them what a good pair of lasses they had been. A light drizzle began to fall and he guided them over to a large, canvas-covered area for shelter. With a horse either side of him they stood together for a short while; a group of friends waiting for a tram.

'Tell y'what, when this slows we'll slip over yonder 'n' get a quick brush down. 'Ow's that suit?'

After a few minutes the shower did indeed slow. George had just stepped out of the shelter, when he was confronted by the Sergeant.

'Radcliffe! No good you 'idin' in 'ere!' He pointed to a cart a few yards away. ''Ook up that munitions cart, join up wi' Gordon an' them two 'orsemen from D Comp'ny. They're be'ind rations tent. Then get them loads up to 'Ill Twelve, above th' river!' The Sergeant turned to leave. 'They're waitin' on yer, so don't 'ang about!'

Looking through the drizzle towards the hill, once a distant danger now a dangerous destination, George indicated the state of both him and the horses.

''Idin'? Don't want t' start a war or nothin', Sarn't, but 'avin' just done a stint 'f four hours on me own, can I ask 'ow come D Company 'orsemen're 'ere f'r thirty seconds an' c'n commandeer 'elp...an' where's their bloody tanks anyway? D Company's Tank Division, or so rumour'ld 'ave it!'

The Sergeant spun back round on his heel.

'They're 'ere because they're 'ere, Private, an' unlike others I could mention they obey orders first time o' tellin'! Tanks're all committed!'

'Like th' rest 'f us should be. Tanks! Cee Three th' lot 'f 'em! They still can't 'andle th' wet like an 'orse can. Bag o' feed an' a brush an' y're away.'

'An' it'll be you as'll be away if yer don't obey orders 'n' get up that bloody 'ill, Radcliffe! Any more o' this an' yer'll not be usin' th' brush, yer'll be wearin' it! Now, move!'

Unlike the present weather, George was aware bonhomie was beginning to run dry.

'Yes Sir! Where'd y' say, Sarn't?'

'Back o' th' munitions tent. D' yer need a map?'

'No, Sir!'

'Best be off then!'

Saluting rapidly, George led Diment and Clowdy over to the indicated carriage.

'Sorry, Girls, no time f'r a clean up… When we get back, eh?'

He hitched up the cart and moved off to the munitions area. As he rounded the tented screen, George saw Sam then the D Company horsemen with him. Both had their backs to him, but there was no mistaking it. George shook his head and smiled.

'Should've listened t' you all them years ago, Daniel Long.' Daniel let go of the draw bar he was inspecting and spun round. 'Y'were a bad lot about most things, but y'were right about one.'

Daniel was as surprised as George.

'Bugger me! If it ain't George Radcliffe! Right about what?'

'Y' said y'd see me in 'ell, an' 'ere we are.'

Daniel clocked the two Shires.

'Bloody Norah! Are them th' two 'orses you 'ad back on Shirley Lodge? By, y' must've pulled some strings t' get them 'ere.'

'No strings, Daniel, just luck.'

'Yours maybe, Radcliffe, not theirs.'

'This y' usual then?'

It was Sam who first spotted the imminent arrival of the Sergeant and who began to look busy as Eric, the other D Company horseman, joined in the conversation.

'No, we're usually V.A. staff.'

George laughed out loud.

'Vet's Assistants! Ha-ha! Now why am I not surprised at 'earin' that about you, Daniel? Any excuse t' put an 'orse down an' you'd use it.'

'You c'n laugh, Radcliffe, but as far as I'm concerned this one's got me in at th' wrong end 'f th' battle.'

Eric frowned.

'You two know each other then?'

Arriving behind them, the Sergeant said in matter-of-fact tone, 'My very question.'

Eric saw the Sergeant and moved rapidly to his horses but, before he had realised who had asked the question, Daniel answered it.

'Y'could say that…'

The Sergeant cut Daniel dead.

'I could but I won't because this ain't an old-pals reunion it's a bloody war! Radcliffe! I might've known it'd be you 'oldin' court in shirkers' corner! Now, not wishin' t' put yer all under too much pressure, but King and Country would be eternally grateful if th' four 'f yer would be s' kind as t' put down yer tea 'n' biscuits, line out, an' get up that bloody 'ill!'

All four men snapped to attention as one.

'Yes, Sir!'

Quickly gathering loose reins and tattered dignity they all moved out of the uneven shelter of the tents and headed up the track towards Hill Twelve.

George saw the gathering rain clouds ahead.

'Looks black over th' back o' Bill's mother's, Sam.'

'An' 'ere we are, we're walkin' up this' 'ill an' straight into it like a pair o' sacrificial goats…' A couple of shells landed in the distance. '…An' 'ark at that shellin'…where the 'ell were we when they 'anded out th' common sense, George, eh?'

'Not payin' attention, Sam, that's where. Spent too much time lookin' out th' window.'

As they moved further away from the compound, Daniel looked back.

'I see we're without Sergeant's company f'r this 'un then.'

Sam glanced over his shoulder.

'On important work, that one. 'E's on LFT duty all week.'

'What's that when it's at 'ome then?'

'Leadin' fr'm tent.'

With shells falling ahead and the mud and bloody artistry of war all around, eager momentum and joie de vivre were missing from the quartet. As they drew closer to their destination, each man retreated into his own cocoon of coping. George, second in the line, talked constantly to Diment and Clowdy, encouraging them, letting them know what progress they were making. They were a couple of chain away from the summit when Daniel broke their self-imposed survival routine.

'A Minnie! Ge' down!'

A whistling shell homed in…it was going to be close.

All three of George's companions dropped to the ground using their carts and horses as cover, but George moved quickly to Diment and Clowdy's heads.

'Bloody 'orses can't get down, y' daft sod!'

The in-coming shell's whistle grew in intensity.

Daniel shouted back.

'You can!'

Then, just before landing, the whistle ceased.

'You're th' daft…!'

The split-second of silence was as shattering as the explosion that followed. Landing about sixty yards away to their right the detonation shook the ground, uprooting two previously shattered trees but, miraculously, left all the travelling party, horses, carts and men totally unscathed.

Up and full of comment on the near miss, a voice called out to them from the trench-line ahead.

'Get that ammunition up here, horsemen! Move!'

They knew the voice of authority and responded in like manner.

'Yes, Sir!' But George's add-on to Diment and Clowdy gave outlet to their real feelings. 'Christ, girls…it's an asylum up 'ere.'

Reins collected with a little more alacrity than usual, they moved their horses up the remainder of the slope and on to the doubtful shelter of the few remaining pine trees and nearby rear trench-line. As they arrived above the river, at the crest of Hill Twelve, George called to his team.

'Whoa! Stand-On, girls!'

The panorama of brutal destruction was laid out before them. The trenches, the mud, the displaced and shattered machinery, the carelessly strewn wire and, in the distance, desultory shells continuing to fall, bullets to whine and whizz. The familiar sight never ceased to hone George's emotions…as indeed, did the reaction of his two horses.

Through this, as in all their previous encounters with such panoply of shocks, Diment and Clowdy remained true to their last order. Standing stock still, unfazed and trusting, their concentration was fixed, their massive strength and training totally focused on the job in hand. On this particular mission, at this particular time and no matter what the surroundings, danger or distractions, their role was to keep the chains taught from harness to cart and so hold the carriage at the top of this slope; and that was exactly what they were doing.

George patted Diment's neck.

'Some scruffy ploughin' down there, my girls, eh?'

The voice came again, closer and more insistent.

'Unload! Unload!' A Captain appeared from the disturbed structure of a previously damaged trench. '…Unload, you men; into trench three here!'

Several soldiers appeared from that same trench and helped to carry the ammunition back into it. All munitions off, the delivery team were preparing, gratefully, to return down the hill.

The Captain halted all thoughts and actions on that particular front.

'Where d'you think you lot are going?'

George answered him.

'Sir?'

The Captain indicated a stack of boxes a short distance away.

'Gather up those report boxes and take them down with you, Private!'

'Yes, Sir!'

'Back to trench three the rest of you. Get those horses to pull out those collapsed supports; we'll need them ahead. My men will help…stack them by the remains of those pine trees!'

The other horsemen and various soldiers voiced as one.

'Yes, Sir!'

They split up to their various tasks.

George, singularly unhappy that the report boxes were closer to the action than he would otherwise have liked, moved his team forward and away from the cover. Heaving the last box onto his cart, a shell whined in…exploded to his left…massive…a direct hit on the rear portion of trench three and its recently stored ammunition.

Body parts, soil, wood, shrapnel…all were launched in every direction. George was thrown to the ground by the force of the explosion as stones and rocks from the shattered ground and slaps of munitions boxes zipped across the ground and showered the horses' heads and backs from on high. At the same instant, Diment kicked out hard as the half-inch, jagged metal spike stabbed into her haunch.

Jumping up, ears ringing, blood coming from his lower lip and forehead, George moved to Diment's side.

'Steady-On, lass, an' 'old tight.' To the sharp snort of Diment and with a deft flick of his bayonet, he dug in and removed the shrapnel, poured water from his flask onto his old, blue-and-white-spotted 'kerchief, and staunched the blood flow. 'Nothin' a dab o' this won't put right. Good lass.'

Pressing down on the 'kerchief and casting a glance around, George saw all six other horses had been scythed down, one of them still twitching in its death throes such was the suddenness and size of the blast. Their bodies had been the protective wall for George and his team; and not just horses. Eric's upper body and head lay across a horse's neck; of his legs there was no sign. A further look at the carnage told George that Sam and Daniel were missing too.

Another shell announced its arrival and intent, exploding slightly further down the hill. The faint voices of other men reached George now, some calling for action some calling for mothers, God or death to relieve them.

A movement beyond the dead horses and wrecked carts caught George's attention.

An arm?

A hand and arm…projecting through the soil… twitching?

No; waving?

Without thinking, George released his pressure on Diment's wound, the flow now dampened to ooze, and moved towards the hand's grim beckoning. Yet another incoming shell, whistling a permanent lullaby for some, dropped sixty yards further along trench three.

The Captain's voice cracked through George's fuddled senses.

'Get out! Get out of here you bloody idiot, they've got the range! Get those boxes down that hill!' George hesitated, the arm dropped limp, signalling its last farewell. 'Now, Private!' He released chains from cart and snatched a length of rope from off a stack of boxes nearby. The arm's last movement attracted the Captain's attention. He looked across, quickly realised what was about to happen and barked across. 'Soldier!'

Two further shells landed nearby and an enemy machine-gun opened up, the bullets raking the shattered trench three, their slaughterous cacophony drowning out anything further from the Captain. George kept on with his intention and called back.

'You sort them buggers out, you've got guns! I'll sort this lot out, I've got 'orses!'

Gathering up the reins, George clicked Diment and Clowdy down into a natural hollow near the bombed-in trench three and the now stationary hand and arm. A second enemy machine-gun joined its partner, and falling shells greedy for carrion now began to land at regular intervals. The Captain yelled out, 'Covering fire!' as he dropped back under some dubious shelter. Rapid return fire began as George and his team arrived in the base of the hollow which gave them all a modicum of shelter.

'Stand-On girls!'

Up the dip's slope to a carbine ovation, rope in hand, keeping low to the ground, he arrived at the remains of trench three, grabbing the limp limb as he did so. It reacted immediately to his contact, fastening round his hand like a gin-trap. George forced the hand free.

'You 'old on, Sam; just you 'old on.'

Clearing the soil with his bare hands, George dug deep into the soil. A dismembered hand, lacerated reins still gripped between death-frozen fingers, came to the surface. He sat back in surprise.

'Jesus Christ! Not some o' you, Sam? I bloody 'ope not!'

He pushed the hand to one side, looped the rope round the cleared timber then moved back to his horses with the loose end. In the dip, he tied the rope to their chains and wheeled the Shires round.

'Got t' show ourselves a bit now, girls. Let's 'ope that Captain's doin' 'is job.'

Halters in hand, George backed up the slope as he led them all into view. The chains tightened.

'Haul-On my girls, Haul-On!'

With impeccable timing, both Shires and man arrived at the top of the slope to be greeted by a shell landing close by. A previously blasted tree-trunk between impact point and emerging trio took the full brunt, the explosion's force splintering and shattering it, sending stabbing and hacking blades of wood and shrapnel in all directions. Several of these found their mark. Clowdy, the closer of the two horses to the tree, shied at the pain and surprise as she took a five-inch sliver of wood to the neck and several only slightly smaller ones to her flank and rear legs. George was blown over once again and the hoof of Diment's left-rear, whacked hard by a large, skipping-stone, was flicked away by its impact causing her to collapse to her knees, onto her side then back down the slope as a hailstorm of soil, rubble and stones rained down on the trio.

The sudden loss of Diment's strength on the pull, plus her weight moving backwards down the rain-drenched slope, now told on the precarious footing Clowdy had and she, too, began to slide backwards, her rear legs stretching out behind her in a graceful arc. The combined weight of both floundering Shires easily dragged George with them and, in a slow-motion toboggan, all three gently slid back to the base of the hollow.

George was back on his feet in a trice, ears ringing, stomach churning, legs shaking.

'Hie, Hup-Hup, Diment, Hup; Clowdy! Hup, girls!'

Both horses rose unsteadily and uncertainly, well covered in forest debris and soil. He tushed Clowdy then gently drew the splinter from her neck. Blood oozed and trickled out of the wound and George spat on it, amazed he could conjure up enough moisture. He pressed his already damp and bloodied 'kerchief to the wound in an effort to slow the bleeding. Red wheals were beginning to show on the grey's head from the stones that had hit, and mud plastered both horses' sides, chest and front legs.

George spoke as much to calm his own pulsating terror as theirs.

'Bloody 'ell, girls but that were close. We'll cold-tub that 'oof afore supper, Diment; that'll about cap your day. Right, let's get timber shifted an' the 'ell out 'f 'ere. My fault, girls, sorry. I'll shorten th' line; give us a bit more cover eh?' He released the pressure on Clowdy's neck. Blood continuing to trickle as he moved to the slackened line, unclipped chains, shortened them, then re-clipped. Back at their heads he grabbed the halters. 'This time, my girls.'

Once more they moved up the slope, taking in the slack. The noise from competing machine guns grew in intensity as he rose into view and the line tightened.

'Haul-On, girls! Haul-On!'

At his urging call they both strained to shift the dead-weight of timber and soil behind them. Releasing the halters, George ran to their rear and pulled on the chains too.

'Home-Home, my ladies! Home-Home!'

Hauling forward with extra force on the up-slope, Diment and Clowdy gradually dropped to their knees in their efforts. On the lip of the slope and the edge of defeat, their determination was rewarded. The timber slid rapidly out of the trench's collapsed-earth grip sending Diment and Clowdy staggering up and over the top, fast. Their speedy appearance over the crest lifted George off his feet, dragging him up the slope and along the ground for several feet before the horses could gain a steady foothold and control the initial surge of their release; all this activity transmitted itself back to the once-limp hand which flailed wildly once more.

'Stand-On! Stand-On, girls!' George stumbled and slipped to their heads. 'Back-Back! Back-Back!'

Backing down the now well-churned slope into the dip, George halted them and rushed back to the trench. More shells began to fall and increased enemy fire sent bullets cavorting off the uprooted timbers which were giving him some welcome cover. Grabbing the partially revealed, gesticulating arm, George heaved and the loosened soil finally released its grip.

With a mighty pull he disinterred the would-be corpse of Daniel. Spluttering and coughing his face clear of debris, he squealed out.

'Ahh! JesusChristAlmighty! Me leg, me bloody leg! Go easy!' Then he saw who had rescued him. 'Fuck! Go easy, Radcliffe!'

Despite these roared protests, George continued to roll Daniel back into the hollow of what was once trench three and out of machine gun's harm, the blood flow from Daniel's shattered leg staunched only by the soil that clogged it. They fetched up in the trench's dip, side-by-side.

'F'rget it, Long! Nothin' as 'appens now'll save it; that leg's buggered!'

'You 'ad t' remind me, eh, Radcliffe! Did y'think I'd f'rgot? Twat; an' you'll be waitin' a long time f'r thanks!'

'From you? I'd not expect nothin'!'

'Then you'll not be disappointed, will y'r?' Daniel grabbed his leg. 'Aaahhfuck that 'urts! Those bastards nearly killed me!'

George offered him his water-bottle.

'They're makin' 'n 'ash o' th' job is all I c'n say then, y'still breathin'. I were lookin' f'r Sam, if I'd've known it were you I'd've left y' there.' Daniel took a swig, flushed his mouth and spat the water into the soil. George snatched it back. 'Oi! Easy wi' that! I've wounded 'orses'll be glad 'f it!'

'Y' thoughtless bastard, Radcliffe! Y' want me t' swallow shit?'

'Why not? Y've been talkin' it f' years!'

Another two shells landed, shaking the ground in their brutal mining and enemy fire took an increasing interest in their position sending bullets, stone and soil skipping and dancing over their heads and forcing Daniel to disregard George's last remark.

'Fuck me, ain't there another battle they c'n be at? Aahhhh…!… Bugger me if that leg don't 'urt! Give us another drink, Radcliffe, I'm chokin'!'

George pushed the water bottle back into Daniel's hands.

'Good. 'Ere…' He moved rapidly away from the relative cover of the shattered timbers. '…Don't spit it free, don't lose that flask, an' don't go runnin' off neither.'

'Oi! Where the 'ell're you goin' Radcliffe? What th' fuck 'appens t' me if you get shot?'

George's voice floated back through the gunfire as he dropped down the dip.

'Y' die, Long, that's what!'

'You bastard…!'

Out of earshot of Daniel's invective, George reached his horses and rallied them.

'Hi-Back-Back, Clowdy, Diment! Hi-Back-Back!'

Diment and Clowdy reversed up the opposite slope a little. The tops of their rumps showed and Daniel saw them and called out.

'Now y' thinkin' Radcliffe; 'orses'll get us back th' sooner!'

'Stand-On Girls, Stand-On!'

George ran back past the horses, dropping just short of Daniel to quickly re-tie one end of the rope to the debris that was still embedded in the trench's remains. Daniel finally realised George was doing something other than prepare for their immediate, equine evacuation.

'What th' fuck're y' doin' Radcliffe?'

'There's others under 'ere somewhere; they need diggin' out too.'

'Fuck them! I'm free you're free; let's get th' fuck out 'f 'ere!'

'Your compassion overw'elms me, Long! Stay where y'are 'n' wait y' turn.'

'It is my fuckin' turn…! Rad…?' George was deafly and fully occupied with the task in hand. '…Radcliffe, Oi!'

Back in the dip, he led the two Shires forward up the opposite slope again.

'On-On, Girls!'

With horses half-way up the bank and encouraging them throughout, George ran back to the disturbed timbers as Diment and Clowdy continued to haul on free-rein. 'On-On, Girls! Haul-On!' He dropped down amongst the wooden supports and shattered woodwork, pushing and pulling with the horses. The unpinned planking moved a little easier; from under what would have been their graveyard soil but for the scrambled timber, a further two wounded soldiers emerged. George called to his team above the melee of exercising armament. 'Stand-On! Stand-On!' They did. 'Back-Back, Girls, Back-Back!' They did. 'Stand-On!' They did.

George gave a cursory inspection of the two coughing, spluttering soldiers.

'Can y' walk, either 'f y'r?'

Both soldiers, one whose teeth gleamed against his explosion-blackened face, showed signs of being dazed but coherent and obviously had no intention of staying put.

'Ar. Shoulder's not good but me legs'll carry me away from this lot.'

His mate added, 'If I 'ave t' bleedin' crawl.'

George began to gather them up.

'Well said.' He called to Daniel. 'Right, you stay where y'are, Long, I'll come back f' y'.' He indicated the group of abandoned and shattered carts. 'You two wi' me, off t' th' back o' them carts.'

Daniel could not believe it.

'What…? Oi, Radcliffe! 'Ow come I'm left be'ind? I'm wounded too!'

'Because they c'n walk an' I can't do three 'f y' at once, that's why! Now sit tight 'n' stop y' moanin'!'

'You bastard, Radcliffe! I were found first…I c'ld die 'ere!'

George lifted the one soldier to his feet. 'Y're only sayin' that t' cheer me up.' With that they left; the two wounded soldiers, one being supported by George, crawled, staggered and rolled their way over to the cover of the recently blasted carriages. Propping them both up, George made to leave. 'Two down, two t' go. Sit tight, both 'f y'.'

The fire-fight had maintained its intensity and now, as he scrambled and zigzagged his way back, George could have sworn he actually felt the wind from the bullets as they zipped past him, the staccato rattle of machine guns discharging their spite from both sides became deafening.

Daniel shifted his position as George approached him once more, eager for support and escape.

''Bout fuckin' time too!' Daniel's face fell and he flopped back under cover as George went straight past him and further into the bombed-out trench. 'F' fuck's sake…! Radcliffe…! Fuckin' 'ell, Radcliffe!'

George did not hear him. Apart from the noise of gunfire he was already scrabbling about in the shell-mined trench.

'Sam! Sam? Samuel! Where the 'ell…?'

The lower part of a leg and an arm protruding from the debris stopped him short. George gasped as he saw the solid gold wrist watch!

'Sam!'

Grabbing hold of both limbs, George heaved. With no body attached to them they came out the soil easily, suddenly, depositing him into a heap on the ground. For a couple of seconds he looked at the limbs then dropped the leg.

'Bloody 'ell, Sam.'

Scrambling up the slope of the disembowelled trench still holding the arm, George arrived at its top on his knees. After a long look, George placed the arm on the ground, almost reverentially, and began to move away.

In spite of his damaged leg, the danger, his pain and the noise, Daniel saw the watch on the dismembered arm. Rolling over to the limb, he grabbed it and relieved it of its jewellery.

Still somewhat dazed at the outcome of his supposed rescue mission, George saw this as if through a veil; then his eyes widened. A glance around the butchered remnants of the shell-disturbed trench revealed a discarded rifle and he rolled over to it. Snatching it up, he knelt and pointed it at Daniel.

'You put that watch down now, Long! Put it down or so 'elp me, I'll by-pass enemy 'n' shoot y' meself…'

Seeing the rifle but reckoning he was on safe ground, Daniel tried to brazen it out and folded the watch into his palm.

George reiterated the point.

'Now, Daniel!'

Daniel manoeuvred the watch towards his pocket.

'F' what? It's no use to 'im.'

George's voice was icy-cold and level.

'Y' know me well enough, Daniel. Put it down; now.'

'Oh, I see, you're th' new owner are y'?'

This was a serious misjudgement. He realised it when he saw the blood drain from George's face.

'Put…it…down…now, Long.'

The reality of what might be about to happen finally dawned on Daniel but, even in this predicament, he still tried to slither his way out of the impasse.

'Alright, alright, so not you, but…f'r Chrissake, Radcliffe, if I put it down some other bugger'll be along 'n' scoop it up…German pro'bly!'

'They've turned me into a lot 'f things, Long but I aint no grave-robber, an' I'd rather the Devil hiself got it th'n you.'

'Grave-robb…!...fuck me, Radcliffe, what you talkin' about? This aint no churchyard this is a fuckin' charnel'ouse.'

'That don't mean we stop doin' the right thing Daniel, an' if other folk had've done the right thing a few year ago we'd not be 'ere now, but we are...so, do you put it down and do we get out 'f 'ere, or do you 'old on to it an' I save meself th' carry?

The two men continued to hold their gaze, rifle and watch.

'An' shootin' me is the right thing t' do is it?'

'I'll live with it...shame you won't.' Daniel's jaw dropped as George slipped off the safety catch. 'Your choice, Daniel.'

'By fuck…you'd do it an' all, wouldn't y'?'

George's aim wavered not even fractionally.

'Some'ow, damned if I know 'ow but some'ow, I've got through this war so far without killin' anyone; never even fired a gun in anger... But if you never believe owt else, Long, believe that I will kill you.'

Daniel began to lower the watch to the ground.

'Alright, alright, I'm puttin' it down! Christ, it's only a fuckin' watch!' But the barrel of the rifle stayed trained on his head and a level of panic now entered Daniel's voice. 'Look! I'm puttin' it down, Radcliffe! Now put that bloody safety-catch back on!'

George's aim remained straight and steady until Daniel let go of the watch completely. George shuffled forward and flicked the watch further into the trench with his hand, the severed arm rolling after it. He looked at the parted companions then at Daniel.

'You pick it up again, Long, an' you'll not 'ear th' bang. Got that?'

George slipped the safety-catch back on and flipped the rifle's strap over his shoulder. He called Diment and Clowdy back as he re-entered the dip, moving round to their heads to check on their injuries and remove some of the splinters from Clowdy's flank.

'That neck'll need a poultice, lass; just be patient.' Shells began to land around them again and a torrential sleety-rain began to fall. George looked at the local carnage then up into the heavens. 'Ain't this bad enough f' y'?'

Looking down from the top of the dip, where he had now crawled in order to force a two-man retreat, Daniel's plaintive voice reached George.

'F'r fuck's sake, Radcliffe, get up 'ere 'n' 'elp me away! Y've found what's left 'f y' mate, now let's bugger off!'

More shells landed nearby as George moved alongside Daniel and lifted him to his feet in a single action.

'A way wi' words you 'ave, Daniel.'

With that, George half-carried, half-supported him to the other soldiers by the wrecked carts.

Just as suddenly as the intensive shelling and gunfire had started so it ceased, just the odd distant crackle of small arms fire punctuating the air.

Setting Daniel down, George winked at them all.

'No dancin' now you three.'

He left and Daniel grimaced at the other two.

'No, dancin! Jesus, me fuckin' leg's in three bits an' e' says no dancin'…? 'E's a funny fucker, ain't 'e, eh? Laugh a-fuckin' minute 'e is…bastard!'

George returned to Diment and Clowdy.

'Bit 'f a lull, girls, let's get out 'f 'ere an' fast!'

Out of the dip and over to the cart he had loaded earlier, he hitched up and took it past the injured soldiers to the deeper cover of the firs. Moving back, he organised them to leave.

'Right, Daniel, let's get you strapped up, patched up an' back in them trenches so's y'c'n get shot again, eh, an' by someone wi' a better aim next time?'

'Fuck you, Radcliffe.'

'An' a big thank-you t' you too.'

One of the soldiers frowned at George.

'You two in th' same unit?'

George lifted him up.

'No, just th' same war.'

Daniel's reply came back fast.

'Too close f'r me.'

'Mutual.'

With that, George helped all three across and onto the cart, Daniel needing the most support, and sheeted them over from the worst of the weather. The continuing lull in the gunfire allowed him a quick check of Clowdy's wounds and now he was ready for the off. It also allowed the Captain to leave his trench and move over to them. He was pleased to see all was ready for departure.

'Now will you fall back and get down that bloody hill, Private?'

George saluted.

'Yes, Sir, wi' pleasure, Sir.'

'And well done. A mighty brave thing you did, in spite of orders.'

'Orders, Sir? I 'eard no orders, Sir, nothin' above th' gunfire, Sir; otherwise I would've obeyed them, Sir.'

The Captain looked at him and smiled slightly.

'That so, horseman?'

'Yes, Sir!'

He looked at George's face.

'That lip's bad. Shrapnel?'

George realised his lip did indeed hurt, a lot.

'No, Sir. Clacked me teeth t'gether when that shell landed earlier; bit a chunk out 'f it.'

'Teach you to keep your mouth shut then, won't it? Get it seen to.'

'Yes, Sir.'

The Captain smiled, stroked Diment's head.

'Well done.'

George saluted.

'Thank you, Sir, just doin' my job.'

'Not you, you fool, the horses.'

'Yes, Sir, sorry, Sir.'

'Name and Number?'

George put his hand onto Clowdy's lowered nose.

''Orse 310816-6 Diment an' 'Orse 310816-5 Clowdy, Sir.'

'Not theirs, yours, idiot!'

'Yes Sir, sorry Sir. Private 41341 Radcliffe, sorry, Sir.'

'Right, Private 41341 Radcliffe, and Diment and Clowdy, I suggest you move back to base before you each catch your death...' He looked at Clowdy's wounds. '...Get those seen to as well; before yours.'

'Yes, Sir, I will, Sir; an' thank you f' th' coverin' fire.'

'Pleasure, Private Radcliffe; me just doing my job.'

They both smiled and saluted.

Away down the hill the firing opened up afresh and with devilish intensity. The Captain, after the briefest of hesitations, moved back through the rain to the savagery and his men.

George turned to Diment and Clowdy.

'Fine line between bravery 'n' madness, ladies. What you did were brave...' He indicated the fast disappearing Captain. '...Not sure which side 'e's on...nor us lot.'

The shelling picked up again and a volley landed a hundred yards further along the now empty trench three. Daniel's voice roared from under the sheeting.

'Come on 'orseman there's wounded folk in 'ere! D' we 'ave t' fuckin' walk back?'

George gathered the reins up.

'We'll make it t' base, you're all three safe, never worry.'

'They're not my worry, Radcliffe, I am…an' you c'n g' to 'ell!'

'We're there, Long, remember? Now shut y' face an' let me concentrate!' He flicked the reins. 'Haul-On, ladies, Haul-On!'

Under the canopy, Daniel began to sound off to the other soldiers.

'Let 'im concentrate? 'Ark at 'im…'

Both horses reacted to George's call and set off down the rutted tracks of Hill Twelve, leaving behind its continuing battle and taking with them a still cursing Daniel.

'…I'll give 'im fuckin' concentrate. 'E's only got t' steer 'orses t' base. What's th' bettin' 'e fucks that up so's 'e can rescue a flower or summat……!'

42

16.04.17

The view across the field of ploughing for Sarah, sat aloft Lizzie, was all encompassing.

Over the hedge, lapwings tottered across fresh-sprung barley to their carefully disguised nesting scrapes, and beyond, where a group of hares thumped out their differences by a far hedgerow, a pair of stretcher-bearer crows rasped out their judgement on each contest.

Emily called Lizzie to a halt and looked back at the furrow long and straight. She arched her back, pushing her knuckles into her sides and rolling her neck as she walked to Sarah. The days were full, no doubt about that.

She smiled up at her daughter.

'As wet as it's been, Sarah, that's as good a line of plough as any. Mustard's turned in a treat. What do you think, plough-girl, do you think Daddy would be pleased?'

Sarah cocked her head to one side and considered the point.

'We could ask him.'

'Not really, Sarah.'

Sarah considered this too.

'I could send God to tell him.'

Emily looked at what remained to be done.

'I suppose, but He's very busy these days, God, what with the war and all; just like us.'

This came as a surprise to Sarah and she took a while to assimilate it.

'Shall I stop asking Him things then, if He's busy?'

'No, no. You keep trying, Sarah.'

Emily patted Sarah's leg.

'Hold tight.' She collected the reins. 'On-On, Lizzie; On-On!'

43

08.08.17

'If Daddy's not here then why do we still make wobble, Mummy?'

At the sink, Sarah, on a low stool, and Emily were washing containers for that year's beer brewing.

'It isn't just Daddy who likes wobble, is it? Grandpa likes it too, remember, and we've always kept a few bottles back each year for when Daddy comes home, then he'll know what clever folk we've been, won't he?'

'Yes, Mummy. Clever aren't we?'

Nodding in agreement, Emily glanced up from the sink and out, through the kitchen window. At the far end of the track she could see a figure moving towards the farm.

A man's figure.

Whoever it was, he was limping…then she recognised Daniel Long.

Quickly wiping her hands on the cloth hanging over the sink, Emily lifted Sarah off the stool and patted her in the direction of the stairs.

'You go off to your room now, Sarah, tidy those dolls up. We'll finish this later.'

'Promise you won't do wobble without me, Mummy.'

'Promise, no wobble. Now, off you pop.'

Sarah skipped to the bottom of the stairs as Emily moved to answer the door-knock.

'Door, Mummy!'

'Yes, Sarah, I heard. Tidy those dolls.'

She opened the door on Daniel who stood with his weight on one leg, his arm resting on the porch's cover-support.

'Daniel. Didn't know you'd been returned.'

'No, Missus, well that's th' way 'f it. No one knows nor seems t' care neither. I'm lookin' f'r work 'n' I 'eard my old gaffer's not about.'

'Mister Arch? No, he died about eighteen months ago. He was ill for…'

'I know that, Missus, no point tryin' there; is there chance 'f a start 'ere?'

Emily raised her eyebrow a little.

'Ever the pragmatist…we've something of a history, Daniel, had you forgotten?'

He coughed.

'Ah-ha! Reformed character, Missus, war's seen t' that.'

Emily saw the need for stalling.

'Call back this afternoon and I'll let you know. I'll speak to Father.'

'What sort o' time, Missus?'

'About three. We'll be back from Grant's Meadow by then.'

—⁓—

At three o'clock on the dot, Daniel was back at the farm's kitchen door.

'Well, Missus?'

But he already knew the answer by Emily's expression.

'Father and I have discussed it, Daniel, and I'm afraid there's not to be work for you here; I'm sorry.'

'And why's that, Missus? Is it th' leg…or summat else?'

Placing her hand on the door and moving back inside fractionally, Emily hopefully conveyed her intention of bringing the conversation to a close.

'I don't wish to discuss that with you, Daniel. You've asked, been given consideration and an answer.'

'Some answer! Short 'n' sweet…'ail th' conq'rin' 'ero? Ha!'

'You've served your country, Daniel, and you've a right to be proud of that. I hope your experience has steadied your temperament and I'm sure you'll get fixed up soon, just not here.' Daniel continued to stand on the doorstep, a look in his eye that Emily recognised and found very disquieting. 'Look. I hear Mister Gray, new man at Broad Farm, he's on the look-out for staff. You know the land; why not give him a try?'

Daniel smirked at his victory.

'Ar, maybe. Y' don't like me much, do y', Missus?'

Emily saw the time for pleasantries had just passed.

'Goodbye, Daniel. Get across to Broad Farm, and if you get the start I hope you don't spoil it.'

Closing the door, she heard Daniel's rejoinder.

'How c'n y' spoil what's already ruined, Missus?'

She moved back to the window and watched him leave. It was Sarah's arrival back in the kitchen clutching a doll that broke the moment.

'Who was that, Mummy?'

'Oh, Sarah! That? Oh, no one; someone; a man, looking for work…'

'Did you find some?'

'No. No, Sarah, I didn't. What's the matter with dolly?'

'Her arm's twisted and I can't get it back.'

Emily went to the kitchen table and sat gratefully in a chair, beckoning Sarah to join her.

'Let's see what we can do for dolly then, shall we?'

—⁓—

Turning the corner into the yard, Edward almost collided with Daniel who quickly exploited the situation.

'Last person you expected t' see, I'll bet.'

Edward was horrified.

'Stay off from me, Daniel! You're bad lot an' give me t' trouble!'

'That right, stupid? I'll bet y' wished I'd copped it in France, eh? Well this ain't no ghost. I'm back.'

Edward looked nervously round the yard.

'Missus won't want bother.'

Daniel took a step towards him.

'Don't you try any o' y' tricks from be'ind th' Missus' apron wi' me y' dim-wit! She'll not stop me, an 'ero 'f th' battle-field, tellin' you, a coward o' th' barley-field what's what.'

Edward choked at the reminder.

'I tried t' do war, I did! They'd not take me!'

'No, they wouldn't take y'r. Know why? Because y' too stupid, that's why! T' think I fought f' your safety, an' you, y' just slunk back 'ere an' took th' jobs. Christ, I spiked mules as deserved t' live better 'n you.'

Discursive abilities at an end, Edward could only repeat.

'War wouldn't take me, Daniel!'

Daniel moved in very close to Edward's face.

'Well I'll take y'r, y' thick little shit, I'll take y' into th' Forty-Acre an' 'ang y' from one o' them elm trees by a white sheet if y' so much as cross my path again. Understood?'

Out of arguments and courage, Edward tried to by-pass Daniel but was grabbed by the lapels, twisted round and had Daniel's arm wrapped round his neck before he could call out. Daniel tightened his grip and stretched back his jacket sleeve to reveal a solid gold wrist watch which he pressed into Edward's face.

'See that? Look at it!' Edward tried to twist his head away only to have it forced back by Daniel. 'Look at it y' stupid fucker!' He now enunciated slowly, for maximum effect. 'It belonged to a German; I killed 'im f'r it. Crep' up on 'im an' slit 'is fuckin' throat, took th' watch while 'e were still twitchin', still…bleedin'. Like 'im, y'll never 'ear me comin'. I can get t' you an' that bitch 'f a mistress o' yours any time I like. Don't you never f'get that!'

What little resolve Edward might have had now gave way as the spectre Daniel conjured up invaded his imagination.

'Stop, Daniel, stop! Th' Missus…'

'An' you shut y' mouth, y' moron! She may think she's boss o' th' county but she's just another snob who needs t' be brought down a peg 'r two, an' it'll not come fr'm cowards such as you!'

Edward was now beside himself with panic.

'Leave 'er, Daniel…she's good t' me!'

'Yes, I'll bet she is; 'er likes 'em stupid.' Daniel twisted Edward back round to face him. 'Get where y' belong!' With that, he punched Edward hard in the midriff.

Well winded, Edward stumbled gasping, floundering into the muck pile as Daniel limped off through the gate.

'No work, eh? We'll see some fuckin' work yet!'

17.09.17

Just outside of Zillebeke is a part-destroyed farm whose yard cobbles may still bear the scar where Diment scraped her foot.

Standing at attention and in full military dress, George turned slightly and rattled her reins, remaining at attention as he whispered to her.

'Shush, Diment. Stand-On.'

Long periods of idleness were never a favourite pastime for Diment or Clowdy, not for George either. After an interminable wait the Captain entered the yard and approached George.

They saluted.

'At ease. Well done, 41341 Radcliffe.'

He pinned the Military Medal to George's chest and they saluted again, and then moved along to Diment and Clowdy. To George's surprise, onto each horse's bridle next to the regimental cap badge, he fixed a small silver star.

'Sir? That's a general's star…but…?'

'Goes with the cap badges…wherever you got those from.'

'Found 'em, Sir.'

'Yes, in common with the rest of the British army, I have no doubt; they must be spread about like daisies. Do you not think they deserve the recognition?'

'Yes, Sir. More so th'n me, Sir.'

'And I agree with you, that's why they've got them and you haven't, and why I called in a favour or two for that very reason; understand?'

'Sir.'

'Their names are on the back, got a local chap to scratch it on; the same one you men use for your sweetheart buttons, I'd suggest?'

'Names, Sir?'

'Yes…Diment and Clowdy wasn't it?'

'Er…yes, Sir.'

'Surprised I'd have the brains to remember, me being a chinless toff?'

'I'd not say that Sir! I'm sure y'got t' where y'got through merit an' not through fam'ly connections…not that th' thought ever entered…just…'

'Stop digging, Lance Corporal Radcliffe and keep them safe; medals and horses. Those two are the best friends you'll ever have.'

'Yes, Sir, I know; we're a team.'

'Are you? Well, you deserve them but I'm not so sure they deserve you.'

'No, Sir.' Stepping back the Captain saluted again and George snapped to attention and returned it. 'An' thank you, Sir, fr'm all 'f us.'

Clowdy snorted, loudly and Diment rapped the cobbles again.

The Captain patted Diment's neck.

'That your view of proceedings then?'

'Not used t' standin' still f'r so long, Sir. Like t' be busy…'ard t' stop most times…well…as y' know y'rself, Sir. Apologies.'

The Captain smiled again.

'Accepted. Well done, all three of you. Right, service rest over, back to it.'

George saluted again and Diment rattled her harness.

- 45 -

28.09.17

Dispatch riders attract attention, even in towns. Out in the sticks of Allingham they would stir up a veritable whirlwind of comment.

This particular dispatch rider was so early however that, even as he swung into the yard of Shirley Lodge, removed his gloves and took the envelope from inside his shoulder-bag, so the two farm cockerels were still announcing their intent and suitability to all in hen-county.

Up half-an-hour before first light as usual, Emily knew of his imminent arrival long before it happened and had spent the several minutes awaiting his appearance with her heart firmly lodged in her throat. She anticipated his knock and opened the door.

Her outward sigh at the sight of the buff envelope and the dispatch rider's smile was audible.

'Thank you.'

'That's my pleasure, Mrs Radcliffe.'

And he meant it too.

Closing the door to the sound of the departing motorbike, Emily went to Sarah's bedroom and gently roused her.

'Sarah…Letter…Military letter…from Daddy.'

A sleepy Sarah slipped on her dressing gown, grabbed a doll and followed her mother into the kitchen, where Emily read the contents of the telegram out loud.

'LANCE CORPORAL GR RADCLIFFE ALLINGHAM LEICESTERSHIRE STOP AWARDED MILITARY MEDAL STOP CONGRATULATIONS STOP'

Sarah stood silent for a moment then rubbed her eyes.

'Is Daddy coming home now, Mummy?'

Scooping a towel off the stove, Emily gathered Sarah into its warmth, cuddling her close.

'Not just yet, Sarah. He's very busy at the moment, but he's been a very good boy and the army people have written to tell us that he's been very brave.'

'Like me when Diment and Clowdy went to war?'

'Just like you, Sarah, yes. We're Radcliffes aren't we?'

'Yes, and he's a daddy Radcliffe.'

'Yes, he is, only now he's got a Military Medal, that's an M.M., Sarah. That's very important.'

Sarah yawned and considered this.

'Daddy Radcliffe em-em. Is that his prize for being brave?'

'Yes, and it makes him a very important person, sleepy-head.'

'Will he be too important to remember me?'

Emily held Sarah out at arm's length.

'Oh, no, Sarah. That's why he's been very brave; for you.'

Sarah snuggled back into the towel and Emily's arms.

'And for you, Mummy.'

'Yes, for both of us.'

They hugged silently. After a short pause Sarah spoke from within the towel.

'Is Edward a Radcliffe?'

'No, Sarah, why?'

''Cause he was very brave when Diment and Clowdy went to war too, wasn't he?'

'Yes. He was.'

Sarah lifted her head out of the towel.

'Do you think Diment and Clowdy are being brave too?'

'Wherever they are, Sarah, they're being very brave, don't you think?'

'We're being very brave too, aren't we, doing all the work? We're all being brave… Can I have a prize too?'

Emily smiled at her.

'You've got your prize, haven't you, and Daddy to look forward to when he gets home. That's enough for anyone, don't you think?'

'Yes, but I'll have to share.'

'Well, that's a good thing, isn't it?'

'Yes,' holding the arms of her doll she turned it over and over, 'but couldn't I have my own prize as well, like Daddy em-em?'

'That's how dolly's arms get broken, Sarah…'

'Couldn't I, Mummy?'

Emily considered this for a moment.

'I'll make you your own medal. How would that be?'

She pulled away from Emily in her excitement.

'Yes, please, then Daddy will know I've been brave!'

Emily gathered her up again.

'Yes he will…and yes you have.'

46

11.10.17

The temperature had dropped sharply and now it felt like a good frost was in the offing.

In the stables, however, the grooming and clearing of Lizzie and her stall had warmed Emily up and she had discarded her top-coat. In open waistcoat and shirt sleeves, Emily bent over the edge of the feed barrel to scoop out Lizzie's evening bait.

'I see y' still strugglin' wi' the 'orse work then?'

Pulling herself out very quickly, Emily exchanged bucket for barrel lid. Annoyance fuelled her surprise. By the look on his face, Daniel had been there for a few seconds before speaking. She instinctively pulled her waistcoat closed.

'Daniel! What are you doing here? What do you want?'

He smirked at her discomfort.

'Old man Gray sent me over, wants t' know if 'e c'n 'ave a lend 'f th' disc-'arrow t'morrow, break that ploughin' down on Langley's Field.'

Fastening the waistcoat buttons was Emily's displacement activity.

'You're with Mister Gray then? I'd heard you'd got in there…staff shortages must be biting hard.'

'War's got most, dead 'r alive. What's about's women now; took all th' jobs 'f us men…an' makin' a mess 'f it f'r their pains too. Disc-'arrow?'

'Yes, of course. Tell him I'll drop it by.'

'Don't trouble y'rself; we're a long way up th' valley.' Daniel smirked. 'I'll collect it.'

Now recovered sufficiently, Emily wrestled the conversation back to her satisfaction.

'I said I'll drop it by, Daniel, thank you.'

Lizzie was standing in her stall still patiently awaiting her evening feed, and Daniel pointed at her.

'Wi' what, that nag? I 'ad 'er at Arch's an' she were useless then! She's about fit f'r th' knacker that one.'

Emily was fully focused on the conversation now.

'Your answer to every horse ailment, Daniel, from strangles to a stone in the hoof. Now, if that's all….'

'Who says so?'

'Me for one, George for another; the only other I need to ask, now, if…'

'Not about now though, is 'e? War's still got 'im; see what I mean?'

'Here or not, in life as well as livestock he's far and above your master, Daniel. Now…if that's all you came for, can you leave and I can get on.'

'Think you've got all the answers, don't y'?'

'Daniel…'

'Well I'll tell y' summat y'don't know…I saw y' precious George…in France.'

Emily sucked in her breath at this revelation.

'You saw George!' Then she saw beyond it and shut down. 'Why? Why are you saying this?'

Seeing the effect pleased Daniel and he filled out the picture.

'Saw 'im in France, diggin' f'r favours in trenches full o' dead men.'

'How dare you, Daniel! How dare you say that to me! Get out right now and don't come back, sober or civil!'

'Ha! Is that what y'think this all about? Fuckin' 'ell! It's not th' drink, lady! Th' job I've got wi' old man Gray leaves me precious little money nor time f'r that, nor no lack o' civility. You've no idea what goes on over there, 'ave y'…eh…?' Seeing the shift in Daniel's face, Emily took half a step backwards, lifting the feed-bin lid further as his rant continued, '…None! Sat back 'ere in comfort 'n' warmth talkin' about y' darlin' 'usband, y' simple workers dotin' on y' beck 'n' call. An' 'im, y'r precious, stupid 'usband? 'E takes too many risks; 'e'll only be 'ome in a fuckin' telegram!'

Daniel's rage was building and Emily scanned the area for escape and moved to put the feed barrel between her and him.

'Get out, Daniel! Get out, now!'

Daniel spat on the floor.

'Don't fret y'rself, I'm goin'. T'night I do need a drink, t' wash away th' taste 'f y'r ign'rance.'

He left the stable, slamming the door as he went. The catch missed and the door shook and rattled in its freedom, echoing Emily's shocked and unsteady stance.

She was angry now. Angry at herself and how she had let the situation and the imagery conjured up by Daniel take her over. She rapped the lid back onto the feed barrel. Grabbing her jacket and fiercely wiping her eyes on its sleeve, she moved toward the stable's door to close it properly. As she reached it the door burst open, cracking her on the forehead as Daniel barged through it.

Grabbing Emily round the throat, his rage lending him extra strength, he pushed her brutally back in amongst the tools and feed barrels, upsetting one in the process. Her foot caught on the dragging jacket unbalancing her further and only serving to assist Daniel as he forced Emily back onto this overturned barrel.

Ripping open her waistcoat and shirt front, screaming in her face, he grappled with her clothing.

'Master o' me! I'll show 'ow much a master 'f me 'e is, Missus! I should've done this six year ago!'

'Daniel…please!'

Daniel's reply was to slap her viciously across the face.

Forehand! Backhand!

Then he flipped her over onto her stomach. His close, short punch entered Emily's right side deep, hard, brutal, leaving her gasping for breath…then a second. He leant over and spittled into her ear.

'Now you concentrate on that m'lady, an' I'll take what's mine.'

His forearm across the back of her neck, he forced her head downwards and, snatching at her waistband, he pulled down her trousers and camisole knickers in one movement such was his rage. Unbuttoning his trouser-fly he forced his erection into Emily, causing her to squeal loudly at the pain…

The click of the latch a minute later registered with Daniel, forewarning him of someone else arriving on the scene.

'Missus…?'

Pulling quickly out of Emily, Daniel pushed his now slack manhood back into his trousers.

'…What y' doin' wi' th' Missus, Daniel?

Daniel was over and immediately onto Edward with his drawn knife, pushing him very firmly back against an aisle pillar. Still gasping from the blows to her kidney, Emily slid down the barrel to the floor.

Up very close, Daniel laid out the details.

'Now you listen t' me, y' stupid fucker! Y' saw nor'eard nothin', understand? If you so much as breathe a word o' this to a livin' soul, I'll deny all, denounce y' f'r th' simpleton everyone knows y'are an' slit y' fuck-in' throat in th' night…!...'

Daniel's speech was cut short as the spade struck him across the back of the head. He fell to the floor as if he had been pole-axed, the dropped knife somersaulting across the floor in its freedom as Emily followed up her first blow with two more. As she lifted the spade for a further hit, so Edward snatched it from her and Daniel's body convulsed to the rhythm of his four fast blows….

And eventually twitched… … ..

To stillness.

The immediate silence was broken by the scrape of Lizzie's hoof.

Her forehead and gashed lip still bleeding, her side throbbing, Emily drew in courage through one deep breath. She moved to the doorway and looked out; all clear. Thinking on her feet now, she looked across the yard then turned back to Edward.

'We've to get him over to that muck-heap, now.'

'Muck-'eap, Missus?'

'Yes, the far end, the well-rotted.'

'Yes, Missus…carry 'im.'

'No, we'll get blood over us and everywhere, there's enough as it is…and I don't think I could carry him right now, even with your help. No, we need….' she caught sight of one of the large barley sacks, '…that sack and a rope; you get the sack, I'll get the rope.'

She moved to fetch it, hastily adjusting her trousers as the button on one side of the waistband was missing, then together and in a single movement they rolled Daniel's corpse face down onto the sack, folded the sack's two corners over his ankles and tied all together with the rope. Emily pointed.

'To the door, Edward.'

Taking hold of the feet they dragged Daniel's body closer to the yard door. Another glance outside confirmed continued lack of company and Emily gingerly collected the dropped knife and pocketed it.

'We'll be needing that, now you wait here.'

She crossed the yard, uncoiling the rope as she went until she reached the base of the muck-heap, then hissed across to the shadowy form standing by the half-open doorway.

'Pull the bottom door wide and come over here!' Edward joined her. 'We need to listen out as we get him across; I'll cut off visitors…that's the last thing we want right now.'

'Yes, Missus, don't want no 'elp 'ere.'

'None.'

They both took hold of the rope and hauled on it hand-over-hand. In the stables, Daniel's body jerked away and his left arm slid off the sacking to trail behind, his whitening knuckles skipping and bouncing over the stable's rough stone-floor; his late request to leave the room.

A noise from the direction of Henry's farmhouse stopped them, Emily's breath coming out in short, controlled gasps. After a few moments they heard a door close and looked at each other, Emily letting go a deep sigh of relief.

'Let's get this done, Edward; come on!'

They hauled with extra effort now and, as the body emerged fully from the stable, so the trailing arm scraped along the space between ill-fitting door frame and cobbled stable floor…

…Emily and Edward continued to pull…

…the wrist watch jammed…was stripped free of its transport and fixed, deeply, firmly, into the gap.

At the muck heap and to Edward's inward gasp, Emily took out the knife and stabbed three punctures into Daniel's stomach with it.

'We both know what happens to pigs in hot muck heaps if their belly's aren't stuck, don't we, Edward?'

'Yes, Missus. Bang!'

'Right, Edward. Bang! And everyone will know what's what then; don't want that to happen, do we?' Without waiting for a reply, Emily walked quickly along the muck-heap and grabbed two forks that were jammed in it. Back to him, she handed one to Edward and climbed the heap. 'Up here! Dig!'

Following Emily, Edward helped her dig a trench near the summit of the huge steaming pile then between them, and with some effort, they dragged up Daniel's body, untied the rope and inserted corpse, barley sack and knife into the makeshift grave.

'Just a sprinkling, Edward. Let's get those blowflies to do a bit of the work.' They covered the body with a light top-dressing of the rotting muck. 'I'll come back up in a couple of days and refill it; eggs will be well on the way by then.'

Edward looked at her alarmed.

'But, Misses...folk t' see!'

'What, up here? Whoever would want to climb up to the top of our muck-heap, Edward? It's well hidden now and I'll make sure I leave it no longer than two days.'

'Yes, Missus.'

Down on the cobbled yard, she gave the forks to Edward.

'Push those back into the heap where they came from, then get me some buckets of water.' She began re-coiling the rope and Edward came back empty-handed and stood watching. 'Buckets of water, Edward, from the stables!' On his return Emily swapped rope for full buckets. 'Now that back too, feed stall, by Lizzie's harness; Lizzie's harness.'

Edward returned to the stables as, with bass-broom, pail and water, Emily began sluicing and scrubbing the line of Daniel's last journey. Edward now joined her to help, and it was only when they were back in the stables and had emptied the last bucket of soiled water down the drain that he spoke again.

'We killed-ed him, Missus. 'E's dead an' we killed-ed 'im!'

Emily put her hand onto Edward's shoulder.

'And if not, what then?'

He thought for a moment.

'Kills us, Missus?'

'Exactly. We'll not tell on each other because we're both guilty, but only guilty of ridding this earth of a scoundrel and a bully…and you've not seen Daniel for weeks, understand?'

'Yes, Missus?'

Emily forced the point home.

'Not…for…weeks.'

Edward cottoned on.

'Yes, Missus; weeks.'

The adrenaline Emily had been operating on finally gave out. Like a paper plane running out of breeze, she slumped slowly and gracefully to the floor.

Edward was in a panic, but she reassured him.

'Out of breath a bit, Edward, just the shock. Give me a few minutes and I'll be alright. Tell you what, let me just stay here for a while and get my breath. Can you feed Lizzie for me, if you will? She must be starving.'

Glad of the distraction, Edward nodded.

'Yes, Missus.' He began to walk away, then turned and smiled. 'Weeks, Missus; now never.'

Emily smiled weakly back.

'Yes, Edward, now never.'

With the yard to herself, she drew in deep breaths to concentrate her challenge to the pain and her realisation of the events. After a few minutes, she stood up using the wall as support and followed its line to the yard's spring and trough. Gently she knelt and, clenching her teeth in expectation, dunked her head into the trough that held the spring's fresh, clean, cold pool. The water was October temperature. With her face under the surface, her shoulders flexed and her stomach contracted with the initial shock. She snatched her head out quickly at the intensity of the pain.

She knelt there, totally unable to do anything else other than pant.

Eventually she took her 'kerchief out, dipped it into the trough and began to gently wipe the wetted blood from off her face. Her lip felt as big as a horse-collar and had sealed tight with the water's cold, but her gentle rubbing had caused the cut on her forehead to reopen. After dabbing up the excess, Emily breathed in deeply and plunged her head back into the trough. She held her face under for as long as breath would allow, the bitter cold of the water shrinking the cuts and numbing her face in seconds. Pulling her head out of the water and panting for air once more, Emily hung her head as the moon-lit, rose-coloured water ran off her face and out of her hair.

She'd present a strange sight to anyone entering the yard, kneeling as if in prayer at the side of the trough, her head drooping and dripping, so she forced herself to move. Both hands on the trough's side, she raised herself up. After three or four deep breaths, as deep as her side would allow, she used the wall for support once more and limped into the stables.

The skewbald Shire dropped her head over the stall door in greeting.

'Hello, Lizzie, soon be at trough, lass…'

That comment drained her of all strength. She made it to the far end of the stables and sat gratefully onto an upturned bucket, her breathing coming in short shallow gasps as, through clouded eyes, she watched Edward feeding Lizzie.

—◦◦◦—

After she and Edward parted company that night, Emily had travelled from stables to cottage and not known how. One minute she was gritting her teeth, closing the stable door, gauging the distance to get home; the next she was leaning, gasping on the architrave in the hall, blinking back the shooting pains in her side.

The silence was piercing.

It took Emily by surprise, this utter quiet; then she remembered; Sarah was spending the night at grandpa's house. Her initial reaction of disappointment gave way to gratitude at not having to face their enquiries concerning her wet, breathless and bruised state. After that walk home it would have been too much to bear.

Once inside the closed-door cottage, Emily attempted to clean herself up with flannel and soap. Taking off trousers and knickers, she opened the range and threw her soiled undergarment onto the embers. Opening the tap, she part-filled the sink and began to wash, but the combination of balance, cold water and pain quickly had its effects on her breathing, forcing Emily to stop and grab hold of the cold tap for balance. Her grip tightened; she looked at her white knuckles…the tap…and, to dripping-water background, she stood at the sink, towel to face, and wept…and wept…

Tears of frustration changed to tears of grim determination as she called herself to account and completed her ablutions, but even this simple task left her not only breathless but also completely exhausted.

Unwilling to turn the pain-mangle any more than was absolutely necessary, she put on clean knickers and slipped under the eiderdown, partially clothed, to lay panting, staring into her starless ceiling.

No sleep was granted her that night for now the pain in her side had time and space to gain her full attention; it made the most of it.

47

12.10.17

After two hours of painful restlessness, Emily decided to get up and take a long and very hot bath.

Stoking and re-building the range's fire was a real challenge to her determination. Once it was fully alight and by some deft balancing, she was able to transfer some of its coals to the parlour fireplace where she built a second fire, using them as the base. Moving four buckets of freshly drawn water from sink to range, dragging the large tub in front of the parlour fire and transferring boiling water from range-top to tub made her wince further; her lungs grab at air. Several times she had to stop, but refusing to make room for tears and with full concentration on the job in hand, she managed, finally, to get sufficient water into the bath.

Slipping off her waistcoat, shirt and bodice-slip was fine; it was the final item of clothing, her knickers, which caused the still moment. As they dropped to her ankles their crumpled state caught Emily completely off-guard. Standing in that deserted fire-lit parlour at the edge of that tin bath, naked and fearful, suddenly and with no warning she could not stop shaking and, for a moment or two, was convinced death would swiftly follow.

It was only when she caught sight, in the parlour mirror, of the bruising to her side, its rainbow discolouration and size, that her pain was given understanding. The shaking fit slowed. Her determined reasoning that the thumping in her chest was not the knocking of death but the result of delayed shock adjusted her panic to logic and stopped her falling to the floor in a dead swoon.

When her breathing and self-control were fully restored, she flipped the knickers to one side with her foot and gently stepped forward into the tub, sinking gratefully into the water's embrace…

To answer her father's initial question and concern, Emily made up a part-true tale about a quarrel with a horse and a stable door. She changed the subject as soon as possible, assuring all that she was fine and telling Henry and Sarah how she intended to get the wheat she normally reserved for home-use milled early this year, 'Probably as early as next week'. Stretching the discussion beyond interest and through Sarah's yawned responses, she talked them both through the levels of grinding she wanted for the various amounts of wheat and how she would use the various types… This ploy lasted throughout breakfast and, after giving further assurances that all was well, she left Sarah in her father's capable care and went out into the yard to start the morning's chores with not a little trepidation.

Everything had to appear as normal; for Sarah, for her father, for the world in general.

- 48 -

20·10·17

As the days moved on, Emily's ability to cope with the pain was helped by the time of year.

The approach of winter meant there was a natural slow-down in the demands of the farm, so she was able to reduce her own, usually prodigious workload out of respect for her aching side without it drawing undue attention.

On this Saturday, Emily announced to Henry and Sarah that she intended to take a little time out for her and her daughter and had arranged the day accordingly. She had been in the corn barn for ten or so minutes that morning when Edward arrived.

'Mornin', Missus.'

'Good morning, Edward, early again, I see.'

'Yes, Missus?'

'Your start-time is seven-thirty.'

He smiled at her.

'Yes, Missus.'

'It's only seven.'

'Yes, Missus.'

She shook her head and smiled at him.

'Never mind. Not too much to get done today, eh? Take it just a little easy shall we, so no horse-work and an early finish.'

'Yes, Missus, easy.'

'Right, I'm going to sweep out and tidy the corn barn. Take a scythe and trim those thistles in the far corner of Castle Meadow; the goldfinches have stripped them now and they just look a mess.'

'Yes, Missus, scythe thistles at meadow…'

'Castle Meadow.'

'Castle Meadow, Missus.'

'Right; then come back here and fill the twenty small sacks with wheat from the large pen.' She held up one of them. 'These sacks. I've laid them out ready, over there. Tuck this one in your belt then you'll have a reminder.' She handed it to Edward. He unbuttoned his top coat, untucked his knitted waistcoat from his trousers and pushed the sack into his waist-band and belt.

'Fill sacks, yes, Missus.'

He began to re-tuck his waistcoat and button his jacket.

'Yes, then take the full sacks and stack them under the lean-to at the back of father's house. You know the lean-to?'

'Yes, Missus. Wheat at Mister 'Enry's.'

'Where, Edward?'

'Mister 'Enry's lean-to, Missus?'

'You're on the bridle today, Edward, well done! Mister Henry will be taking the wheat to the mill tomorrow for grinding. I'm baking new season's bread on Wednesday for us, some for your mother too.'

'New bread f'r Ma; yes Missus.'

Blinking a couple of times, Edward stared at Emily without moving.

'So, it's thistles scythed in Castle Meadow and corn to Mister Henry's. Got that?'

'Yes, Missus. Thistles cut an' sacks t' Mister 'Enry.'

'Then it'll be lunch.'

'Yes, Missus.'

'And no need to hurry back after lunch.'

'No 'urry, Missus?'

'No, Edward; you go home for a long lunch eh? Tell your mother you're not wanted here again until two o'clock.'

'Two o'clock.'

'And tell her this time. You forgot about the late start on Monday, didn't you?'

Edward thought for a moment or two, then looked expressionlessly at Emily.

'Don't remember, Missus.'

'No, I know that, Edward. You turned up here an hour before Monday's start-time; too early.'

'Yes, Missus, too early.'

'Didn't you realise it was still dark when you left home?'

'Don't remember, Missus.'

'No, I know. Well this time, tell your mother.'

'Yes, Missus.'

'Then when you do get back, at two o'clock, we'll have a go at Lizzie's coat. She looks like a used hayrick.'

Edward laughed at this.

'Yes, Missus; used 'ayrick.'

'She does. So, concentrate now, Edward. Thistles. Wheat. Then lunch until two o'clock, right?'

'Yes, Missus.'

'I'll let Father know about the wheat and tell him to put the kettle on for ten; I'll give you a call, eh?'

Edward smiled again.

'Yes, Missus, f' tea.'

'Thought you'd need no reminder about tea.'

Edward grinned.

'No, Missus. Tea.'

The thought struck Emily and she muttered to herself.

'I'll get him to cut a slice of boiled fruit cake too…'

'Yes, Missus. Fruit cake.'

Emily laughed.

'Tea and cake. Two words you never fail to remember. Off you go, Edward, tea at ten and I'll see you at two o'clock for Lizzie. Tell your mother, right?'

'Yes, Missus, two o'clock for Lizzie…' He smiled at her as he left the barn. 'After tea 'n' cake.'

Emily followed him, calling out as she did so.

'And scything thistles and bagging wheat!'

'Yes, Missus, then tea 'n' cake.'

She watched as he collected the scythe and headed out to the meadow, knowing full well he would forget at least one thing by lunchtime.

Into the corn barn, Emily set about the cleaning, but using the bass-broom on walls and floor soon began to tell. It was with some relief that midday arrived. She had not seen Edward since ten so, after ascertaining he had left for home, Emily made her excuses from lunch and returned to the corn barn. By sipping spring water and sitting quietly in the barn, she eventually felt sufficiently in control to do a little light work again, 'But out in the yard,' she thought, 'in the sharp autumn air.'

—⁓—

'Christ, they live like their animals out here! Is there no other way round?'

'Yes, Sir, at th' back o' th' stables, off that field, that one wi' bull in it.'

Detective Sergeant Edson Garrard, young, fresh-faced and very intense, eyed the alternative route proffered by Constable Graham Ferris, the size of the animal and shook his head.

'No, thank you, Constable, this is bad enough.'

Picking his pathway, D.S. Garrard, Constable Ferris just behind him, endeavoured to enter the stable yard by not touching the ground with his well-polished brown brogues. His exaggerated progress presented an amusing site to Emily, piling fresh stable cleanings from wheelbarrow to huge, steaming manure heap. In an effort to cover his discomfort, D.S. Garrard began talking some distance away.

'Afternoon Miss?'

Although she recognised the Constable, Emily was immediately on her guard concerning the stranger.

'Good afternoon…and it's Mrs.'

'Beg your pardon, Mrs…?'

The Constable joined in.

'Well it were Carter, weren't it? Emily Carter?'

'Yes it was, Constable Graham Ferris.'

'Now Mrs Emily Radcliffe?'

Emily smiled at him.

'Guilty.'

Constable Ferris smiled broadly back and D.S. Garrard looked at them both.

'You two know each other?'

Emily nodded.

'We do.'

D.S. Garrard shook his head.

'Everybody knows everybody else. As thick as thieves out here, you lot are.'

Emily looked at him.

'We were at school together.'

Constable Ferris laughed.

'An' a little toughie y'were back then an' all.'

Emily smiled.

'There's a back-handed compliment if ever there was one.'

'It is too, Mrs Radcliffe!'

He indicated the man with him.

'This is our new Sergeant, sorry, Detective Sergeant, so 'e'll not know the 'ist'ry…'

'Constable?'

'…When I were first got t' school, Sir, she were what, third year? I were first an' shy as a nun. Big boys gave me trouble; Emily 'ere, Mrs Radcliffe, took me under 'er wing…'

'Constable!'

'…I considered us t' be sweet'earts from then on, y' know? Devastated when I 'eard you was married! Our Mary told us. Was only when I found out it were t' George Radcliffe that it were made alright…sort of…'

D.S. Garrard cut in.

'Constable…! As pleased as I am to have effected your reunion!' He turned back to Emily. 'Now, Mrs Radcliffe, I believe you have a friendship with a Mister Long; Daniel Long?'

Picking up the introduction of authority into the conversation, Emily reacted accordingly.

'No, Sergeant.'

'You deny that you know him?'

'No, Sergeant, I do know him but not as a friend, just a casual labourer who had some involvement with the farm several years ago.' Henry entered the yard. 'Ah, Father, these two officers want a word, about Daniel Long.'

Henry strode across to them.

'Daniel? Is something wrong?' He saw the Constable. 'Ah, Graham Ferris! Haven't seen you in many a year, how are you?' Henry and Constable Ferris shook hands as Henry continued, 'Heard you did some good work a few months back, over those poachers on Lord Ardingley's estate?'

'Yes, Mister Carter, we got lucky I s'pose, an' lucky we didn't get shot too!'

'I heard Godfrey Musto's lad was involved.'

'Ar. We let 'im off wi a caution though; 'e's barely thirteen…'

D.S. Garrard talked over their greeting.

'That was months ago, Constable!' He turned towards Henry. 'We're interested in right now, Sir. A little matter of Mister Long's whereabouts, Mister Carter, is it?'

Henry held out his hand and they shook.

'Yes, I'm Henry Carter. You are?'

'Detective Sergeant Garrard, Mister Carter.'

'Pleasure to meet you, Sergeant Garrard.' He looked across at Emily. 'Do you want lunch, Emily? I was about to feed Sarah and…'

'If lunch could just wait until I've asked a few questions, Mister Carter, I'd be extremely grateful. This is official business…and it's Detective Sergeant Garrard, Sir.' He paused for effect, then continued, 'Now, Mrs Radcliffe, can you tell me when you last saw Mister Long?'

Emily looked at Constable Ferris.

'What's this about?'

'Just some stolen silver from The Grapes, Emily, Mrs Radcliffe, Friday fortnight past. Now both silver an' thief 'ave gone.'

D.S. Garrard cut in.

'Yes, thank you, Constable! That's police business, not for ordinary folk! I believe he came here looking for work when he was returned from the forces, Mrs Radcliffe, and that you sent him on to Mister Gray's. Is that right?'

'Yes, that's correct.'

'You didn't want to set him on here then?'

Henry joined in.

'No. Emily thought it best not to. She was well aware of his past; well, we both were.'

'Worked here before though, hadn't he, Mister Carter?'

'Yes, before hostilities broke out. His reputation stretched further afield than most, but at harvest and such like, pooling labour as farms do, he was a useful hand, until he muddied the waters that is.'

'Indeed, so I gather. His reputation found a home here, at haymaking, I understand, Mrs Radcliffe?'

'Meaning, Sergeant?'

'Well, if gossip is anything to go by…'

'Gossip is a trap the locals set for the simple or the unobservant, Sergeant. After you've settled in here we'll find out if you're either of these by just how quickly you learn not to set too much store by it.'

'In my work gossip gives leads, Mrs Radcliffe. That's how I discovered you'd 'recommended' Mister Long to Mister Gray's employ.'

'As I said, local gossip is a trap; not 'recommended', Sergeant, 'suggested'.'

Henry backed up Emily's comment.

'Even with his history, he'd served his country, Sergeant, so should be given a chance.'

And Emily completed Henry's.

'Just not here.'

D.S. Garrard looked from one to the other.

'Hm… And you've not seen him since?'

Emily stressed her earlier statement.

'Not since he first turned up here and asked for work, as I said.'

'So, two months ago?'

'Yes, Sergeant, not since…'

'So how do you account for the fact that Mister Gray says he sent Mister Long here a week last Thursday to ask if Broad Farm could have use of your disc… erm…yes, disc…'

333

Emily frowned.

'Harrow?'

'…Harrow.'

'You need to learn more agricultural vocabulary.'

'Mrs Radcliffe, I know all I need to know…'

'And you also need to learn to be more open in your dealings with local folk, Sergeant. You'll not gain their trust through subterfuge.'

'No, Mrs Radcliffe, you're very wrong there. A certain amount of discretion has to be exercised. So, what have you to say to Mister Gray's statement?'

'That he may have been sent, Sergeant, but I can assure you that, for whatever reason, Daniel Long never arrived here.'

'Then you'll have no objection if we take a look around.'

'For what reason, Sergeant?'

'Mister Gray was insistent that Mister Long was sent here.'

'And I am equally insistent that, to the best of my knowledge, he never arrived! What do you think, that we're hiding him here?'

It was obvious to D.S. Garrard that Emily was no pushover; but then, neither was he.

'Mrs Radcliffe. There's a popular but misguided belief that we 'coppers' just blunder around the county until we happen to trip over the criminals; we don't. We, in the police force detect things by looking for them, looking carefully and diligently. I'm in charge of that, that's why I'm called a Detective…Sergeant, and why I ask you, again, that,

with your permission, I'd, like, to, look, around…
Mister Carter?'

'Yes, of course. We don't mind, do we, Emily?'

Emily's smile was saccharine.

'No. No, if the Sergeant insists, please. And let us
know if you find him. If he's been hiding here for over a
week he'll owe rent.'

'Thank you, Mrs Radcliffe, and it's Detective
Sergeant…'

Signalling the conversation was at a close by turning
her back on D.S. Garrard, Emily spoke over her
shoulder as she left them.

'Is it.'

Back at the muck heap, she picked up the fork and
continued with her work.

Breaking the awkward silence, Henry rubbed his
palms together.

'Can I be of any help? Do you want me to show
you round?'

D.S Garrard shook his head.

'Thank you, Sir, but no, I'd rather we took a look
around on our own. So much easier to concentrate, and
we can look at what we want to and not at what we're
directed to…if you understand. No offence meant, Sir,
it's just easier.'

Henry nodded.

'And none taken. Right, well, if I can't be of any
further help, I'll be in the house. Emily! I'll go and see
to the corn milling order and get lunch for Sarah, you
sure you won't join us?'

'No, thank you, Father.'

'Right, well, if you want me.'

'Yes, Father.'

Henry rubbed his hands together again and turned back to the Constable.

'Right. Nice to see you again after all these years, Graham. Don't be a stranger. Detective Garrard…'

D.S. Garrard sighed.

'Detective Sergeant, Mister Carter, it's Detective Sergeant…'

But Henry was already leaving the yard.

After a long annoyed sigh, D.S. Garrard indicated that they should get on.

'Right. You make a start in the corn house.'

'Barn, Sir. Corn barn.'

'Yes, right, you check in there, I'll check the stables.'

'Yes, Sir.'

They parted.

Inside the stables, D.S. Garrard's attention was alerted to the fact they were not all empty when he heard a clattering sound. What appeared to be an exploded mattress was chewing meditatively on some hay. Then Lizzie made a couple of bristling paces towards the stable door the better to inspect this interloper.

'Hello, old fella, not going to disturb.' Moving away rapidly from the advancing Shire, D.S. Garrard tripped on the uneven surface and fell backwards onto the stone floor. 'Bugger!'

Turning over quickly, he was about to rise when his eye was caught by something fixed underneath the door frame… A glint of something…part-hidden, amongst the dirt and chaff…something…?

Dropping nearer the floor to get a better view, D.S. Garrard's eyes widened and for a moment he couldn't believe what he was seeing.

…It was gold…gold…? Gold! Of a…?

He stood up quickly to look through the window. Emily was still forking muck onto the heap, and Constable Ferris was moving out of sight, round the rear of the stable block. D.S. Garrard grinned…he had been unobserved. He was about to drop back to the floor to remove the item when he stopped, and with a sly smile muttered softly to himself.

'No, no. You just stay right there my pretty.' He looked out the window again. 'Right, Madam, let's see just how sharp you country folk really are…a pound to a pinch o' snuff says you're mine; ten minutes maximum!'

Aware of his arrival, Emily continued to work as D.S. Garrard stood silently for a moment or two: then he coughed.

'Ahem! No job for a lady, that, Mrs Radcliffe.'

Emily worked on.

'Not always the lady, Sergeant, as you seem to have decided for yourself.'

'Not me, Mrs Radcliffe, gossip. From Constable Ferris…your school history?' D.S. Garrard watched Emily work as he continued, 'I didn't know Daniel, as you called him, Mister Long, at all. I've only been in the district for a couple of months now. Came up from London to take charge, called here by Chief Constable Allen himself, as you'll probably know.'

'No, I didn't, Sergeant, my social circle excludes me from mixing with the likes of Chief Constables.'

'Oh? Then strange you didn't know about me from others; that no one told you of my arrival, you all seeming to know each other's business like you do.'

'Well, yes, indeed, you're probably right. Can't imagine how I missed it. A person of greater intellect than me might have guessed straight away you were new to the district…and you having to work on a Saturday like us ordinary folk too, what a thing.'

She started forking the loose edges of the heap, throwing the rounded piles of well-rotted manure towards its peak as D.S. Garrard replied.

'Hard work's never bothered me, Mrs Radcliffe; hard work nor dirty work neither.'

'Yes, but I wonder that you should've had to come all the way out here from such a place as London to put that into practice.'

'You think I'm green, don't you? That I come from London so know nothing'

'No need to think it, Sergeant. The naïveté you've shown since your arrival on this farm bears witness to it.'

Reaching forward he grabbed the handle of Emily's fork as he snapped out his reply.

'City folk, stumbling about out here in the sticks, is that what you think? Well you're wrong! In London I deal with real criminals, Mrs Radcliffe…and one of them would be far sharper than a whole village put together out here. Criminals who think themselves clever…' He leant in close. '…and I deal with this scum by being cleverer. Like the animals they are, I trap them in snares of their own making. It's my job, Mrs Radcliffe…' He dropped his voice further. '…And nothing gives me greater pleasure.'

D.S. Garrard raised one eyebrow and nodded at his diatribe's conclusion.

Emily shrugged it off.

'I wonder then, why you ended up out here, 'in the sticks' as you so quaintly put it, amongst us simple folk.'

'To get a command under my belt, Mrs Radcliffe. A couple of years in charge here then I'm back to London. A district waiting for me there, oh yes. But while I'm here, I'll shake this place up. I'm here to sort out the messes that you local folk are either too lazy, too stupid or too incompetent to sort out for yourselves; to sort out your criminals, no matter what their excuses.' Emily smiled. It annoyed him and he talked through it. 'I'm good at my job, Mrs Radcliffe, and that makes me right. I was right to come out here after my initial enquiries, and now? Now I'm not just right, I'm certain…certain that things here are not what they seem.'

'I wonder you can sleep soundly at night with such a head full of ability, Sergeant.'

'Sleep? You mean like Constable Ferris, your school friend? Mrs Radcliffe, your Constable's been sleep-walking his way through the real crime hereabouts for years. All those long nights out 'chasin' poachers' tires him out no doubt.'

'He's not my Constable…'

'He got to know Mister Long well, your Constable. Finally knew him for what he was; a thoroughly bad lot. I read the notes, you see. No need of gossip for this one.'

'I've said once before, Sergeant, he's not my Constable.'

'And I've also said, several times before, that I'm a Detective Sergeant, Mrs Radcliffe. One of us seems not to be listening to the other, do we?'

'I heard you perfectly well, Detective Sergeant. Your derogatory comments about Constable Ferris taking an interest in the crime that afflicts us; poaching. Does that make him wrong?'

'Not wrong, Mrs Radcliffe. Weak…it makes him weak. He's so wrapped up in the pithy goings-on round here that he fails to see the bigger picture; that lad Musto? He'll come back to haunt him, I know. No, no room for pity in this game, Mrs Radcliffe.'

'What, none?'

'None, otherwise the country would be full of murderers with sob stories; entertaining to listen to but very dangerous to live in…'

'And what about justice?'

'Ha! What would folk round here know of that? They live so much in each other's pockets they're blind to it.'

'That's a sweeping generalisation about the people of this district don't you think…and justice too?'

'You want to know about justice? Right. I've missed out on the dubious benefit of the town's inbreeding, Mrs Radcliffe; I can read. I've read the notes. Add them together with the gossip and they spell de-tec-tion. So now, having spelt it out for you, we both know what we're talking about this time, don't we?'

Emily remained silent. She was now fully aware that there was another agenda going on here.

'Young I may be, Mrs Radcliffe, but far from stupid, and what I've worked out from gossip and those files is that, though he was a lot of things, he was never wasteful, our Daniel. Always on the look-out for trinkets and such, mostly to sell in order to buy drink, of course… But, just very occasionally, he took a shine to certain things…on a whim…kept them, these certain things, like…well, like wrist watches.'

D.S. Garrard's pause demanded some reply. He waited.

Finally, Emily answered him.

'Wrist, watches?'

D.S. Garrard smiled at her fashioned reply.

'Yes. Wrist watches. You have seen one before, haven't you? Rare things round here, much like honesty. I'll draw a picture of one if you like.'

'That'll not be necessary, Detective Sergeant…'

'Good, I'm not much of an artist. So, to continue. See, a man of his reputation, our Daniel, when he shows off something unusual, of real value…something out of place on such as him…like a solid gold wrist watch? Well, people take note.' Entering the yard from the rear of the stables, Constable Ferris wandered across it and moved slowly along the muck heap as, receiving no flicker of recognition from Emily, D.S. Garrard continued, 'Difficult to follow for country folk, this level of reasoning, I know. Lot of new-fangled things in it. Let me put it in easier terms for you, shall I? Erm…it's like…like you're walking down the high street…and you pass a turkey carrying a shotgun. Stands out, see? You'd notice it, you country folk. Well that'd be the same as a gold watch on Daniel Long's wrist…to folk with intelligence, folk like me; that's your turkey with a shotgun, see; it was noted, commented on by several folk hereabouts, his gaffer in particular.'

'Sorry, Sergeant? I don't follow your turkey and wrist watch analogy.'

'Shotgun, Mrs Radcliffe, turkey with a shotgun. Daniel had the wrist watch.'

'Oh.'

D.S. Garrard was well into his stride now and moving to the kill.

'Yes, a bad lot, Long. Violent…wrong-headed, particularly where women were concerned. Particularly when things didn't go his way, I'm told. That gossip thing again, I'm afraid…that and the 'incomplete' files on Miss Ferris… and a couple of others… Funny thing that isn't it? That he should be such a thug to women and yet never seem short of them? Some say, not me you understand, but some say that a lot of women like, er, 'a bit of rough', is that the phrase, from time to time; Why's that, do you think? Does it remind them of what a real man is like; is that it?' Emily stayed silent. These suppositions were cutting deeply into her recent experience at Daniel's hands. 'What, nothing to add, Mrs Radcliffe? That surprises me. I'd've thought you'd have plenty to say on this matter. But then, that's the thread running through Mister Long's involvement with all his women hereabouts; none of them have the courage to help us get him arrested when it comes to it, so, away he goes to do it again…until, one day, maybe, one of them gets jealous of a rival…or has enough of his brutality?'

'Forgive me, Sergeant, but is this any concern of mine? I've told you that Mister Long has not been on these premises for two…'

D.S. Garrard chorused with her.

'…Months. Yes, so you said.' He paused. 'Forgive me drawing attention to it again, Mrs Radcliffe, but my information is that you and Mister Long have something of a past, particularly at haymaking time? Your husband, Mister George Radcliffe? No love lost between him and Mister Long, is there? Had cause to put him on the straight-and-narrow a while back?'

'Yes, before we were married…'

'Long time ago for you maybe, but he bears a grudge does our Daniel, did you not know that?

'No.'

'No?' He smiled that smile again. 'Well let me assure you he does…sometimes for years. Likes to get payment. Then I arrive here on your farm, following in the footsteps of this man, a violent man, and what do I find? I find you, one of his…unfulfilled conquests…?'

'Detective Sergeant, how dare you!'

'Local gossip, Mrs Radcliffe. Not my words…'

'You have no right to speak to me in such a way!'

'I can assure you I do Mrs Radcliffe! This isn't some case of a few missing ducks, this is a missing person, possibly even a murder, enquiry, and you do nothing for your defence by playing the part of a simple country girl!'

Now Emily was taken aback, and her voice and face said as much.

'My defence?'

'Mrs Radcliffe, there are certain things…'

'Did you say my defence?'

'…Your forehead and cheek? Looks like you lost in a recent fight, say, what, about two weeks ago, judging by the bruises and healing? Lose a lot of things in fights, you know, apart from your dignity…your temper perhaps?' He paused for a reaction, got none, and so homed in on the nub of his enquiry. 'So there we have it, Mrs Radcliffe. Your injuries…a man with a history of violence against women but whose history seems to excite women for his company; a man known to you, turned down for work here…but, according to gossip, coming back here for a disc…thing, and, well, who knows what else…now missing?'

D.S. Garrard saw her hackles rise and Emily's sarcasm was cutting.

'Is that what you think? That because I'm a woman on her own, husband away in the army serving his country, that I'd be foolish enough, shallow enough, to become involved with an ex farm-worker just because he has an exciting past…? Is that it, Sergeant?'

D.S. Garrard was pleased with her reaction; things were going well.

'Faulty memory again, Mrs Radcliffe; its Detective Sergeant, and…'

But Emily spoke over him.

'…Your view of women is somewhat askew and does you no favours, Detective Sergeant. And, as for my bruising? Let me put it in simple terms for you. As I told my father, our horse backed into the stable door ten days ago and unfortunately it was off the latch. Even more unfortunately, I was behind it and took the full force of its opening. The latch caught my forehead, the door my cheek and lip. I would guess that you'll not take a mere woman's account of events so, please, feel free to ask my father about it at anytime you like.'

'I will, Mrs Radcliffe; I will.' Constable Ferris had sauntered along the muck heap to join them as D.S. Garrard continued with his interrogation. 'But, before I do, is there nothing you want to change or add? No visits from volatile, local ex-farmworkers then? No…'indelicate situations?'

'It may be that others you deal with find themselves party to 'indelicate situations' as you so baldly put it, Detective Sergeant, but I can assure you I do not.'

D.S. Garrard took his bowler hat off.

'Then would you accompany me to the stables, Mrs Radcliffe? Constable, get out your note-book and accompany Mrs Radcliffe and myself to the stable block, would you?'

A puzzled Constable Ferris took out his note-book.

'Yes, Sir.'

Now in full official mode, D.S. Garrard continued, 'And I would remind you, Mrs Radcliffe, that although you are not at this present time under arrest, anything you may say will be taken down and may be given in evidence.'

Emily looked at them both.

'Under arrest?'

Waving his hand dismissively, D.S. Garrard replaced his hat.

'All in good time, Mrs Radcliffe. Traps take time to spring.'

Emily's heart was thumping as the three of them walked across the yard and into the stables. D.S. Garrard pointed down to the base of the door frame.

'Would you just take a look down there, Mrs Radcliffe, and tell me what you see, jammed, between the door-frame and floor…please?' Emily stood for a moment. D. S. Garrard indicated the spot again. 'Please?'

Bending down, Emily glanced under the door frame then stood up.

'Straw?'

D.S. Garrard let go a world-weary sigh.

'Very well, Mrs Radcliffe, if you insist. Constable?'

Looking into the indicated spot, Constable Ferris eventually stood up.

'Straw, Sir. A knot o' straw. A poppet by th' looks…'

'A what? What did you say?'

'A poppet.'

'What's a poppet?'

'What's under there, Sir; that's what it is…a poppet.'

D.S. Garrard shoved Constable Ferris roughly to one side.

'Out of my way, you fool! Look! Here!'

Scrabbling underneath the door, D.S. Garrard eventually stood up holding a knot of new, gleaming barley straw carefully folded into the shape of a miniature human being and liberally dusted with chaff and dirt.

Constable Ferris reached across and tapped the debris off it as he spoke.

'There, Sir! a poppet!'

There was an astounded silence.

D.S. Garrard turned to Emily.

'What've you done…what have you done with it?'

Emily showed genuine bewilderment.

'With what?'

'The watch! The gold wrist watch…I saw the gold…I saw a strap…!'

Emily shook her head.

'I have no idea what you're talking about, Sergeant… Is this the watch the turkey had?'

Constable Ferris looked confused as D.S. Garrard's temper of foolishness rose.

'Don't you try and get clever with me! You know very well what I'm talking about, Mrs Radcliffe!'

Unsure how, Emily was aware she had gained the upper-hand.

'How could I possibly? It's a poppet, Sergeant, a corn dolly left there to guard the door after harvest! You'd not know these local customs, being a Londoner and unfamiliar with our country ways, and the light isn't very good in here… If you'd removed it straight away and asked me, or probably your Constable here, you could've avoided this embarrassment.'

D.S. Garrard began to bluster.

'Mrs Radcliffe, the watch…'

'Is not here, Detective Sergeant, and we have the Constable to verify that, do we not?'

'Yes, Sir; Mrs Radcliffe. I 'ave t' say, Sir, there were no watch…th' poppet were there alright.' He then added helpfully. 'An' I've seen no sign 'f a turkey neither.'

D.S. Garrard threw the corn dolly across the stable.

'Never mind the bloody turkey, Constable, I know what I saw! We're going to turn this place upside down, Constable. I know its here!'

'Excuse me, Detective Sergeant, but I think that you've looked around enough on the strength of my goodwill…'

'Mrs Radcliffe…!'

'…And any further searches will require an official request from you, in writing, Detective Sergeant. I think I've been more than accommodating up to now, and I'll be sure to inform your Chief Constable Allen of this. This foolishness has to stop somewhere!'

D.S. Garrard's expression told it all as they each looked from floor to discarded corn dolly and then back to each other. Eventually D.S. Garrard spoke coldly, bluntly.

'Mrs Radcliffe, there's some sharp practice gone on here; I know it and you know it too, and like scum it'll come to the surface. I'm sure we'll be seeing each other again very soon. Constable, we're leaving!'

D.S. Garrard turned on his heel and strode out of the stable leaving Emily and Constable Ferris staring at his fast disappearing form. After a brief pause, Constable Ferris retrieved the poppet and joined Emily in the yard.

'I don't know what went on 'ere, Emily, Mrs Radcliffe, wi' Daniel I mean, an' though my Sergeant is an ass 'e's a tenacious ass an' 'e wants this one solved. Means a lot o' points on 'is card… Mister Long were a nasty piece o' work, Mrs Radcliffe, nasty in its meanest sense.'

Staring at the now distant Detective Sergeant, Emily replied distractedly.

'Is he?'

'Yes, 'e were, y'know 'e were…you've 'ad cause t' find that out, an' I've 'ad cause t' pick up some 'f 'is messes over th' years, y'know that too. Not many secrets in this village, remember. I'd 'ate f'r you t' become another one 'f 'is messes, Mrs Radcliffe, so, if y'do see Daniel, Mister Long…or 'is watch.'

'Or a turkey?'

'Ar. What were that all about?'

'Cleverness overreaching itself Constable, but don't ask your Detective Sergeant about it, not if you ever want to make Sergeant yourself. And if I do see him again, Daniel that is, not the turkey, you'll be the first to know, Constable; the very first. As for a watch, I know nothing of that.'

'You've access to a telephone out 'ere?'

'Indeed we do, Constable, at the Post Office, and as slow as your Detective Sergeant may seem to think we are, we've managed to master its use.'

Constable Ferris smiled at her.

'Oh, I think you're far from slow, Mrs Radcliffe, we're all very far from slow round 'ere.' He handed her the poppet. 'T' ward off them evil spirits…'

D.S. Garrard's voice reached them from the far end of the lane.

'Constable Ferris!'

'Comin', Sir!' After a couple of paces he turned back. 'I 'ear George, Mister Radcliffe, were decorated. That right?'

Emily half smiled.

'Not many secrets in this village, Constable Ferris, as you rightly said, even though we try to keep them so. Yes, he was.'

'An' very proud you must be, Mrs Radcliffe.'

'Yes; I am, very.'

'We were 'quainted, y'know, me an' Mister Radcliffe. 'E were one o' th' first t' know I'd thought t' join th' police. Wished me luck, unlike most, an' signed as a witness t' me good character, followed it up when Chief Constable contacted 'im too; made all th' diff'rence that, that an' the encouragement; Y' didn't marry me, Emily Carter, but y' married a good 'un by th' sound.' Emily pocketed the corn dolly. D.S. Garrard was now out of sight as Constable Ferris continued, 'Well, I'd best be gettin' off. Thank you f'r y' co-operation…an' thank Edward f'r me too would y'? I forgot t' say…when I left 'im out back.' Emily's eyes widened. 'Good o' y' t' take 'im on f'r all these years. There's precious little starts f'r sound chaps, let alone one such as 'im… Y' didn't know 'e were back on th' farm, did y'r? 'E's be'ind th' stables, in the old sty.

350

Must've got back early…from lunch?' He winked at Emily. 'Got th' time wrong, I 'spect, even though 'e's got a watch now.'

Emily was rooted to the spot for a few seconds then took a couple of steps forward.

'Constable Ferris…Graham…' She framed her thoughts. 'My husband, George, has been in the armed forces serving in France since the outbreak of war, as you already know.' Constable Ferris nodded. 'He left me in charge, here, to look after our daughter, the farm…and our marriage, until he returned. There's nothing I wouldn't do to safeguard those responsibilities. Nothing. Do I make myself clear?'

'As spring water, Mrs Radcliffe.'

The beginnings of tears were in her throat, which she fiercely held in check.

'I'm a good wife, Graham; as good as I can be, even when all the signals say otherwise…Battles don't stay comfortably behind borders, as you well know. They often stray closer to home, and when that happens…'

He completed her sentence.

'…We take th' necessary action? Ar, well, you've dodged the explosion, just watch out th' shrapnel don't catch y'r.'

They stood looking at each other for a few moments then Emily moved back to the muck-heap and, picking up the fork, began her work again.

'You take care o' y'rself as best y'can, Emily Carter. War-wife's a lonely old business, I'd guess, but, remember, we take friendship serious round 'ere, look out f'r each other we do; an' that's not gossip, that's a fact.'

He saluted in her direction and walked briskly away along the lane.

Emily turned towards the stables. Standing at one of its windows was Edward. He waved to Emily, a gold wrist watch clearly visible in his hand.

Emily's jaw dropped then, eventually, her eyes widened and she took out and waved the poppet at Edward. She looked along the now empty lane, dropped fork into barrow and re-entered the stables.

'Well, that was all very tricky, Edward.'

'Yes, Missus.'

'You were back early then? Didn't tell your mother, did you?'

'Tell 'er, Missus?'

'Never mind, Edward. How on earth did you know? About the watch?'

'I saw police, Missus…not Mister Graham; I knows 'im. The other police, th' young 'un. Saw 'im lookin' at door from back way, Missus. Lizzie felled 'im. 'E never saw me…'e'd gone, I were a mouse…I crep' up an' found it. Went back as mine…I were a mouse.'

'Yes, but how did you know, about it being Daniel's watch?'

''E showed it me.'

'Who did?'

'Mister Daniel.'

'When did he do this?'

''Ere, a time off. After war.'

'After the war? You mean when he came home from the war?'

'Yes, Missus, in our yard 'e showed me. Said 'e'd killed-ed a German man dead f'r it, would kill me too.'

'Well we know that won't happen, don't we, Edward?'

Edward looked out of the window and towards the muck heap.

'Yes, Missus.'

'What made you think of this?' Emily took out the poppet. 'That was very clever, Edward.'

'Poppet, Missus? No, Missus, I took a watch…I were a mouse.'

Emily looked at the innocence on Edward's face.

'Yes, Edward, you were a mouse…and Detective Sergeant Garrard was no cat. I'd better take it and dispose of it later.'

'Yes, Missus.' Edward handed her the watch. 'Don't want no dead German man's watch in 'ouse.'

Emily turned it round in her hand.

She saw an inscription on the back and read it out loud to Edward.

TO SAMUEL
ON YOUR TWENTY-FIRST BIRTHDAY –
GOD BLESS YOU SON

'Some German!' She put it in her waistcoat pocket and looked at the poppet again. 'Did the other policeman, Mister Graham, did he see you with it, the watch?'

'Yes, Missus. Saw me, said founder's keepsit but young police might take it. 'E sent me t' th' sty.'

'He sent you in there? The policeman, Mister Graham did…into the sty?'

'Yes, Missus.'

Emily lifted up the poppet and took the watch back out, holding it up so Edward could see both.

'With the watch?'

'Yes, Missus.'

'Not the poppet?'

'No, Missus. I'd no poppet…I knows 'im.'

'Yes, Edward, you said.'

'I were a mouse.'

'Yes, Edward, you were a mouse.'

Emily returned the watch to her waistcoat pocket.

'Right. Thank you, Edward. Now, let's get Lizzie sorted, shall we…and remember…' She gave him the corn dolly. '…it was a poppet under the door, not a watch.'

Edward nodded again and smiled broadly.

'Yes, Missus, no watch; a poppet.' They began to sort out brushes and buckets. After a few moments, Edward looked back along the stables. 'Where'll we put turkeys in 'ere, Missus?'

49

29.01.18

Winter had been slow in coming but arrived with fairy-tale whiteness by day and bitter temperatures by night.

Just as Emily knew for certain this snow would be white so she knew, and also for certain, that things were going badly wrong inside her. In the days immediately following Daniel's attack, she had passed much blood, at times fearing for her life so intense was the pain. The cessation of her usually very regular period also prepared her for the inevitable. Daily hot baths, as hot as she could stand and taken in front of roaring fires, and doses of fresh willow pith gave Emily some respite from the pain, but not a cure for the deep loathing she felt for the man who had robbed her of her femininity.

Then, just one week ago, there had been a return of the deeper pains. Not to the crescendo of earlier, just a deep-dull throb, and she knew...after the first forty-eight hours...she just knew the life within her was dying

At twenty minutes past nine on a Tuesday night, after Sarah had been given the surprise treat of an overnight stop with grandpa, Emily retired to one of the empty stable stalls. Biting on a leather rein to stifle her cries of pain and distress, Emily miscarried of herself a still-born child at precisely eleven forty three. For a long while Emily held it close, this tiny stranger, weeping quietly but uncontrollably at the pitiless tragedy of it all. It was the hot breath of Lizzie, her head drooping over the barrier, which shook her from this misery.

Without a word, Emily slowly rose from the straw and, removing her shawl, wrapped the tiny form in it. Lizzie dropped her head further and Emily reached to her, stroking her muzzle; the Shire whinnied quietly.

The yard was empty.

Staying tight to the hedgerow of the roadway, Emily made off towards the Forty-Acre. The snow was thick on the ground as she kept to the shadows of the half-moon's shroud of light. Slipping through the open gate and into the field's ditch, she moved purposefully along its damp, still-soft base, passing under the cobwebbed reflections of bare elm branches. Two elms along this tree-lined hedge, in the shelter of the tree whose shade she had shared with her family so many summers ago, Emily excavated a tiny grave. Her hands turned over the moist, fine tilth and leaf mould, the years of decay and regrowth.

As she placed the tiny corpse in the damp and fertile ground and covered it over so fresh snow began to fall, a mask for her fresh tears.

50

11.02.18

Loading from heap to cart for this first day's muck-spreading took a shorter time than they had anticipated.

The majority of the snow had melted and, with Edward alongside, Emily led Lizzie onto one of the Forty-Acre fields designated for spring barley, scattering the finch-flock that was eagerly searching sustenance in the part-thawed soil and uncovered seeds. Setting off across the field, with Edward stood atop the load forking off the muck and debris, Emily moved to and fro along the ploughing. Rooks, crows, starlings and seagulls now joined the returning finches in anticipation of easier pickings.

Loaded again and returned to the Forty-Acre, Emily looked at the amount of ground the first spread had covered.

'We'll get about sixty-odd loads out of that heap, Edward. Enough to do all the field, I think.'

'Ar, Missus, good muck.'

'End each day with a couple of hours muck-knocking then a run over it with the disc-harrow and we'll be ready for planting, weather being kind; what do you think, Edward?'

'All finished, Missus?'

Emily smiled at him.

'Yes, Edward. All finished.'

Lizzie was clicked on for this second run, the gulls circling; land-locked sea-vultures, dipping, weaving and seizing on anything that attracted their attention, no matter how unpromising. Gannet-face-yellow against the snowflake gulls, the nicotinic shoulder bone flung from the cart arced across the February sky and bounced off the frost-frazzled ploughing. Snapped up in the feeding frenzy by a Greater Black-Backed Gull the bone was transported, assessed as inedible en route and dropped by a nearby hedgerow, its carrier quickly returning to the fray.

Edward smiled at its progress.

'All finished then.'

—〰—

Lizzie looked smart, harness shining in the winter sun that had melted all but the last of the snow. Emily checked the marker pegs left from the ploughing of earlier, adjusted the disc-harrow and fixings to suit the conditions then clicked the mare on.

'Haul-On, Lizzie, Haul-On!'

The Shire moved off, the harrow slicing and crumbling the plough furrows, folding the soil together with the recently spread manure. A gull-flock drifted and dipped behind them, selecting morsels from the freshly exposed soil.

After two hours or so Emily stopped the harrow mid-field. From out of her shirt pocket she took the solid gold wrist watch, looking at the inscription once more.

'Hope you understand, Samuel, whoever you are.' With a swift glance around the field, she tossed it into the furrow ahead then called out, 'Haul-On, Lizzie! Haul-On!'

The harrow jerked forward burying soil, manure and watch together as the blades passed over it...

51

20.04.18

The sodden, ruptured battlefield just outside Villiers Bretonneux had seen considerable, rain-soaked action on the previous day.

George, Clowdy and Diment had been fully involved on the periphery of it, hauling ammunition and hardware around sites of particular brutality but now, with skirmishes still clearly audible but their centre subdued and distant, they were on a pre-dawn return to base camp, hauling a field-gun along a deeply rutted and muddy track.

Over the past few days land had been fought over, gained, lost and generally ruined, the picture becoming so confused at times that he and others, leaders included, were sometimes not quite sure just on which side of the line they actually were…this track, for instance. That it was an old drover's road was certain, what was uncertain was whose possession it was in? Certainly not the long absent farmer that was for sure.

Creaking leathers and the rumble of gun-carriage-wheels were joined by the dawn chorus as day-break ripped the blanket of a cloud-covered sky. The sun seared through the opening, bathing all in its early light. Even in such circumstances, this event brought a smile to George's face.

'Haul-On, girls! We may even get a bit o' dry t'day. Make a change, eh?'

The early sun began to chase off the previous days' damp and whisk it into peaks of mist as the trio eventually reached the outskirts of a wrecked farm.

'Whoa, Girls! What's this?' The track ahead was blocked by a large fallen tree. 'Knew it were too good t' last. We'll go round it then, eh; 'ave to.'

George veered his team off to the right and together they made their way through the farm's blasted buildings and out, beyond its dismembered barn and onto a field; a huge stubble field…? Its condition was so surprising that George halted at its edge. This one field had, for reasons best known to the military on both sides, been left totally unscathed.

The ripe wheat had been scythed down and collected, the stalks remaining untouched since harvest and now, rising away to a false horizon, its fast-faded golden hollowness was gradually being swamped by a green tide of weaker offspring and weeds, all struggling to reach adulthood. Daisy and meadow buttercup, interspersed with red clover and the odd hedge-bound, snow-slash of greater stitchwort, spread over the ground like scattered wedding confetti and the early-day sun glistened across the mist-soaked, cobwebbed ground ahead.

The horse's recent efforts showed in the early, chill-spring air, and those few distant trees that still clung to life showed their first efforts of this year's growth, their colour made all the more garish by the skeletal remains of their charred near-neighbours.

George breathed in deeply and slipped his rifle from off his shoulder, placing the butt against the toe of his boot.

'That felled tree were delib'rate, lasses; made us go this way, I reckon. What a sight, eh?'

Gazing across this field, forgetting just for a moment the reasons and incidences, he could almost have been back in Leicestershire at the start of a ploughing day.

He scanned the field and patted Clowdy's neck.

'This'ld turn a good furrow 'n' grow a good crop, I reckon, girls; wha'd'y' say?'

Clowdy shook her head and snorted. A covey of mid-field, creaking partridges completed the reminder…it was the odd shell clumping in the distance that ruined his reverie.

'Another time, eh? Shame t' spoil it but we've t' get on.' He slipped the rifle back on his shoulder and gave a gentle tug on Diment's halter. 'Walk-On, ladies, Walk-On.'

The horses took up the strain and leant into the task, their hooves swishing through the field's familiar, stubbled firmness, their hooves bruising the herbed greenness and enveloping them all in a haze of spring perfume…

They had taken barely a score of steps when, just a hundred and fifty yards away, a German tank lumbered over a rise in the field. It halted on the crest, a swaying motion the legacy of its hurried stop.

'Oh, Christ…this 'ain't our ground Clowdy!' George froze, holding all still. The horses' breath bled into the still air. 'Stand-On, girls, Stand-On. It's a tank…we've th' wall as background; might just dodge a bullet 'ere, if God's about an' we're lucky; Stand-On.'

Clowdy tossed her head, seemingly in agreement…

The sun's rays caught the regimental cap badge and star on her harness, flashing a sun-kissed Morse signal far and wide. George saw the message…then the actions of the receiver as the tank swung his way and the gun elevated.

Frantically he pushed back at the horses.

'We're found! Hi, Back-Back! C'mon my girls, c'mon! Jeeesus, c'mon! Back-Back!'

Diment and Clowdy pushed back against the heavy field-gun, their muscles rippling, their hooves sinking, their breath gushing out of widened nostrils. The gun's wheels dug into the soft ground denying any help or mercy.

A light from the front of the tank flashed…!…

George saw it…heard it…it exploded a split-second later!

Face bloody, his shattered shin bone sticking out through the gaping wound in his right leg, George rose up on his elbow to see both horses lying nearby. Their harness was still intact, the field-gun torn away, dumped twenty yards distant by the explosion, the whole scene wreathed in smoke.

Diment was already dead, he had seen it often enough to know, but Clowdy lifted her head in acknowledgement of George's movement. He crawled across and looked along her flank. Despite her terrible wounds to hips and back, she lifted her head and neck in an effort to get up…Unable to maintain this position, she snorted as her head flopped to the ground, condensation's kiss dusting George's face.

Leaning across to his rifle lying some three feet away, George collected it then reached over and rubbed Clowdy's ear.

She flicked her head, snorting at his touch.

'Good Lass…my lovely Shire lady.'

In his swoon at the rifle's recoil, George missed the arrival of the three British tanks as they ploughed across the pristine stubble field.

Staggering to a halt they crowded a volley of shells onto the German tank, sending it into a fancy display of fire and flashes…

52

11.09.18

She had feared her first reaction would be to burst into tears and this was not what was required right now.

As the train pulled into the afternoon sunshine of Allingham station, Emily took a little time to compose her emotions. After a short wait, and through the steam of the engine's recent effort, she saw him, limping along the platform; stick in hand, a strong and upright ploughman had returned with a lined face and eyes that burned with the look of the lost. A few seconds later and she knew he had seen her, Sarah too, standing; waiting.

George halted a few paces from them and the trio hovered, unsure of what to do, quite how to react.

In spite of her heart's desire she smiled her biggest, sunniest smile.

'Hello, my love. You look tired.'

George took a long time to answer.

'Ar. Long journey to 'ome… 'Ello, Em.' He looked around. 'Mam not 'ere?'

'At Shirley Lodge, with Father. It's a fair step for them both, but in truth I think they wanted us to have this time together; kindness itself, they both are.'

George looked at Sarah.

'An' who's this young lady?'

'I'm Sarah, Daddy em-em!' She whispered loudly to Emily. 'He doesn't remember me, Mummy.'

George heard it.

'Course I remember y'r. Just y've growed so big. An' who's Daddy em-em?'

'Your decoration, George.'

'Oh, that. Ar. Th' stick goes wi' it; they're a pair.' He saw Sarah's gaze settle on the stick. 'Never mind th' stick, Sarah, 'ow about a hug-lee f'r Daddy?'

That word made the contact point for Sarah, for them all, and she rushed forward.

'Daddy, Daddy!'

George used his stick for support and squatted shakily to receive Sarah's long hug. After a few moments he held her at arm's length.

'Let's 'ave a look at this young lady 'f our Shire then.' He noticed the gold disc pinned to Sarah's cardigan. ''Ello then, what's this?'

Sarah beamed.

'It's my medal, Daddy. Mummy says I'm an EmDeeBeeGee.'

Emily made her first steps towards them as George touched the gold disc and spoke over Sarah's shoulder.

'What were this f'r then?'

'For being Mummy and Daddy's Brave Girl, George. And she was.'

At George's side, Emily reached out her hand and rubbed his hair gently, then took Sarah's hand in her other. After a few seconds, George began to stand shakily, picking Sarah up as he rose and putting his full weight on the stick in his other hand. Emily looped her arm helpfully through his and, once he was upright she enfolded him and Sarah in a long embrace.

They stayed like this for some time, until Sarah's weight got the better of George. He returned her gently to the ground and she tugged at Emily's arm.

'Can we show Daddy now, Mummy? Can we?' Then she turned to her father, unable to contain her excitement. 'Daddy em-em, can we show you our surprise! Can we?'

'Let Daddy catch his breath, Sarah…Mummy too.'

George smiled at them both.

'Breath all caught up now; you good f'r it, Em?' She nodded. 'Ar, right, Sarah, I'll see y' surprise, but can we go by th' Forty-Acre t' get to it, summat I'd like t' do?'

Emily was puzzled.

'Forty-Acre?'

'Are you going ploughing, Daddy?'

'Not ploughin', Sarah, just a bit o' diggin'.'

Emily tried to forestall this trip.

'But, George, you've only just got back.'

Sarah carried on her insistence, jumping up and down in excitement.

'Then can we show you the surprise, Daddy? Can we?'

Emily tried to continue over her.

'And your leg…'

George shushed Sarah and calmed Emily.

'We'll go an' 'ave a look-see at y' surprise, Sarah, as soon as I've finished at Forty-Acre. Leg'll put up, Em, summat I need t' see to.'

Emily eventually nodded.

'Yes, alright, George.'

They left the station hand-in-hand, walking in silence for a while, George looking over the remembered familiarity of the landscape.

'I see nothin' much 'as changed round 'ere.'

Emily was glad of the conversation.

'So much you know. There's a lot gone on before us.'

'Oh, Lor'; what's th' roll-call?

'Eric Abbot, Robert Clarke, Cecil and John Mayhew, Martin Stallard… all three Jenkins boys…'

'All three?'

'Each and every one. Godfrey Ewart, Gilbert Adams, the Missus Amiss, Mrs Groves.'

'Crikey, is there anyone left in th' village? I'd no idea so many 'ad gone on.'

'Hardly surprising the amount of letter-writing you did! Three post-cards, three, in the whole time you were away, George Radcliffe! Never knew where you were or what you were thinking.'

'Army 'ad strict rules on that, Em, so what I wanted t' say would've been crossed out or landed me on a fizzer…'

'Well other wives were getting letters and such, so their men must have written something, just not me. I would've told you so much more if I'd known where to send it.'

'Ar. Sorry, Em. Just not good at settin' pen t' paper, an' things were a might busy…sorry.'

'You're forgiven. Having you home more than makes up for it.'

Her thoughts drifted a little as she looked over the panorama. Sarah, bored by this lull in the conversation, tugged at George's hand.

'Watch me run, Daddy. I can run very fast now. Watch!'

Without waiting for permission, Sarah set off running along the lane for the sheer pleasure of the exercise. Emily called after her.

'Don't go any further than The Lowry, Sarah.'

Without stopping, Sarah called back.

'Yes, Mummy. Watch, Daddy!'

George watched Sarah for a few seconds then looked at Emily.

She felt his gaze and returned it.

'You've done some job on 'er, Em.'

She flushed slightly, and then her face faded pale.

'They've not all fared as well, George.'

George knew by her tone this was a late extra, knew it was of real significance.

He waited.

Emily looked across the fields then said simply.

'Edward's gone too.'

The news was like a shot to George.

'Oh, Em…not Edward!' He thought for a moment. 'Should've guessed; why'd y' not let me know…Oh, right, letters…ar, I see… What 'appened?'

Emily's grip on George's hand tightened as she recounted the events.

'Do you remember those two young girls of Victoria Mason's, the butcher's wife?'

'Ar, think so…Lottie an'…?'

'Elisabeth, right. They went into Crantock's Lake, the bottom of Long Acre, for a swim. Edward was doing some hedge brushing in Thomson's field right next there. Heard them yelling, saw them splashing and such and, of all things, waded in to help.'

'But, Edward can't swim, Em, never could!'

'We knew that, George, but Edward? In he went. You remember how soft the bottom is there and how sharp it shelves off on Thomson's side?'

'Ar, I do. David Keen lost a bullock there fifteen year ago, bogged into th' mud 'n' sank wi' out trace; ten seconds it 'ad; they never even got a rope to it, so I were told.'

'Well, Edward drowned right there too.'

'Oh, Lor'…'

'The Mason girls got out on their own and raised the alarm. There's irony, they raised the alarm for him! Turns out they were only playing, you know, larking about? Edward thought they were in trouble, didn't think to run round their side and ask. Waded in, like a hero, tried to swim across.'

'But, 'e can't… When were this?'

'Four months ago. I'm so sorry, George. I didn't want to worry you with it while you were convalescing. Wouldn't have changed things if I had.'

George shook his head.

'Just about th' level 'f 'is luck, that. No war an' no 'ero.'

'Depends how you justify heroism; just because he didn't make the war doesn't mean he was less of a man. He's a hero to others, George; to me. Struggled every step of the way. Endured all he had thrown at him and still had the gumption to risk it all for a couple of girls he hardly knew, who would've called him names had they met him on the street.'

Emily's eyes began to fill and George gave her his white-spotted, blue 'kerchief.

'Ar, 'e never 'ad it easy. Folk bewildered 'im most o' th' time, but 'e loved 'is 'orses did Edward, an' 'e got it returned at odd times…where's 'e laid, I'd like t' pay 'im a visit later?'

'In Allingham Churchyard, row next to your dad. I took a rooted cutting of late Buff Beauty last week and planted it on the top…six of us at the funeral; his mum and the vicar, your mum…Grace went, bless her; she's not well but made the journey. Not much for a life is it?'

They walked in silence again until George ventured his next comment.

'Well, that's some roll-call, Em; is that all…as if it's not enough?'

'Mister Arch? He died over two years ago.'

'Who, Daniel's old boss?'

'Yes. We bought his old skewbald.'

'What, Lizzie?'

'You remember! Yes, the very same.'

'Don't know much, but know 'orses. Lizzie, eh? By, old man Arch 'ad 'er when I were last 'ere. She c'ld still do a bit o' work then?'

'Did us proud. She's back at the farm and going on strong. All the ploughing you see is down to her.'

'An' a bit t' you, I've no doubt.' Emily returned his smile. 'Ar, I'd reckon she's 'avin' a better life 'ere than under Daniel, no matter what age she is.' George thought on for a moment. 'I saw 'im in France…Daniel. Got wounded an' baled out.'

'Yes, I know.'

''Ow d'y' know?'

'What?'

'That I saw him in France. I didn't write it.'

'Er…I don't, I didn't…you didn't. I meant, I know he got wounded and baled out…because he turned up here.'

'What, Alling'am?'

'Yes, but I mean 'here'.'

'Shirley Lodge! 'E's got some brass neck comin' back 'ere, that one. What was 'e after?'

'Work, what else?'

'Ha! An' th' rest! When were this then?'

Sarah had started to run back towards them as Emily filled in the details for George.

'About a year ago. I sent him off to Broad Farm. A new man, Mister Gray, he'd taken it over after Albert Grosvenor passed on so didn't know Daniel Long's ways. Stupid to think he deserved the chance.'

'Just like you that is, too soft by 'alf you are.'

'Maybe. You never said, in the couple of letters I did get from hospital, you never said you'd met up again.'

'T' what purpose? What were the outcome 'f it all then?'

'Police followed hot on his heels.'

'Sounds about right. Leopards 'n' spots come t' mind, did they catch up wi' 'im?'

'Not that I heard. By the time the police came he was beyond them. Graham Ferris and a new chap in charge, a Detective Sergeant somebody or other.'

'Ar? Big guns then.'

'Seemed so. Not a local. From London. Gone back there now, I heard. Couldn't work out the way folk are round here.'

George thought for a moment.

'Sweet on you at one time, I seem t' remember, Ferris, so gossip would 'ave it. Still out at Thrensham?'

'Yes, he's still out at Thrensham, and yes he was sweet on me, when he was five year old, George Radcliffe!'

'Never trust a copper.'

'Well, he was one of the good ones, George, you knew that too, and he remembered you fondly.'

'Must 'ave th' wrong man then is all I c'n say; good at that are th' police. 'Ad a bit 'f a past 'ist'ry, Daniel 'n' Graham, summat over 'is sister, Mary, weren't it?'

'Yes, no friend of Graham's, I'm sure of that.'

''E were still trouble then, Daniel?'

'Not to us, no; no trouble at all. Some silver missing from a pub, then him; he's not been seen since, that was several months ago…'

Sarah arrived back, her face shining from her recent efforts.

'Did you see me run, Daddy em-em, did you?'

'I did too! You'd give a whippet some good sport.'

Sarah took his arm and said teasingly.

'We've got new stock, Daddy em-em. Mummy bought it.'

'New stock? What's this then? This th' surprise?'

Emily took Sarah's hand.

'A new bull, George. We call him William. I bought him at the last autumn sale to replace Joshua.' Emily talked smilingly on through George's puzzled expression. 'No, you didn't see him either; yes you've been gone that long. He's in the home farm bottom field.'

'I'd ask if 'e's any good but I reckon that's a daft question. You always were a good judge o' stock, Em. Turned down a copper an' married me f'r a start.'

They laughed, easily, softly, and Sarah, happy in their happiness, released George and Emily's hands and skipped ahead of them. George looked across the land once more, his expert eye, even though he had been away for so long, taking in the relevant information.

'Fields look in good order. Y've been 'ard at it too, I'd think. Lookin' forw'd t' seein' th' furrow y've ploughed. Does y' dad do anythin' at all on th' land now?'

'No, not for two years now. In truth, his arthritis gives him gyp if he walks too far. He'll still do the weekly market but not the farm-work, not now. He's content to leave all that to Sarah and me. We're the ones to blame; us and that scatty skewbald.'

George smiled at her.

'No blame 'ere, not f'r any 'f y'r, Em. I'm just sorry to 'ave been away on 'oliday an' left it all t' you.'

'So were we, George.' She brightened and turned to Sarah. 'Yes, that's the last time we let you go away 'til Christmas on your own, isn't it, Sarah?'

Sarah wagged her finger at George.

'Yes, Mummy. Last time, Daddy em-em.'

George laughed at her gesture as she skipped off again.

'An' Mam?'

'Not bad, all things considered. Still suffers from the headaches, but she drives her way through them; a tough old bird, as you well know. Spends a fair bit of time with us now. A real help with Sarah she is.'

They walked in silence for a short while.

'If I remember the age o' that skewbald aright, Em, well be needin' new stock soon; youngsters. What's the 'orse market like?'

Emily had known the subject would come up, but its sudden introduction into this happy day still came as a shock and it took her while to answer.

'Not good, George. What's desirable's unavailable and what's available's undesirable.'

'Ar. Saw th' cream 'f it lyin' on them fields in France…'

There was a further long silence now before Emily spoke again.

'Diment and Clowdy, George…in the two letters you did write me.'

'Ar, an' I'll bet they made no sense neither! 'Ad time in 'ospital, see. Nothin' else t' do in France but wait to 'eal an' get used to a life wi'out fear an' shells.'

'Yes, I understand that, and thank you for the letters you did write. Couldn't believe it when I read they'd found you.'

'Found me?'

'Edward said they'd get home; may have been France but home to them was where you were; see, he was right.'

''E said that, about 'orses?'

'Yes, when they were collected by Remounts.'

George raised his eyebrows and sighed.

'Some 'omecomin'.'

Emily squeezed his hand.

'That second letter, when you were convalescing …you just wrote they'd died…I'm just so sorry. My poor, beautiful Shire ladies…'

George thought on for a moment before speaking.

'When they turned up in our detail, Em…I don't know… I were so full 'f it, t' get 'em back… I'm no believer, Em, y' know, but that were some miracle right there. To 'ave covered all that distance and to 'ave ended up in my battalion of all places and in th' very stockade of my troop? Should've let 'em pass, best never to 'ave known… An' no sign 'f Ben, no idea what become 'f 'im; I'd like t' think 'e fared better th'n th' rest.'

Emily's eyes began to fill again and she cut in.

'Please, George, stop. I don't want to hear about it. Please.'

'Ar, sorry, Em. An' now y'know one o' th' reasons I didn't write so much. 'Ow can y' send those thoughts 'ome, eh? What t' write? "It's sunny 'ere an' ev'rythin's fine"? Well it weren't…an' it weren't.' He stopped for a moment as memory cleared space for reflection then he sighed. 'After all their efforts… Y'got so used to it, used to it all.'

Sarah looked from one parent to the other.

'Used to what, Daddy em-em?'

'Nothin', our Sarah. 'Orses. Got used t' seein' 'orses.'

'Horses are lovely.'

'Ar, they are that our Sarah.' She seemed satisfied and skipped off again. When she was a few yards away, George spoke again. 'News got back then, did it, about the army's surplus livestock?'

'Yes.' She stopped, breathed in deeply. 'So, given those options, I know exactly where our two ladies would rather have been at the end, George Radcliffe; and so do you.'

George's eyes remained fixed on the distant horizon.

'Ar, maybe... Y'know, 'til they arrived I'd th' feelin' my life were goin' on somewhere else...sort 'f, wi'out me...d'you understand? About as good at this as I am at letter-writin', Em, sorry.'

'No, no, it's fine; you're fine. Carry on.'

'I don't know...I just felt I should be there wi' it...an' if only I could just, I don't know...just, connect somehow...? Then they arrived an' we were all t'gether again; me, those two Shires an' through them, you too.'

His hand tightened on Emily's. She tugged it gently in recognition and they lapsed into a further silence.

Eventually they arrived at the Forty-Acre field gate and Sarah skipped back, squeezed between them and took their hands as together they crossed the field, the long stubble crackling in return conversation of their tread.

'Good yield off 'ere, Em?'

'Near enough two tons to the acre, George. Best year yet, and some full grains saved for our nineteen eighteen vintage beer too.'

'I'll look forward t' th' thrashin' then, shall I?'

'And the drinking, George! We saved a dozen bottles from each year you've been away, didn't we, Sarah?'

'What, Mummy?'

'Wobble, for Daddy, we saved some each year.'

'Yes, we saved plenty of wobble, Daddy.'

'I'll look forward t' that too then, shall I? Will that be after th' thrashin', Milady?' He held Sarah's hand. 'Thank you, Sarah.'

'Mummy helped!'

'Yes, and Mummy too.'

Reaching the far hedgerow they walked along its length, Emily all the while growing not a little anxious as, the further along its length they progressed the heavier her legs became. Eventually, and to her great relief, George halted at the base of the first in the line of elms.

Emily looked along the hedgerow.

'Here, George?'

'Ar, 'ere'll do, under Ben's tree.'

Emily looked at him. 'Ben's tree?'

'Ar, d' y' not remember? It's where Edward tied 'im when we broke f' lunch at mowin' time, afore the war…' George saw Emily's expression of incredulity. 'Memr'y like an elephant, Em.'

'Pity it didn't stretch to you remembering to write home then, isn't it?'

George smiled at her reply then, with the aid of his stick he stepped into the ditch and squatted down. Digging a small hole in the soft, rich soil with his hands, he removed a piece of sacking from his coat pocket and unrolled it to reveal two horses' ears; one grey, one bay. Emily drew in her breath. Sarah looked round her mother and into the ditch.

'Is that Diment and Clowdy, Daddy?' George stared at the ears as she repeated. 'Is it, Daddy?'

'Ar. Back 'ome now Sarah, where they belong.'

Sarah began to sniffle.

'Don't cry now, Sarah.' He stood up and took her hand. 'Look…this is just summat f'r us t' think on; our secret. Their spirit never left 'ere, Sarah, an' now land's got 'em back their journey's complete, eh?'

'Not ploughing though, Daddy.'

Even under these circumstances, George smiled.

'No, not ploughin', Sarah, but growin' all th' same, eh?' He looked up at Emily. 'First field we did plough on this farm though. D' y' remember, Em?'

Emily had recovered enough to speak.

'Yes. It was the first time I really saw you three. I came past with father. We watched you working; he said the horses didn't seem to need you.' She smiled. 'Thought of the money he'd save.'

George smiled back at her. Stooping down once more, he dropped the ears into the hole.

'Ar, 'e were right about them two.'

Reaching into his other pocket he took out a medal, two silver stars and two regimental tunic buttons from a small box.

Emily realised what was to follow.

'George? Is that your medal?'

'Ar, an' theirs.'

'Are you sure, George?'

'Never surer, Em.'

Sarah was intrigued.

'What's those, Daddy?'

'Their bravery, Sarah.'

Emily squatted and put her hand on George's shoulder.

'Your bravery too, George.'

He dropped them into the hole alongside the ears

'No, Em; they were brave. I chose t' be there.'

'Can my medal go in with them too, Daddy?' Emily looked up at Sarah, hand to mouth and the beginnings of yet more tears in her eyes. Sarah began to undo the medal. 'Can it, Mummy?'

'Sarah…you really do catch Mummy off guard sometimes. I'd say of course it can. George?'

'Would be th' perfect end to a long journey, Sarah, an' they'd be proud t' share their bravery wi' yours. In 'ere, look.'

Emily helped Sarah undo the clasp on the back of the medal. Sarah held it out for George.

'No, lass, that's f'r you t' do.'

With Emily's help he lifted Sarah down into the ditch alongside him then, kneeling down, Sarah placed her medal carefully alongside the insignia and ears then stood up as George took her hand.

'There; restin' t'gether now, Sarah. Almost fam'ly. You got anythin' y'want t' put in th' grave, Em?'

Her tears now falling freely, Emily shook her head, unable to voice any reply.

'Ar, enough buryin', Em. Enough.'

Gently back-filling the hole, George stood up and lifted Sarah up to Emily then climbed out to join them. They looked at the fresh soil, the view, each other. Emily took his hand and wiped her tears away determinedly with George's 'kerchief.

'Some memory here, George; these trees, the fields. They'll be here forever; we're all just passing through…'

Taking hold of her other hand, George turned her to face him.

'Passin' through maybe, Em, but we've stood up straight 'ere, made our mark. Nothin'll change that. As long as folk recall us in their chat, that's our immortality.'

Emily looked along the hedgerow again.

'Will they remember us, George?'

'Course, Em… We've put down our footprint, eh?'

'And more…'

'Ar, an' much more f'r some, I'd guess; th' likes 'f Edward an' others… Land always wins in the end, you remember that our Sarah. Treat it right, that earth, or it'll swallow you up an' leave no trace 'f you ever bein' 'ere.'

'Land always wins, Daddy.'

'Ar, it does.'

Emily shuddered and shook herself out of her melancholy.

'C'mon! We've something to show you, haven't we, Sarah? Something to cheer Daddy em-em up, cheer all of us up. You skip off to Grant's Meadow, Sarah, you know where to go. You good for the walk, George?'

George smiled, glad of the distraction.

'Leg pains a bit but I'd not miss this. Grant's Meadow? I thought y' said bull was in 'ome farm bottom field?'

In the bird-and-bee song that passed for cacophony in nineteen eighteen England, Sarah set off as George and Emily followed, holding hands. The sound of their footfall changed from the crackle of stubble to the sharp click of George's army boots on the newly surfaced road which they followed.

'I see Council finally got round t' met'llin' this road then, an' made summat 'f a pig's ear 'f it. When were this?'

'Last July. They used that new bitumen and crushed chippings; did it in the full of summer and with a new gang of chaps who'd not know hay from a bull's foot.'

'That's 'cos the other lot'd buggered off t' th' war…an' on full pay at that! What 'appened?'

'They used that big roller from the cricket club to squash it down. What with the heat and the pressure, most of it was shoved down the slope and into the dip there; made a second hill!'

'Ha! I reckon Council an' army are related! God alone knows what sort o' pups they'd throw if we'd ever let 'em breed!'

This joke brought a smile to Emily's face which stayed throughout the gentle walk to the gate of Grant's

Meadow. Sarah was nowhere to be seen and George looked around.

'Ay-up, where's our Sarah got to?'

Releasing George's hand Emily's pace quickened a little. As she reached the gate so she called out.

'Sarah! Sarah, Daddy's here!'

She leaned on the gate and George, taking his cue from her relaxed attitude, rested his arms alongside her on the top bar of the gate. Emily was gazing across the meadow and George, after a further cursory glance around, looked in the same direction.

Gradually, rising into sight over the crest of the hill that ran the breadth of Grant's Meadow, the head of a grey Shire filly appeared...then the whole Shire horse together with Sarah running alongside it and holding its leading rein.

Lifting his arms from off the gate, George dropped his stick and stared, his eyes and mouth wide open in disbelief.

'That's Clowdy... 'Ers? By, bloody 'ell! All this time an' y' never said, Em!'

Emily retrieved his stick.

'No, well, we thought it'd be a nice surprise.' She laughed at his expression. 'That'll teach you not to write won't it, George Radcliffe; nice surprise?'

'Surprise? This is...a...a surprise...it's that alright!'

Slowed to a walk now, a smiling Sarah and the Shire approached the gate.

'This is our baby. I've broke her a bit but she'll need your guiding hand, George.'

George put out his hand and, to his amazement, the filly dropped her head allowing him to rub her ear. For several seconds he could only stare, his hand moving rhythmically, his thoughts racing.

Eventually he cleared his throat.

'Uh-hum. Like I said, Em, a way wi' stock you 'ave…an' a way wi' surprises too our Sarah.'

'She's called, ClowdySky, Daddy, after her mummy. Nice surprise, Daddy em-em?'

'Ar, y' could say that. Stumped me complete.'

Taking his stick off Emily, he stepped back the better to look at the Shire.

Emily nudged Sarah.

'Look out, Sarah, judge's here. Now we'll know the verdict.'

'I'd recognise 'er stamp anywhere, Em. Dead ringer f'r 'er mam. She's a grand shape, an' if I know right, there's a Draughtsman in there somewhere.'

Emily laughed.

'Typical horseman! Might not recognise his own children but can pedigree a horse in ten seconds. Yes, Mister Bullock's stallion, over in Staffordshire.' George nodded in recognition as Emily continued, 'Well, you'd done all the hard work. It seemed a shame to waste it…but no need to dwell on it now, plenty of time for all that.'

'What you called 'er f'r th' book?'

Emily coloured a little.

'Best just say that she's not registered at present.'

'Not registered? But, she'd 'ave t' be, otherwise…?'

'I knew this would get difficult, Sarah.' She faced George. 'If I say she was stillborn, would you understand then?'

George was still confused.

'A stillborn? But…?'

Sarah's excitement got the better of her.

'C'mon, Daddy em-em! Walk her. Walk her!'

Flicking the gate's catch, Emily pulled at George's arm, guiding him through it.

'Do as you're asked, Daddy em-em, and walk her!' George went through and stood stroking ClowdySky's neck. 'Do you need your stick?'

'I reckon I could fly right now, Em…'ere.'

He gave her the stick.

'But…'orse like 'er, 'ow come she's missed all th' call ups?'

'Oh, alright, you'll not leave it, will you? Tell Daddy how she missed the call ups, Sarah'

'Because we hid her Daddy…' she put her finger to her lips. 'Shhhhhh!'

George was about to say something, but Emily cut off any reply.

'Not now, George; enough! Walk her!'

He took the leading rein and, using the Shire as support, set off across the field at as stiff a walk as his leg would allow. Sarah climbed atop the gate and Emily stood behind, her chin resting on Sarah's shoulder, arms folded round her.

'Will Daddy's leg get better, Mummy?'

'Probably never be right, Sarah, but I'd say the sight of that filly has helped no end, wouldn't you?'

'Yes, no stick with a horse.'

Gradually George's limping pace quickened and ClowdySky broke into a gentle trot alongside him as they moved across the field as one. After going about fifty yards, George turned the filly round and walked her back. With just twenty yards to the gate and to Emily and Sarah, the silence was slowly but emphatically drowned out. George halted ClowdySky's progress mid-field. Over a rise in the road a steel-wheeled traction engine, hauling a plough and hawser-line, trundled and rattled down the slope, belching out smoke and fumes. ClowdySky flicked her head and George put a little pressure on her halter and raised his hand to her head.

'Steady, my Shire lady, nothin' t' concern. Steady, lass, Stand-On.'

The Shire snorted and fixed the traction engine with an attentive eye.

The black-smoke legacy from its roaring furnace had streaked the clear blue sky; it lingered along the road's line as the traction engine rumbled on, past the field and gate, on into the village and out of sight, Emily, Sarah, George and ClowdySky staring after it ....

07.09.07

……Richard's lips silently trace the rusted letters.

TO S..UEL
O. YO.. TW…Y-FI… ..RT..AY
G.. .L.SS Y.U SO.

'Their bad luck, my good; this looks like gold, and from under the straw…'

Then out loud, causing a Mexican wave along the recently settled but alert bird-mass.

'…Ha! I'm Rumpelstiltskin, and rich beyond the dreams of average now!'

Disc in his back pocket, his soiled hands remove the straw canopy and he picks up the play-dead leveret. A look across to the hedgerow confirms the continued presence of the doe hare.

'So, yours then? Late one too. By, you're a brave lass; you must be scared squitless.'

Over to the hedgerow, leveret in hand, the doe hare remaining true, scared squitless but true to her filial duty, Richard places it under a drooping tuft of dry grass.

'Here you go. You've earned it.'

As he moves back to the tractor the doe hare hops her way to the outline of folded grass with a stuttering gait which can only be reproduced by the terrified. Once there she is up on hind legs, front paws flicking a poor man's emblem rampant, then drops down to inspect the crypt.

The resurrected leveret snuggles out. A cursory reciprocal sniff then both exit through a hedgerow gap, away to an unseen and uncertain freedom.

Climbing back into the cab, Richard glances at his particular three graces; computer screen, fuel gauge, wrist watch.

'Enough to get through to lunch.'

He sits…then rises and takes the disc from out of his back pocket. Tossing it onto the dashboard, he sits again and reaches out through the tractor's open rear window to retrieve the horseshoe.

A short piece of baler twine, left over from last Wednesday's partridge shoot and threaded through a hole in the 'shoe's centre, acts as a hanger. He loops this over the tractor's sun-roof handle.

Pressing *Headland Re-align* followed by, *Performance Memory 1* and *Auto-Steer* on the computer's touch-screen, Richard sends the engine from tick-over to hysteria in one movement of his hand.

He flops the gear mechanism into *Drive*, setting the tractor into motion, and gives the rear-view camera screen a quick glimpse as he jigsaws the ploughshares back into their furrows.

'Gee-up, you bugger!'

Headphone and iPod resplendent once more, Richard re-enters the world of *Harvest Moon* and Mister Young.

The patient gulls rise and slip alongside the plough to restart their rudely interrupted squabbles and feeding, the ground yielding once again to the massive plough's mighty demands, the horseshoe dancing to the movement.........